Paula Brackston is the *New York Times* bestselling author of *The Witch's Daughter* and *The Winter Witch*. She has an MA in Creative Writing from Lancaster University and is a visiting lecturer for the University of Wales, Newport. She lives in a wild, mountainous part of Wales and much of the inspiration for her writing comes from stomping about on the mountains being serenaded by skylarks and buzzards. In 2007 Paula was shortlisted in the Crème de la Crime search for new writers. In 2010 her book *Nutters* (writing as P. J. Davy) was shortlisted for the Mind Book Award. Visit her author website at www. paulabrackston.com

The Shadow Chronicles

The Witch's Daughter
The Witches of the Blue Well
The Winter Witch
The Midnight Witch

The Silver Witch

PAULA BRACKSTON

CORSAIR

First published in the United States of America by Thomas Dunne Books,
an imprint of St. Martin's Press, New York, 2015

First published in Great Britain in 2015 by Corsair

1 3 5 7 9 10 8 6 4 2

Copyright © 2015 by Paula Brackston

Designed by Molly Rose Murphy
Illustrations by Ellisa Mitchell
Author photo credit: Michael Taylor

The moral right of the author has been asserted.

A CIP catalogue record for this book
is available from the British Library.

ISBN: 978-1-4721-5065-3 (paperback)
ISBN: 978-1-4721-5066-0 (ebook)

Printed and bound in Great Britain by
CPI Group (UK) Ltd., Croydon, CR0 4YY

Papers used by Corsair are from well-managed forests and other
responsible sources

MIX
Paper from
responsible sources
FSC
www.fsc.org   FSC® C104740

Corsair
An imprint of
Little, Brown Book Group
Carmelite House
50 Victoria Embankment
London EC4Y 0DZ

An Hachette UK Company
www.hachette.co.uk

www.littlebrown.co.uk

For my mum

The Silver Witch

PROLOGUE

It is as if she has always known that one day it would come to this. One day she would have to face it. Her darkest fear has been there to test her from a distance all her life. Years of imagining, thinking, wondering what it would be like to be swallowed up by the waves, or swept away by a fast-flowing river, or held beneath the sunny surface of a sparkling swimming pool, all have led to this place, this moment.

Gingerly, she moves toward the edge of the boat house jetty. Her fingers are already losing their colour in the damp chill. She crouches then sits, lowering her feet into the water. The intense cold is a shock. Her breathing accelerates as she twists around and lowers herself over the edge and in. The ancient, neglected wood is slimy with algae and her fingers start to slip. She gasps, clawing at the wet wood, but cannot get a firm grip. With a feeble splash she slides into the water, bursting into tears of relief and terror as her feet find the silty lake bed. The water level is just above her waist. Raising her arms, elbows bent, she edges toward the entrance, inching her way along the uneven surface. The sloping uneven surface. By the time she reaches the gable end of the boat house the water is up to her armpits. She knows she is in danger of hyperventilating. Of being sick. Of fainting.

No, no, no! Mustn't trip, mustn't stumble. Small steps. Come on, feet, pretend we're running. Running in slow motion. Fleet feet. Strong steps. One foot in front of the other.

She pushes through the reeds, causing small waves to bounce back at her from the timber walls. She raises her chin as the water sloshes against her face. With every step she fights rising panic. Panic that threatens to send her falling into the water. Panic that might be the finish of her.

She reaches the low boards that block the exit. The moment has come. Now she must dive beneath the water, push through into the unknown, fight the tangle of weeds and swim to the outside. She knows if she thinks about it any longer she will not move, so in one desperate, sudden action she forces herself under the surface. The sensation of going beneath the water is more than she can stand. She loses her balance, falling through the twisted undergrowth, her feet sliding so that she disappears into the brackish blackness. She reacts as she has always feared she would, as she has always imagined so vividly in her nightmares. She inhales. The mouthful of water becomes a lungful in a soundless scream of terror. Tilda feels time stop. Her intellect tells her she must get up, must break the surface, must push up, grab something, find air. Her instinct tells her to fight and flail and clutch and claw. But the blackness is enticing, the silence seductive. And the cold, the bone-deep cold, has her in its tight embrace, numbing her will as well as her body.

1

SEREN

All is darkness. Blessed night. Freed from light and troubled vision, my thoughts are fed instead by the howling of the wind outside. The sound forms pictures in my mind, where I see the trees moving in the raging air. Willow and hazel pull at their roots as they dance. Birch and ash bow to the mighty force from the skies. But the oak will not bend the knee. He stands stubborn and steady. Would sooner break than yield. My mind is like the willow; it flexes and springs. My heart is a knot of oak. Let them try to wound me. Let them try.

TILDA

Feet find firm ground, thudding into dry mud. Nike on hard earth. Breathe in. Breathe out. In on second left footfall. Out on second right.

Lengthen stride, a couple of inches, no more. Pace, rhythm, run, step, the poetry of movement, of exertion.

Tilda loves to run. Tilda needs to run. Her style is loose, fluid, easy, but with power and purpose. And with every step she lets her mind overlay the beat with plump, juicy images – images she will gather together for when she returns home, a crop harvested from the amber autumn landscape through which she now runs. All her best work has been created this way. Running charges her body and her mind. If she does not run, her thoughts become composted in her head, overheated and overcrowded, potentially fertile but unusable. Too much of a mass to be employed as separate artistic ideas. She turns off the woodland track and follows the slender path out of the trees and across the open fields.

Breathe, pace, breathe, pace. Heart strobing against ribs. Lungs efficient, trained, strong. Turf opening up, stretching out. The vista is uplifting. Lush, plush, velvet grass. Green is the colour of life.

Her left foot hits a small stone and her mind is momentarily jolted out of its meditative state, her rhythm disrupted. Cold air stings the back of her throat. The day is cool but dry. The year is turning the corner away from summer, but the fertile rot of autumn has not yet taken hold of the landscape. The smell of fungi is just faintly detectable. The crunch of broken nut-shells underfoot still only occasional. Another full moon will see shortening days and lengthening shadows.

Tilda's long legs stride over the meadow to the bordering hedge. She finds the narrow gap and squeezes through, her breath loud in her ears as she stoops to pass beneath the brambles. A squirrel dashes out and fluffs its way up the nearest trunk. Tilda picks a glossy blackberry and pops it in her mouth, then presses on, winding a now-familiar route between neglected hazel and blackthorn. At last she is in the open again, alongside the lake. A smile, as involuntary as a hiccup, curves her mouth. As on each occasion that she runs here she is reminded of how she is drawn to what she fears. Deep water is the nightmare of her childhood that she never grew out of. Nothing she can imagine would induce her to step off the path and break that silky surface. And yet she loves to run here, to be close, to be fascinated by the terror and the beauty of it. Laughing at her fear a little each time. Like the thrill of watching a horror movie. A reminder of what it means to be alive. And how close at hand death is. Any death. His death.

Mustn't think of it, not now. Mustn't falter. Quicker now. Up a gear. Legs and arms help each other. Calf muscles tightening, ignore that. Run, girl, run. Fleet. Fast. Foot sure. I see you, waiting water. I see you. One more mile. Turning for home.

Home. Though she forms the word in her head it is still hard to think of the cottage as anything other than the place where she lives. For, what is home? Surely more than a set of rooms, a roof, an address? Home suggests belonging. Suggests warmth, safety, companionship. Love. When Mat died, all those things died with him. So she returns to the cottage. It is the place where she lives now, has lived for a month, almost. It is the place where she must live. Where she will work. Where she will simply be. Home is too much to ask of it. For now.

She has not completely circled the lake today, but loops back, so that she passes St Cynog's church and the Old School House a second time. The church is solid Norman, boxy and stout, built to withstand time and the damp air from the lake. Its graveyard is kempt and well-used, but even so there are some ancient tombstones which lean toward each other at angles that give away their age.

Like so many old men huddled in conversation after a few pints.

The Old School House is a building out of place. A nineteenth-century idea of rural perfection, with its mullioned windows, low eaves, and rustic charm. No longer a school, but the cozy home of an evidently proficient gardener. Tilda jogs on by, taking the footpath to the lane beyond. She crosses the narrow road that will be busy with visitors to the lake at weekends and leans into the steep slope to the cottage.

Ty Gwyn is a humble farmworker's cottage, positioned high on the hill and approached via a testing climb. It sits steady and serene, and ever-so-slightly smug, as if enjoying the view, and laughing just a little at the puffing people who struggle up to its blue front door. The whitewashed stone gleams in the autumn sunshine, sharp against the fading colours of the mountain pastures, while the slate roof is an exact match for the stone walls that mark the boundary of the garden. Breathing heavily, Tilda unlatches the wooden gate at the end of the bumpy track and secures it behind her against opportunist sheep. She reminds herself that one day she will enjoy tending the modest lawn and flower beds and recovering the neglected plants. One day. A path of uneven flagstones leads around the side of the little house to the back door, which she unlocks with the chunky key she keeps beneath a pot of thyme. The temperature inside is not noticeably warmer than out, but she is too warm from her run to mind. She raises the blinds to let the young day into the low-ceilinged room and places the filled kettle on the hot plate of the Rayburn stove. The aged beast heats so slowly it will take some time to boil. Already, in the few short weeks she has been here, she has formed habits. There is comfort to be had in the repetition of simple tasks. Reassurance to be found in ritual. Routine has a way of helping to make the new familiar, of filling the mind with purpose and, in doing so, leaving less room for unwelcome doubts and fears. She takes milk from the fridge and pours herself a glass to drink where she stands, leaning against the sink. She can feel her heart begin to steady after its exertion. The milk refreshes and chills her in equal measure. She glances at the kitchen clock and notices it has stopped.

Another dud battery. So much for value brands.

Tilda levers off her trainers and heads upstairs to the tiny bathroom. The shower is old and temperamental and coughs unpromisingly when she turns it on. She leaves the water spluttering and pulls off her beanie and running clothes before deftly undoing the heavy plait that has restrained her hair. Steam begins to mist the mirror, so that her reflection is even more ghostly than usual. She wipes the glass and peers at the pale young woman who peers back at her. Swirls of vapour blur the image.

I could fade away entirely. It wouldn't require effort. Just grow a little fainter every day.

She steps into the shower and lets the hot water cascade over her. Her white-blonde hair becomes slick, darkening to pewter. Her skin flushes. Now she is the most coloured, the most opaque she will ever be. She should have come with instructions: To render visible, add warm water. Her mother once told her that when she had first held her baby daughter in her arms she doubted anything so fragile, so thin skinned, so seemingly insubstantial, could survive. But Tilda had shown her. Had grown tall and strong. Had proved her wrong. As in so many things.

By the time she has dressed, dried her hair so that it hangs straight and loose, a crystal curtain down her back, the day is properly awake. She takes her mug of tea and steps out onto the small patio of mossy flagstones beyond the front door. As always, the view is like a deep breath of pure oxygen.

This is why we bought this place. This.

The flat piece of garden extends only a few paces to the low stone wall that separates it from the dizzying drop to the valley below. The landscape falls away abruptly, so that Tilda is gazing down upon a thick copse of trees – still more green than gold – and beyond to the sweep of small fields that lay around the lake. The water is glassy and still this morning, undisturbed by any breeze or activity, save for the movements of the families of waterfowl that have made the place their home. Beyond the lake, the Brecon Beacons rise up, an ancient shield of mountains against the wild weather and people of the west. When she and Mat had discovered the cottage, had stood on this very spot for the first time, he had taken her hand in his and they had ginned at each other in silence. They had both known, in that instant, that this was the place they would start their married life together, would live, would work.

Except that fate had other plans for them.

Three rooks are startled by some unseen danger and fly from their perch, flapping and squawking. The sound is sharp and discordant and provokes in Tilda a fierce reaction. She is taken back to the moment of Mat's death with such brutal speed and vivid colours that she is forced to relive those heartbreaking seconds again. She is no longer in the garden beneath the September sunshine, but back in the car, Mat's car, on their way home from their honeymoon, rain lashing the windshield; watery lights of the motorway traffic flashing past. It was she who had been driving, she who had felt the pull on the steering wheel as the tire rapidly deflated, she who had slowed and halted on the hard shoulder. Mat had got out, walked around to examine the tire. She can see him now, in the cruel memory of her mind's eye, stooping to look in through the window of the driver's-side door. The rain, pouring onto Mat and the glass, has washed his features into a blur. He opens his mouth. He is speaking, trying to tell her something, but there is too much noise. She cannot hear him. He points, forward, and toward the edge of the road. She wipes the inside of the window with her hand, frowning to make him out, to make out what he is saying. And then, in a heartbeat, he is gone. Vanished. She has never been able to recall so much as the colour of the truck that swept him away. She was told, later, that it had been empty, returning to the continent after a long haul, its driver not negligent, but not as vigilant as the speed and conditions required.

Tilda shakes her head, rubs her eyes, gasps against the pain of the vision, the renewed shock of the realization, the dragging weight of grief, all assailing her for the hundredth time.

Again. Again. And for how long? More than a year now and still every time as clear and as violent as the first. Will it never ease? Will it always be so unbearable?

She keeps her eyes closed for a moment longer. When she opens them the brightness of the sun makes her flinch. She tips the last of her tea into a pot of geraniums, turns on her heel, and heads back into the cottage. Once inside again she is reminded by the boxes in the narrow hallway, and in the sitting room, and indeed all over the house, that there is still unpacking to be done. She cannot imagine what she can own that fills so many boxes. She has not yet missed any of it, though soon she will be forced to search out a winter coat and some warmer bedding. The cottage is plenty big enough for her needs, but its rooms are small and cannot be used comfortably while the packing cases remain. Tilda knows it is a job she will not enjoy, but she will feel better for having done it.

Like a visit to the dentist, or filing your tax returns.

She can hear her father gently nagging her on both counts. Soon her parents will insist on visiting. To see she is all right. To make sure she has settled in. She must make sure every last book is unpacked by then, if her mother is not to shake her head and purse her lips.

Soon, but not quite yet. Today I begin work. Proper work.

The little barn attached to the cottage had been used as a garage for years before she and Mat became its owners. It had been a fairly simple matter to change the door – fitting in glass sliding ones to allow plenty of natural light – sweep it out and move in shelving, bins for clay and glazes, a Belfast sink, extra lighting, a small wood-burning stove and, of course, the kiln. Tilda regards the iron oven warily, wondering how long it will be before she is ready for a firing. In their old studio, before they had ever thought of moving out to Wales, so many times she and Mat had waited on tenterhooks for the thing to cool sufficiently to be safely opened, and to reveal the success – or otherwise – of the firing. At two thousand degrees Fahrenheit, the heat inside a potter's kiln would reduce a human hand to charred bones in a matter of seconds. Such terrifying temperatures are necessary to create the required chemical reactions within the glazes so that they are transformed from dull dust to colours of shimmering brilliance and mesmerizing intensity. Tilda is ceaselessly amazed by what transformations can occur amid that heat. The process of firing clay within such a domesticated dragon is a timeless and mysterious alchemy. Raw earth is slabbed from the ground, then worked and pounded, then teased and caressed, before being persuaded into forms to suit the craftsman's wishes. The piece is subjected to a biscuit firing, rendering it, as the name suggests, dry, brittle and ready to receive its glaze. These magical powders mixed with water in a thousand variations – a pipkin more antimony oxide, a pinch less chrome, or a spoonful of cobalt to a measure of manganese – cling somberly to their given bodies, awaiting the crucial application of fire to bring about their chrysalis-to-butterfly moment. Every opening of the kiln door is an instant pregnant with expectation and hope, an occasion that will reveal the results of weeks of work and thought and art. It is a moment of exquisite agony every bit as intense as the heat inside the crucible itself.

Well, Mat, at least you are spared any more disastrous firings. I'll just have to face those on my own, won't I?

A part of Tilda believes it might, in fact, be easier. Easier not having to suffer Mat's disappointment as well as her own. She can recall all too well the occasions where they had both despaired of the wasted months of work when a glaze had failed to behave as it should, or a volatile piece exploded and wrecked the entire firing.

The Silver Witch

And now she needs to begin again. To find the pace and rhythm of her work, as sure-footedly as the pace and rhythm of her running. She rolls up her sleeves and takes a lump of earthenware clay from the green plastic bin beneath the sink. She drops the smooth, heavy clod onto the scrubbed wood of the bench and begins to knead it, letting the repetitive action of wedging the muddy substance steady her mind. Lifting and slamming the clay down with increasing force, she can feel the texture begin to change beneath her palms, the material begin to yield. Lift and slam. Lift and slam. Pummel, turn, scoop, lift and slam. Dull thuds of weight and effort growing louder with every focused, determined movement.

2

TILDA

The dawn light is soft on Tilda's eyes as she follows the path around the top of the lake. Still she wears her protective tinted lenses, as she always does. This morning a mist rises slowly from the surface of the water, deadening sounds and blurring the edges of the trees as she runs past them. In the gloom she can just make out the fuzzy silhouette of the ramshackle disused boat house at the top of the lake. Everything appears smudged and indistinct. Tiny droplets of water settle upon her black beanie and her long, pale plait that swings as she runs. She glances at her watch, wanting to check her pace on the specialized timer. To her annoyance she finds it has stopped working. She halts, her heavy breath chasing away the mist as she exhales. The watch had been a present from Mat. A serious runner's watch for a serious runner. Tilda taps it, frowning, but the hands stay stubbornly still, the tiny dials refuse to move.

I told him it was too complicated. Too many parts waiting to go wrong.

Except that it has never gone wrong before, not in the two years she has been using it. It has always kept perfect time, and the stopwatch diligently recorded her progress. Until now. Now it is dead. Tilda closes her eyes tightly, bracing herself against another flashback, another vivid glimpse of Mat's death.

No. Not again, not today, not out here. Please.

She opens her eyes. The mist moves in eddies about her, but no heartrending vision comes this time. She leans forward and sets off once again at a smart pace. As the day breaks properly more of the lake is exposed, its shroud of vapour rising to reveal the silky surface shimmering beneath the autumn sun. Once again she experiences the frisson running close to the water gives her. It is as if by looking at it so frequently, by treading so near, she is controlling her fear of its depths, managing her phobia. For phobia it is, she has never been under any illusions about that. Her father had done his utmost to help her. Notes had been coming home from school — Tilda refuses to set foot in the swimming pool. Tilda must learn to swim but cannot be made to leave the changing room. Her mother had scolded and tutted and refused to have any patience with such silliness. Her father had taken it upon himself to Do Something Constructive. This involved Saturday mornings spent at the local baths, the two of them sitting on the wooden benches beside the baby pool, she in an inappropriately cheerful costume and tightly inflated water wings, he in beige checked shorts and baring an expanse of fuzzy chest and pasty belly. He had squeezed her hand firmly.

'There is nothing to be frightened of, Little Rabbit. I'm here. I won't let anything happen to you. It's very shallow, you know. You could walk from one side to the other. Why don't we just try that? A bit of walking, hmmm?'

'But the water . . .' Tilda, at eight years old, had been unable to make anyone understand what she felt. It wasn't really that she believed she would drown, it was the water itself. The look of it. The way it moved. The feel of it as it pulled against her legs, disturbing her balance, threatening to topple her. And then, what? She had never been able to put her head beneath the surface, even in the bath. What would she do if she went under here? She caught her breath at the very thought of it. It would be like death, she was certain of it, like death swallow-ing you up, in a silent, airless place. People weren't meant to go there. It was meant for fishes.

'Daddy,' she said at last, 'I'm not a fish.' It was the best she could do.

He looked at her, eyebrows raised, laughing not unkindly, patting her hand.

'No, little one,' he agreed. 'You're not a fish.'

She never had learned to swim, and even her father, the most tactful man she knew, had been unable to hide his astonish-ment that she should choose to live so close to a lake.

Ah, the things we do for love.

Today she enjoys the stimulation of the proximity of danger. Of fear managed. She runs on, and has gone only a little farther when she becomes aware of voices. Though muffled by the mist, they are clearly raised, angry voices. Slowing her pace she peers into the gloom. She has never encountered anyone on her early morning circuits of the lake. The voices are com-ing from the field to her left. She can discern two men, both cursing, but not, she thinks, at each other. A sudden yelp reveals the target of their rage. Tilda reaches the patchy hedge and clambers more through than over it in time to see the taller of the youths land a second hefty kick on the skinny grey dog with scruffy hair that cowers on the ground in front of him.

'Oy!' she shouts before she has time to think of the wisdom of confronting two angry strangers when she is alone. 'Stop that! Leave the poor thing alone.'

The men look up and see Tilda as she emerges from the mist. Her appearance startles them, and for a brief moment they stare, but are quickly over their surprise.

'What's it got to do with you?' the shorter one growls.

As she gets closer to the dog, Tilda can see a trickle of blood coming from its mouth. It is shaking with fear but unable to run away, as one of the men has hold of a chain that is fastened around the dog's neck.

'Why are you hurting her? What has she done that is so terrible?'

'She's useless,' the dog's tormenter tells Tilda. 'She won't do her job.'

'Her job?'

The men exchange glances and Tilda realizes whatever activity they are engaged in is probably without the landowner's permission.

'Were you after foxes?' she asks, though she knows this can't be right.

'Huh!' the shorter man sneers, 'this thing couldn't catch a cold, never mind a fox.'

'She's a lurcher,' the other youth points out, as if this explains anything. When Tilda remains blank he goes on. 'She's supposed to catch hares.'

'Hares. But . . . why?'

At this both men lose their patience. 'Look,' says the nearest one, 'it's none of your business, okay? You don't know about dogs.'

'I know you don't teach them anything by kicking their teeth out,' she says, putting her hands on her hips.

The taller man yanks on the dog's chain, forcing it to stagger to its unsteady feet. 'Come on,' he says to his companion, 'let's go. Stupid bitch!' he spits, and Tilda can't be sure if he is addressing the dog or her. The poor animal glances back as it is dragged away. It is still bleeding from the kick to its mouth, and also has a pronounced limp. The sight of its suffering is too much for Tilda.

'Wait!' she calls after them. 'If you don't want the dog, I'll have it.'

The men pause and turn. 'What do you want with it? Why should we give it to you?'

'You've just said it's useless at . . . hunting. Must cost a lot, feeding a dog like that. I'll take it off your hands.'

'Oh yeah? How much?'

'What?'

'How much are you gonna give us for her? She's from a good line. They cost money, you know, working lurchers.'

'Even useless ones?'

Both men scowl and begin to walk off. Tilda trots after them and catches up with the tall one holding the lead. She instinctively puts her hand on his arm.

'Look, I haven't got any money on me. But I'll give her a good home. Save you the cost of the dog food. And the vet's bills.'

The youth looks down at her hand and sees her watch.

'I'll take that for her,' he says.

'My watch? Oh, but it's . . .' She is going to say *broken* but then notices the hands are moving; it is working again. '. . . It was a present from my husband.'

The man shrugs. 'Do you want the dog or don't you?'

She hesitates for only a moment, thinking of Mat and how pleased he had been when he found the watch for her, and then knowing what he would want her to do. Slipping the watch from her wrist, she hands it over and takes the chain before the man can change his mind. She whistles softly at the dog to encourage it to go with her and is relieved when it limps along beside her quite willingly. She is aware of the men watching her as she struggles to help the dog over a low bit of hedge and back onto the path, and finds she is only breathing steadily again once she hears them stomping off across the field in the opposite direction.

It takes an age to reach the house, as the dog is lame, sore, and undernourished. Tilda's running clothes are unequal to the chilliness of the morning without the warmth exertion would produce, so that by the time they arrive at the cottage both she and her new house mate are shivering. It follows her inside meekly. Only now does she realize she did not ask for the dog's name. There is no tag on its chain collar, which has started to rub, so she takes it off.

'What am I going to call you, pooch? You are a weedy thing. All skinny and grey and tufty. I know; Thistle! Yes. That'll suit you. Now, what would you like to eat, eh, Thistle? What do lurcher dogs eat, I wonder?'

It feels strange, the sound of her own voice in the house she has only ever been alone in. Strange, but nice. She fetches a saucer of milk and the dog gives her a look that clearly says *I'm not a cat*, but drinks it all the same. Tilda empties a tin of tuna into a cereal bowl. It is wolfed down in seconds. The sight of the dog licking hungrily at the empty dish reminds her that she will have to buy more supplies soon. Without a car, this is not a simple task.

When Tilda had informed her parents of her intention to live at the cottage without Mat it was the first thing her mother had brought up.

'How can you possibly live in such a remote place if you refuse to drive? Really, Tilda, it's just not sensible. How will you shop?'

'There's a post office and stores in the village.'

'You can't live on canned food and chocolate bars.'

Wrong again, Mother.

Thistle stands on her stringy legs, head on one side, watching Tilda quizzically.

'Okay, maybe you will need proper food. Later on I'll have a look on the Internet to see if there's a supermarket that delivers around here, okay? Later. Now, we need heat.'

Tilda opens the door of the Rayburn and pokes at the smouldering fire inside. She takes a log from the basket and feeds it in. There is a great deal of smoke, but very little warmth. Shutting the stove door, she pulls a cushion from one of the kitchen chairs and calls the dog to lie on it. But the cushion is small, and however tightly Thistle tries to curl herself up onto it, her legs still dangle over the edges onto the cold kitchen floor.

'Now you're making me feel like a bad dog owner. Don't you know how lucky you are? I haven't time to fuss over you. I have work to do. A studio to set up. Orders to fill.' The dog regards her with a woeful expression.

With a sigh Tilda drags the electric fan heater out from the corner of the room and positions it close to the dog's bed. She switches it on, expecting a cheerful light and a gentle puffing of heat. Instead there is a nerve-jarring bang and all the lights go off.

'Damn!'

In the gloom of the hallway, she squints at the ancient fuse box. It is a tangle of wires and dusty fitments, but she is eventually able to find the master switch. She flicks it down, and light is restored.

Feeling quite pleased with herself, Tilda returns to the kitchen.

'Right,' she tells the dog, 'I've got to get into the studio. You'll just have to make do with the Rayburn. I'm not risking switching that heater on again.' As she heads for the door she is painfully aware of a pair of beady brown eyes following her.

Will it be lonely? Should I take it with me? Oh, this is ridiculous.

'I'll be back in a couple of hours,' she calls to Thistle, her hand on the latch of the door. She is just about to go out when there is a second loud bang and the power goes off once more.

'Damn it! Again?' She turns and strides through the kitchen. Not seeing that Thistle has got up from her cushion she stumbles into the dog, tripping, her knee connecting with the edge of a wooden chair. 'Stay in your bed! Ouch, for pity's sake.' Cursing further, she sits heavily on the floor, clutching her knee. The dog is back on its cushion, making itself as flat and small as it can. Tilda is filled with remorse at having spoken harshly. She swallows a sob and closes her eyes tight. She knows if she lets herself cry – properly cry – grief will claim her again.

You are a self-pitying fool, Tilda Fordwells. Get up, girl. Get up and get on!

She wipes her face with her sleeve and stands up, allowing herself two deep breaths before she opens her eyes again. Thistle is peering up at her from beneath shaggy brows. Immediately, Tilda is swamped by pity for the dog. Slowly she moves close to the scruffy hound, crouching beside it, stroking the animal's head and ears gently.

'I'm sorry. You poor old thing. And your mouth is still bleeding. Tell you what, I'll put the kettle on the stove, make me a cup of tea and you some warm water so I can bathe your face. Then we'll phone an electrician. The cell phone might not work up here, but at least the landline does. Upside of keeping the old telephones that don't need to be plugged into the main power supply. What d'you say, sound like a good idea? Might even be a biscuit or two to go with the tea. You could help me with those.'

Thistle replies with a feeble but friendly wagging of her tail, the movement sending up little clouds of dust to swirl and dance in the narrow beam of sunlight that falls through the window.

'Who needs electric lights anyhow, eh? Not me. And certainly not you,' Tilda decides, noticing how soothing the feel of the dog's fur is beneath her fingers. She sets about her tasks and begins to achieve the sense of calm that comes from gently restoring order; from attending to the small details of life that ease the passage of time. When at last the dog is tended to and settled and the electrician called, she slips out of the house and into her ceramics studio.

SEREN

The sun has gone to sleep and left shadow-making to the torches that burn bright in the still of the evening. From where I sit, at the entrance to my small lakeside house, I have an unbroken view of the crannog. The small island sits upon the water as if held there by magic, floating, the weight of the hall and the other buildings apparently supported by some unknown glamour. In truth, it is a solid thing. It was not magic that brought it into being but hard labour, sweat, and toil. It is not suspended at all, but sits stoutly on layers of rock and wood, hauled into place over many months, constructed to the design of clever, ambitious men.

Many more torches than is customary are lit to night, the better to show the way to the gathering in the long hall. And the better to show off the finery of those who will attend. How people snatch at the chance to parade in their expensive garments and gaudy jewels. They pretend to hurry to their prince's side, to show their support, to listen to his every word. In truth their loyalty is not as great as their vanity. And is not the crannog itself a display of pride? That man can make an island! Not content to build his hall and smithy and houses on the shore, he must construct his own isle, must sit atop the water, as if he has conquered the elements so that he alone is able to float his impossibly heavy buildings above the eels and fishes. As if his feet are too tender, too royal, to set upon the gritty earth.

The lake itself is quiet to night. The trifling events of those who dwell within its reach do not trouble it. A wind might stir its surface into jagged waves. A freezing might glaze it with bitter ice. The sun on a summer morn might lift from it a mist. But man's splashings and flailings are fleeting disturbances only. Prince Brynach considers himself ruler of his own land, and that may be so, but he no more rules the water of the lake than the stars in the sky or the thunder in the clouds. No matter how many crannogs he builds.

They are hurrying to the gathering now, eager to take the best seats, close enough to the fire to be illuminated, to be seen, but not so close as to suffer the choking smoke more than they must. They will greet one another warmly, but those smiles will slip to sneers behind turned backs. The prince has his royal home, his floating palace, and it attracts the ambitious like so many moths to a flame. It is his own fault that he is surrounded by men who would as readily fight with him as for him. He is a good prince, with good intentions, but unwilling to see the truth sometimes. He has eyes to melt your heart, peat-dark and flecked with gold, and steady in their gaze, but he cannot see the treachery before him. It falls to me to show him.

I take my time. Let them bluster and settle. I have no interest in observing pleasantries. The night is cooling and I am glad of my wolf-skin cloak and headdress. My appearance among the prince's people always causes unease. The sight of me reminds them of things they do not understand. Of things they fear, and yet need. But to night I must present myself not merely as Seren the Seer, Seren who lives apart. Who lives alone. This night I must stand before my prince and make him hear me. Make them all hear me. I am Seren Arianaidd. Seren who calls the Afanc. Seren the Prophet. Seren the Witch. My pale hair beneath my wolf's mask headdress is braided with bright green reeds from the banks of the lake. Under the fine animal skin I am naked except for my short woollen tunic and my leather armour, the silver at my throat and wrists, and the pictures on my flesh. My feet are bare, though my steps ring to the sound of bangles of bone and shell at my ankles. My blade is at my waist. I have painted my eyes so that their glasslike lightness is particularly striking, and I have studded my brow and cheeks with beetle wings. Wings that will flutter and shine beneath the glow of the fire as I move around it. They will look at me and be afraid. And that fear will make them listen. Before I leave the sanctuary of my little home, I step into the lake, let it gently lap my feet. I need the calmness of the water if I am not to be riled beyond endurance. This is not a moment to let my temper steer me. When my mother was schooling me in the ways of the shaman and the skill of the witch, how often she would chide me for my want of control.

I make the short walk from my own house to the wooden causeway swiftly and silently. Most have crossed the water to the crannog already, so that the solitary guard watches me warily as I pass. He is the only one on the narrow wooden crossing that links the island to the shore to witness my arrival. The sight of me makes him start, makes him stare, then quickly look away again. It is a common reaction to my appearance. At least I have no need to identify myself, and he steps aside wordlessly to let me pass. The smaller buildings are quiet – the smithy, the barn, and the house with its byre – all their occupants having gone into the hall to take their places. The prince's horses are at rest in their stable; the long-horned bull slumbers, head low; tired working dogs are too weary to bark. I wait outside the hall and listen. Hywel Gruffydd, the prince's stalwart captain, is up on his hind legs, barking gruff words of welcome at the gathering, reminding them of the greatness of their ruler, informing them of recent gains in territory or status for the prince, and bidding them salute his wise leadership and bravery. His words bring forth an easy cheer. Hywel falls quiet, and even from this rump of the heavy oak door I can picture him setting his broad rump on the seat to his master's right, shifting his weight to one side, as is his habit, to ease the pain in his fattening leg. He is not the warrior he once was, though it would be a foolish man who chose to remind him of the fact. And now people stand, in turn, those who have come with a question, a quarrel to be solved, a dispute over livestock, a broken promise, an accusation of theft, a plea for alms. They pick their words with care when addressing their prince, but the music of their voices is strained, their throats tightened with anger or heartache. If others interrupt to argue or shout down the complainant, they are swiftly silenced by Hywel, who will have them dragged from the hall if they do not conduct themselves as they should.

So Prince Brynach listens. I know he listens, though I still stand without. I close my eyes to see him more clearly, his strong body finely robed, his crown upon his head, his eyes thoughtful, his expression purposefully blank. He will guard his own thoughts, not letting them show on his handsome face. He is not afraid to let others see his passions or his cares, but he knows he must appear more than a mere man to his people. He is their prince, their protector, their provider, their wise man, their shelter and their sword. He must not reveal himself to be as they are.

Yet I see the truth. See the man who is flesh and blood, soul and heart. See the truth he veils from others.

I judge the moment right and make my entrance, flinging the door wide and striding into the hall. The guards draw their swords but stay their hands the instant they recognize me. All eyes turn toward me and I level my gaze at as many as will meet it. The quiet that greets me is a marrying of respect and fear with its mistress, hatred, though none would profess such a thing. Even Hywel will silence his blustering. I am permitted to walk to the centre of the gathering and stand before my Prince. He inclines his head, a gesture of cool regard. I dip my staff and bow low, so that I am lower than my chief, though the farseeing eyes of my wolf-pelt headdress will remain level with his own. There is no other man living I would defer to in such a way. And this he knows.

'Seren Arianaidd,' he says, 'you are welcome. We are honoured that you grace us with your presence.'

I straighten and look about me. While the prince's words are sincerely uttered, there are many here who would wish me as far away as their imaginations could send me. And the most ardent of my detractors sits in the finely carved seat to the left of our ruler. Princess Wenna. Unlike her husband, she wears her opinions plainly for all to see, so that now her beautiful, high-born face and her eyes, green as the leaves of young holly, are darkened with her loathing for me. By her side sits her toad of a brother, Rhodri, whose refined exterior hides a warty soul. He is a man I would not trust to mind a cooking pot, let alone a princedom, and yet Prince Brynach, out of loyalty to the princess, in truth, trusts him with the royal coffers. One day Rhodri brother-of-the-princess will let slip his mask.

'Won't you sit with us?' The prince asks. He summons a page. 'Fetch wine for Seren Arianaidd.'

The boy scurries to do his master's bidding, but I shake my head.

'I come not to drink, but to speak,' I tell him.

There is an uneasy silence in the room now.

'We are always ready to hear your words,' the prince assures me with no more formal courtesy than is expected of him.

'I bring a warning.'

At this, Hywel cannot stop himself asking what they are all wondering, 'You have had a seeing?'

'I have.' The gasps and anxious mutterings that greet this news mean I must raise my voice to be heard. 'A vision, clear and bright as a full moon.'

'What did you see?' Hywel demands, unable to wait for the prince to speak, his own nervousness making him forget his manners.

'I saw the crannog desolate, empty! The houses long gone.'

'And the people?' comes a cry from the back of the hall.

'Not a child remained. Neither beasts nor birds, for the place was barren and nothing grew in it or round it.' Now a woman begins to weep and men set to questioning, clamouring, begging for my interpretation of the seeing. They need the truth, but they fear it. As well they might. 'And in the dust and ashes of the palace there were broken eggshells.'

The prince leaned forward on hearing this. 'What manner of bird did the eggs belong to? Was it an eagle? A falcon?'

'Would that were so, my Prince. Alas, this was a nest not of birds, but of vipers.'

Now Princess Wenna speaks. 'Then surely there is no cause for alarm,' she says, letting her hand rest upon that of her husband. 'In the old religion, does not an adder signify both wisdom and fertility? The very continuation of life. Is that not the case, Seren?'

I resist bridling at the familiar way in which she addresses me but it gives me pause, and in that space the priest leaps up to remind us all that there is a new faith to be followed now.

'The serpent is to be feared,' he insists. 'We were thrown out from a state of grace, from the garden of Eden itself, when Eve fell prey to the viper's slippery words. Man has learned to beware the serpent.'

Hywel Gruffydd grunts. 'Man might have, but there are still a few women who can be charmed by a snake if it be of sufficient size!'

At this the tension in the room is broken and laughter erupts. As is often the case, people are keen to make fun of what scares them. To scoff, to laugh off the danger. I see Prince Brynach throw his aide a look, but even he struggles to keep a smile from his face. The priest shakes his head and frowns in my direction. He must realize he has unwittingly talked himself into agreement with me. Not a position either of us is comfortable with.

The prince declares himself a Christian, and so those under his protection are happy to follow his faith of choice. There are fine churches hereabouts, and monks aplenty. But many still secretly hold to the old religion. To the ancient wisdom that has served us so well for centuries. Else why would I be tolerated? It cannot be avoided, then, that our different creeds should sometimes be at odds, sometimes in harmony.

'Princess Wenna is right,' I say into the heightened mood of the hall, 'we have nothing to fear from the vipers who share their home with us, save the odd nip. And a snake in a vision can foretell a fertile time of plenty. But these were no earthbound serpents. What ever hatched from the shells in my seeing were foul, evil creatures, bent on destruction.'

The merriment in the room disappears as quickly as it began. Even the priest stills his tongue.

'Mark my words,' I go on. 'The seeing was a warning. The crannog is under threat.'

'We know this,' Prince Brynach waves his hand dismissively in an attempt to dampen any panic that might be kindling among the gathering. 'There are ever those who want what we have and would take it from us. We live with war as our cousin and our neighbour, who may visit us without invitation. These are not peaceful times.'

'You may float your palace on the water,' I say, 'and you may build your barricades and man them with guards with swords of iron, and, yes, that will keep your enemies at bay.' I take two strides forward with such urgency that a guard draws his sword, but the prince raises his hand in a signal for him to stay back. I lean toward my noble ruler until my face is but a hand's breadth from his own. He meets my icy gaze. He is one of the few who is able to do so. I keep my voice low and level. 'But nothing you can build will save you from the danger that comes from within.'

His eyes widen but he does not move nor look away. 'You say I have an enemy . . . inside my camp?'

'The vision was strong, the message clear. You are in a nest of vipers, my Prince, and they wish you dead!'

3

TILDA

Tilda feeds another log into the Rayburn in the kitchen and is yet again thankful for a solid fuel stove. Having spent a candlelit night at the cottage, she was surprised to find she did not miss the tele vision, the radio, or even her music, but was content to read until the daylight and candle were insufficient for the print of her chosen novel. The memory of Mat attempting to convert her to an e-reader prompted a wry smile. Why not go to bed when the sun did? She was an early riser anyway, preferring to run with the dawn.

Early to bed, early to rise. Who needs watches to tell us when to do something, or lights to stop us going to sleep?

In addition, the quiet and gloom seemed to help her sleep, so that, for once, she has slumbered long past daybreak and done without her morning run. Since knowing the insomnia that so often keeps grief company, she cannot remember waking feeling so rested and refreshed. She knows, though, that an electricity-free house would quickly lose its charm were she not able to make a morning cup of tea. The kettle begins to sing softly. Tilda finds the low light of the kitchen strangely soothing, and realizes she has forgotten to put in her contact lenses. The less light there is, the less need she has of them, after all. But they have long been a part of her daily disguise, her defence against prejudice and fear. Her colourless hair and her pale skin don't cause too much interest. Eyes that have only the tiniest hint of blue pigment, however, so that they appear pink, unnerve people. They are what make people stare, and look away, then look again. Tilda is accustomed to a range of reactions to her albinism. Perhaps alone on the hill she will have to deal with them less. She leans against the stove and regards the shaggy shape of Thistle, who remains curled upon the inadequate cushion, watching her new mistress's every move.

'You don't look ready for a run yet,' she says to the dog. 'Still sore?' She wonders briefly if she should have taken the animal to see a vet, but quickly dismisses the idea. The nearest veterinary practice would be in Brecon, ten miles away. How would she get her there without a car? She crouches down beside Thistle and ruffles her fur gently.

'Not exactly on a bus route here, are we girl? You'll be okay. How about some sardines, eh? Would you like that?' Tilda gropes in the cupboard for the right shaped can, opens it, and kneels on the floor to empty the contents into what has become Thistle's bowl. The dog gets stiffly to its feet and comes wagging over. 'There you go. Better than dog food any day,' she says, reasoning the animal must be on the mend if it has a good appetite. At that moment Thistle stops eating, lifts her face from the bowl, and stares hard into the half-light of the hallway. The whole dog tenses. The fur on the back of its neck stands up. Tilda is aware of her own heartbeat racing. Thistle does not move or bark, but begins to emit a low, menacing growl. It is such a raw, basic sound that it transforms the dog from domesticated pet to potential killer in an instant. Tilda listens and squints into the gloom of the hallway, but she can neither hear nor see anything.

'What is it, girl? What's wrong?' she asks, her voice a whisper.

The loud knocking on the front door is so unexpected that Tilda lets out a small scream. Feeling foolish, she walks briskly down the hall. 'Just a minute,' she calls out as she wrestles with the aged key and the bolts, which have become sticky through lack of use. When at last she gets the door open, she finds a wiry-looking man in a cycling helmet standing on the door-step. On seeing Tilda, surprise registers minutely on his face. She is accustomed to watching the reaction of strangers to her appearance. Used to seeing herself seen for the first time. Time and time again. Seeing the curiosity. The unasked questions. Sometimes even a little fear. She remembers that she is not wearing her lenses, and so is impressed that her caller does so well to mask his feelings. He even manages a smile.

'Sorry,' he says, unbuckling his chin strap, 'I should have gone round the back. I'm Bob,' he offers her his business card. 'You called me about your fuses.'

'Oh! The electrician. Of course. Somehow I didn't expect you to arrive on a bike.'

'I like to cycle when I can, if I'm going somewhere I can manage without my ladders.' He shakes his head, gesturing back toward the track. 'Mind you, it's quite a climb you've got there. Think I'll bring the van next time.'

Tilda lets him in and shows him to the fuse box. Thistle slinks in from the kitchen to inspect the visitor, decides he is not a threat, and returns to her cushion by the Rayburn. Tilda fetches Bob a cup of tea and hands it to him when he has finished checking the system.

'Well? Is it hopeless?' she asks. 'It's bound to be ancient, but we had a survey done when we bought the place, and I don't remember reading that it would need replacing.'

Bob shakes his head. 'It's not in bad shape, really. Must have been rewired fairly recently. Someone did a pretty good job of it.' To make his point he throws the main power switch and light is restored.

'So why does it keep tripping out?' Tilda finds herself

blinking, her eyes taking a moment to adjust to the new level of brightness.

Bob shrugs. 'Must be something you've got plugged in. Something you've installed.'

'There isn't anything I can think of. Only my kiln, but I haven't switched that on yet.'

'Be careful when you do. Have you got it on the right circuit? Those things are pretty heavy on power.'

'Yes, the manufacturer sent someone to set it up.'

They both stand in the hall, waiting. Tilda finds herself almost wanting the fuses to blow again, just so there is something for Bob to actually fix.

'Now I feel stupid,' she says. 'Seems like I dragged you up here for nothing.'

'No problem.' Bob finishes his tea in a few gulps. 'The ride down that hill will be worth it.'

'What do I owe you?'

'Nothing too terrible. I'll pop an invoice in the post. Call me if you have any more trouble.'

She watches him descend the lane with increasing speed. It is still early, and there is a fluffy mist sitting over the lake today. The mountains beyond rise up through the froth of white, their peaks dark and sharp against the lightening sky. Thistle pads out to join her in the front garden. She wonders if the dog will be well enough for at least a walk in a couple of days.

'Well, if either of us is going to be up to exercise, we are going to need some proper food. Come on, let's see if I can't magic up groceries on the Internet.'

Back in the kitchen Tilda switches on her laptop and starts to feel quite excited at the prospect of fresh fruit, meat, interesting salad, perhaps some sinful puddings, and a bottle of her favourite wine. The computer *chirrups* encouragingly, displaying the home page so brightly she is forced to dim the screen a little. She is just on the point of selecting a supermarket offering deliveries in the area when the screen goes blue, then grey, then, with a pathetic whirring sound, darkens completely and falls silent.

'Damn.' Tilda slumps back in her chair with a sigh. Before she has time to do more than shake her head there is a sharp bang and all the lights fail again. Seconds later she feels her leg being nudged and looks down to see Thistle, who has tiptoed over to stand beside her. The dog nuzzles her and wags its tail anxiously. That the animal should be so sensitive to her emotional state touches Tilda.

'What a pair we are,' she says, gently stroking the dog's velvety ears. 'You all lame and creaky, me unable to get on with the simplest things. And both of us living in a house that doesn't seem to want to have electricity in it anymore.' She takes a deep breath and snaps shut the lifeless laptop. 'Okay, we can't go on like this,' she tells Thistle. 'You stay here and . . . well, get better. I'm going for a late run that'll take in the village shop. I promise I'll return with food. We can have a proper meal, and then I'm going into the studio to do some work. That sound like a plan to you?'

Thistle answers by padding back to her bed and curling up, nose on paws, tail on nose, clearly settling for a nap.

Outside the air is fresh in the sunshine but drops several crucial degrees to become chilling once Tilda descends into the mist. Even though the hour is later than her usual run time, there are no other walkers out braving the damp and gloomy conditions along the lake-side footpath. Tilda falls into the rhythm of running, finding solace in the repetition of easy, fluid steps. Footfalls crunching on fallen beechnuts. Step, step breathe. Step, step breathe. Heart strong and steady, lungs working calmly.

No need to think. No need to feel. No need to remember. Just here and now. Just this. Only this. You are strong. You are strong. Tilda loves to run. Tilda needs to run.

She takes an unfamiliar route, but follows a clear path. To her left, set back among the marshy side of the lake, she can just make out a small, dilapidated building, so overgrown it is almost entirely hidden by ivy and brambles. The closer the path gets to the water, the denser the fog becomes, so that soon she is running as if within a narrow tunnel through the miasma. Sounds become muffled and distorted. A cawing crow, its voice flattened and stretched, flaps from a low branch, the movement of its wings disturbing the swirling milkiness around it. Some way off, a tractor rumbles across a field, one second sounding close, the next very distant. Tilda can make out the honking of geese upon the water, but visibility is limited to a few yards, so that she can only see the reedy shore and the shallows of the lake's edge. As she runs on she notices that her eyes are struggling to make sense of the floating landscape around her. Low branches across the path seem to stretch out like so many arms reaching for something unseen. The gritty track beneath her feet appears to rise up and fall away as she strides over it. Among the sounds of birds and the tractor she can discern something new. A noise from the surface of the water, rhythmic and fluid. Splash, swoosh, splash, swoosh.

Oars. Someone is rowing. In this? Why would they do that? Can't be for the view. Fishing? Are they fishing?

The sounds grow a little louder. Stronger. Closer. Tilda stops and peers through the murk toward the body of the lake. Slowly a shape begins to form, as much of the mist as out of it. She squints and tries to refocus her unreliable eyes. At last, she can make out a small boat containing three shadowy figures. The vessel is wooden, low in the water, and of a curiously rustic construction. Two of the people in it are rowing, sitting with their backs to Tilda, pulling toward the shore. The shape and clothing of the third person are indistinct still, yet suggest a woman. Tilda blinks away the droplets of mist clinging to her eyelashes and wipes her face with her hand.

Into her watery vision, as she stares harder, come the striking features of the passenger in the boat. Now Tilda can see that this is a young, beautiful woman, her hair concealed beneath twists of leather and some sort of animal skin headdress. Her skin is pale, but the light is too poor, the air too disturbed with mist, for Tilda to make out her eyes or her expression. What becomes clear is that all three in the boat seem to be dressed in some manner of costume, as if decked out for a historical reenactment, or a scene from a movie.

But why on earth would they do that now? Here? On their own?

They are so close now Tilda could call out to them easily. She raises her hand to wave, but something stops her. Something causes her scalp to tingle and the breath to catch in her throat. She can hear drums now, coming from farther around the lake. Suddenly the mist parts, clearing in seconds, so that she can see the expanse of water before her and even the far shore. But things are not as they should be. Instead of the low roof of the visitor's café on the north side of the lake, she can see huts, clustered together, and smoke rising from small fires. And horses. And cattle. And strange figures moving about. There are no cars. No motorboats. No trailers loaded with canoes. Nothing is as she knows it to be.

Tilda's heart starts to pound, although she is already beginning to feel cold from standing. Her mind is spinning.

Am I dreaming? How low must my blood sugar be? I must be dizzy from running and it's making me see things?

The sound of oars being raised from the water and shipped snatches her attention back to the oarsmen. The boat has reached the shallows and the reeds, and the men are allowing it to coast as far in toward the shore as it will go. Every instinct in Tilda is telling her to turn and run, but she finds she cannot move. She is transfixed by what she is witnessing. By the impossibility of what her eyes would have her believe. And, most of all, by the strange figure now standing in the prow of the boat. The woman is tall and her movements graceful. There is such a quiet strength about her. As she waits for the boat to come to a halt she turns her head, slowly, scanning the shore as the mist melts away before her steady gaze. Tilda holds her breath, sensing the inevitability of what will happen next. She wants to move, to flee, but she can no more run than fly as the phantom woman continues to turn, until at last, unmistakably, her gaze falls on Tilda.

There is an instant of connection. A moment where all else seems not to exist, nothing but that moment of seeing and of being seen. It is both wonderful and terrifying. Something inside Tilda snaps and fear galvanizes her. As she spins on her heel and sprints away she hears shouts. Clear, loud, urgent shouts, as those in the boat alert each other to the presence of a stranger. There is a short silence, quickly followed by several splashes.

They're getting out of the boat! They are coming after me!

Now Tilda runs. She finds a speed and power she did not know she possessed and pounds along the path. She can hear heavy footsteps behind her. She can feel the shuddering of the earth as the runners begin to close the gap. Frightened beyond reason, she increases her speed still more, even as the trail twists away from the lake, even as the mist returns to swallow up the fields to her right, to shorten her view to a few yards once more. Still she runs, blindly, wildly, though she can no longer hear her pursuers. And as she rounds a narrow corner she all but barrels into a tall, solitary figure standing firmly in the centre of the path.

SEREN

Two days have passed since I delivered my words of warning at the gathering. The weather continues gentle, the lake is tranquil, but I can feel the discord and alarm on the crannog. People are afraid, and with good reason. The vision was strong, its meaning plain. They harried me for more detail, pestering me with who? and when? and why? Of course I cannot tell them, though as the danger grows stronger there will be more signs. Of that I am certain. As to the who . . . many of them would not believe me if I told them my thoughts, for that is all I have to give; the wisdom of my mind. They will all listen when I bring them a seeing, but some still doubt my own word. As if their prophet is nothing more than a cypher!

But then, I must allow that I am a mystery to them. I cannot expect them to understand all that I do, all that I am. I have followed my mother's calling as a shaman, and it was she who showed me the path of the seeker of visions. She who taught me how to read what I saw. Our strangeness marked us out, and we have always been respected as different, as having a connection to the old religion, to useful talents and gifts. The title of witch they accept less readily. There are too many tales of wickedness attached to my kind, and the combination of seer and witch is rare. My mother knew the day I was born that I carried magic within me. That I had been doubly blessed. But my skills were not enough to keep her in this life. When the sickness took hold of her, she could not shake free of it, and I was too young, too green, my gifts too undeveloped to save her.

The moon is high, sacred darkness claiming the land. There are few clouds, so that a silvery light descends upon the surface of the lake. The water slips and slides in small undulations beneath it, moving in the wake of a scurrying water vole, or the sleepy paddling of slumbering birds that rest upon it for safety. The air smells fresh, cool, yet with the warmth of decay as reeds and rushes begin to die back for another year. From the woods, I can hear my sister owls, cutting the night air with their sharp screeches, or wooing one another with their breathy calls. And now there is something else. My eyes work better without the harsh sun to hurt them, so that I am able to see the darkening shadows forming on the lake, near the centre. I steady my own thudding heart and wait. The silky water does not stir, but I sense a presence. My skin tingles, my pulse grows stronger, louder. I feel a coolness cloak me. She is near. I feel the immense weight of her beneath the surface and my soul dances to know that I am in her company again!

'Seren?'

The voice behind me is as unexpected as it is unwelcome. Even as I wheel around I know that the connection is broken. I hear a low rumble from deep within the lake, fading as it swiftly moves away, and I know that she is gone. I frown at my visitor. He may have donned a monk's robe to disguise himself, but his height and regal bearing give him away to any with the wit to look at him properly. I dip my head, irritation at this interruption preventing me from showing further deference.

'My Prince,' I say, and then, 'You are welcome,' even though he is not. Not at this moment.

'I cannot fool you, can I Seren?' He smiles, pushing back the hood of his habit.

'I would not be worthy of the name "seer" if I could be so easily blinded to the truth.'

'Indeed.' He steps forward. He stands close now. When he speaks again I can feel his breath upon my cheek. 'I wished to come sooner, but, well . . . I have been much occupied . . . .' He waves a hand, vague and apologetic.

'It is the business of a prince to calm his subjects when they are agitated.'

'They ask me questions for which I have no answer.'

'You know the Mercian army stand ready to threaten us at any time. You were quick to tell me this is not news.'

'Queen Aethelflaed will bide her time yet.' He shakes his head. 'She herself is much occupied.'

'Making trysts with Vikings?'

'Trysts. War. One or the other. Both at once. Her plans change direction at the lightest breeze it seems, but that is to our favour. We are not, for the moment, her main concern.'

'You see how at times it is best, after all, not to be the centre of all things?'

Prince Brynach gasps, and then laughs, louder than he meant to. Louder than he should. A nearby coot is startled from its reedy bed and splashes out onto the safety of the open lake. 'Why, Seren, my revered prophet, I believe you are chiding me for vanity!'

'If the crown fits . . .'

He laughs again, more softly this time, and reaches out to put a hand on my shoulder. It is a gesture of friendship, casual, the reflex of a soldier, or one man to another. But I am not a man. And the instant his palm alights on my shoulder I feel the tension in him. He lifts his hand, hesitant, unsure, before moving to touch my hair. I am not in my ceremonial garb now, but wear my workaday woollen tunic. My hair, unbraided and loose, reflects the moon's beams. My arms are bare and the prince's hand is cool against my flesh. His touch is restrained, but there is no mistaking the catch in his breath, nor the widening of his eyes.

'I trust Princess Wenna is in good health,' I say.

At the sound of his wife's name Prince Brynach drops his hand. His manner alters. He becomes brusque. The friendliness is gone. He is a Prince once more, and I his advisor, nothing more.

'At the gathering,' he says, staring out over the lake as he speaks, 'when you told of your vision, you said there were others who threaten us. Others besides the Queen of Mercia.'

'That is what was shown to me in the vision, yes.'

'How? How was it shown?'

I shrug, shaking my head, as if I must explain the obvious to a child. Again. 'There was more than one egg,' I tell him.

'And that signifies multiple enemies? You can be certain?'

'Visions would be of little value were they to mislead, to shroud their meaning in mystery,' I point out.

'Yes. Yes, I see. But how can you know from where these other adversaries will come?'

'The nest within your own fortress clearly suggests your enemy is close to you.'

'But Queen Aethelflaed is not. She is not of my court. She resides a hundred miles from here.'

'Then there is a connection. Something, or someone, links you with a chain of ambition to the Mercian queen and her army. Someone you trust.'

'Someone close to me will betray me?'

'There is more than one manner of closeness, my Prince, as you are aware. A person might live within the same region or cantref. Or the same crannog, perhaps. Or that person may enjoy your trust. Your friendship. Your love, even.'

Anger flashes across Prince Brynach's face. 'You would accuse my wife? Tread with care, Prophet.'

'I accuse no one. I recount my vision. I interpret its meaning for those not able to read the message themselves.'

'But there is nothing – nothing – that speaks of the Princess!'

'There are the facts! Your wife's family makes no secret of their dislike of you.'

'Ours was an arranged marriage! They chose to betroth their daughter to me.'

'In the same way a farmer with a failing farm and one shabby mare puts her to a sturdy stallion from a fine stable.'

'Now you go too far!'

'The alliance of your two families benefitted Princess Wenna's kin far more than it did your own! Your father agreed to the match to avoid a possible uprising. Four years ago there were still men who supported her clan. Your father acted to ensure peace. But times changed, allegiances shifted, and Wenna's family lost their own power. It was she who had the better end of the bargain in the end. And her brother, Rhodri! That creature is more buzzard than man, the way he watches you, waiting for any sign of weakness. He's not bold enough, or foolish enough, to challenge you directly, and he knows there is no necessity. He will bide his time, and the day will come when you are under attack and he will sit on his sword hand sooner than come to your aid. He will do nothing, nothing but watch and gloat and then take pleasure in picking over your bones!'

'And you think Wenna would allow this?'

'What say has she in the matter?'

'She is my Princess!'

'And what is a princess for if not to provide her lord with an heir?'

Silence. He has nothing to say to this. For what can he say? I am right. But being right does not make my words any less poison to his ears. He struggles to hold his temper.

'My wife has my trust. Her family is allied to mine. I will honour that alliance unless or until I am given a reason to doubt it.'

'Have I not just given you such a reason? Did not the vision open your eyes to the truth?'

'Some might say the interpretation is . . . unreliable.'

'You would prefer to doubt the word of your shaman than hear harsh truths about you wife?'

'Who is to say they are true? Some people might say that the interpreter has forgotten her art, her gift, her place, and has shown herself to be nothing more than a jealous woman!'

Now it is my turn to have to master my anger. I speak calmly, though I do not feel calm. 'And anyone who listens to such people, to such talk, is a fool.'

The prince opens his mouth to respond, but I do not wait to hear his argument. I turn on my heel and stride out, away from my camp, away from the light of my fire, away from him. Unaccustomed to being dismissed, but wary of sending his raised voice after me for fear of giving away his whereabouts, Prince Brynach stomps with furious footsteps in the other direction, back to the crannog. Back to his princess.

4

TILDA

Gasping, Tilda steps back from the figure – who is most definitely solid, as her bruised wrist and ribs assure her – and tries to shake the chaos from her head.

'I'm sorry,' she splutters, focusing on the elderly man she has just collided with. 'I wasn't looking where I was going.'

The man smiles at her calmly, a steadying hand still on her arm. He is tall and wiry, with bushy white hair that is partially covered by a tweedy hat. He sports an equally abundant beard and a pair of luxuriant eyebrows. His coat has evidently been chosen for reasons of practicality rather than style. He carries a walking stick with a bone handle carved to resemble a swan, and around his neck hang expensive-looking binoculars.

'This mist can be confusing,' he says, his accent lilting and softly Welsh, taking the hard edges off his words and giving the slightest hiss to each 's'. 'And you were running very quickly.'

'I run most days,' she tells him.

'At such a speed? My goodness. How wonderful to be so strong and nimble. My own running days are over, I fear,' he adds, and then, with a broadening grin, 'unless I was being chased by something, of course. I like to think fear could still lend wings to my heels.'

Tilda tries to read the expression of this stranger.

What did he see? Did he see those . . . people, too? Does he know I was running away from them?

She cannot decide whether this notion makes her more anxious than the idea that the trio in the boat was the conjuring of her own imagination alone.

'I . . .' She hesitates; she cannot discuss what she has seen, what she *thinks* she has seen, with this apparently sensible, normal person. He will think her mad.

Perhaps I am. Perhaps I am losing my mind.

The man's voice cuts through her thoughts.

'Are you quite all right?' he asks. 'Forgive my saying so, but you look a little upset.'

Tilda shakes her head and tries to pull herself together. This is her new home, where she will have to live with her neighbours. She does not want them writing her off as the loon on the hill just yet.

'I'm fine, thank you. I think I overdid it a bit, that's all. Made me a little . . . light-headed.'

'Strong, sweet tea. That's what my late wife would have recommended.' He raises his walking stick, pointing into the mist along the path behind him. 'We are very close to my house; won't you come in for a moment? I'm a poor cook, but I am quite capable of brewing a reasonable pot of Darjeeling.'

'Oh no, thank you, I couldn't possibly . . .'

'Of course you couldn't, what was I thinking? I haven't even introduced myself.' He offers her his hand. 'Professor Illtyd Williams, local historian and keen bird-watcher, resident of the Old School House these past thirty years. Delighted to meet you.'

Tilda manages a weak smile. 'Tilda Fordwells, ceramic artist, resident of Ty Gwyn cottage about five weeks.' She takes his hand and shakes it in what she hopes is a firm and sensible way.

'Well, there we are, then,' says Professor Williams. 'Now that we are acquainted it seems only good manners that we take tea

43

together.' So saying, he turns and begins to stride out with surprising vigour.

Tilda hesitates, hearing her father muttering about not taking sweets from strangers, but then reasons that this gentleman must be eighty years old at least, and is, after all, a neighbour, not a stranger. And besides, she is still unsteady, shaking a little, and there is something so very comforting in the thought of tea with this real and sensible person. On top of which, the idea of returning to the cottage, of more time alone, does not appeal to her. Not yet. Ordinarily, she welcomes solitude but this morning has not been ordinary. Tea, no doubt out of china cups and accompanied by light conversation, is possibly exactly what she needs.

In less than a minute they have reached the stile and climb over it to step onto the lane that winds up from the lake. The tarmac feels firm beneath Tilda's feet, and with each passing moment she begins to doubt what she saw, to find it easier to believe that the mist and the eerie light were playing tricks with her feckless eyesight and overwrought mind. The narrow road takes them past the church and immediately to the little dwelling next to it. Even as a newcomer to the area, Tilda can see that Old School House is unusual, and not built in the conventional architecture of the region. It is constructed of the same blue-grey stone as the church and is roofed with slates, but there the similarities cease. Every window, up and down, is mullioned and set in deep sills. There are pointy arches above the front door and the door set in the wall to the side. The house is approached via a little iron gate and a short path that leads through the most flower-filled garden Tilda has ever seen. Climbing roses scramble up pergolas and walls, as do wisteria, clematis, and jasmine. Even so late in the year and so early in the damp day, the air is filled with the aroma of flowers. Fine examples of hydrangeas and mock orange bushes vie with all manner of shrubs for space between the low wall that runs along the lane and the front of the house itself. Tilda can see that the garden continues around and behind the cottage, with tall and ancient trees to the rear adding shelter and shade and a sense of an enclosed and secret place. A place of beauty, of peace, and of safety.

'Come in, come in.' The professor drops his stick into an umbrella stand and drapes his coat over it. Tilda wriggles out of her waterproof running jacket, hands it to him, and then pulls off her muddy sneakers. 'The sitting room is through there,' he says, waving a hand at a door to their right. 'You make yourself at home and I'll make tea.' With that he disappears into what Tilda assumes is the kitchen and soon she can hear a kettle humming and china being put on a tray.

The hallway is low-ceilinged and in soft light from the latticed windows, but it is still clear that Professor Williams is a man given to collecting things. Every shelf, every wall, every cupboard is crammed with bits of brass, or pieces of china, or paintings, or bric-a-brac of a wide and dizzying variety. In the centre, at the foot of the wooden staircase, stands a very fine grandfather clock, its steady tick-tocking offering a soothingly slow rhythm by which to live one's life. Tilda steps forward to examine it more closely. Its casement is burnished wood, dark red, walnut, she decides, and the clock face decorated with mother-of-pearl and gleaming brass hands. It is about to strike the hour, and she hears the preliminary whirring from deep within its workings as the hammers ready themselves to strike ten.

And then it stops. Completely and suddenly. No chiming. No ticking. Nothing. Tilda feels the hairs prickle at the nape of her neck and she knows, simply *knows*, that it has stopped because of her. She glances toward the kitchen and can still make out her host bustling about. Quickly, she goes through the low door into the living room. The space is clearly organized for the comfort of someone who enjoys reading. There are shelves lining two of the walls, and further cupboards and stacks of hardback volumes about the place. A small sofa is positioned near the fire, with reading lights above, and there is a worn armchair in the window, angled to make the best of the view into the garden and to the lake beyond. As with the hall, much space is devoted to housing all manner of objects and curios. In the moments Tilda spends waiting for the professor and trying to shake off the feeling of unease that has increased again with the stopping of the clock, she spots an ancient record player and beside it a box of vinyl disks; a fearsome wooden mask hanging on the wall; an ornate camel saddle; and on the mantelpiece a large ammonite she cannot resist touching. As she turns to watch the door for the promised tea, her eye takes in the broad desk in the corner of the room. On it, an old map is pinned down at its corners with two glass paperweights – a brass donkey, and a tin that once contained peppermint creams. She is leaning over it when Professor Williams arrives bearing a tray laden with the paraphernalia of teatime.

'Here we are. Oh, I see you have found my map of the lake. A fine example of early nineteenth-century cartography, I think you'll agree. Now, where shall I put this? Would you be so kind as to clear the coffee table of its debris? Thank you so much.' He sets the tray down, the china giving an alarming rattle as he does so.

Tilda has taken off her beanie, so that now her unusual hair is more noticeable. She is pleased to see that if her host registers anything unsettling about her appearance, he does not show it at all.

'It is a wonderful map,' she agrees. 'I can't see that the place has changed much, though the lake does look as if it was bigger then than it is now.'

'You are right about that.' He takes his spectacles from their resting place on the arm of a chair and leans over the desk. 'The church itself was nearer the shore, and so was the vicarage . . . there,' he explains, pointing as he does so. 'It's a retreat house now, and there's a good stretch of land between it and the lake. There are parish records recording the water sometimes flooding considerably farther out. And there, on the far side, you can see the crannog marked. The man-made island. They are quite common in Ireland, but this is the only one in Wales. Not that much of it was visible when this map was drawn up, but people knew it was there.' He gives a small chuckle, a soft, merry sound. 'Well, they *should* have known about it – it'd been there long enough.'

'I read about it, when we came here to look at the cottage.' She pauses, realizing she has given the impression there is still a 'we'.

Have to get used to being just 'I'. Have to start.

'My husband and I, we bought the cottage just before he died,' she explains.

'Oh, I am terribly sorry to hear that.'

'It was sudden. A car accident. We were going to start a new life here . . .' She does not want to be talking about this, not now, not here.

The professor smiles gently. 'I think you'll find being here helps. Eventually. The lake, this valley, it is a very healing place. At least,' he goes on, 'I found it so when my wife, Greta, passed away.'

Tilda returns his smile, grateful for his sympathy and his tact. 'So,' she says as brightly as she can, 'you were going to tell me about the crannog. Everyone says it's important, historically, but to be honest, it looks pretty small to me. I can't imagine much of a settlement on it.'

'Ah, well, people in the ninth century had a different idea of scale, you see. The population was so much smaller then, and construction so much more of a challenge. It must have taken a great deal of time and effort to build. Layer upon layer of stone to begin with and then timbers laid on top, bound together. Imagine making a base sufficiently stable to withstand buildings and people and their livestock.'

'They kept animals on there too?'

'Indeed.' He snatches up a pencil and a piece of paper and begins to make a sketch of what the settlement would have looked like. 'There was the long hall, here, like this. A building about the size of a barn, if you can picture that, single storey, but quite a high roof, sloped to keep the good Welsh rain off it. They would have used the hall for important gatherings, celebrations, meetings of various visiting princes and so on. Historians have established that the palace was built for Prince Brynach, who was ruler of the region at the time. He and his family and extended family and guards would have lived there. And, of course, if the community were to come under attack the rest of the villagers would leave the shore and hurry onto the crannog to take refuge in the hall. We think there was another building here, probably providing living quarters for more soldiers and their families, with room for some of the more prized beasts to be stabled. Next to that, at an angle' – he squints through his glasses as he makes rough marks on the paper '– like this. That would have been the blacksmith's work-shop. Very important.'

'For horse shoes, I'm guessing.'

'Partly, though not all the horses would have been shod. What made the smithy so crucial was that this was where weapons were forged. Swords, daggers, shields, helmets and so forth . . . Those were dangerous times. The prince had to be ready to defend his territory.'

'You certainly seem to know a lot about it.'

'Oh –' he shakes his head – 'a historian can never know enough about his pet subject. The lake has always fascinated me, as it did my wife. Greta was an anthropologist.' He waves an arm at the more exotic artifacts in the room. 'Most of what you see here was collected on her travels. It was she who first fell in love with the lake. She insisted we move here. Said she felt an affinity with the place. And I'm very glad of it. The lake provided us with so much to think about. People have lived here for centuries. Millennia, in fact. It is such an ideal spot for a settlement, d'you see? Fresh water, fish, the shelter of those hills over there, fertile soil; it has it all. Prince Brynach, when he built the crannog for his royal dwelling, well, he knew what he was about. And, of course, there are so many lovely legends and myths attached to the place. It has its own magic, I think it fair to say. One could study it a lifetime and not know everything.' He returns to the tea tray. 'Now, sugar? Milk? Chocolate biscuit? And perhaps you'll tell me what it is that a ceramic artist does?'

Half an hour passes swiftly in the old man's company. As Tilda sits on the squishy sofa, her feet curled beneath her, the reviving tea and the friendly conversation with the professor have such a restorative effect upon her that she soon feels quite differently about what she thinks she saw at the lake. Their talk has taken them from the history of the area to the abundance of wild birds that now live there, and the fact that the far side is a thriving example of local tourism, with its campsite and boats for hire and sailing lessons. It all sounds to Tilda so reassuringly normal, and convinces her that her fanciful mind had been working with her tired body to trick her, nothing more.

Not enough breakfast. Pushing myself too hard. Too much time spent on my own.

As she forms the thought she remembers she does not, actually, live alone anymore. She has a shaggy hound as a house mate, one that might be in need of letting out by now. She puts her cup on the tray and stands up.

'I ought to get on,' she says. 'Leave you in peace.'

'My dear girl, I have nothing but peace, these days. Your visit was a most welcome distraction from the day-to-day. Please do drop in on me again.'

They make their way into the hall, where Professor Williams notices that the clock is no longer working.

He peers at it, tapping the glass that houses the face. 'Strange. It's usually such a reliable timepiece.'

Tilda watches him as he opens the casing and adjusts the weights and chains inside. She is aware of some of her earlier anxiety returning. 'Perhaps it needs winding up,' she suggests, even though she knows nothing about clocks, and is fairly certain the professor is the sort of man who would look after such a fine antique with great care.

'No, no, I don't think it's that. Let me see . . .' He minutely alters some setting which Tilda cannot see. There is a pause, and then the hallway is once again filled with the steady rhythm of the grandfather clock. 'There!' The professor shuts the door to the workings and gives the thing an affectionate pat. 'Lovely craftsmanship. Look at the inlay, can you see from there? Here, thin strips of a lighter-coloured wood cut and set into the walnut casing. Beautifully done. You'd think it was painted, the joins are so flawless. If you run your fingers over it the surface is as smooth as marble. You try,' he says, standing back.

Tilda finds she cannot step forward. The calm that she has acquired while with Professor Williams is leaving her, minute by minute. Her pulse begins to race as if she has just run up the hill to Ty Gwyn, for she knows beyond doubt that if she touches the clock it will stop again. And this time there will be a witness to the madness. The professor will see that it is she who is causing the clock to stutter and fail. Just as the lights failed at the cottage. Just as the computer failed.

Because of her.

And I won't be able to pretend otherwise any longer. Not even to myself.

'I'm sorry,' she blurts out, 'I really have to go.' Hurrying to the doorway, she jams on her sneakers, hat and jacket as the professor chatters on about tea and clocks and the fog having lifted outside.

She scarcely hears what he is saying as she mumbles a good-bye and hurries through the heavy oak front door, breaking into a run the second she turns in the direction of home.

Two days after meeting Professor Williams, Tilda steels herself to visit the busy side of the lake. Ordinarily, she would avoid the bustle of such a place, with its boats for hire, ice-cream van, café, sailing club, campsite, and so on, but the more she thinks about it, the more she knows she must go there. However much tea and a chat with the professor helped her to shrug off what she saw in the mist that morning, time on her own has forced her to think again. Try as she might to convince herself that what she saw was nothing more than a trick of the eerie light combined with low blood-sugar levels, she cannot shake off the feeling that there was more to it than that. On top of which, her own effect on the grandfather clock still disturbs her. She cannot see how, *if*, the two things are in any way connected, and yet there is a niggling sense that they must be. On her return to the cottage that same day the lights had fused again. Not when she first arrived home, but after she had been there an hour or so.

Something is going on. Either I'm losing my mind, or there is another explanation.

She is relieved not to be having to explain her actions to anyone. She is aware how unformed her ideas are. How unfounded her theories. She is acting only on a hunch, and has no real notion of where it will lead her. Or even what it is she is hoping to find. Last night she sat in front of the fire in the snug sitting room of Ty Gwyn, sipping a glass of daftly expensive wine from the local shop, with Thistle stretched out on the hearth rug, and tried to pull together what she knew. Or at least, what she thought she knew. Her flashbacks – or waking nightmares as she had come to think of them – of the moment of Mat's death are not new. She has been having them for over a year now. But recently they do seem to be more vivid, more horribly, cruelly real in every heartbreaking detail. And then there are the electrics in the cottage. Bob found nothing wrong, yet the fuse box continues to trip out so frequently that Tilda has given up resetting the thing. She and the dog muddle along without electric light or the computer or any other plug-in appliances. The solid fuel range in the kitchen means she can continue to boil a kettle or cook the few food items she has left. And it heats the water to lukewarm, too. The open fire in the sitting room stops the house from becoming uncomfortably cold, even if upstairs is getting increasingly bleak as the temperature outside drops. Tilda is certain that it was her own proximity to the professor's clock that caused it to stop, so she cannot pretend that the wiring at the cottage is faulty. It makes no real sense, but the fact is, *she* is the common factor in both cases.

Sitting next to Thistle, gazing into the flames, Tilda had tried to recall what she had seen – or thought she had seen – at the lake. Three people in a boat. Two men, one woman, rowing for the shore. Dressed outlandishly. Or rather, outdatedly.

By several hundred years.

And the far side of the lake utterly changed. No café, no boat house, no sailing club. No buildings that made any sense. Just a collection of huts. As if everything had been washed away by the mist and replaced by another land entirely. The most obvious cause for what she had seen, Tilda had decided as she drained her wine, was that grief had finally unhinged her. She was losing her flimsy hold on her own sanity. It was not a conclusion that brought her any comfort. And the only way she could think of to disprove it, to come up with something, *anything* else, was to go to the north shore and reassure herself that everything was still there, still as it should be, in all its slightly tacky, hot dog and paddleboat normality. That her hallucination, if such it was, amounted to nothing more than the febrile workings of a troubled mind. Her grief counsellor, all those months ago, had advised her to accept her flashbacks as a part of the grieving process. Was this latest vision simply more of the same?

So here she is, duffle-coated against the late autumn chill, woolly hat pulled low, her pale plait tucked into her collar and Thistle walking a little stiffly at her side on the end of an old leather belt that stands in for a lead. Although it is late in the year, it is the weekend, and plenty of people have taken the opportunity to come down to the lake. The little car park is nearly full, and the bicycle racks bristle with mountain bikes and racers, their riders sitting nearby to eat their lunches, or wandering closer to the shore to view the lake. There is a family of swans being fed by some walkers, their cygnets grown large but still sporting some of their grubby brown feathers. Pushy mallards waddle onto the small tarmac quay in the hope of sandwich crusts or maybe the stub of an ice-cream cone. A harassed woman shepherds her own brood of young children away from the water's edge, luring them toward the café with the promise of hot dogs. A party of teenage canoeists busy themselves unloading their boats from a trailer.

All perfectly normal. Solid people. Real buildings. Of course.

Tilda walks past the concrete boat launch and follows the path to the recently constructed crannog centre. Unlike its ancient namesake, this little thatched building is a modest single-storey room, with glassless windows set into its curved walls, constructed to give people better views of the lake. Like the original crannog, it is reached via a wooden walkway, the whole thing supported by stout wooden stilts. Standing on the decked and railed area that encircles the hut, Tilda has the curious sense she is above and yet upon the water. She can hear ripples lapping against the wood. Coots and moorhens scoot about below her, bobbing on the gentle waves the light breeze has stirred up, or hurrying into the cover of the reeded area of the shore. Thistle creeps nearer the edge and peers into the water, ears alert, following the progress of a water vole as it gathers weeds for its nest. Looking across the lake, Tilda can make out St Cynog's Church and the Old School House on the far side, and the bird blind a little farther around. This enables her to pinpoint where she must have been standing when she saw the people in the boat. The air is clear today, visibility excellent, and all there is to see is the reedy shore, the path, the fields with cows grazing peacefully, and the small area of woodland to the right.

A sightseer comes to stand next to her, scanning the water with expensive-looking binoculars. Tilda makes a mental note to rummage through the as-yet unpacked boxes back at the cottage to find her own pair. Following the visitor's line of vision, she sees what it is that has caught his attention. To the west of the lake, a hundred yards or so from the shoreline, are a minibus and a van and a cluster of people; a small knot of activity on a usually empty part of the landscape. It is not a campsite, yet she can just about make out a large tent pitched beside two portable toilets. She does not feel bold enough to ask the man if she might borrow his binoculars, so instead she forces herself to speak.

'What's going on over there?' she asks. 'Can you tell?'

Without lowering his glasses the man replies, 'Archaeologists. Some sort of dig, according to the bloke hiring out the boats.' Only now does he look at Tilda.

Look. Look away. Look again. Standard reaction number three.

Into the awkward silence comes a woman – the man's wife, Tilda thinks – holding a small girl by the hand. While the adults seek refuge in talking about nothing, the child stares openly from beneath a floral sou'wester. Tilda holds her gaze, waiting.

She has her contact lenses in place, but she had not bothered with mascara or any sort of makeup for weeks now, so that her white lashes and brows are clearly visible. At last the girl, swinging her mother's hand, asks loudly, 'Why is that dog on a belt? Haven't you got a proper lead? And why are your eyes funny? Are you blind?' The mortified parents hasten to smooth over their daughter's inadvertent rudeness.

'I'm so sorry,' says the woman, reflexively pulling her child back a pace.

'It's all right,' Tilda says.

'She shouldn't ask questions like that.'

'Really, it's fine.'

The girl frowns deeply, causing her rain hat to drop a little lower on her brow. 'But, Mummy, why does she look like that? And why hasn't the dog got a proper lead and a proper collar?'

Tilda glances at Thistle's makeshift leash, and has to agree that the belt buckle looks uncomfortable on the dog's slender neck. She crouches down in front of the child. 'You know, you're right. She does need a proper collar. And a lead. I'm going to go and buy her one right now. What colour do you think I should get?'

The girl gives the question serious consideration and then says firmly, 'Pink.'

'Right. Pink it is. I'll see what I can do.'

'Can I stroke her?'

'I think she'd like that,' Tilda says.

The child moves closer, her nose only just higher than Thistle's shoulder. She gives the animal a gentle pat. Both dog and child appear to enjoy the experience.

Tilda straightens up, smiling a practiced smile.

The parents breathe again. The moment of embarrassment has passed. The little family moves on with their day, the child turning to wave at Thistle. Tilda sighs and returns her attention to the lake. The archaeologists are pushing a small boat out onto the water and placing some sort of floats or buoys at measured distances. Looking to the north, in the space between their camp and the car park, now Tilda can clearly see the original crannog. It is a small island, with little to give away its unique origins; the fact that it is the only such man-made island in the country, and is still there, settled onto the silky waters of the lake, over one thousand years after its construction. Now it is almost completely covered in trees, and is inhabited only by some of the more timid waterbirds that benefit from its protected status. The oaks and willows, their branches just patchily leaved now, are reflected prettily in the water, and Tilda at once finds herself thinking how she might use such shapes and patterns in her work. It has been a while since she felt inspired to try something new, and a tiny spark of hope inside her lifts her mood.

Maybe now. Maybe here. Those twisted boughs and shadowy trunks . . . soft greys mingled with the fading gold leaves. I could do something with that.

A nearby mallard quacks loudly for no apparent reason, causing Thistle to jump. Tilda notices that the hound is shivering a little.

'You're still not properly better, are you, poor thing? Come on, we'll buy some chips in the café on our way home.'

Their route takes them past a shop selling camping equipment, fishing rods, and similar leisure supplies. There is no sign on the door barring dogs, so Tilda is able to take Thistle inside in search of a collar and lead. Minutes later the pair emerge with the dog sporting a rather bright pink-with-blue-paw-prints ensemble.

'Sorry about the colour,' Tilda tells her, 'but that must be a bit more comfortable, at least.'

Thistle regards her new mistress with a quizzical expression, her ears cocked and her head a little to one side, but otherwise keeps her opinion to herself. Together, they head for home.

SEREN

It is restful here, inside the single room that is my house. I do not have ornately carved chairs, nor costly tapestries, nor silver goblets. Mine is a simple existence, but I have all I need, and I am content. No man tells me what I should do or how I should be. I choose to live alone. To live separate. Some wonder that I do not crave the protection or the company life on the crannog offers, but what need have I of protection? True, there are those who wish me gone, but they are too afraid of me to act upon those wishes. And if they were to conquer their fear, still they would hold back, for in their hearts they know they need me to be here. For am I not, after all, their protector?

And as for company . . . I do not crave the companionship of other women, for I have never found one who did not judge me against herself and find me either to be envied or pitied. As for the friendship of men . . . well, when the day comes when one is man enough to treat me as his equal, then, only then, will I allow desire to be my guide.

And beyond all this, I have the company of my visions. When I see, when I travel to those places others cannot, I am surrounded by all manner of wondrous beings, from times past and yet to come. They welcome me, and offer me their friendship and their counsel. How then, could I be lonely? How could I feel a lack of solace and kinship? What use have I for love? I have witnessed the foolishness it engenders in the most steadfast of people. I have seen sensible women lose their wits to a handsome stranger. I have marvelled at good men debased by their passion for an unsuitable woman. I would rather keep my own company than permit myself to be so unraveled by another.

My little house is cozy on these cold nights. The walls are thick wattle and daub, darkened by woodsmoke inside and weather outside. The roof is a dense thatch of reeds with low eaves to keep off rain and snow. There is a single doorway, closed by a rug in summer and a wooden door in winter, and a hole in the roof for the fire to smoke through. The floor is earth, packed and trodden to a hard, smooth surface, which I cover in rushes on one side beneath my bed of wood pallet and wool sack, covered in sheepskins. I keep a small fire in the centre of the space, ringed by stones. I like to burn sweet wood or herbs to fill the room with soothing scents, and to night an apple bough crackles in front of me, while sprigs of thyme singe slowly above it. I have a wooden stool, two padded bolsters, and a simple rug upon which to sit or recline. Above my fire stands a slender spit so that I might roast fowl or a piece of deer meat, or suspend a pot for stew, or to simmer my infusions. A roughly hewn chest to one side keeps my precious items clean and dry: my ceremonial robes, my braids, my blood letting blades, my bones for telling, my ground spices and preserved tinctures. Nearby sit two stout jars, one empty, one filled with honey, and a shallow bowl in case I have need of warm water to bathe wounds or otherwise offer treatments. All else I hang upon the walls: my wolf headdress, my staff, my drum, my axe, my hazel basket, an animal skin for water. My boots stand by the door – one soft leather pair, another sturdier against the cold. Next to them on a high peg I keep my hooded cloak of fine, dark red wool, a gift from the prince to show the grati-tude of the community after a foretelling saved them from the worst of a storm. Tonight, alone and at my ease, I wear a plain woollen tunic, tied loosely at the waist with a broad twist of hide, a string of painted clay beads, and a bracelet of polished ram's horn. When I am alone I leave my hair to hang free. I do not adorn my body greatly unless I am presenting my visions as shaman. When I am at rest, I am content to let simple jewellery and the ancient patterns worked onto my skin be my only decoration.

I am soon for my bed, but I become aware of footfalls along the path outside. I listen, head cocked. Three people. One striding bold and loud as only a young man can, rudely waking everything he passes. The others are softer. Women, I believe. I slip on my cape and step out of the hut. As I do so I am hailed by my visitors to warn me of their proximity, as if I were unaware of their approach! The youth I recognize as Siōn, the son of the princess's brother, the family likeness marked with his green eyes and dark complexion, who is evidently accompanying his elders to afford them the enormous benefit of his protection. He steps to one side and stands feet apart, arms folded. His stance is arrogant, but his body is that of a boy, not yet hardened by years or the grit of manhood. The women come forward. Both wear deep hoods in some small effort to mask their identities, but the ruse is pointless, given the expensive fabric of the taller woman's garb, and the stout girth of her companion. A simpleton in his cups would know them.

I stand tall. 'Princess Wenna, good evening to you.'

'Forgive us for disturbing you so late, Seren Arianaidd.' Her use of my full name – not her habit – suggests she is eager to win my favour. She wants something from me, that much is plain. Her maid, Nesta – for it can be no other – stomps her feet against the cold and her mistress takes the point. 'I would speak with you,' the princess goes on. 'Perhaps your house would afford us more privacy?'

And more warmth. I nod, holding open the door so that they may enter, but shaking my head when Rhodri's boy attempts to join us. 'We would all feel so much safer with you standing guard,' I tell him, and he smiles happily, having not the wit to hear the mockery in my voice.

The room feels crowded with the three of us standing. I indicate the stool and bolsters and we arrange ourselves at comfortable distances from each other. The two women look about them, Nesta with her perpetual sneer, Princess Wenna with practiced blankness. She lowers her hood to reveal her hair coiled sleekly upon her head, a band of silver-threaded braid across her brow. She is beautiful, yet the prince does not love her. Does it gnaw at her heart, I wonder? Or does she care only for his affection because it makes her position more secure? Why has she come? Why has her maid agreed to accompany her? Nesta's contempt for me is widely known. She is a wise woman of sorts, offering herbal remedies and assisting at births. All for a price, of course. Nesta sees the value of everything measured in silver. To her I am a rival in the business of cures, and she is jealous, both of my magic, and of my standing. And there is more besides, for she is the keeper of a knowledge of dark spells. Witchery of a dangerous kind, little known or practiced now. She has no call to use any of her talents, and she should be thankful for that. Such poisons and hexes as she has inherited would not endear her to anyone. Yet I know she resents my position of trust. She is envious of the respect afforded me. And she is no servant, in truth, but her mistress's cousin, and, as such, is not given to unquestioning service. But still, the princess trusts her. What has compelled them to visit me? For does not Princess Wenna, too, have her own reason to despise me?

I push another stout log onto the fire, sending up a small shower of sparks. There is a moment of smoke before the bark begins to burn and new flames lick hungrily at the wood. I turn to the princess, waiting for her to speak. She meets my gaze – one of the few who will – and keeps her voice level.

'I will not insult you by talking of trifles, Seren Arianaidd. I have come here to ask for your help because no other can give it.'

At this, Nesta fidgets and her sour face sours further.

'How can I be of service, Princess?' I ask.

She hesitates, the slightest in-breath, yet her composure does not falter.

'Prince Brynach and I were wed four years past, but our union has not been blessed with children.'

Nesta can remain silent no longer. 'I have said, my lady, 'tis not a question of time. Were you to follow my advice—'

'I have had sufficient of your vile concoctions and undigni-fied instructions!' Princess Wenna cuts off her maid. 'No more.' She turns back to me. 'The prince requires an heir, that is the fact of the matter. It is I who must provide him with one.'

So, she has come to me on this! This most personal of all business. And yet, of course, for a princess there is more than what is private to be considered. And nobody knows this better than Wenna. For if there is not love to bind her to her prince, and no child, then all that is left is the fickle bond of politics. Should it suit our leader to no longer be allied to his wife's kin, what price for her slender crown then? How much has it cost her to seek *my* help? Pride might have stopped her. Or the desire not to admit her failing to me. But I am being foolish, for her barrenness is not a secret.

'Can you help me?' she asks. 'Are you able to serve your prince in this way?'

Now I understand. Clever woman indeed! By placing her malady in my hands she has ensured that any failure to pro-duce an heir could be laid at my door. At the same time, she knows that, should I succeed and she give her husband his longed-for child, she will take the credit. She will be lauded and revered, her position secured. Perhaps she will even earn his love. But should I fail, should no babe appear, then the shortcoming will be mine, even if it must be put about *secretly* that she sought my assistance. She will no longer be seen as the sole reason for a childless marriage. It could even happen that in such a case Prince Brynach would cease to find my company so desirable. Could that be her hidden motive? Clever woman indeed, for I cannot refuse her.

I stand up and take my knife from its hook on the wall. Both women start, their eyes wide, their bodies taut. Quickly, I turn the knife in my hand so that the blade points toward me, and offer the handle to the princess.

'Cut me a lock of your hair,' I tell her.

She takes the knife, and Nesta fumbles with the pins securing her twisted hair. At last, some falls free.

'You must cut it yourself,' I explain.

She does so, with purpose, not taking some tiny wisp, but a bold hank. She means my magic to work, then, that much is plain.

I take the hair from her, coiling it tightly. In my wooden trunk I find a small leather pouch to keep the precious lock. Tying the drawstring firmly, I slide the pouch into the pocket of my tunic.

I remain standing and the others get to their feet.

'Have you any instructions for me?' Princess Wenna asks. 'Is there any action I should take, anything . . .'

She casts her eyes down, and for the first, the only time, I see the vulnerable young woman beneath the mask of privilege and position.

I shake my head. 'I will do what needs to be done,' I tell her.

Outside we find Siôn blowing into his hands and stamping his feet against the cold. He is making so much noise all by himself I doubt he would have heard an approaching army. At the sight of us he becomes brisk and arrogant, taking his place beside the princess importantly.

The women pull up their hoods. Princess Wenna takes a velvet purse from her robe and offers it to me.

'Your payment,' she says, 'for your trouble.'

It is as well that the darkness shades the expression on my face. There is a silence charged with my own anger and the expectation of the three who stand before me. When I speak, I am aware my ire colours the sound of my words. The princess knows well how to insult me, and chooses to do so with her nephew as witness, so that the slight will be reported back to Rhodri.

'I work for Prince Brynach's betterment,' I tell her. 'For his safety, for his favour. I require no pieces of silver. A seer cannot be hired for coin. My gifts are not for sale.' As if to give weight to my sentiment, a heavy cloud swallows up the bright moon so that the blackness about us deepens. There is no more to be said. The princess gathers her pride and her followers and turns for the crannog. I stand and watch as the three figures melt into the night.

5

TILDA

A steady drizzle has rendered the landscape grey and blurred, so that Tilda is happy to be shut in her studio, turning her attention to her work. The feeble sunlight has compounded her lighting problems, however, so that she has resorted to candles and a storm lantern to light the space. She put a match to the fire in the wood-burning stove more than an hour ago, so that now the room is warm enough. Thistle, who has become her grey shadow, settles herself on the rag rug in front of the stove. The studio already has a familiar, cozy feel to it. Tilda sits in a dusty, glaze-stained chair by the patio doors, sketch book on her knee, attempting to reproduce the shapes and patterns she saw among the twisted branches of the crannog trees. She works with quick, confident strokes, her stub of soft pencil creating thick marks on the paper. She tries to recall the way the limbs of the trees entwined and crossed through and over one another.

As if winter winds have tied them in knots.

Her intention is to fashion her trademark large, bulbous pots, and to work onto them these intricate, flowing designs. She has not yet decided on colours. Should she use mottled, natural finishes, or opt for deep, rich glazes? As she chews her pencil in thought, her eyes look up from the page, so that she is unable to avoid staring directly at her cold, inert kiln. The sight of it brings home an inescapable fact.

Without a reliable power supply, she cannot switch the kiln on or, should it work long enough to reach the needed temperature, risk firing her work inside it.

No power equals no firing. No firing, no pots. No pots, no money.

She frowns, biting hard on the wood of the pencil, resisting the voice in her head that is telling her that drawing anything is pointless because she cannot, as things stand, translate her designs into ceramic objects. With a sigh she turns and squints out of the window. The rain is lessening, and the grubby cloud is beginning to lift. She can barely see the lake, but there is a glimmer on the tops of the hills beyond that suggests the weather is, slowly, improving. Remembering her binoculars, she leaves her sketch pad on the floor and goes in search of them. There is a stack of boxes in the corner of the studio, which seems as good a place as any to begin. She opens and closes several packing cases, bracing herself for photographs of Mat, or momentos of their time together. Mercifully, she finds what she is looking for within minutes. Standing at the picture window, she adjusts the glasses to her eyes and scans the lake. The church is easy enough to find, its tower a dark grey shape amidst the almost monochrome landscape. Even the water of the lake itself has lost all vestige of colour, leaving it a pool of liquid metal dotted with smudged birds of indiscernible type. The crannog is similarly drab today, and even the powerful lenses do not reveal any helpful detail.

A movement catches Tilda's eye. She shifts her focus to the west of the lake and follows the jerky progress of a minibus approaching the site of the archaeological dig. She recalls noticing it for the first time during her visit to the populated side of the lake. The thought of excavating the past in such a way both intrigues and disturbs her somehow. As she watches, the vehicle parks next to the large tent that appears to be the centre of operations. Five people get out and are met by two others who emerge from the tent. Together they walk quickly to the staked-out area nearer the shore. Tilda turns the dial on the glasses to keep the scene sharp. The figures crouch low on the ground, and even in these conditions, through the poor light and the water-filled air, Tilda can tell that there is excitement among the group, with a deal of gesticulating and nodding and pointing going on. She wonders at people's ability to become so animated over what seems to be merely a misshapen hole in the mud. Her eyes are becoming tired with the strain of looking at such distant and indistinct objects, when, more suddenly than makes any sense, her field of vision is filled with a face. It is a face so terrible, and so hideous, and so close, it makes her scream and drop the glasses. But in that split second, in that instant when the image filled her view, the awful details of that face have been seared into Tilda's consciousness: the bulging eyes, the smashed jaw, the swollen and bruised flesh, the mouth open in a silent scream, the whole so distorted and disfigured she cannot even tell if it is a man or a woman. Tilda takes a step back, expecting to find this fearsome person standing inches away on the other side of the window. But there is no one. Just the view and the weakening rain. Her heart is jumping and her mouth dry. Nervously, she glances over her shoulder, but Thistle continues to sleep undisturbed. The binoculars lie at her feet. She forces herself to pick them up. Lifting them, hands trembling, she puts them to her eyes once more, holding her breath as she does so.

Nothing. Just the lake. Fields. Trees. Nothing . . . more.

Yet again she finds herself struggling to make sense of what her eyes – her unreliable eyes – are telling her mind.

Is my brain becoming as fragile as my eyesight now?

She directs her gaze to the crannog, but it remains a tangle of blurred branches. A small flock of inland seagulls descend from the clouds and land upon the water. The farmer has decided to bring in his cattle, and two black-and-white sheep-dogs race across the field to gather them in. The archaeologists continue to enthuse about their brown patch of excavated soil. All is as normal and as unremarkable as it could possibly be. All except Tilda's galloping heart.

Her nerves are so tautly strung that the ringing of the telephone makes her jump again. She snatches up the receiver on the workbench, more than a little surprised to find it still working.

'Hello, Little Rabbit.' Her father's voice brings its habitual comfort. 'Not interrupting great work, am I?'

Tilda closes her eyes, picturing his dear face, fighting to blot out that other, terrifying one and replace it with her father's, gentle, reassuring features. She is grateful for the normality his conversation will bring.

'No, Dad. You're not interrupting anything. How are you? And Mum?'

'As ever. I am between crossword puzzles, and your mother has gone out to do battle with the local planners over the possibility of fracking, I believe.'

'Poor planners.'

'I think it safe to say the people of North Somerset can rest easy in their beds.'

'It's good for her to have a project.'

'Other than we two, you mean? Indeed it is. I have even been left to watch the rugby unharried.' He pauses, then asks, 'And you, Tilda? How is life up there on the mountaintop?'

'It's only a hill, Dad, and I'm nowhere near the top.'

'Even so, not many neighbours, not a lot of folk passing . . .'

'I'm fine. Stop worrying.'

'I fear it is written somewhere in the terms of my parental contract: Fret frequently about well-being of offspring.'

Tilda bites her lip, knowing that she cannot even begin to tell her father of the things she has seen. *Thinks* she has seen.

Or the fact that she has no power in the cottage. Or how only moments ago she was frightened half out of her skin by something that wasn't really there.

'I'm fine, really. I'm fine.'

'That's what you always say.'

'That's 'cause I'm always fine.'

They both know this is not true, but that Tilda says it because she loves her father and doesn't want him to worry, and he lets her say it because he loves her and doesn't want her to have to talk about difficult things if she doesn't want to. Which makes her love him even more.

'Your mother is talking about a visit,' he tells her.

'Ah.'

'Yes, ah.' The line becomes crackly, but Tilda can just about hear the smile in his voice. 'All the same, it would be nice to see you, Little Rabbit.'

And now Tilda smiles. Smiles at the thought of having her father close by, even if it does mean putting up with her mother too. Smiles at his use of her pet name again. The name he gave her when she was old enough to ask about the way she looked, about difference, about why one thing is thought ugly and another thing beautiful. He had taken her to a pet shop and helped her choose a snowy white rabbit with pink eyes, the pair of them agreeing it was the most beautiful thing either of them had ever seen.

And now she smiles with relief at the discovery that she is, after all, still able to smile.

'A visit would be great, Dad,' she says. 'Really. I'd love to see you.'

By the time she puts down the phone she is feeling altogether stronger. The rain has stopped completely, at last, and she decides a run will chase away bad thoughts and strengthen her further.

★ ★ ★

As always, the meditative rhythm of running, coupled with the sense of well-being exertion brings, added to the uplifting effect of the landscape through which she moves, act both as balm to Tilda's troubled mind and tonic for her body. She lopes down the lane, crosses the road and speeds past the church, forcing herself to return to the place where she experienced her curious sighting of the people in the boat. There is no mist today, but the weather, which earlier seemed to be clearing, has changed its mind, so that by the time Tilda reaches the narrow path on the south side of the lake the rain has set in once more. Her lightweight running gear is no match for the deluge, and she silently berates herself for not wearing her waterproof jacket. There is no wind and the rain pelts down hard onto the surface of the lake, causing it to seethe and sing. Soon visibility is reduced to a few strides and Tilda is forced to slow her pace.

Run steady, run strong. Head down, work arms, work. No need to rush. Nothing to run from. Nothing to run to.

Just as she is starting to shake off the memory of the face that had so startled her earlier, she senses rather than sees something moving in the water to her right. From the corner of her eye, not daring to turn her head, she follows the ripples that glide along beside her. She fights conflicting desires; the first being to run faster, to put as much distance as she can as quickly as she can between herself and whatever it is that is stirring beneath the water. The other instinct, the stronger one, as it turns out, the one that wins, compels her to stop. To stop and to face the danger. She stands firm, hands on hips now, looking braver than she feels, watching the surface of the lake as it undulates in shallow waves that are still speckled and peppered by the incessant rain. Her ears are filled with the hiss of water falling on water, to the accompaniment of her own pounding heartbeats. Rain washes over her face, distorting her vision further. She wipes her face with her hand, determined to look, determined to see whatever there is to see. Slowly the eddies and swirls cease their forward motion. The water is disturbed in one place only now, directly in front of Tilda, only a matter of yards from where she stands, her breath held, her fists clenched.

Whatever it is, let it be real! No more ghosts. No more madness.

As she stares hard at the boiling lake, rain running unchecked into her eyes, down her cheeks and dripping off her jaw, a shape begins to emerge. Something dark. Something smooth, reflecting the weak, silvery light of the water-filled day. Tilda gasps, and then, suddenly, she is standing face-to-face with a diver, complete with mask, breathing apparatus, and wet suit. Tilda did not know what she was expecting – or dreading – but it was definitely not this. Not this slightly comical figure, which is now removing his mouthpiece and lifting his diving mask, to reveal a young man, dark skinned, with bright green eyes and a ready grin.

'Good morning!' he calls to her over the noise of the rain. He is close to the shore but he treads water rather than standing and stumbling in the mud that must be beneath his feet. 'Wet day for a run,' he says, taking in the drenched state of Tilda's clothes. 'You should get yourself one of these,' he adds, indicating his wet suit.

The sudden relief, as fear and tension melt away, leaves Tilda quite drained and not altogether in the mood for banter with a stranger.

'I don't imagine you can see anything down there,' she says, pointing to the lake. 'It must be so muddy, and dark, and churned up by the rain.'

He lifts a large underwater torch, making Tilda feel a bit stupid.

'What are you looking for, anyway?' she asks.

'Ah, well, I won't know that until I find it.'

She nods, deciding that she has done her bit by way of being civil and can now reasonably move on. But as she turns and starts off the diver swims alongside her. 'You should try it,' he says. 'Diving. It's quite something, beneath the water.'

'I prefer dry land,' she tells him, caught between staying and going.

'You call that dry?'

The question makes her awkwardly conscious of how she must look, soaked to the skin, flushed from running, beanie plastered to her head.

As if sensing her discomfort, the young man says, 'I could give you a lift, if you like.' He gestures into the gloom and now she can make out a small boat bobbing a little ways behind him on the lake. It has an outboard motor and is evidently anchored so that he can return to it after his dive. She watches as he swims out to it, takes hold of the side and pulls himself aboard. The little boat rocks wildly but rights itself once he is in. He slips off his oxygen tanks and pulls down his rubber hood, revealing a mass of black curls. 'Come on, I'll take you across the lake,' he tells her.

She shakes her head. 'No. Thanks. I want to finish my run.'

'I can bring the boat nearer the shore if you like. You won't have to swim. Though, actually, I don't think you could get any wetter.'

His teasing begins to rankle. She knows how bedraggled she looks, and now she is being made to feel more than a little silly. Soon he will detect her fear of the water, she is sure of it. And then Tilda has an idea. A startling, wild idea. An idea that makes her pulse quicken again, and fills her with a curious excitement.

Crazy, girl. Too much time on your own. It'd never work. You can't do it. Can you?

She stills her thoughts. With no clear notion of what it is she is doing, only a clear picture in her mind of the end result she is aiming for, she focuses her attention on the boat. She forms no words in her head, utters no whisper beneath her breath. She is simply still, simply pulled into this one place, this one moment, this one visualized wish. And suddenly, as if a key has turned in a lock, or a switch has been thrown to connect a circuit, Tilda knows that it is done. Her amazement at the knowledge of this certain fact brings from her a short bark of laughter. The diver looks at her, puzzled. She waves goodbye and turns to go. He calls after her.

'See you on the other side, then?'

But she shakes her head, calling back over her shoulder, 'Not unless you plan on swimming.' And as she runs on along the lakeside path her footsteps are accompanied by the sounds of the young man trying to start the outboard motor on his boat. Trying and failing. Trying and failing. Trying and failing.

As Tilda had known he would. Only when she has reached the stile to the lane, when she has put some distance between herself and the motor, does she let go the captive image of the static motor. She releases her grip on the thing, setting it free from her influence. There is a pause, then the sound of the pull-chord being worked again, and Tilda allows herself another smile as she hears the engine at last successfully fire into life.

SEREN

I wait until the sun is directly above me, and then take my basket and head toward the woodland to the south of the lake. It is a dry day, mild for the time of year. Others are no doubt welcoming the brightness of the sunshine, but it is a trial for me. I wear my hooded cloak so that my eyes, sensitive to such harsh light, are afforded at least some shade. As I walk across the water meadows, the noises of busy lives upon the crannog start to fade. With each step the laughter of the children, the hammer of the blacksmith, the coaxing calls of the cowherd, all recede as if into memory, to be replaced by the less insistent sounds of the copse. The trees here are carefully managed. None may be felled without the prince's permission, so that there is always heavy timber for building houses, or slender ash for making arrows, or logs to keep the people of the crannog and the village warm in the chill of the night.

There are few leaves left on the branches now, but still the light alters as I leave the open grassland and step between the tall trunks. There is sufficient shattering of the sunlight to allow me to lower my hood. I am aware of the heat of the sun on my face, still, and resolve to make a balm of chamomile and honey when I return to my house to guard against blisters. The woodland floor is yet a tangle of plants – ground elder, brambles, ivy, the remnants of rosebay willow herb, all tumble over one another in their scramble for space. Above me birds make the most of the fair weather. On an oak bough three lazy crows spread their wings to soak up the warmth of the sunshine through their glossy black feathers. In a holly bush a plump robin, full of his own importance, sings to claim his territory and warn off any rivals. A mother blackbird, browner than her name suggests, flits past at knee height before trilling her warning of my approach. How much more tuneful are the birds of the woods than the birds of the water. Ducks and geese make their raucous racket without once finding a note of sweetness, whilst these tree dwellers are practiced in the art of melody.

I cast my eyes to the ferny floor in search of what I will need for the princess's vision and spellcasting, for my gifts are twofold. The first is that I am able to work as a shaman, to enter a trance in which, should I be blessed, a vision will come to me. A seeing that foretells the future, or answers a question, or offers guidance. There are times I find my visions in the flickering flames of my fire. At others I see them rise from the moonlight reflected on the lake. They can come to me unsought, or I can chase them, in which case I prefer to aid my quest with the use of certain mushrooms or herbs. Today I look for the bright red caps of the elfin toadstool, which I will simmer in milk and sip in silent contemplation. The measure is of vital importance. Too little, and it will prove in effective. Too much, and it will prove fatal.

My second talent is for the casting of spells, and for this I am called witch. Some put a spit in that word, others whisper it. I care not. The magic was bequeathed me by my mother, as she had received her own from my grandmother. All of us born to dwell in the moonlight, marked with the silver eyes and milk-white hair of our kind. Our spellcraft and talents are born of the lake, so that we know how to use its pure water and the plants and herbs that grow in and around it for our cures and spells. But only I was touched by the Afanc, our wise and ancient mother-of-the-lake who dwells deep in the cold waters. How proud my mother was to have her daughter so blessed! What an honour that I was chosen.

My skills allow me to act upon my seeings, and for that I, and those who need me, should be grateful. Princess Wenna will have subjected herself to Nesta's remedies, some of which might have worked, had the problem been a simple one. But I suspect there is a strong obstacle to her fertility. One that even I may not be able to remove.

Still I shall endeavour to help her. For my prince. And for my reputation. I stoop and pick moist moss, dropping it into my basket, and reach further for the tiny leaves of the wood sprite, a shy plant that hides itself beneath its bigger, bolder cousins. As I crouch low my senses respond to the musky scent of the damp earth and rotting stems of the more tender growths that will retreat beneath the soil for the winter. On a warm day such as this these smells are powerful, and a pungent warning of the bleak months that lie ahead.

A rabbit, grey-furred and bright-eyed, hops slowly into the glade. He is intent on his feasting, and has not noticed me. And if he did, he would not fear me. He would recognize a fellow forager, recognize a kindred spirit. He has not the strength and speed of his sister hare, and there is something in his vulnerability that causes me to be uneasy, yet I have an affection for his kind. How could I not? Of a sudden, he tenses, raising his head and ceasing his nibbling in one sharp movement. For a second more he is as still as the dead bough behind him, then his ears twitch once and, in half a heartbeat, he is gone, bounding away through the foliage, a grey blur. Here, then gone. Visible, then vanished. I hear it, too, the approaching horse. Its hooves thud into the ground slowly but heavily. It carries a rider. I straighten up but do not turn. Soon I can hear the clinking of the iron bit the horse works in its mouth, and the creaking of the fine leather of the saddle. The crows flap away from their perch. The robin falls silent. The horse stops. Its rider dismounts.

Without turning, I offer my greeting. 'Your horse is moving too slowly, my Prince, you will never catch anything.'

I can hear the smile in his voice. 'Ah, I am not engaged in hunting this day, my Prophet.' He treads through the under-growth and comes to stand beside me.

Only now do I face him. He is dressed casually, his hair hanging forward to partly cover his dark eyes. He wears no mail and carries no shield, but bears his sword on his hip. His smile broadens.

'Have you come, then, to check for invading armies?' I ask. 'If so I fear you will be disappointed, for I have not seen a single Viking all morning,' I tell him.

'What Viking would dare confront Seren Arianaidd, even with an army?'

I glance in the direction he has come from, but cannot see any more riders.

'You appear to have lost your own men,' I point out. 'Some might consider that a careless action for a prince.'

'I rode alone.'

I do not ask why. I can see he is hoping I will do so, but I will not play his game. I busy myself with picking more plants, as if his business is of no concern to me. In truth I know he has sought me out. In my chest, my heart gallops, threatening to betray my feelings. Does he truly know me? Can he see the longing inside me? If so, why does he torment me, for we both know we can never be more than we are to each other.

He follows me. 'Are you not curious?' he asks. 'Have you no interest in your prince's reasons for being alone in the woods? I would know what brings you here.'

'I mind my business,' I reply, giving him a stern look over my shoulder. 'Most people of good sense would do the same.'

He laughs off the rebuke.

'Very well, seeing as how you wish to know . . . I saw a lone figure taking the path alongside the lake, and to my surprise I knew it to be my Seer. What is this? I asked myself. What manner of emergency can compel Seren Arianaidd to go about beneath the brightest sun we have seen in many a long week? Seren who favours moonlight for her excursions almost exclusively.' When I do not respond to this he goes on. 'I had to find out for myself what it was that brought you from your solitary home. What is it that calls you to the trees when the sun is at its highest and the light is so sharp and so hot?' He steps in front of me and stares at my hair as a shaft of that same sunshine falls through the boughs above and illuminates me. 'You are a very vision yourself,' he murmurs.

Does he know that last night his wife came to me for help?

I doubt it. She will not have discussed the matter with him. Her humiliation runs deep enough as it is. I could tell him, tell him that the reason I am gathering ingredients for a vision quest and a spellcasting is to make his seed quicken in the belly of his princess. I could. But I will not.

'I was about my work,' I say. 'If you will stand aside, I would continue.'

But he does not stand aside. Instead he moves closer and stretches one arm out against the trunk of the silver birch to my left. 'I would detain you but a moment more,' he says gently. I keep my gaze fixed on the ground at our feet as he slowly, cautiously, reaches forward and touches my pale hair, letting his fingers follow its sweep down onto my shoulders. Onto my breast. His fingertips stray across to the narrow gap of bare skin my tunic reveals at my throat. His touch is warm. 'You are like . . . no other,' he says. 'You are moonlight made flesh.'

I raise my face and force myself to look into his eyes. And he to look into mine. He does not flinch, only returns my stare with such intensity I fear for an instant that my own resolve might weaken. That I will let down my guard and reveal the depth of my own feverish wishes. But I must not. Still I do not trust myself to speak, for a woman's heart can be a faithless mistress of her mind, and her tongue is more than able to betray them both!

The prince, too, stands silent for a moment, but then words come tumbling from his hungry mouth. 'Do you not know that my mind is filled with you? When men speak to me I do not hear their voices, but *yours*. I see not their faces, but *your own*. In sleep there is no escape, for you haunt my dreams. And what dreams they are! You and I . . . alone . . .'

'My Lord, you must not say these things.'

'I must speak what is in my heart, else it will burst!'

'You are a prince and should have command of your heart at least.'

'I have not! It is in your thrall. You have bewitched me.'

'I would not misuse my gifts so!'

'And yet it is the truth. Whether you bring it about with purpose or not. I am a man sick with passion . . .'

'You are not a man!' I insist. 'You are protector of your people. Ruler of this land. Husband to your wife.'

'Yes, I am all these, and yet I am good for none of them if my soul is in torment.'

'Do not speak to me of souls. Your pain lies a little farther south of your heart, I believe.'

'Does mocking me serve you well, Seren?'

'I seek only to remind you of what is true. You are my prince,' I repeat, though now I cannot meet his gaze. 'I am your shaman, your prophet, your witch. Our destinies are linked in *these* ways *alone*. I will be your guide, your most faithful ally, but I can never share your home. Nor your bed.' I push at his arm, making to stride past him, but in a swift movement he traps me against the tree, his body pressed against mine, his breath hot upon my cheek as he whispers urgently.

'Then I will meet you in the wildness of the woods, or on the soothing shores of the sacred lake, or under the gentle cloak of darkness. Wherever, whenever you will it, just so long as you do not turn from me again!'

He notices me tilt my head and I know that he, too, has heard the galloping horse that approaches. His own steed pauses in its grazing and whinnies to its stable mate. Prince Brynach wrenches himself from me, cursing as the sturdy figure of his faithful captain, Hywel Gruffydd, rides into view. I stand straight, resisting the impulse to scurry away through the trees, willing my heart to return to a more stable rhythm.

'My Prince!' Hywel calls out as his wide-rumped mount slows to a jarring trot. 'I was not aware you wished to ride out. Forgive me for not being at your service,' he pants.

'No matter, Hywel,' the prince replies with a practiced casualness that belies the turmoil I know him to be suppressing. 'I had a wish to take in some of this rare sunshine. My route crossed that of our Seer.' He gestures toward me and his captain nods curtly, grunting a greeting that might have earned him a cuff around the ear had we been in more formal circumstances.

'I bid you both good day,' I say, and, without allowing either the time to respond, I march past the prince's patient horse and walk as quickly as I can away from that scene of such tightly bottled tempers as might cause the lake itself to seethe. It takes me all my wits not to run. Back to my home. Back to my seclusion. Back to the place I belong. Alone.

6

TILDA

Tilda lies awake in her bed, listening to the moaning of the wind that has been gathering strength all night. The temperature in the cottage is noticeably colder now, and she has already been driven to finding extra blankets. There is something snug about being in a warm bed, heavy with covers, in a cool room. Daylight hours have shortened unhelpfully, so that she has been working in the studio more and more by the uneven light of candles or storm lanterns. She has not attempted to fix the electrics in the house again, nor to call back Bob the electrician. In her heart of hearts, she knows there would be no point. She knows that she is the reason behind it. She is somehow triggering surges or splutterings in power that cause the system to overload and fail. The same way she caused the professor's clock to stop. The same way she disabled the diver's boat.

Except that I meant to do that one. Pity I can't decide to fix things. Just break 'em.

From the corner of the room come sounds of Thistle digging at her bedding in an attempt to get comfortable. Tilda had done her best to dissuade the dog from coming upstairs, reasoning that she would be warmer in the kitchen by the Rayburn, but Thistle became distressed at being separated from her mistress, so that in the end she had sacrificed a spare duvet to provide her with somewhere to sleep at the foot of her bed. Outside the last of the clouds have been blown far away, so that the light of the full moon falls through the window. Tilda has long since given up closing the curtains, growing ever more accustomed to making use of what natural light there may be, and increasingly following the rhythm of the short winter days. In the silvery illumination she is shocked to see her own breath forming thin puffs.

If it gets any colder, we shall both be sleeping downstairs.

She peers over at the dog. Even in the half-light she can see the poor hound is shivering.

'Come on, girl. Get your skinny self up here,' she says at last, patting the bed beside her.

With surprising ease, and needing no further encouragement, Thistle springs up onto the bed, tail wagging.

'Well, you certainly seem pretty well healed, don't you? Want to come for a run with me in the morning, hmm?' She ruffles the dog's fur and it settles down next to her, a warm presence and welcome draft excluder. Thistle wriggles deeper into the bedding, and gazes up adoringly at her mistress with a look of such trust that Tilda is moved by it. Never having shared her home with a dog before, she finds she is frequently surprised at the rewards this symbiotic relationship brings. The unexpected velvety softness of the animal's fuzzy, cocked ears, or her silent but attentive presence as Tilda works in the studio — such things are small but real pleasures.

The two manage a fitful sleep. Tilda is disturbed by the raucous wind, and unaccustomed to sharing her bed. Each time she moves, however minutely, Thistle adjusts her position so that the gap between them is closed. Tilda remembers how soundly Mat would sleep, scarcely stirring all night. She notices that the memory no longer causes her physical pain. The customary jolt that has, until this moment, accompanied each and every recollection of him is absent. The realization brings mixed feelings. There is relief, certainly, but also a strange sense of guilt, as if by not hurting she is allowing him to become less important to her.

And why now? With all this weird stuff going on . . . Don't I need him now more than ever?

She is too sleepy to try to make sense of it all. When she did what she did to the boat motor; when she dared to harness and use the bewildering ability that has come to her seemingly from nowhere, Tilda was briefly frightened, but then, to her own astonishment, she felt exhilarated. Empowered.

Happy? For heaven's sake, yes. Happy. Here. Like this.

She finds she is not fazed by living without electricity, though she knows that when her parents arrive for their promised visit they will be appalled, and that she will have to do something about a non-electric kiln. The bizarre nature of what is happening to her unsettles her less than she might have expected it to. What does disturb her, however, the thing that does still cause her to jump at sudden noises, or make her heartbeat race when something on the periphery of her vision snags her attention, are the inexplicable things that she sees. As she lies beneath her warm bedding, Thistle snuggled close, the wind wailing around the chimney pots of the cottage, she forces herself to list those things. To name them. To face them.

The waking nightmares of Mat's death.

She forms the thought calmly and acknowledges that the flash-backs to this terrible moment, though more vivid when she first moved to her new home, have now lessened. In fact, she cannot recall the last time she experienced one.

The people in the boat.

They had seemed so real at the time. Even now, though her recollection of the two men rowing with their backs to her is faint, she can clearly see the striking woman who looked straight at her. Who must have seen her.

But who was she? She looked young, and yet ancient at the same time. Was she a ghost then? Is the lake haunted?

The word brings with it the memory of the horrendous face that so shockingly filled her vision more recently. A face so different from the serene and beautiful features of the first. So close, so terrible, so raging. If ever Tilda harboured an idea of what a terrifying ghost might look like, that was it. She turns her head in the dark, instinctively trying to turn away from the image she has brought to mind, knowing that closing her eyes will make no difference. Instead she looks down at the sleeping dog by her side, letting her hand rest on its grizzled fur.

Do you see them, too, girl? Do you see the ghosts? Or is it just me?

She makes herself apply logic to the puzzle as best she can. The lake has been inhabited for centuries. What better place to be sprinkled with wandering souls? She has always been a little sensitive to eerie atmospheres in certain houses or places, and as a teenager was given to being easily spooked, but she never thought of herself as someone who actually saw ghosts. Since she moved to this house that sensitivity has significantly heightened, so that now she encounters the inexplicable. Here things are crucially different. True, the year spent at her parent's house recovering from losing Mat had been filled with the singular visions of that fateful day, and she had felt herself at times unhinged by sadness. But she had not adversely affected the electricity supply whilst staying in Somerset. No machinery had failed to work in her presence. And she had not once seen apparitions. Had never encountered such apparently real people in her waking moments, all the time knowing that they were *not* real. No, the plain fact was, everything changed when she moved to Ty Gwyn. Everything inexplicable began when she came to live by the lake. So the ghosts, if ghosts they are, must somehow have their origins here too.

For even ghosts must surely have their beginnings in something real.

Outside, a doughty blackbird announces the start of a new day. Tilda sits up, fired with a determination to look for reason. For sense. For explanations. She believes the answers to the questions she has not yet properly formed lie with the lake, its history and its people. And luck, or something like it, has thrown in her path the perfect person to help her discover its past.

'Come on,' she nudges Thistle. 'That feeble glimmer in the sky out there is what passes for sunrise in these parts. Best time of day for a run, so if you're coming with me, shake a leg.'

Outside the wind has vanished with the night, and been quickly replaced by a light frost. Tilda pulls on her warmer running fleece and a thermal scarf to keep the icy air off her throat. She clips the pink collar and lead onto Thistle and they set off at a gentle pace. The dog looks sound and eager, and the pair are soon covering the hoary ground with ease. The wintry landscape begins to sparkle as the sun rises, so that the lake and its surrounding fields are rendered postcard pretty. Tilda takes the shortest route, and watches her new running companion closely for any signs of lameness or fatigue. She is impressed at the way the dog is able to lope along beside her, not once getting in her way or pulling on the lead. As they near the little wooden bird blind, she sees a figure emerging from it and recognizes Professor Williams at once. She waves to him, slowing to a halt, and waits on the path. Despite his years, the professor moves with strong strides, waving back, his binoculars around his neck, walking stick digging firmly into the ground with each confident step.

'Good morning,' Tilda calls to him. 'You're up early.'

'Ah, dawn in winter is an excellent time for bird-watching,' he tells her. 'The migratory water fowl have either departed or arrived, and all have settled into their new habitats. Even so, the shy newcomers like to be up early to feed so as to avoid their more boisterous competitors.' He indicates the dog. 'I see you have a new friend.'

'This is Thistle. She's . . . been unwell. This is her first time out for a while.'

Professor Williams touches the brim of his tweed hat. 'I'm delighted to make your acquaintance,' he says to the dog, who wags her tail politely by way of reply.

'I'm glad I found you,' Tilda says, seizing the moment. 'I . . . I want to ask you more about the lake. About its history. I was wondering . . . if you could spare the time . . .'

'My dear girl, nothing would make me happier. May I suggest tea? I have a fire laid in the hearth at home. Your courser will look very fine in front of it.'

'My what?' Tilda asks, falling into step beside him.

'Your lurcher. She is a hunting dog, is she not? A hare courser?'

'Oh, well, she was supposed to be. She wasn't any good at it, apparently.'

'Probably just as well. There are few enough hares left as it is. In any case, she has the look.'

'She does seem to like lounging about in front of fires like something out of an old oil painting. You know the type, expensive rugs, stag's head on the wall, hounds sprawled in the warmest place.'

'On such a chilly day, and after brisk exercise? I cannot fault her thinking.'

The reassuringly sensible company the professor offers has such a restorative effect on Tilda that she all but forgets about the grandfather clock until she is standing next to it in the hallway of the Old School House. She sees that it is working again, and hurries on into the sitting room in the hope that she can escape causing the thing to break down. Professor Williams strikes a long match and sets it to the neatly twisted paper in the grate, and soon the sticks and coals have caught. He leaves Tilda examining the old map that appears to have a permanent home on his desk, and goes to make tea. Thistle stretches out on the hearth rug with a contented sigh. Tilda studies the details offered by the faded, beautifully drawn representation of the lake and its surroundings. The cartographer's date stamp says 1908, which explains the absence of many of the buildings she is familiar with, particularly on the northern, busy side of the lake, but for the most part things are unchanged. She finds St Cynog's church again straightaway, with the Old School House next to it, and the Vicarage a little ways off, all set safely back from the shoreline. The crannog is marked, but only as an uninhabited island. Farther back, on the far side, various constructions in the village of Llangors itself stand out − another church, two inns, a lowland farm and a scattering of houses. Tilda studies the map closely without knowing what it is she is hoping to find or expecting to see.

A normal map of a normal place. A bit too recent for 'Here be dragons'.

The professor returns quickly with the tea, clearly eager to discuss his favourite subject. 'Was there any particular period of history you were interested in?' he asks, setting the tray down on the cluttered coffee table. 'That map is finely drawn by a cartographer of some renown, but I have earlier renditions. Or perhaps a book would better suit your needs?' He picks up his wire-framed reading glasses from the mantelpiece and begins to scan the nearest bookshelf. 'I have many excellent volumes that might be of use . . . let me see . . . there's Thomas Jones's *The Lake.* An unimaginative title, I grant you, but the text is reliable. Of course, if you were looking for an emphasis on the art of the area . . . for your own work perhaps . . . ?'

Tilda gives a rueful shrug. 'To be honest, I'm not sure where to start. I . . . I think I'd like to get an idea of who lived here long ago.'

'How long, precisely?'

She tries to recall the people in the boat, to bring to mind what they were wearing, what tools or weapons they were carrying, but the recollection is unhelpfully hazy at this moment. All she can clearly see in her mind's eye is the young woman with the animal skin hood or headdress, the leather straps on her legs. Her hair covered, more leather twists and braids . . . and tattoos.

Yes, she had ink!

'Did any of the people who settled here use tattoos, do you know?'

'Well, I don't think I've ever been asked that before!' He gives a low laugh. 'I daresay there are one or two youngsters sporting such things even now, but . . .'

'These . . . the ones I'm interested in . . . they weren't coloured. Just black. Shapes, rather than objects, I think. Twisted together. Like tangled branches or vines, I suppose.'

'Ah, that sounds very much like Celtic knot work. In which case' – he squeezes behind the sofa in order to get to another shelf – 'you could do worse than take a look at Bartlett's *Celtic Britain*. He's a little wordy' – he removes a chunky book and blows off the nonexistent dust – 'but knowledgeable. And there are illustrations aplenty.' He takes the book to her. 'Good references for an artist like yourself, I should imagine.'

'Thank you,' says Tilda, flicking through the pages, taking in glimpses of dozens of images. 'Yes, these are just right. Exactly right.'

She browses further for a moment, and then looks at the professor, hesitating before going on. 'The people who would have worn designs like these, when would they have lived here?'

'Oh, that's difficult to answer with certainty. Celtic artwork such as this was used over centuries, you see. I'd need a little more information . . .'

'They had a boat, a small one, but big enough for three people.'

'I'm sorry, who had a boat?'

Tilda realizes she has given just enough information to be cryptic. She wants to say more, to explain, but how can she? How can she tell this sensible person that she is chasing the identity of some ghosts?

'I mean,' she tries, 'I imagine they would have a boat.' This still sounds lame, so she adds, 'I saw a picture once, of a woman, and two men, in a boat. There was a Celtic feel about it. The woman was . . . striking. Like a warrior, or someone powerful, anyway, but not dressed in finery. More . . . earthy, somehow. She had tattoos.'

The professor waits for more.

Tilda shrugs. 'I thought I could use patterns like that in my work. I just wanted to get the context right.' She turns back to the map. 'There would have been other buildings here centuries before this, wouldn't there? Different ones, of course.'

'Well, if you're talking about the Celtic people, yes. Nothing that remains now. That's the trouble with huts built of sticks or wattle, they don't leave much for we historians to work with.' He comes to stand next to her. 'We know now that there were people living around the lake before the Romans came here, and long after they left, naturally. It's a good place for a settlement. There were monks and villagers here, and even royalty, such was the appeal of the place. I think I mentioned Prince Brynach to you on your previous visit. He went to all the trouble of building the crannog here precisely because he recognized what a splendid place to live the lake provided.'

'There are just a few trees left on the island now. Was there really a palace there once?'

'Not one you and I might recognize as such, but yes. It was a royal dwelling, built to impress. It was known as the long hall, or sometimes the great hall – a simple construction, timber framed, with wattle and daub. We are not entirely sure what materials were used for the roof, most likely some sort of reed thatch from the lake. The large space inside could accommodate gatherings and meetings as well as providing a relatively warm and comfortable home for the prince.'

'It must have been cold, surely? On the water like that. When it was misty or frozen, wasn't it damp and horrible?'

'There is evidence they used a large fire in the centre, and later another at the far end, though this was before the idea of fireplaces set into the walls with proper chimneys. They would have had to dress against the cold.' He smiles, 'Don't forget how much heat people themselves generate, all in one space together. And there would have been more people living around the lake. They could have retreated to the crannog for safety if the settlement came under attack.'

'And did it?'

'Oh, quite frequently. The centuries we used to call the Dark Ages were dangerous times in which to live. Vikings were claiming more and more territory, and warring princes and kings across Britain were constantly doing battle with one another.'

Tilda reaches forward and touches the map where the small area of green upon the lake signifies the crannog. 'Strange. To even think about living on the lake like that. Weren't they worried the thing might sink? It had to support houses, all those people, horses . . .'

'Evidently any such fears would have been unfounded. The island still stands a thousand years after it ceased being inhabited. No, the greatest danger to the people of the lake came not from their surroundings, but from man's inability to live in peace with his neighbours. An unchanging fact, sadly.'

They are interrupted by a sudden movement by the fire. Thistle scrambles to her feet and lets out a low growl as a man walks into the room. Tilda recognizes him at once as the diver she encountered a few days earlier. He is tall and lean, his unruly black hair more ringlets than curls, and his skin the colour of warm honey. Now that she can see him properly, without his wet suit hood or mask, she is struck by how unusual he is. His dark complexion and bright green eyes suggest a mixed ethnicity, as does the glossy blackness of his hair oddly matched with his angular European features. Realizing she is staring at him, and conscious of the irony of this, she experiences a niggling shame about what she did to his boat.

'Ah,' the professor beams, 'Dylan, come in, come in.'

'I will if your visitor promises not to bite me,' he says, nodding at the dog.

Tilda slips out from behind the desk and goes to Thistle, putting a hand on the animal's head. 'She won't hurt you,' she says. 'She was just startled. You woke her up.'

Professor Williams laughs. 'And you know what they say about letting sleeping dogs lie! Tilda, this is my nephew, Dylan.'

'We've met,' Dylan says with a grin. 'Though I remember you as . . .' He pauses, then says, 'wetter.'

'How's your boat?' Tilda asks, struggling to meet his gaze. She is annoyed to find she feels self-conscious; aware of being in her unflattering running clothes and mismatched spotty socks, with her hair flattened from her hat. Thistle has stopped growling, but keeps her eyes fixed on the newcomer.

That's two of us he's making nervous. Ridiculous. We should get out more.

'There's tea in the pot,' says the professor. 'Tilda has moved in to Ty Gwyn. Marvellous views from up there. My nephew is on a rare visit home, not on my account, it has to be said.'

'Now Uncle Illtyd will give you a hard-luck story about how he never sees me.'

'More important things to do than spend time with his aged relative, of course.'

'I'm a diver. My job takes me abroad a lot.'

'But on this occasion his work has brought him to my doorstep.'

'I've been hired by the archaeologists at the far end of the lake.'

'Oh,' Tilda is suddenly interested, 'I've seen them there. What is it they're looking for?'

The professor laughs, 'Well, Dylan has been searching for the Afanc since he was a boy.'

'The what?' she asks.

'Just Uncle Illtyd's little joke,' Dylan assures her. 'The diggers are after the usual – you know, bits of buildings, weapons, coins, jewellery . . .'

'And bones,' Professor Williams puts in.

'Bones?' Tilda wants to know more.

The professor hands around cups of tea as he tells her, 'Every archaeologist will assure you they are searching for treasures that reveal secrets about people long dead. We fondly imagine these to be piles of gold or valuable gems, but in fact, nothing tells us more about a people than their bones. Science has made such strides . . . When I was at Oxford we had to content ourselves with measuring things. Now, tests can be done to pinpoint exact dates when people lived or died, their age, their nationality, what they ate, what diseases and parasites afflicted them . . . all from the smallest fragment of a smashed skull, or perhaps a few teeth in a broken jawbone. Remarkable, really. Shortbread, anyone?'

At that moment the grandfather clock begins to strike the hour. Tilda tenses, listening.

Three, four, five, six . . .

The chiming stops. She knows it was after seven when she left the cottage. When the professor comments on how curious it is that the clock has stopped, she cannot think of anything to say that will not give away the consternation she is feeling.

What next? I have to leave. Now.

'I . . . I should be going,' she says, coaxing Thistle from the rug.

Dylan looks surprised. 'Aren't you going to drink your tea?'

'It's late. I hadn't realized. I have work I should be getting on with. I'm sorry.'

'Me too,' he says, just as his uncle comes back into the room.

'Most peculiar. I've had that clock, ooh, twenty years or more, and it's been completely reliable. In these last few weeks however . . . Oh, are you on your way?'

'I should be in my studio. I've rather a lot to catch up with, you know, what with the move . . .'

'Of course. Here, why don't you borrow these?' He hands her the two books he had selected for her, and then quickly takes another from a high shelf. 'And this one, I think,' he says, nodding to himself. 'Yes, I think this might have something of what you are looking for.'

'Thank you. You've been really helpful.' Tilda hurries to the front door and struggles into her running shoes and fleece as quickly as she can. Thistle, too, seems eager to go, and fidgets as she tries to clip on her pink leash. 'Stand still, daft dog.'

Dylan has followed them into the hall. 'I wouldn't want to wear that, either.'

'It was the only colour they had,' she lies.

'Dog like that wants to run, anyway. I don't expect she really needs to be on a lead, do you, girl?' He reaches out slowly and carefully but Thistle moves away with another quiet but alarming growl.

Tilda experiences the embarrassment of being the parent of an ill-mannered child and can't stop herself explaining. 'She's been badly treated. I think she's nervous of men. They hurt her.'

'I'm sorry to hear that,' he says, but when he speaks he is looking not at Thistle, but at Tilda.

Outside, the day has brightened and instinctively Tilda flinches as the sunshine hits her eyes. As she reaches the garden gate Dylan calls after her. 'Come to the dig. If you're interested. I'll show you around.'

She pauses, hand on the latch, and manages a polite smile.

'Thank you,' she says. 'That would be . . . lovely.' She fumbles with the gate and hurries on her way.

Lovely? Hardly the word for looking for ancient bones. Get a grip, girl.

By the time they reach the field below the cottage both Tilda and Thistle are puffing small clouds of warm breath into the frosty air. They slow to a walk, and Tilda wonders if the skinny dog hasn't overdone things a little for her first proper run. She considers an idea, biting her bottom lip, and then pulls gently on the lead.

'Come here, little one. I'm told you don't need a lead. What d'you think about that, eh? Let's have this off you, shall we?' So saying, she undoes the collar and slips it from the dog's neck. Thistle shakes herself briskly and gives a brief wag of her tail.

The two of them continue their journey, and Tilda decides it is rather pleasing to have the willing company of a trusting hound. Just as the thought forms in her mind, she sees Thistle's head shoot up, ears pricked. She follows the direction of her sightline and sees what it is that has her so transfixed. A large, brown hare stands motionless on the path in front of them, not more than a dozen paces away. Tilda has never seen a hare close up before, and is struck by the wild, ancient look of the thing. This is not some timid, fluffy bunny, but a creature of the mountains, something knowing and wise. Its enormous, bright eyes do not flicker as it takes in the odd pair who have happened upon it.

What a wonderful thing. A truly wonderful thing.

Too late, Tilda remembers what manner of dog she has at her side. And that that dog is no longer on the lead. In another heartbeat, Thistle is racing forward, any hint of fatigue vanished, all the animal's instincts telling it to chase, chase, chase!

'Thistle, no! Stop!' Tilda shouts, but her cries are pointless. The hare turns and bounds away, its powerful hind legs propelling it across the hard ground with astonishing speed. Thistle is a dog possessed of a single thought now, and soon closes the gap between herself and her prey. The hare jinks and twists, leading its pursuer in zigzags up and down the hill. Tilda runs after them, hampered by the heavy books she is carry ing, and with little hope of either catching the dog or getting it to listen to her. The hare darts off the path and around a corner, so that in an instant both creatures are out of sight. Limbs aching, muscles burning from the effort, Tilda forces herself to follow as fast as she is able. She rounds the bend, dreading what she might find, half expecting to see her dog savaging the defenceless hare, tearing it limb from limb, its beautiful fur bloodstained and gory. Never in her wildest imaginings could she have conjured up the scene that greets her. The hare has stopped running and sits, apparently unperturbed, as Thistle bounces around it playfully, tail wagging, clearly having no intention of hurting it. Tilda stares at the bizarre spectacle of a lurcher, a dog bred over centuries for hunting hares, rolling on the sparse meadow grass, ears flat, paws outstretched toward its new playmate in an attitude of utter submission and friendliness, while the hare sits inches away, calmly washing its whiskers with its tiny paws. Tilda stands stock-still as the hare slowly lollops toward her. It comes closer and closer, until at last it is only inches in front of her, and Tilda has the strangest sensation that it is somehow *studying* her. Just as she wonders if she could reach out and touch it, the hare leaps in the air, twisting so that it lands facing in the opposite direction, speeds off back down the hill and disappears through the hedge at the bottom of the field. Thistle comes panting to stand next to her mistress.

Tilda regards her pet with amazement. She shakes her head and smiles. 'You are one very strange dog, you know that? Come on, there must be something left at home we can call breakfast.'

7

TILDA

Later the same day there is a dramatic drop in the temperature. After a frustrating session in the studio, where nothing seems to want to go right, Tilda shares the last tin of chicken soup with Thistle, and the two of them retreat to the sitting room. Tilda banks up the fire, wondering how long the log supply will last if she has no central heating to back up the wood fires and stoves in the house. She pulls cushions off the small sofa and hunkers down on the rug as close to the crackling flames as is sensible, with Thistle curled up beside her. She has lit a paraffin storm lantern, which smells more than a little, and gives out a low light that is helpful, but not steady or strong enough to read by. A moment of inspiration drove her to dig through the unpacked box of camping gear to find a headlight. Tilda has put new batteries in it and adjusted the headband to make it as comfortable as she can, and now the thing provides a narrow beam that neatly illuminates a page at a time as she leafs slowly through the books Professor Williams lent her.

The images of Celtic knot-work are quickly becoming familiar to her. There are standard shapes and patterns that seem to have been employed in a variety of ways. Animals, birds and flowers are often incorporated into the designs, twisting and entwining with one another, their heads and bodies stylized and elongated, their eyes always watchful and sharp.

Yes, these. On my pots, these would work. The animals, in particular, I think.

But it is too late in the day, and too dark in the sitting room, to attempt sketching. Instead she puts the book aside and chooses the next. A moment's turning of the pages reveals impenetrably dense text regarding the history of the lake. Tilda feels unequal to the task of reading it. She knows there must be fascinating facts hidden somewhere in the plodding prose, but she is not in the right state of mind to tackle it.

The third book is the one the professor chose for her, almost as an afterthought. Only now has she had the chance to look at it. She reads the title out loud to Thistle.

'*"Myths and Legends of Llyn Syfaddan."* Hmm, what d'you reckon, girl? Might answer a few questions?'

Tilda has learned enough to recognize the old Welsh name for Llangors Lake. The book has a hardcover that creaks slightly as she opens it. There are slightly fuzzy black-and-white plates showing maidens with flowing hair, dark-eyed men on horse back, hunting dogs by the pack and one singularly strange beast. Checking the figure reference, Tilda explains to her uncomplaining audience: 'That's an *Afanc*. Scary-looking thing. Like a cross between a dragon and the Loch Ness Monster. Well, well. It seems our lake has its very own water-horse.' Reading on, she learns that the *Afanc* has several legends surrounding it, some making it out to be a benign, misunderstood creature, others portraying it in a less flattering light. In one version the water-horse, which had the ability to walk upon the shore of the lake, was coaxed from its hiding place by a brave young girl of the village. She sang to it as it laid its head in her lap, and the local men were able to capture it. It was then either removed to another, distant lake where it could no longer devour the villagers' cattle, or slain, depending on which story you chose to believe. Tilda runs her fingers over the largest picture of the beast, which shows it to have overlapping scales, a long, sinuous neck, and enormous eyes. Although at first glance she had thought it frightening, she now decides it was, in fact, a gentle thing, without fearsome teeth or claws, and had probably just wanted to live peacefully in the clean, deep waters of the lake. She catches herself believing the creature to have actually existed, but is not surprised.

Why not? If magic is possible, visions, ghosts . . . why not fantastic beasts too? What else lives in those ancient waters, I wonder?

With a sigh, she realizes the book has not, in fact, provided answers, but instead it has raised even more questions. And there are only two ways Tilda knows to work through a problem.

Run or work. And I've done a great deal of running lately, and precious little work.

'Okay, Thistle,' she declares, snapping shut the dusty book. 'Work it is.'

For the next five days Tilda works in her studio, wearing many layers of thermals and woollens, her hands clumsy in their fingerless mittens, as the countryside around her freezes. She is able, at last, to fall into that near-meditative state that artists yearn for, where each sketch, each worked slab of clay, each finished piece, seems to move closer to the ideal. Closer to the fervently imagined perfection that skitters on the peripheral vision of her mind's eye. Over and over, she sketches the intricate and ancient Celtic patterns. She starts with dogs, and then birds and then hares silently slip their way into her designs. She builds huge, bulbous pots from coils of clay, each one unique and beautiful in its basic, rustic shape. Onto these she builds her knot-work in thin strips, adding, blending, working, until the pattern stands in relief from its base while still seeming to merge with it. To grow from it. Gradually, over days, the studio fills with these generous shapes and their detailed, symbolic decoration.

Such exciting progress cannot be interrupted by mundanities like food and rest, so that all accepted rhythms to her day are slowly shed. She no longer bothers to fashion something from the dwindling store cupboard into a meal, but snacks and browses on whatever comes easily to hand, remembering to find something for her long-suffering dog when she does so. She does not go to her bed, but naps in the chair in her studio, or curled in a sleeping bag on the hearth with Thistle. She does not bathe, nor brush her hair, and even her running is abandoned. The act of creation is everything now, and she will not step out of it for a moment. For such a blissful state is an elusive and flighty thing, and could be gone in an instant. So it is with something approaching panic that Tilda eventually realizes she can go no further. Her own lack of planning, her refusal to face up to and deal with what has been happening to her, and the effects these changes have had on the way she lives, these things now force her to stop. For the next step is to test her dreamed-of glazes and fire her pots. And still she has no power for the kiln.

Draining the last of her mug of tea, she moves stiffly over to her sleeping bag and wriggles inside it. Her hands are dry and rough from working with the clay. Her shoulders ache from hours hunched over her workbench. Her stomach growls from lack of sensible food. Thistle comes, wagging, to snuggle up beside her, and within minutes the pair are drifting into a restless sleep. Just as the sharp edges of wakefulness begin to dull, Tilda is jolted awake. At first she thinks she has heard something, but then she realizes, with a flash of fear that sends adrenalin shooting through her veins, that she has sensed somebody close. Somebody is in the studio with her. Thistle lifts her head and begins to whimper. Nothing could so effectively have increased her mistress's alarm. In the half-light of the winter's afternoon, Tilda scans the room, not daring to move even her head as she does so. Slowly a shape in the far corner comes into focus. It is a figure, a woman, judging by the heavy skirts. There is little else to identify her as such, as she wears a hooded cape and her face is obscured, partly by the heavy cloth of the hood, and partly by the shadowy quality of the available light. At her side, Tilda feels Thistle tremble. Cautiously, she inches her way out of her sleeping bag until she is kneeling on the rag rug, never for one second taking her eyes off the motionless, gloomy figure in the corner of the room.

Is it the woman from the boat? Is it her? I can't tell. I can't be sure.

Whoever it is, Tilda is certain that her visitor did not enter via the door. She never did anything as ordinary and reassuring as lift the latch and tread the frosty day onto the concrete floor of the studio. There emanates from the figure a vibration. An energy that, whilst it is most definitely human, is not of the real and everyday world. Tilda searches for her voice and her courage. She forces herself to speak.

'Who are you?' she asks. 'What is it you want?'

The figure does not answer, but straightens slightly, seeming to become taller as she does so, and moves forward on silent feet. Tilda wants to flee, to scramble from her vulnerable position on the floor and turn and run faster than she has ever run in her life. But she finds she cannot. It is more than fear that keeps her pinned down. It is as if the approaching apparition has exerted an invisible, vicelike grip upon her, so that she is unable even to stand up. Thistle crouches low on her belly and has ceased her whimpering, her ears flat against her head, her whole body tense, whether for flight or attack Tilda cannot tell. Soon the looming figure is fewer than two strides away.

'What do you want!?' Tilda demands again.

Now the visitor lifts her head and the light of the dying day that falls through the patio doors reveals her face. Tilda lets out a shriek of horror. This is not the first time she has seen this terrible face. It appeared to her once before. This is not the lithe, youthful woman from the boat, but the brutalized, bloody and smashed face that showed itself as Tilda looked through her binoculars. It is an image she has been trying to forget ever since, but such a thing is not easily erased from memory. The nose has been broken, so that it is both flattened and twisted. One eye is closed with blood, the other bulges in its socket, sickeningly bruised and swollen. The lower jaw has been smashed by some terrible force, so that white bone can be seen through the mess of a mouth that remains, the teeth either broken or at impossible angles. The woman's skin is a ghoulish grey only where it is not black or purple from bruising and swelling. Matted hair, encrusted with blood and dirt, falls forward from beneath the hood of the cape, which Tilda can now see is saturated with blood.

Fighting the urge to retch, Tilda falls back, her hands behind her, and attempts to scurry away, but there is nowhere to go. A foul stench bursts from the woman's ruined mouth as she opens it and screams '*Llygad am lygad! Bywyd ar gyfer bywyd!*' An eye for an eye, a life to a life!

At the sound of the rasping, shrill voice, Thistle leaps at the figure, snarling and snapping as she flies through the air. Tilda watches as the dog connects with the woman, expecting to see more blood and devastation wreaked upon her broken body, but, in a heartbeat, the apparition dissolves. Thistle lands, growling and biting at nothing. Nothing.

Gone. My God, she's gone!

Tilda struggles to her feet, her whole being in a state of shock, her stomach turning over, her heart thudding as if she has just run up the mountain. But she is alone, save for the bewildered and frightened dog. Whoever it was, whatever it was, that came to deliver its message, has vanished.

Tilda puts a calming hand on Thistle's head. It was obvious that the dog was terrified, and yet she had found the courage to try to protect her. She falls to her knees and takes the still trembling hound in her arms. 'It's Okay, girl. You brave thing. You scared her off, see? She's gone. She's gone.'

In the hours that follow the visitation, Tilda knows she has to take control of her fear. It would be all too easy to pack a bag and leave.

Hurrying back to Mum and Dad, tail between my legs. Couldn't do it. Couldn't live the life we had planned. Couldn't hack it on my own.

They would welcome her. They would understand − or believe that they understood − without asking unanswerable questions. Her father would enfold her in his boundless affection, and she would be safe. But then what? What would she do with her life? Would she have to live forever with her parents? Would she always be too afraid, too damaged, too unstable, too fragile to lead her own life? And what if the visions, the inexplicable things she did and saw and felt, what if they continued wherever she went? Perhaps this was a time when running was not the answer.

This is my home, dammit. This is my life.

And so she finds it is possible to be brave for hours at a time, particularly when she keeps busy. But then the wind rattles a windowpane, or a draught slams a door, or the darkness is simply too deep and too long, and Tilda feels panic rising. Panic at the thought that the ghost, if such it was, will come back.

What did she mean? What was she trying to say to me? What can whatever happened to that poor woman have to do with me?

Tilda has done her utmost to recall the strange words the woman spat at her. She is fairly certain they were Welsh, but this is an opinion formed from listening to the music of the language between modern-day Welsh speakers in the area. She knows no Welsh herself, and can only remember fragments spoken by the apparition, and perhaps one word clearly. A word that seemed to be repeated and sounded something like 'bewit'.

A search through her pocket Welsh dictionary – a house-warming present from her father – has proved fruitless. She is unable to relax, to let down her guard, and yet she finds the thought of leaving the house difficult. Worse, the ghastliness of the apparition, its vehemence, the aura of despair and anger it brought with it, all have combined to halt Tilda's progress with her work completely.

On the second morning after what she prefers to think of as a vision, rather than a ghost, Tilda decides she must go out. There are things she has to do. The situation cannot go on as it is. She forces herself to write a short list of what it is she must tackle. It reads:

> *Get translation of Welsh word*
> *Find out about any local murders or ghosts*
> *Get food*
> *Start construction of wood-fired kiln*

The last of these missions came to her in the sleepless watches of the previous night. Her sanity, and ultimately her livelihood, depend upon her producing finished pieces to sell. And soon. She can bring her mind and nerves to bear on fixing the electricity to work her kiln, or she has to find some other way of firing her pots. Once the idea of a wood-fired kiln presented itself the choice was easy. A firing done outside, beneath the stars, heat generated by wood grown in this very landscape, her work brought into being via a method so natural, so ancient, so somehow of-the-place, it was, after all, the perfect solution. The prospect of building her own kiln excites her, and the possibilities the process offered – the curious, slightly random results such firings were known to produce – these things appeal to her more and more now that she thinks about them. She will use natural glazes, work them with salt to produce free and flowing patterns of texture and colour.

These pieces could be something special. Something really special.

She has the space in the garden, and there is plenty of wood. She built a kiln of this sort whilst at art school, and recalls being delighted with the resulting pots. A few more pointers regarding glaze mixes at such uncontrolled temperatures would be helpful, but otherwise she knows she is more than capable of constructing a kiln that will perfectly suit her needs.

She pulls on her duffle coat, a woollen hat, and thermal gloves, and chooses hiking socks and boots rather than trainers. The sun is bright and sharp today, but the ground outside is still frozen, and the temperature low enough to bring on a toothache. She pauses in the doorway to speak to Thistle.

'You sure you want to come? It's very cold, and I'm not going to be running.'

The dog looks at her quizzically, head tilted.

'There'll probably be a fair amount of hanging about.'

Thistle gives up trying to make sense of her mistress's babble and squeezes past her, through the door, and starts trotting around the garden, her decision clearly made.

'Have it your way, then.' Tilda stuffs the leash in her pocket, shuts what little warmth there is inside the kitchen, hitches her backpack onto her shoulder, jams on her sunglasses and strides purposefully after her dog. She has a clear plan in her head, and such method and action have given her some much needed courage. First, she needs to find out about women who were murdered, or maybe killed in battle, in the area, particularly if there are any ghost stories about them. If she is going to deal with being visited by someone so frightening, she has to know who exactly it is she is dealing with. Next, she needs to try to get those Welsh words, or at least the one she can recall, translated. As she is unable to use her own computer, she has decided to call on Professor Williams again. This time her questions will be considerably more specific. She knows this may mean she will end up talking to someone she barely knows about being visited by a terrifying phantom, herself being the cause of electrical and mechanical mayhem, and the other visions that have troubled her these past few weeks. He may think her quite mad. It is a chance she is prepared to take. Later, she will go to the village stores and stock up on food, as the cupboard at home is now depressingly bare.

The easy downhill walk is both warming and invigorating. As they descend into the valley, the ground is a little warmer, but still sparkling with frost, and the lake itself bears a thin glazing of ice. All the water birds have been forced to paddle on the icy shoreline. There is no wind, but only a distant, cooling winter sun, and Tilda and Thistle puff clouds of hot breath before them as they walk. The brightness and beauty of the landscape lift Tilda's spirits, but her happier mood is short-lived when she finds that the professor is not at home. Having knocked on the low oak front door several times, she walks around to the mullioned kitchen window, pressing her hand upon it as she peers in. There is no sign of either light or movement. Thistle busies herself sniffing out a mouse trail in the vegetable patch.

'Damn,' says Tilda, only now aware of how fragile her new-found positive frame of mind is. For a moment she considers returning to the cottage, but a gnawing hunger tells her she must continue on the next part of her mission. She walks along the short stretch of road past the church and down to the lake, intending to turn left and loop around to the village that way. But when she reaches the shore, her attention is taken by the activity from the north end of the water, where the archaeologists appear to be particularly busy. She still cannot bring herself to look through her binoculars, so she has not been able to follow their activities. She remembers Dylan's offer to show her around the dig and wonders if he will be there.

Surely he wouldn't go diving through the ice.

Before she has time to change her mind, Tilda climbs the gate to her right and follows the stony path that winds through the water meadow. As she nears the sight of the excavation, she can make out voices and counts at least five people, all of whom seem to be focused on a patch of earth set a short way back from the waterline. They are so intent on what they are doing that no one notices her approach until she is standing only a few paces behind them. Thistle keeps close, suddenly tense and alert, reminding Tilda that the dog has suffered at the hands of men before and might well be nervous of raised voices, mistaking excitement for anger. She briefly considers clipping the lead onto the dog's collar, but reasons that restricting the animal might make it feel panicked.

'It's okay, girl.' Tilda strokes her ears gently but Thistle shows no sign of relaxing. A familiar voice makes Tilda turn toward the large canvas tent that serves as the operations room for the dig.

'Hello,' says Dylan as he makes his way toward her. 'Come to witness the great event?'

'Sorry?'

'They are hoping to exhume the skeleton today. From the grave they found. Or at least, that was the plan. I'm told the weather may hold things up.'

'A body? Shouldn't the police be here?'

Dylan smiles at her line of thinking. 'I don't think they work on cases over a thousand years old.' He points toward the huddle of students, archaeologists, and hangers-on. 'They reckon the burial took place somewhere between the ninth and eleventh centuries. They'll know much more once they can start testing the bones.'

'Isn't it strange to have a single grave like that? Why wasn't the body buried by the church?'

'Aside from the fact that it wouldn't have been there then, you mean?'

Tilda shoots him a look, not enjoying having made herself sound dim.

'Sorry,' he goes on. 'It's a fair point. Saint Cynog's might not have been built until the twelfth century, but there was a monastery here before that. So yes, you're right, it is strange the poor person was planted out here on the boggy side of the lake all on their own.'

'I remember the site of an old monastery being marked on your uncle's map,' Tilda says, pleased to be able to offer some intelligent comment. They stand and watch the diggers for a little longer. 'Nothing seems to be happening,' she points out at last.

'The ground may be too frozen. They could damage the skeleton if they force it from the icy earth. There was some talk of warm water but that just opened up a whole debate about what evidence might or might not be corrupted. Academics, eh?' he adds with a shrug, and then nods in the direction of the grave where Tilda can now see Professor Williams. He notices her and hurries over.

'What a moment you have chosen to arrive! Such an exciting find. The skeleton appears complete. When Dylan told me what was planned for today I had to come and witness it for myself.' The old man pushes his hat a little farther back on his head. His eyes are bright, his cheeks and nose flushed in reaction to both the cold and the excitement.

Dylan smiles at him. 'Only you could get so worked up over a few bones in the mud,' he teases.

'A few bones in the . . . !' The professor is aghast. 'This is the most momentous discovery since the crannog itself. The body has lain for centuries in an unmarked grave. We can only begin to imagine what insights might be revealed upon examination of the remains,' he explains, waving his walking stick to emphasize his point. He beams at them, shaking his head. 'Can't you feel the coming together of past and present in a moment like this? Another mystery of the lake about to reveal itself to us. Fascinating!'

Tilda experiences a sudden moment of dizziness. She closes her eyes for a second.

Steady. Should have found something to eat before I left the cottage.

She takes a breath and forces her attention to what the professor is gabbling on about. Somewhere in the flood of information and theories he is putting forward could lie the answers she has been seeking.

'But why has it taken this long for anyone to find the grave?' she asks. 'I mean, people have known about the crannog and the settlements here for ages. How did this body stay hidden for so long? And why has it been found now?'

'Well, there was no marker, no indication at all that there was anything here,' Professor Williams says, clearly pleased by her interest. 'All previous digs have been close to the crannog, or the monastery. This area is very boggy, and often underwater, not really suitable for a grave. Particularly if any grieving relatives would want to visit.'

'Not someone with much of a family, then,' says Dylan. He reaches out to pat Thistle, but the dog moves fractionally away from him, pressing against Tilda. He lets his hand drop.

'That's one possible explanation,' the professor agrees. 'Someone alone, with no one to contribute to the upkeep of a grave in the grounds of the monastery, perhaps. And yet it does seem a singularly odd choice of plot. Almost as if the person being buried was being pointedly kept at a distance from the inhabitants of the crannog. And from the monks and priests.'

'So what made anyone decide to dig here now?' Tilda steadies herself through another wave of giddiness.

'Aah, well, you see, a very rare thing happened this year.' He chuckles. 'We had an exceptionally dry summer. There was a severe drought. The shoreline of the lake on this side receded by . . . oh, thirty yards or more. This phenomenon coincided with a field trip for students from Lancaster University – they were visiting the crannog – and one eagle-eyed young man noticed something unusual about the newly exposed area of land. Exceptionally bright student. He's leading the dig now. That's him over there . . . Lucas Freyn.' The professor employs his stick as a pointer this time.

Tilda sees a tall, wiry young man, dressed against the cold, talking in an animated manner with his colleagues.

'If there's anything more you want to know about the find,' says the professor, 'he's your man. I'm sure he'd be delighted to talk to you.'

As they watch, the group turns away from their precious excavation and begins to move back toward the tent. The professor hails them.

'Lucas! Molly! There is someone here who would very much like to meet you.'

When Lucas lets his gaze fall on Tilda as he shakes her hand, she has the distinct impression she is being studied rather than stared at, as if she, too, were an unexpected find. Introductions are made, during which Tilda learns that the pair are both working on their doctorates at the university, that Molly is married and has left her two small children at home with her husband in order to be part of the dig, and that Lucas is every bit as passionate about the find as the professor. She does her best to take in everything she is being told, but she is feeling increasingly unwell. She is aware of Professor Williams explaining, somewhat sketchily, her interest in the history of the lake, but his voice is growing distant, and her legs feel in danger of buckling beneath her.

'I'm sorry,' she says. 'I'm not feeling very well. I . . . I think I probably just need something to eat.'

'Excellent idea,' says the professor.

Dylan nods. 'The Red Lion does the best steak and kidney pudding in Wales. Have you tried it yet?'

'No, I . . .' The idea of a cozy pub, a proper hot meal, and a chance to sit and talk in company is hugely appealing.

Lucas steps in. 'Well, we've had to shut things down here for the day. Temperature is just too low. Can't risk moving anything while the ground is this frozen. We might try to get some heat into it tomorrow, if there isn't a thaw. Meantime, lunch sounds like a plan. Happy to fill you in on what we think we've found. If you're interested,' he tells Tilda.

'Yes, I am. That'd be great. Oh, can I bring Thistle?'

Lucas regards the dog as if he has only just noticed her. 'Well, I don't know if she'll be allowed in,' he says.

'I know the landlord. Mike'll be cool about it. If I ask him,' Dylan assures them. The point made, he leads them all in the direction of the village pub, Lucas falling into step behind him, the professor picking up the subject of the skeleton as they make their way along the muddy path.

SEREN

The moment has come. The moon is full, its beams pure and strong, touching the surface of the lake with silver. The night is at its deepest now, and all on the crannog, save the bored watchmen, are sleeping; the cattleman curled around his plump little wife; the blacksmith warm in his forge; young brothers and sisters heaped together like puppies, snuffling and squeaking as they chase sleep; the new mother dozing with her babe at her breast; even the horses slumber, eyelids drooping, resting a hind hoof, heads low, minds slowed and numbed to the world. And my prince, he will be snug beneath his fine cloths, his princess at his side, the two of them private behind the drapery of their princely bed. She will dream of a future filled with children. Their children. Each one a promise of loyalty, of protection, of respect, of continued privilege and position, as they scamper about the great hall carrying his likeness and his blood into the next and future generations.

And will my prince dream? Does he dare to? So great are his responsibilities. So many have put their lives, and their families' lives, into his strong hands. Dare he let his secret thoughts run free in the haven of his nighttime imaginings? Will he allow himself there, and then, to be a man before he is a prince? To be young? To follow his heart? Or would to do so weaken the prince in his waking hours? Would he yearn for that other, fleeting happiness? Might he risk diminishing himself so?

I know that I must not.

And this night I am engaged in work that serves to remind me well of my place. Of my purpose. I seek a vision for the princess. I search for a seeing. For an answer to her question. For a way for her to have what it is she desires more than any silver trinket or jewelled necklace or gold-threaded gown. This night I am her prophet and her servant. Though she does not truly love Prince Brynach, nor he her. Though he would choose another if he were free to do so. Though I do not trust her intentions. I do not believe her to be loyal. Despite all this, I will do what I can for her. I will do what I must.

I have kept my fire well stoked, and even now the logs burn bright on a bed of scarlet embers. My outdoor fire pit is three strides from my front door, and five from the lake. Earlier I gathered and prepared everything necessary for my vision quest. I have spread my finest deerskin upon the gritty ground, so that I might lie in comfort as my spirit travels, and so that I will be accompanied by the spirit of the departed deer. The night is cold enough to freeze a shallow puddle, but not so bitter as to bother me while I lie still beneath the stars. I am close enough to the fire to benefit from its heat, and over my tunic I wear my fine woollen cape, its hood pulled up to keep my head warm. I might have chosen my wolf skin, but its own music would be at odds with that of the deer whose assistance I am hoping for. This is to be a gentle quest, not a hunt. Besides, the cape was a present from the prince. It is fitting that something of him should accompany me on my journey.

I have assembled what tools and ingredients I require. My drum is placed within reach on the deerskin. In a jar to one side is an infusion of mosses and mint, which I will take to revive and soothe me upon my return. The plants and herbs within it, strengthened by a spell given for healing, will go some way to easing my pain after the vision, and to restoring my body and mind as it readjusts to the weight of the common world. In my black cooking pot, suspended over the fire, the concoction simmers. I have used mare's milk this time, as it is sweeter than cow's, and gentler. Into this I have crumbled the dried fairy toadstool I collected a few days ago under the glare of the full sun. The bright red of the caps has softened and turned the mixture to pink. It smells of the forest floor, of the earth, of something strange and dangerous. As indeed it is. Too little, and there will not be sufficient to aid my vision. Too much, and it will send me into a dark place of pain and fear from which I will not return. I have judged the measure with great care. I am of no use to my prince dead.

Before beginning, I stand firm and tall in front of the fire and raise my arms to the heavens. I offer up ancient words taught to me in secret, and held in my memory for safekeeping, to be used only with a good heart, for the benefit of those in need, without hope of gain for myself, my assistance freely given. The words have magic in them. Magic of the Celtic elders, who have studied the ways of man for centuries alongside the ways of the underworld. Magic of the shamans, who have travelled this path before me seeking answers and wisdom. Magic of the witches, who are born with the light of spellcasting in their bones. And as I speak I feel my own spirit stir, my own essence shift and change and tremble in anticipation of what is to come.

Next I pull the pot from the fire and place it on the ground. I take my cow's horn cup and dip it deep, scooping a helping of the precious liquid as full of the bewitching toadstools as can be. Pungent steam rises from the cup as the cold night air cools it. I take my place, cross legged, upon the deerskin. I ask my spirit guides to join me, I offer thanks to the woodland that has given up its bounty for me to use, I form my question, clear and plain, speaking it aloud into the dancing flames of the fire.

'I seek Wenna's progeny. Show them to me, or show them not to be, but bring me to the truth of it. If there be a way to coax such offspring into this world, let me know the manner of it.'

So saying, I raise up the cup, close my eyes and then down the foul liquid in three hungry gulps, closing my mouth and throat swiftly afterward, lest my stomach rebel against the poison I am inflicting upon it.

All is good. It is begun.

I sit at my drum and pick up a steady beat while I await the effects of the draught. I let my palms strike the drum skin, flat and slow to start, feeling the sound and its vibration enter my body. As the minutes pass, the fairy toadstool enters further, deeper, wider into me, into my mind, my soul, so that I increase the pace of my drumming. Faster now. Faster! I feel a darkness grip me. The lake and the crannog, the woodlands and the meadows, all have faded to nothing. I am removed from them, and they from me. I exist only inside my head, until the magic will release me on my journey. Pain twists in my belly and scratches at my throat. My breath burns through me. There is a noise, a fearsome roaring of a storm, building, building, building until I must surely burst with it! Burst or die! It is so strong. As if my body cannot withstand what I have forced it to endure. Shall I be smothered, pushed into eternal darkness?

But no! There! I am released. My journey is under way.

Of a sudden, I am leaping through the summer hay meadow, the flowering grasses high above my head as I crouch, tickling my belly as I spring and bound. I am not being chased. I run for joy, for the wonder of the day, for the blessing of the ripening harvest, for the warmth of the sun. As I am, my eyes are not stung by the light. As I am, my skin does not burn nor blister in the golden heat. What freedom! No longer forced to dwell in the shadows, no longer a creature of the darkness, I can run with the singing birds, dart past the grazing cattle, twist through the fragrant flowers and herbs that release their sweetness in the daytime.

I pause, sniffing the air, my keen ears alert, listening, my bold eyes watchful. A movement against the sunlight horizon. A deer, fine-legged and with a gleaming coat. My fellow traveller. It regards me for a moment, and then raises its head, ears twitching. There is something. A sound. A woman crying. I move silently toward it, keeping cover in the tall grasses, taking care not to give myself away. I come upon a figure, bent away from me, kneeling on the ground at the edge of the lake. I cannot see the woman's face, but she is weeping pitifully, and in front of her is a baby's crib. It rocks on wooden rockers, but there is no sound or movement from within it, for it is empty. As I creep closer, wanting to see who it is who sobs so for what is not there, another sound stops me. A shuddering of the earth.

A galloping. Many horses, and approaching at speed! The deer, too, has felt their thundering through the ground and turns, leaping, running fast away. Now the horses charge into view. Fifty? One hundred? Two hundred? Too many to count. I lay flat on the ground, still as a stone, forced to trust that the charging horses will not set their great iron-clad hooves upon me. The soldiers on their backs shout and roar and wield their heavy swords as they charge, and in front of them, a lone figure. A young man, alone, upon a red horse, its neck wet with sweat, its mouth foaming. The man wears no armour, carries no shield, nor any sword. He is defenceless. I fight for breath as I see it is Prince Brynach! The soldiers close upon him. The woman lifts her head. She sees, but she does not call out to him. She does nothing. Nothing. And the attackers race on, so that the prince must turn his horse into the water. Deeper and deeper into the lake he rides until the horse must swim, and then, when it can swim no more, it sinks beneath him. And he with it. So that the waters close over his head, and the lake swallows him up.

8

TILDA

The Red Lion sits in the centre of the village of Llangors, a sturdy, whitewashed building with black-painted window frames and doors, and three smoking chimneys. It appears unchanged by time, so that Tilda can easily imagine weary travellers or thirsty farmers, knocking the mud off their boots, and dipping their heads to enter through its low front door one, two, or even three hundred years ago. The only concessions to the modern age are the wide car park to one side – though this still boasts a hitching rail for horses, as the inn is a popular lunchtime halt for local treks – and, inside, the availability of free Wi-Fi. Dylan finds some tables in the low-ceilinged black-beamed lounge bar, where a fire burns cheerfully in the hearth, its flames glinting off the many brass fire irons and ornaments that surround it. There is much peeling off of outdoor gear as people move to the bar to place their orders, or take their seats on tapestry-cushioned chairs, or the high-backed wooden settle that runs along the wall from the fireplace to the small window. Tilda stands at the bar, her eyes devouring the list of food on offer. Over the bar hang two blackboards listing the day's menu, promising hearty, home-cooked food. There is a friendly murmur and a gentle buzz about the place, with local residents leaning against the bar enjoying a lunchtime pint, or visitors tucking hungrily into their lunches after a morning's activity in the winter cold.

Everything is so utterly normal, and welcoming, and safe, that Tilda finds herself suddenly close to tears as she reads the menu.

You are ridiculous, Tilda Fordwells. You've been spending too much time on your own and eating too much rubbish, if the idea of pub grub can reduce you to snivelling.

Without warning, the lights dim and flicker.

Oh no! Not here, not now.

They flicker again, and then fail completely. There is a collective groan from the pub-goers. The barmaid busies herself trying switches but nothing seems to be working. Someone goes into the cellar to check the fuse box. Tilda fights the urge to turn and run. She knows she has to do something. Has to at least try. She closes her eyes and steadies her breathing.

Focus. Still your mind. You can do this. You can.

While people around her mutter about sandwiches, stoke up the log fire, or find candles, Tilda stands without moving, keeping herself separate. Making herself picture a spark of energy, of power.

Come on. Work, dammit. Work!

Suddenly there is a fizzing noise, a flashing, the lights flicker again, and then stay on.

Yes!

A cheer rings out through the pub. Tilda joins in, smiling at the thought that no one else can have any idea how happy she is to see those lights working.

'What do you want to drink?' Dylan appears at her elbow. He has an easy smile, with bright white teeth and eyes that have a mischievous sparkle to them. He rubs his hands together and nods at the array of taps on the bar. 'Mike's a real ale man. One or two stunning little beers here. The Mountain Goat's a bit strong, but you might like Hiker's Heaven. Or Sheep Dip, that's popular around here.'

'Sounds like you're a bit of an expert,' Tilda says.

'Oh, I do my best to support local businesses,' he tells her.

'Well, I need to eat something before I have a drink or I'll fall over. I've got to try the steak and kidney pudding.'

'With chips?' asks the barmaid, tapping the order into the till.

'Definitely with chips.' Tilda finds her mouth actually watering at the thought of the food. 'And half a shandy while I'm waiting, please.'

'Lightweight,' Dylan teases, ordering himself a pint of the famous Black Sheep ale.

When she sits on the settle, close to the fire, Dylan slides along to sit beside her, and Lucas takes the chair opposite. Thistle stretches out in front of the hearth, her earlier nervousness appearing to have lessened. The room is wonderfully warm, so that Tilda has to remove her hat, scarf and coat. She can feel a dozen pairs of surreptitious eyes upon her now, her striking hair revealed, her face no longer partially obscured by all her winter clothing, her eyes exposed as she takes off her sunglasses. She senses that Dylan is going out of his way not to stare, not to notice, whereas Lucas is still looking at her as if she were a rare specimen that he might label and exhibit in a museum, given half a chance. She is amused to find that she cares less about them noticing her albinism than she does about the fact that she hasn't washed her hair for an age.

Better odd-looking than scuzzy. Pure vanity, silly woman.

'Professor Williams tells me you are a ceramic artist, so you've an interest in Celtic art, am I right?' Lucas asks.

'Yes, for my own designs. But . . . well, apart from that, I want to learn more about the history of the place. You know, being new here, I'd like to find out . . . stuff.' She is aware how badly she is explaining herself, and knows it is because of what she is not saying.

Ghosts and murders: discuss. Not an easy conversation opener over lunch.

Dylan takes a couple of gulps of his pint and then leans close to Tilda.

'My uncle is pretty much the expert on local history around here, you know. I've never heard anyone ask him a question he couldn't answer.'

'Yes,' she says, nodding and sipping cautiously at her shandy, 'and he's been really helpful already. It's just that, well . . . I'm curious about the dig.' She turns to look at Dylan, just quickly enough to catch him gazing at her hair. He meets her eye and then looks away, mumbling an apology into his beer. Standard embarrassed reaction. But then he raises his eyes again and regards her steadily, his face serious. He sighs, seemingly about to speak, but then does not. There are a few seconds, a fleeting moment, where he is awkward, having been found out, and his guard has dropped. The grin is gone. So is his habit of making light of everything, keeping things upbeat. Safe. She likes this version of him better. Out of habit, she continues talking to smooth over his discomfort, but, really, there is no need. An unspoken apology has been given and accepted. She understands that his interest is not voyeuristic, nor is it morbid curiosity, but it is something genuine. Sincere. 'I'd like to know about the grave.' She turns back to Lucas, who has missed what passed between her and Dylan entirely as he was busy texting. 'Who do you think you've found?' she asks him.

As he speaks, Lucas looks at her without faltering, yet his gaze does not connect. Rather his eyes move to take in all her features, all her strangeness, as if filing it away. 'It would be easy to jump to conclusions, given the pointers we've found . . . Point is, I've learnt from the many digs I've been involved in, things are rarely as obvious as they seem. Human lives are complicated . . . and people sometimes, well, they go out of their way to hide things. Or at least, to make them less simple to discover.'

'Perhaps the dead don't want us digging up their secrets,' Dylan suggests, wiping beer foam from his top lip.

Lucas gives him a hard stare. 'Some people have a problem with disturbing a grave, however well-meant the investigation. If you are one of those, why did you agree to dive for us?'

Dylan shrugs. 'Every man has his price. Isn't that what they say?'

Tilda is unconvinced.

Lucas leans forward, elbows on the worn and polished wood of the table, concentrating on Tilda now, keen to share his theories regarding his discovery with her. 'What we know for certain at this stage is that this is a double grave. There are two people buried here, both interred at the same time.'

'Members of the same family?' Tilda asks.

'It's possible, but . . . well, there are signs that suggest something rather different. You see, the bodies are lying not side by side, but one on top of the other. And only the lower one has a coffin. Which is unusual. As is the fact that there don't appear to be any grave goods accompanying the upper body.' Lucas waves his hands expressively as he talks, needing no prompting to explain further. 'Given the date we believe the grave to have been dug, this is strange. Grave goods were things people put in with a deceased person that they believed they might need with them in the next life. Weapons, plates, jewels, things that would mark out their status, signs of wealth or standing in society as well.'

'And your grave . . .' Tilda corrects herself. 'Sorry, the one you've found . . . there are none of these things in it?'

'There may be some in the coffin below, we don't know yet. But the body nearer the surface appears to have been buried without any possessions whatsoever.'

'Perhaps they were very poor,' Tilda suggests. 'Maybe they didn't have anything to take with them.'

'It is possible, but unlikely. Most people would have had *something*. Or if they didn't, relatives or community members would have provided at least the most basic items. It is odd to find a body with nothing at all. Unless . . .'

'Ah, food!' Dylan alerts them to the arrival of the meals. Tilda is torn between her desire to tuck into the first decent plate of food she has seen in a very long time, and her wish to know what it is that Lucas is hinting at. Muttering thanks to the young waiter, who blushes when she finds him gawking at her, she presses Lucas to finish his thought.

'Unless?'

'Unless the person we've found was executed. If the killing was a punishment, the carrying out of a sentence for some sort of crime, then the culprit would not have been allowed any grave goods. It would have been part of the punishment. An important part, as it condemned the executed person to struggle and hardship in the next life too.'

'I don't want to rain on anyone's parade,' Dylan says, liberally sprinkling salt on his chips, 'but there could be a much simpler explanation.'

'Such as?' The irritation is plain in Lucas's voice.

'The person in the coffin took all the stuff with him or her. The second person, the one on top, wasn't buried at the same time, but a little while later. That person had nothing left, couldn't afford a coffin or a decent burial, but wanted to be in the same place as their loved one. Still happens today, after all, people being buried in extra-deep graves so that their spouse can be laid to rest in the same spot when they eventually die.'

Lucas gives him a weary look and adopts the voice of a tired parent addressing a bothersome child. 'In the first place, we know roughly when the grave was dug – somewhere between 850 and 950 AD – and at that time couples were always buried side by side, no matter how many years after the first one died the second one joined them. Stacking bodies was a tactic employed because of a lack of space. By the Victorian era, for example, there simply wasn't room to put people next to each other, particularly in urban areas. Hundreds of years before that, out in the countryside, when the population was a fraction of what it is now, space wasn't an issue. In fact' – he pauses to enjoy a mouthful of shepherd's pie before going on – 'it would have been much easier to dig two shallow graves side by side than one deeper one. Anyway, there is a more compelling reason to suppose this was a punishment killing.'

Tilda hurriedly snatches at some chips while she waits for Lucas to go on. He has paused again, in part to eat some of his food, but more, she suspects, for dramatic effect. And possibly to annoy Dylan.

'The body near the surface is prone, not supine.' He waits, clearly hoping one of them will ask what that means. Eventually he saves them the trouble. 'It was buried face down, not face up. Hardly a respectful and dignified way to treat a corpse. And as if that weren't enough, a very large, very heavy flat stone was placed on the back of the deceased.'

'To hold him or her in place?' Dylan gives a light laugh. 'Hardly seems necessary if they were dead.'

'But very necessary if they were still alive,' Lucas points out.

'*What?*' Tilda is aghast. 'You mean that the person who was executed was punished not just by being killed, but by being buried alive?' All at once she can feel her appetite fading.

Lucas shrugs and tucks into his meal with enthusiasm. 'Makes you wonder, doesn't it, just what crime they must have committed to have deserved such a fate?'

A thoughtful silence descends on the table, during which Tilda attempts to rekindle her appetite. The steak and kidney pudding is delicious, and soon the nourishing food, the heat from the fire, and the small amount of alcohol in her shandy soothes her into a more pleasant state of mind and body than she has experienced for quite a while. Even so, the notion of such a gruesome execution taking place so close to home disturbs her. Could the ghost be the spirit of the body the archaeologists are so intent on unearthing?

It would explain why my visitor is so angry.

'Will you be able to find out who exactly it is you've dug up?' she asks Lucas as he polishes off the last of his pie.

He shakes his head. 'Highly unlikely. Very few written records exist for tenth-century Wales, and a lot of what there is would have been written sometime after the events, so it's pretty un-reliable. At least if you want specifics. So, no, basically, we are not going to be able to give you name, rank and serial num-ber. What we hope to do – what lovely, lovely science now enables us to have a stab at – is to say male or female, age, cause of death, health and diet during life, and, possibly, position in their community. Given that this looks like an execution, we may get more clues when we reach the coffin below.'

'Would the two deaths necessarily be connected?'

'There is a precedent. There was a grave in the southeast of England found with a similarly dispatched guilty party on top, and studies strongly indicate that the body below was the victim of the crime. So, it's possible our upper-level remains are those of a murderer, and the body in the coffin was murdered by them. But we are getting ahead of ourselves,' he warns her, washing down his food with some mineral water. 'Lots to search for yet. Lots to prove, or disprove.' He might have been about to say more, but Molly looks up from her laptop on the next table and calls him over to see something.

Thistle, relaxed at last, begins to show an interest in the food. She gets up and stretches lazily, before reaching up to sniff the edge of the table, her nose twitching. Tilda smiles at her.

'I'll save some for you, I promise,' she says, handing her a chip to keep hunger pangs at bay.

Dylan watches. 'She's looking better. You've done a good job of getting her right.'

Tilda considers the corner-shop diet she has been feeding the dog, the irregular hours of sleep and the erratic exercise patterns she has been subjected to. 'I think she pretty much got better by herself,' she says. 'Though I can see why the men who had her gave up. No way is she ever going to catch a hare.'

'She looks built for it.'

'Maybe so, but when we came across one the other day she bounced after it and then just played with it. Had no intention of catching the thing. And the hare knew it too.'

'Really?' Dylan raises his eyebrows.

'I swear, it just sat there, washing its face. It knew it wasn't in any danger. Thistle didn't even bark.'

'Well, she wouldn't. Proper coursers don't. They hunt silently. That's why they make rubbish guard dogs. They don't track by scent either – they're sight hounds. Though yours is probably just shy 'cause she's embarrassed about wearing that collar.'

Much as it irks her to admit it, the pink band does look all wrong around Thistle's neck. Tilda leans forward and unbuckles it. 'I don't think you really need this, do you, girl?'

'Much better,' Dylan says.

Tilda looks at him. 'Why are you helping with the dig, if you really don't like what they're doing? And don't tell me it's for the money. Your uncle said you go all over the world diving for people. Doesn't sound like you're short of work.'

He smiles, shaking his head. 'To be honest, I jumped at the chance of an excuse to come home for a while. I miss the place. "Away" is not always all it's cracked up to be.'

'So you're okay with them opening a grave?'

'I can't really disapprove, can I? It is more or less what I poke around in too, a lot of the time. Not formal graves, maybe, but wrecks often end up being the final resting places for many people. Some of them have been there a very long time too.'

'You're surely not expecting to find a wreck in the lake?'

He laughs. 'No. This is more of an exploratory bit of diving. The lake has been fairly thoroughly searched over the years, but now they've found something new so near to the water, well, it's worth having another look. The changing levels of the water, particularly if there have been floods as well as droughts, can shift things. New stuff becomes visible. Just! It's pretty murky down there.'

'I read that the lake has its own water horse.'

'Gorsie, you mean?'

'Gorsie?'

'That's what the locals call it. Nessie in Lock Ness: Gorsie in Llangors. Everyone around here has heard about our very own deep-water monster.'

'Have there ever been any . . . sightings?'

'A few claim to have seen it, mostly after a late night in the pub. I think there are a couple of dodgy-looking pictures circulating.' He grins. 'I'll let you know if I find it.'

Tilda forces herself to return to her list of reasons for venturing out. Despite Lucas's insistence that it is too early to be certain about the find, she feels there may be something there which will provide answers to what she feared were unanswerable questions. Something connecting the body in the grave to her frightening visions. Even if those answers do involve words like *ghost* and *murderer*, and the terrible idea of burying someone alive. It is a start. She glances over at the professor. He is sitting next to Molly, and they are all very busy with something on the laptop. She had been going to ask him for his help, but the thought of fusing that computer, with everyone there, so close. Just because she fixed the lights doesn't mean she can be certain she won't adversely affect things again. Instead she turns to Dylan.

'I wonder, could you do something for me?'

'Bring you the head of the water horse, perhaps?'

'Ha ha,' she responds mirthlessly. 'A bit simpler than that. My . . . my computer isn't working, and I need a couple of books. Any chance you could order them for me online? Here, I've written down the sort of thing I'm after. I need to build a wood-fired kiln. That is, I *want* to build one. I'm trying out a new technique. And new glazes. That's the name of a ceramicist who works this way. If you search his name, other potters and authors should come up. I did build something similar years ago, at art school, but, well, I could do with more information. I was going to ask the professor . . .'

'Happy to help,' he says, taking the piece of paper from her.

'Thanks. Let me know how much they cost and I'll give you the cash.'

'No problem. But you should get your PC fixed. Can't be easy living up there without the Internet, especially as you don't drive.'

'I do. I mean I can drive. I just . . . don't have a car at the moment.'

He appears to be waiting for her to explain further, but she does not, so that the silence between them becomes a little awkward. Tilda begins to feel stupidly tired. Lack of regular sleep, the shock of the visions, the pace at which she had been working, all have combined to leave her feeling drained and lacking in stamina. On top of which, she is unused to spending time in company, and feels the need to be on her own again. She gets to her feet and begins putting on her outdoor clothes.

'Leaving us so soon?' Dylan asks.

'I need to go to the shop. Catch the post before it goes. Thanks for the drink, and for offering to get the books for me.'

'Like I said, happy to help.' He watches her replace her hat and glasses. 'Let me know if you fancy going out on the lake any time,' he tells her. 'I've got a boat.'

Now it is her turn to smile.

'The one with the dodgy motor?'

'It's got oars too.'

She shakes her head. 'I prefer dry land, remember?'

Before he can keep her talking further, she waves good-bye to the others, whistles to Thistle and slips out of the pub. Tiredness aside, she feels more human and more normal than she has in weeks. At the village shop she buys as much food as she can carry in her backpack, including some proper dog food, but not forgetting plenty of soup and chocolate. She pauses at the post office counter, selects a picture postcard, and pens a few cheerful lines to her parents. As she puts it in the letter box she sends a silent wish with it that her parents will be convinced she is all right and that she will be able to talk them out of a visit. Much as she would enjoy seeing her father, there is so much that needs her attention right now, there are so many things she knows she has to face up to and deal with, she really does not want to have to manage their worry about her on top of it.

The winter sun is weakening fast as it dips toward the jagged horizon of the Brecon Beacons. Tilda and Thistle make their slow and steady way back up the hill to Ty Gwyn.

9

SEREN

I wait inside my house. The fire is lit but I keep it burning low to avoid too much smoke in the small space. Today I have fed the short flames with rosemary stalks to aid my memory of the vision, and to lift my dulled senses. I am always weary after a quest. The causes of this lie in some measure with the poisonous nature of the fairy toadstool. Its effects linger in the body a day or more sometimes. But there are other origins to my low spirits and lethargy. Journeying in my other guise tires me upon my return, for my limbs and sinews have been used in unfamiliar and unpracticed ways, so that now my body aches. More, I am downcast by the clear meaning of the vision. Wenna will not bear a child. That much is plain. I do not care for the woman, but I pity her. As a princess her position is now all but untenable in these politically unstable times. As a woman, she will face a barren future, and I would not wish that upon anyone. There is more at stake here, however, than Wenna's happiness, for the vision foretold the possible death of Prince Brynach. To those uninitiated in the ways of reading a seeing, it might appear that all is lost. A hundred or more charging horses bearing soldiers sharp with weapons seen driving him into the lake . . . that must surely foretell nothing less than his enemies' triumph, his own defeat, his very death. But it need not be so. Had he fallen to a sword, or an arrow, or an axe, then yes, I would have read the vision no other way. But he went into the water. He was taken by the lake. In this way he entered that liminal realm where two worlds meet, and from which it is possible to return. So, I pray the seeing shows not his ultimate demise, but a battle lost from which he may, *may*, recover.

I have sent a shepherd boy with a message for Nesta. If the princess wishes to hear my words herself she can choose to come, but I think she will not. It is important for her to keep her fears and her desires to herself, and whilst a visit from Nesta would go unremarked, anyone seeing Princess Wenna calling upon me would be suspicious of her motives. And when people are suspicious they want to find the truth, even if it means gouging out someone else's secrets. Or perhaps, making up truths of their own. Either way, Wenna will not want tongues wagging on account of her business. Nesta will come to me as one wise woman to another, under guise of exchanging remedies, perhaps. She will listen to what I have to say and if her mistress trusts her to repeat my words faithfully, then so must I.

Soon I feel her heavy footsteps thudding through the ground, and moments later she knocks on my door. I bid her enter and she comes to settle herself close to the fire. She is a little out of breath, her short legs having worked hard to carry her stout body over the frostbitten ground at some speed, it seems. I give her a moment to arrange her skirts and remove the hood of her grey woollen cloak. I notice she is wearing a silver broach, pinning her kirtle. It is a pretty thing, a ring of oak leaves and acorns finely worked. A present from the princess I should imagine, and worn today to remind me of the esteem Nesta is held in. Of her position on the crannog. I need no such reminder. I know which one of us is trusted to wash Princess Wenna's small clothes and which one of us is trusted with seeing her future.

'You are well, Seren Arianaidd?' Nesta asks. The sound of my formal name spoken in her voice is unfamiliar to us both. It amuses me. I imagine it pains her.

I merely nod, not wishing to encourage an unnecessary exchange of pleasantries. My head is too sore, my belly too hot, my limbs too cramped, to be bothered with such things. Nesta should know this, if she calls herself healer and follower of the old religion. She should understand. But, in truth, she is an altogether different manner of witch from me. It is true, her remedies have helped those with small ailments and base longings. She does not, however, tread the path of true magic, nor would she dare to seek a vision. There are better hedge witches a day's ride from here, I'd wager. She does the name no service, for though her skills are passable, her heart is greedy. This is not the way of a true witch. Her lack of talent has driven her to follow a dangerous path, a road where dark magic is used for personal gain, each successful spell a stain upon her own soul and that of whoever it is pays for her services. She is seen as a vain and silly woman, I think, but people do not fear her. Their judgement is off. She is more dangerous than they could imagine.

At least she has no more patience for formalities than I, so that her next question takes us to business.

'You sent for me; have you done what Princess Wenna asked of you?'

'I sought a vision on her behalf, yes.'

She leans forward, her deep-set eyes brightened by the firelight. 'What did you see?'

'I can speak plainly to you, Nesta Meredith?'

'I would prefer it.'

'The vision was clear, there was nothing slant or double in it. The princess will never bear a child.'

Nesta takes a wheezing in-breath of shock. 'You are certain?'

'I would not state what I do not know to be the truth.'

'No child? Ever?'

'Not by Prince Brynach, nor any other man.'

'Any other? She would not wish to know of such a thing! You were not instructed . . .'

'Indeed I was not *instructed*! Your mistress asked for my help and it was freely given. I sought an answer to her question – would she ever bear a child? The answer came back no, not for any man, not ever.'

'I recall her also asking for your assistance in conceiving a child!'

'As she has asked you, so many times.'

'You are quick to dismiss my cures . . .'

'And what *do* they cure, tell me?'

'. . . but I see you offer no hope. No help. No remedy.'

'I will not give false hope. I will not offer a remedy where there is none. Unlike some . . .'

'My only desire is to aid the princess. To ease her suffering!'

'And to prolong her wish for the impossible, to keep alive a longing that is the bedfellow only of pain and disappointment. Does this ease her suffering?'

'I act only out of love for my mistress.'

To my astonishment, I see tears glinting upon her cheeks. She quickly brushes them away, and makes her voice level and firm once more.

'I cannot return to Princess Wenna with such news. We must think of a way to . . . to soften the blow, else I fear it could kill her.'

'Can a person die of disappointment?'

'You know full well what is at stake here, and not just for the princess. Her wish to be a mother is not for herself alone. It is for the prince, of course, but also for the future of her people. The future of the prince's domain.'

'All the more reason she should know the truth.'

Nesta shakes her head. 'You are a heartless creature, Seren. People say you do not feel as others, that your soul thrives only in the dark hours. How can you know what my mistress endures? How can you understand?'

'If it were within my gift to change the way things are, do you not think I would do it? My magic has its limits. I was not shown a way to put a babe in the arms of the princess.' I cast my gaze into the fire as I speak, my own heart heavy with the burden of such sorrow. 'She must learn to accept that which cannot be changed. As must we all.'

'Ha!' Nesta is angry now, fearful, no doubt, of her mistress's reaction. 'That is all very well for you to say, sitting here in your lair, distant from the life of the crannog. You will not be the one looking into Princess Wenna's eyes when she learns her future. You will not be the one to sit up nights with her as her heart breaks. You will not be the one to watch Prince Brynach turn from her.' She pauses, narrowing her eyes and jutting her chin at me. 'Or it might be that you *will*. For when he turns from her, we all know who it is he looks to in her stead!'

'Have care how you speak to me.'

'Oh? Would you have the truth buttered like parsnips for you now?'

'I am my prince's Seer, nothing more.'

'*Your* prince!' Nesta sneers. 'That's what you want, you cannot deny it. You would send me back to the princess to throttle the life from her dreams with your vision, when all you have seen is the future *you* desire, and my lady's happiness is not a part of it.'

'You damn me with every word that comes out of your mouth!' I leap to my feet, causing dust to kick up into the fire, which spits and sparks. As do I. 'You call me a cheat and a liar! You question my loyalty to Prince Brynach – and his wife – and more than this, you accuse me of falsifying a vision! You cannot believe I would do such a thing. That I would forsake the sacred trust given me!'

Nesta clambers to her feet. 'People are wrong about you, after all is said and done. You are a woman like any other, and you will abuse your position to get what you want. To get *who* you want!'

'Take yourself from my sight! Do not set one fat foot in my home again. I have told you what I saw, and all that is required of you is that you be messenger. Deliver the truth to Princess Wenna. She, at least, will know it when she hears it, even if you do not.'

But after she has gone I wonder. Will the princess believe me? Or will she, too, see some selfish purpose behind my interpretation? The news I send is the worst she could expect, and carries a harsh future for her. Might she not seek to shine a different light on the scene depicted? Might she not be all too willing to listen to Nesta's poison words, words that themselves serve another's purpose? For many is the tale of a messenger bringing bad tidings who does not live long enough to see them come to pass. If Nesta is fervent in her manner and persuasive in her argument, and Wenna wants only to hear a happier version of her life, why then might she not choose to blame me? She knows where her husband's affection lies. How can she not?

I stamp down the flames of my fire, snatch my cape from its hook by the door, and stride out into the gathering dark. I cannot feel this way, my heart heavy, my head disquieted so, and be confined. I will walk by the shores of the lake and take up some of the tranquility of the waters.

TILDA

The December morning is taking its time waking up, so that even at eight o'clock it is still barely light enough for a run. Though Tilda prefers to go out in the soft focus of dawn or dusk, she still has to be sensible. It would be so easy to twist an ankle or have a fall if the gloom were too heavy. There is another frost today, so that as the darkness begins to lift, the landscape is awash with a curious silver glow. She stands in the garden, mug of tea in hand, watching the world below slowly reveal itself. The lake is not quite frozen, but there is a flatness to the surface that suggests if the temperature were to drop another degree or so it would quickly glaze over again. Into this quiet scene comes the flicker of car headlights through the hedge along the lane, and the sound of an engine labouring up the hill. She watches, and an aged Land Rover growls into view. As it makes its noisy progress up the narrow stretch of tarmac that twists in a hairpin bend to climb to the cottage, she can make out Dylan at the wheel. She goes to greet him at the gate. Up close the vehicle is even more dilapidated and battered than she had first thought. Its bodywork is dented in several places, its paintwork dull and scratched, and an alarming amount of smoke trails from its exhaust. Dylan parks up and gets out, cheerful as ever, apparently unbothered by the car's condition.

'Post!' he calls, waving a brown cardboard package. 'Your books have come,' he explains as she lets him into the garden.

'I didn't expect a personal delivery service, but thanks.' She takes them from him. 'Come inside, the kettle's hot.'

She leads him not into the kitchen, but to the studio, where the wood burner is still going from the night before, a cast-iron kettle singing softly on top of it. What daylight exists is backed up by a storm lantern. Tilda is aware how odd it must look. Thistle stands up when they enter the room but does not come to greet Dylan.

'She's still a bit shy,' she tells him. 'Even without her pink collar.'

'This place is great,' he says as he wanders around, taking in her half-made pots, piles of sketch books, pots of glazes and general potter's paraphernalia. If the lack of lighting strikes him as strange, he does not mention it. 'You've been busy, by the look of it.'

'Things are stacking up. I've gone as far as I can go without a kiln. I'm really pleased to see these books.'

Dylan is now standing in front of what is obviously the large, modern, electric kiln. He looks at it, and then at Tilda. 'This one not working then?'

She hesitates, turning away from him to add milk to his drink. 'I want to try something different. Something . . . older. More in keeping with where the pots have been made, and what inspired them.'

'Cool.' He nods, easily accepting her explanation.

She hands him the mug, letting him help himself to the somewhat damp sugar from the bowl. He seems very at ease, and she envies him his ability to relax with someone he scarcely knows, in a place he has never been before, with a less-than-friendly dog watching his every move. She takes the biscuit tin from the workbench and offers one to Thistle in the hope she might thaw a little, but she won't even take it. Dylan takes two, munching as he talks.

'So, what's the plan? Are you going to build the thing in here?'

'Oh, no. It has to be outside. I think I'm going to use bricks. I'd like to seal it with mud, but the weather's not exactly conducive to trying to dig at the moment, so I may have to use mortar.' She unwraps the books and flicks through the first one until she finds an illustration to show him. 'Here, see? It's a simple system, but you can get fantastic results if you manage the temperature carefully.'

'Can't be easy. I mean, you light a fire under the thing and it burns. Hardly comes with a dial, does it?'

'It's all about controlling the airflow and letting the kiln cool down slowly, which can take days.'

'Days!' He laughs. 'We're going to need more biscuits.'

'We?'

'Thought I'd lend a hand. Can't dive until things warm up a bit out there. The dig's on hold because of the freeze too.'

'Well, I hadn't planned . . . that is, I don't know . . .'

'If you're going to make that thing out of bricks,' he says, tapping the picture on the page, 'you'll have to go to the builder's merchants in Brecon.' He shrugs and smiles. 'I've got the Land Rover, all fuelled up and ready to go.'

'Really? I mean, will it get as far as Brecon?'

He clutches dramatically at his chest. 'I'm wounded. Wounded! That's my fabulous Linny the Lanny – she's been with me years.'

'It looks like it.'

'They won't deliver, not all the way up here. And I can easily get what you need in the back of Linny.' He glances at his watch. 'They'll be open by now.' He slurps his tea and looks at her, head tilted slightly to one side, waiting.

And what do I tell him? That I'm terrified of going anywhere in a car? That if he goes over forty miles per hour I'll have a panic attack?

She knows she cannot. No bricks: no kiln. No kiln: no pots. She needs those bricks, and there doesn't seem to be another way of getting them. She drains her mug.

'Okay,' she says, nodding a little too much. 'Yes, thanks. That'd be great. I'll . . . get my coat.'

As they leave, she expects Thistle to follow but the dog hangs back. She pats her gently. 'Okay, funny old thing. You stay here and guard the valuables. That's pretty much the kettle right now.'

She climbs into the passenger seat of the Land Rover and immediately feels her stomach knot.

Steady girl. Not exactly a speed machine. Only ten miles or so, you'll be fine.

'Right,' Dylan slams his door, sending a shudder through the whole vehicle. 'Here we go.' He turns the key, and nothing happens. He tries again. Nothing. Not even a stutter or a faint whir of battery attempting to fire internal combustion engine. He turns the key a third time. Again, nothing. He frowns. 'Odd,' he says.

'Oh well, never mind . . .' Tilda finds herself ridiculously relieved.

'She's such a good starter. Reliable as the day is long, is my lovely Linny.'

'Well, she doesn't seem to want to start today,' Tilda points out.

Dylan hesitates, turning to look at her, then says gently, 'Or perhaps you don't want her to.'

Tilda feels herself blush. 'What on earth do you mean?' she blurts out, more crossly than she intended.

'Look, I'm just saying . . .'

'It's your car.'

'And it usually starts,' he says. 'Just like my boat usually starts. And my uncle's clock usually works. Usually.'

Oh God.

For a full minute neither of them speaks. They simply sit there, the huge unspoken meaning behind his words squashed between them. Tilda wants to jump out of the car, run back to the house, and shut herself inside. She doesn't want to go anywhere in any car. She doesn't want to have to try to explain the inexplicable to this . . . man. She doesn't want to have to try to explain it to herself.

But if I run now, if I hide now, if I give up now, then what?

She knows things have to change. She knows she has to do something. She closes her eyes, forcing herself to find a kernel of courage.

I do want this bloody car to start. I do!

She steadies her breathing, waiting for the sense that something has changed. And it comes. A subtle shift in how she feels. In how she . . . is. She opens her eyes and stares out through the windscreen, not trusting herself to meet Dylan's eyes.

'Try it again,' she says.

Slowly, he takes hold of the key and turns it. And the engine bursts into life, belching exhaust fumes, juddering the ancient frame of the vehicle, setting up a cacophony of squeaks and rattles, but it works. And it goes on working. Only now does Tilda dare look at Dylan. He smiles at her, not his usual chipper grin, but a softer, reassuring sort of smile.

'Right,' he says. 'Bricks, then.'

'Bricks,' she agrees.

Clearly sensitive to her nervousness, Dylan drives slowly and steadily, so that Tilda finds she is actually able to enjoy looking at the beautiful countryside they pass through. She has spent so many weeks at the cottage that discovering what lies beyond the horizon is an exciting event. The road climbs through the high rocky pass in the village of Bwlch and then dips down to follow the River Usk on to the Brecon Beacons, with their sharp, dark peaks and steep escarpments dotted with tough Welsh mountain sheep. The realization that she is able to even notice the scenery, instead of being in her more common, white-knuckled state, is an immense relief to Tilda. Dylan is an excellent local guide, keeping up a light chatter, telling her about points of interest along the route. By the time they reach the small market town of Brecon, Tilda is smiling properly for the first time in an age.

The first time since Mat died? Can it be? Even now, in a car?

The builder's yard is well stocked with a bewildering selection of materials. Dylan admits to being no fan of DIY, but he is practical, and has helped his uncle maintain his old house over the years. Clutching the book as a reference, Tilda asks for a long list of items, anxious not to forget some vital piece of equipment or raw material. In half an hour the goods are paid for and snugly loaded into the back of the Land Rover. It is a rare treat to have the company of such an easy friend. Tilda is aware she has let most of her friendships slide since moving to the area, and had almost forgotten the simple pleasure of a task shared with a willing helper.

As they set off for home along the short stretch of dual carriageway Tilda allows herself to compare this journey to the fateful one on the way home from her honeymoon. Anxiety begins to tug at the corners of her consciousness as she recalls the heavy rain on the motorway that day, in contrast to the clear skies and sunshine today. And she hadn't been driving fast. Not as fast, in fact, as Dylan is driving now. Perhaps he has forgotten how reluctant his passenger was to set foot in his vehicle, or maybe he, too, is buoyed up by the lighthearted mood of the day. Either way, the battered Land Rover is travelling considerably faster than it had done on the outward journey. Tilda experiences a dizzying wave of panic as the road rushes past her. She begins to sweat, and finds her breath catching in her throat. She focuses on the low hill in the middle distance.

Just a few more miles. The lake is on the other side of that hill, and then just a few more minutes to the cottage. Keep steady.

'Tilda?' Dylan has noticed something is wrong. 'Are you okay?'

She nods, searching for her voice. 'I'm fine. Just a bit . . . it's nothing.'

'You sure? Do you want some air? You have to slide the window open. Here, let me help you.' Keeping his eye on the road, he reaches across her and undoes the fastener on the elderly passenger window before pushing at it to gain an inch or two of air.

As he leans toward her, in that instant, Tilda experiences a confusing muddle of emotions. The sense of such closeness to this strong, attractive young man, who at least in those ways cannot help but bring back memories of Mat, the giddiness brought on by the unfamiliar motion and speed of the car, and her own heightened levels of anxiety, all combine to make her feel light-headed, disoriented, strangely unreal, as if she is floating away from the moment. Or away from herself.

Stupid. It doesn't make any sense. I was fine earlier. Stupid woman, pull yourself together.

'Any better?' Dylan asks, clearly concerned.

Tilda turns to say yes, to attempt to reassure him, and to convince herself, that she is okay. And as she does so she sees what is in the seat behind him. Or rather, who. The dark, shabby, broken figure of the woman from her visions sits as solidly as any living breathing person. Tilda gasps. The woman, the ghost, whatever it is, turns its ruined, ghastly face slowly, slowly, slowly toward Tilda.

And then it springs.

It leaps where there is no space to leap, hurling itself forward, over, no *through* the seats, smashed hands and twisted fingers outstretched as it flings its shattered self at Tilda.

And Tilda screams. She cannot do otherwise. She throws her arms over her head, and screams and screams and screams, causing Dylan to swerve dangerously, the Land Rover lurching to one side, sliding, until he is able to bring it back under control and stop at the side of the road.

Tilda feels hands tightly gripping her arms, and for a moment thinks the ghoulish nightmare has her in its clutches.

'Tilda!' Dylan's voice cuts through her terror. 'Tilda, it's okay. You're okay. You're safe, look, we've stopped. There's nothing to be scared of. Open your eyes and look.'

Panting, gulping air, she does as he says, scarcely daring to glance into the back of the vehicle. The vision has ended. The apparition gone. There is only her and Dylan. He sees her looking into the back of the car.

'There's nothing there, see? Just bricks, yeah?'

'Bricks,' Tilda nods, still trembling, letting him hold her hands now. 'Just bricks.'

Dylan makes a quick stop at the shop in Bwlch to buy what he describes as a medicinal bottle of brandy, so that twenty minutes after arriving home he and Tilda are in the sitting room, clutching mugs of strong coffee liberally laced with the stuff. Tilda breathes in the heady fumes as she watches him light the fire. Thistle has wriggled her way onto the sofa beside her and lies with her head in her lap. Neither Dylan nor Tilda spoke for the remainder of the journey home.

There was too much to say, and the noisy Land Rover was not the place to say it.

Dylan carefully places logs on top of the burgeoning flames before sitting himself down in the chair opposite the sofa. Tilda takes two swift swigs of her coffee, willing the brandy to give her courage.

'So,' Dylan says at last, 'do you want to tell me what it was you . . . thought you saw in the Land Rover?'

'I'm not sure where to begin,' she says at last.

'The beginning's the usual place.'

'Nothing about anything is "usual" anymore.'

'You could plunge straight in to the scary bits.'

'Says the diver.'

'I'll lend you my fins.'

She is on the point of telling him. Of blurting out every-thing that has happened since she came to the cottage: the failing power supply, the way she can influence such things, the vision of the people in the boat, and the terrifying ghost who seems intent on driving her insane. For a moment she is almost seduced by the idea of sharing it all with someone who might listen. Someone who, she senses, would make a good try at understanding the inexplicable. But she can't. It's all too much, too crazy, too personal somehow, and she barely knows Dylan.

How well do you have to know a person before you can tell them you're seeing ghosts? Get a grip, girl. This is ridiculous. Pull it together.

'I'm sorry,' she says as calmly as she can. 'It's been a difficult time. But I shouldn't be bothering you with all this.'

'I don't mind. If I can help . . .'

'I've just allowed myself to get spooked. New house. Spending time alone.' She shakes her head and tries what she hopes looks like a brave smile. 'You must think I'm barking mad.' She finishes her coffee, letting the brandy burn a fiery trail to her stomach, letting it numb her whirling mind.

That's better. Can't afford to lose it. Not now.

He shrugs. 'You haven't given me a reason to think that. And,' he pauses, then goes on, '. . . it seems like you're not going to.'

'I'm sorry. Sorry for screaming like that. Ridiculous.'

'Something scared you.'

'Like I said, I've just got a case of the jitters. I'll be better. I'll be fine. Really.'

He looks at her, regarding her patiently, clearly hoping she will confide in him. But when she says nothing he does not press her further, and she finds she likes him all the more for that. There are some things she finds she does want to tell him about. Some things, or someone. 'It took me awhile to come to terms with my husband's death,' she blurts out, and, realiz-ing how big a subject this is to suddenly present him with, hurries on, 'I think, sometimes, that's why I get jittery. Why I overreact. It's not that I don't like being here, I do. This is where I want to be. It's just that . . .'

'Go on,' he says quietly.

'This is where I was supposed to be with Mat. This was his dream too.' She falls silent, biting her bottom lip hard, keeping her focus on the bright orange flames on a mossy oak log.

'I think you're incredibly brave,' Dylan tells her. When she smiles and shakes her head he adds, 'to move here at all. Uncle Illtyd told me, about your husband. How he died.' A thought strikes him and he smacks his own forehead with his hand. 'God, I am so stupid! The Land Rover . . . is that why you were so reluctant? He, Mat, my uncle said it was a car accident. Tilda I'm so sorry, I'm such a fool.'

'No, you're not. Honestly, I have to be able to get into a car. It's ridiculous otherwise . . .'

'And it's why you don't drive? Why you don't have a car?' She nods. 'Pathetic, I know.'

'You are certainly not that! Like I said, I think you're really brave, to come and live here on your own. After . . . after what you went through. It must be tough. You must miss him.'

Tilda does not trust herself to reply without crying.

As if sensing that her grief might overwhelm her, Dylan gets to his feet. 'Come along,' he says, 'we've got too much to do to sit around here.' He takes Tilda's mug gently from her.

'We have?'

'Yup.' He heads for the door. 'We've got a kiln to build.'

Having unloaded the bricks from the Land Rover, they set about choosing a level space in the garden. Tilda measures out a small square and they dig out the turf and topsoil. The ground is frosty, but not deeply frozen, so that the task is slow but not impossible. They compact the mud that will form the base of the kiln using a concrete slab to form the bottom of the hearth and give them a stable foundation on which to build. Tilda checks the dimensions and quantities in her new books and then mixes sufficient mortar to bind the bricks. They then tackle the challenging job of constructing the main shape over the fire pit. Throughout the rest of the day Tilda finds comfort in the purpose and effort of hard work. Hard work, which will mean she can at last fire her precious pots. She is pleased to discover she remembers more than she could have hoped for of how to construct the kiln. She had worried that some vital part of the process would elude her, even with the new books for reference. After all, building such a thing at art school was a very different proposition to tackling the job without any expert help. Dylan does what he can, and his support is a boon, both practically and psychologically, but it is down to Tilda to know what to do. To make sure the thing has no crucial flaws that could wreck weeks of work and render her pots misshapen, malformed disasters. The more she labours on – positioning the firebricks here, making the angle of the wall just so, slanting the arch of the roof this way – the more her confidence grows, and with it an inner certainty that this is right. This is what she should be doing, what she needs to do. With each passing hour the memory of the frightening apparition fades a little, receding into memory, walled up behind a protective layer of purpose, while her attention is directed at what she is doing. The end result, after much cursing and false starts, resembles a somewhat angular beehive. They have left two air-holes, one at the front, one at the back, which can be filled in once the kiln is loaded. Tilda takes further measurements to ensure that the planks they put in for shelves will leave enough space to house her large pots.

Working steadily, snacking in preference to taking a lunch break, it takes the two of them several hours to complete the kiln, and they know they are racing the fading light. It is nearly four o'clock by the time they have finished and stand back to admire their handiwork.

'I'll come back tomorrow,' Dylan tells her. 'Got to be here to see the inaugural firing up of the little beast. Make sure she'll get up to temperature.'

'It's not very beautiful,' Tilda admits, 'but I think it will do.' She turns to Dylan and smiles, a spontaneous, sincere response to what they have achieved. 'Thanks for helping.'

'Worth it to see you looking happier,' he tells her.

Embarrassed now, Tilda says, 'I'm sorry about . . . earlier. I was a mess.'

'No, you weren't.'

'I'd offer you supper, but, well, there's nothing much worth eating here. You'd get a better meal at your uncle's house.'

'I bet you've got something in that kitchen of yours. Besides, I like a challenge. Years of mustering up grub in far-flung parts of the world stand a person in good stead, you know.'

'Don't tell me you're a chef in your spare time too.'

'I'm pretty confident I can cook anything that's come from the village shop.'

Tilda laughs at this.

'That's the first time I've seen you laugh,' he tells her. 'It's . . . lovely.'

'It's getting cold; let's go in.'

He watches her walk toward the back door of the cottage and then asks, 'Are you scared to be here? On your own, I mean?'

She stops on the path but does not turn around when she answers. 'No. Of course not. Just, well, a little spooked. Sometimes.'

'I could stay tonight,' he offers quietly. 'If you like.'

There is a pause. Tilda fights a confusion of thoughts and feelings. At last, she says, 'Yes. I'd like that,' before continuing on her way to the kitchen.

10

SEREN

A feast day has been declared. Prince Brynach is back from a trip north to negotiate a peace with the Mercian queen. The agreement reached was favourable, and a celebration has been called to mark the beginning of what is already being called 'Brynach's Time of Peace'. In truth, I believe he was but a foot soldier in this war of words, for his ambassador, Rhodri, Princess Wenna's odious brother, was responsible for setting up the meeting. He it was who brokered the deal. He who accompanied the prince to the northernmost border of the realm. He the one who wrote the words on the scroll that must bind all parties to this new peace. But the written words of men are flimsy things indeed. Cast that parchment into the waters of Llyn Syfaddan and they would melt to nothing, first the lettering, then the scroll itself, until all was washed clean away. As if none of it had ever been.

I do not trust the word of the Queen of Mercia any more than I trust that of Rhodri, brother-of-the-princess. And I trust him not at all.

The day of the feast is also the day of the first deep fall of snow this year. For hours the previous night the skies shed their burden until the ground was cloaked in white and all sounds were stilted and robbed of their echo. By morning the clouds were spent, so that the blue of the heavens could be found in the new, glittering surface of the land.

It is midday, and the revelries are set to begin. I reluctantly make my way toward the crannog. I dislike crowds. I more strongly dislike gatherings for the purpose of carousing and indulging any and all vices to excess. Man is a creature who raises himself above his base instincts with effort, and keeps himself there only with continued vigilance. What profit is there in undoing that vital restraint? Why would anyone wish to reduce themselves to their lowest state, and have witnesses to that action? I have donned my ceremonial dress, for it is as Seer I am invited. Each present must declare his or her position, to show the breadth, wisdom, and strength of our prince's company. To have one such as me as his boon is seen as an enviable thing. Something to crow about. But the cock who crows loudest attracts not only admirers but foxes also. Prince Brynach would do well to remember that.

There is much milling about and excitement on the crannog. The whole village has come, as indeed they must. Shepherds have left their flocks. Cattlemen leave their stock to mind themselves. The blacksmith's forge is cold. The fisherman's nets and traps lie in the bottom of his boat. For a few hours, everything will wait on the plea sure of the prince, and it is his plea sure that everyone should have a day of rest, a day of feasting.

Without the movement of horses or the common workaday activities, the snow is largely undisturbed, save for the many footsteps of the eager villagers, so that all appears brightly garbed and fresh, without mud, nor drab grey stone, nor weathered stick fence or winter-bare tree to dull the picture. Smoke rises from the hole in the roof of the great hall, and even from outside it is possible to breathe in the sweet aroma of the roasting hogs within. I feel disquieted as I pause before entering, though I am uncertain as to the cause. I know I will face Nesta and Princess Wenna, and neither will be pleased to see me. I know that I must tolerate the unwelcome company of Rhodri and his pimpled son. I know also that I will be in the presence of my prince. I fear that this last disturbs me the most.

Inside the hall all is colour and noise. The fire at the centre has constructed over it two great spits, turned by damp-shirted boys who labour diligently to ensure the even cooking of the pair of pigs that will feed us all today. For a victory in battle a steer might have been slaughtered, but however festive this event, it is still midwinter, with harsh months ahead, and a few promises do not warrant the same jubilation as a triumph gained by bloody fighting. Nonetheless, many here will be more than satisfied to eat good meat for once. The women have turned out in their finest clothes, with all manner of baubles and geegaws pressed into service to dress up a tired kirtle or pinafore. The men have scrubbed themselves to a ruddy shine and all wear anything that might be classed as a weapon. For whose benefit this mummer's attempt at a show of might is made I am not clear. Their own, I must assume. A top table has been set, with chairs and places ready for our noble family when they see fit to arrive. Down the side of the hall are benches and low tables for the lesser mortals to sit at and take their food and drink. At the far end of the hall is space for the musicians and dancing that will come later. Children dart excitedly between the adults, and there is an air of cheerful expectancy and general goodwill. I am courteously greeted and acknowledged by those who see me. They do not count me friend, for they are too afraid of what I am and what I do. Rather, they see me as a useful asset; one who might divine disaster, so allowing it to be avoided. They know I travel to places they cannot, and that frightens them. Yet at the same time they are pleased to have me act on their behalf, to risk my soul, my safety, for their protection. Do they believe I care for them, as their milksop priest would have them believe he does? He readily professes God's love for them and his own as if they were the same. He entreats them to love one another, to forgive their enemies. I was taught to use my skills against anyone who would declare himself enemy. Forgiveness is for mothers of small children, for wronged wives to give and petty thieves to receive. It is not for rulers or warriors. I do not love mankind. I cannot view the herd as any more than that. I keep my love for those deserving of it, and they are few enough.

One of the minstrels takes up a ram's horn and blows a long, clear note. Prince Brynach and his party are come. A cheer, hearty and sincere, greets him as he enters the hall, the princess on his arm. They process toward the top table, followed by Rhodri and Siōn, his lickspittle son. His loyal swordsman, Hywel is here, of course, though he does not look at ease with such formality, forced as he is into an uncomfortably tight tabard. Following on, Nesta basks in her mistress's position. How secure does she feel in that, I wonder? The prince pauses when he draws level with me.

'Seren Arianaidd,' he nods, and I bow low. He reaches out and takes my hand, bidding me rise. There is a sudden hush. Has he forgotten where he is? Who he is? A prince might take the hand of a highborn lady, perhaps, such as the wife of another prince, or a relative of his own wife, but not my hand! I am not only a woman of no rank, I am Prophet and Witch. To touch me is to connect with all those dangerous and magical things that I hold within me. Is this a deliberate crossing of a well-guarded boundary, or simply a mistake? I am unable to decide. 'We are honoured to have you as our guest,' he declares, not only to me, but to the whole of the hall. It is clear he is making a point of underlining his allegiance to me. Of my importance to him. He turns to address the gathering, and still he holds my hand! Beside him the princess tenses but does not otherwise let her thoughts show. Nesta purses her lips.

The prince raises his free hand for quiet, but this is not necessary. An astonished silence has already filled the great hall. 'This day would not have come about were it not for the wisdom of our Seer. It was her vision that prompted me to take action. Her seeing told of the downfall of the realm, of the destruction of our crannog. I heeded her warning. I sought counsel with my advisors' – here he pauses to incline his head at Rhodri, who is already puffed up like a bullfrog – 'and we found a path to peace. Thanks to the skills of our Prophet we have arrived at this moment without bloodshed.'

There is a spontaneous cheer, born not so much of joyous respect, but of relief for the explanation for the prince's curious behaviour toward me. He lets go my hand and moves on. The princess never for one second loses her composure, though still she manages to treat me to a glance colder than the winter's day outside. Nesta glares at me as she passes, which makes me smile, much to her annoyance. As they take their seats, Rhodri whispers something in his sister's ear, whilst not taking his eyes from my face. I swear if that man were sliced with a blade he would not bleed blood, but ooze bile.

And so the drinking and feasting and dancing get under way. I am given a seat at the end of the high table, elevated, yet separate, so at least this convention is upheld. There is ale aplenty, and soon tongues, belts and minds alike are loosened, so that raucous laughter and loudly recounted tales compete with the singing of the minstrels and the determined playing of the musicians to fill the smoky space. The drums, whistles and pipes struggle to make themselves heard. The food is very fine, and I confess, despite my resistance to such organized jollity, I enjoy my expertly seasoned meat and light, crusty bread. I take some ale, but only a little. I have no wish to lose my wits in such company.

After almost two hours of merriment, when some of the smaller children have fallen asleep with their full bellies, curled up on straw in the corner of the hall, the adults take to dancing. The maids are painfully aware of themselves, torn between their shyness and their desire to make an impact on a possible husband. The young men are equally awkward, but some bolder than others, forgetting how unmanly they might look trotting about to a tune if it means they can woo the girl of their choice. Wives and husbands make the most of a rare chance to enjoy each other without the worry of children or work. The prince dances with the princess, the pair a picture of restrained and courtly elegance. No one dares ask me to dance, and I am glad of that. Another hour passes in this manner. Some of the frailer adults join the infants in belching slumber. Gradually the order of the assembly crumbles so that all mix and talk and joke together, regardless of rank or age. Indeed, I'd wager some are so much in the thrall of the ale they do not know who it is they speak to. In the midst of this muddle, I become aware of a presence by my side and find Prince Brynach has come to stand beside me. A glance tells me Wenna is at the far end of the room, being given instruction on the playing of a lyre. Nesta remains in her seat, watching me.

'Seren Arianaidd.' He keeps his voice low in an effort to maintain some privacy, but in truth there is too much rowdiness, too much commotion all around us, for anyone to hear our conversation.

'My Prince.'

'You are enjoying the feast, I hope?'

'The food was excellent. The musicians are tolerable. The dancing has provided me no small measure of amusement.'

'Wait until Hywel takes to the floor.' He smiles. 'He dances like nothing on God's earth.'

'I cannot agree. I have seen him dance before. I was put in mind of a bear I once saw goaded into a jig at Brecon horse fair.'

'And did this bear sing also?'

'Great heavens, spare us Hywel Gruffydd in song.'

'I do not have your gift of foresight, my Prophet, but I fore-tell Hywel in fine voice before the night is out.' He falls silent, then asks, 'Are you not pleased? I listened to your words, I acted upon them. I have seen to it the vipers of your vision will not prosper here.'

'You let the vipers live.'

'Their slaughter would have come at the price of many good men, and they are slippery creatures. I could not be certain I would slay them all. Better this way, I believe.'

'The slipperiest creature here is a member of your wife's family.'

'Still you persist in attacking my wife!'

'The pact with the Mercian Queen was her brother's idea, was it not?'

'An idea that has spared many men and secured the future of the crannog and the village.'

'So you trust.'

'I do. I gave my word, and I have that of the Queen of Mercia. Do you not trust me to govern? Do you not consider me capable of my princely duty?'

'*You* I know. *You* I trust. Beyond that, I sleep with my blade at my hip.'

He takes in my words and thinks on them for a moment before speaking. 'That you trust me humbles me, Seren. For when I am in your presence I do not trust myself.'

I look directly at him now and the fierceness of his gaze, the unmasked longing in it, quickens my blood. He lifts a hand as if to touch me again.

'My Prince, you must not . . .' I am aghast to feel a tighten-ing in my chest at the thought of his touch.

A roar from the far side of the room heralds the start of Hywel's ale-fueled speech. He has clambered unsteadily onto one of the tables and stands, goblet held aloft, calling on the gathering to listen to him. His hair is even wilder than is normal for him, his bulky frame straining at its seams.

'Prince Brynach, Princess Wenna,' he bellows, swaying and teetering as he acknowledges them with a dangerously low bow, 'my Lords,' he inclines his head, 'my Ladies . . .' He closes his eyes and smiles as if in rapture. The assembled company laughs. His eyes spring open again, 'And all you lowly beggars at the bottom of our fragrant heap . . .' this is met with good-natured booing and hissing, 'pray, take a moment from filling your bellies,' there is a cheer, 'slaking your thirst,' this followed by a louder cheer, 'or putting your hands on the nearest arse!' A comment met with loud laughter and some chastising replies from the women in the room. 'Take a moment, I beseech you,'

'Get on with it!' comes a shout from the throng.

Hywel scowls, 'Stop your noise, and stop debauching for one short minute, is all I ask, you lice-ridden, pox-marked scoundrels!'

'What happened to "Lords and Ladies"?' someone wants to know.

'They left hours ago!' shouts a soldier reclining on a bench.

Another puts in, 'They ran for the door when they saw Hywel get up to speak.'

'Stop your cursed interruptions!' Hywel roars. 'Charge your goblets, tankards, beakers, whatever comes readily to hand' – here he pauses to reach out and cup the nearest bosom to make his point. The room fills with laughter again. 'A toast!' he declares, a little more seriously now. 'A toast to the finest prince a man ever had fortune to serve. Who has delivered us from war. Who has provided this magnificent feast. Who will, one day, I am certain of it, be an even better swordsman than I am! Prince Brynach!' He raises his goblet, wine spilling from it.

'Prince Brynach! Prince Brynach!' the crowd takes up the toast and drinks to their saviour. And as they do so, all eyes turn to look upon him. And find him standing not with his princess, but with me.

TILDA

Tilda sleeps more soundly than she has done in weeks. Months. Thistle lies next to her on the bed, a furry bolster. Through the window the first light of dawn is beginning to lift the sky, bringing streaks of scarlet and vermillion as it does so. There is a curious stillness to the new day. Tilda gets up and peers through the frosted panes, gasping at what she sees. Snow. Inches deep, come secretly and silently in the night to transform the landscape.

So beautiful. As if the world has been born again. I have to go out in that.

She quickly dresses in her thermals and running gear, jamming her beanie on. The cottage has become so familiar to her now that she can move around inside with ease even when there is so little light. Despite the weirdness of what is happening to her, Ty Gwyn feels increasingly friendly. More and more like home. Thistle stretches, wags and follows her down the stairs. Tilda pauses to peep through the open door into the sitting room. Dylan is still sleeping on the sofa, all but hidden by the duvet and blankets she found him the night before. The fire in the hearth has gone out, but the little room is still warm.

Tilda carefully closes the door, not wanting to disturb him, and heads out through the kitchen.

The snow is the stuff of childhood dreams. Even in the low light it sparkles like sugar and sits fatly on every surface, every tree, every gate and fence post. Tilda can just make out the lake below as she finishes her warm-up exercises and sets off. It is teal blue, silky, dark against the lightening countryside around it. It is not cold enough for ice, and the snow affords a reasonable amount of grip. Even so, Tilda has to descend the hill cautiously, taking care to stick to the road and then to the footpath. Once on level ground she can increase her speed to a decent pace, enjoying once again the rhythm of running, feeling her muscles working, experiencing the glow and the lift that rewards such sustained exertion.

Come on fleet feet. Running on a cushion of snow. Step, push, step, push. Tilda loves to run. Tilda needs to run. I have seriously missed this!

Her footsteps thud and crunch through the virgin snow, each lift of a heel giving a short squeak. Thistle, like so many animals, is made frisky by the fluffy substance she finds herself bounding through. She abandons her customary loping to frolic and leap, breaking away from the path every now and then to run crazy loops across the water meadows. Tilda laughs at the dog's skittish behaviour. Such playfulness is catching, and she stoops to scoop up a handful of snow. Quickly forming it into a ball, she waits until the hound comes close again.

'Here, girl! Catch!' she calls out as she throws the snowball high into the air. Thistle leaps after it, snatching at the ball as it passes, shaking her head and pouncing at nothing as it crumbles to flakes in her mouth.

Soon the gaps in Tilda's running programme begin to tell, and she is forced to slow to a walk. A sharp stitch has developed in her left side, so that she stops and bends over, panting, waiting for the spasm to pass. She wonders if Dylan will wake up while she is out. What will he think if he finds her gone?

He knows I run. He'll figure it out. Hopefully, he'll relight the stoves.

Tilda is aware of how much she has enjoyed Dylan's company since he turned up to deliver her books. After her meltdown on the way home from Brecon she had felt so shaken, so defeated, somehow. Working together to build the kiln had been the perfect remedy. She had felt so alone for so long, she had almost forgotten her own need for companionship. For the simple pleasure of a shared objective worked toward with someone it was possible to connect with. When he had suggested staying the night her initial response had been panic, quickly followed by embarrassment at her own assumption.

There was no expectation behind his offer. Nothing manipulative. Just a friend, being a friend.

As promised, he had cooked a meal that consisted mostly of tinned tomatoes and potatoes, which they had eaten by the light of candle stubs and the log fire in the sitting room. It might have been uncomfortably, inappropriately romantic as a setting, but it was really just the most comfortable place to eat. The Rayburn stove in the kitchen was working better, now that she had learned how to get the best out of it, and it cooked food well enough, but the sitting room was cozier in the evenings. The studio became numbingly cold at night since the temperature outside had dropped so far. The sitting room was definitely the warmest part of the cottage. Dylan had once, tentatively, brought up the subject of the lack of electricity. She had found it surprisingly easy to tell him she preferred life in the cottage without a power supply. She realized, as she formed the words, that this was the truth. After her success at restoring the supply in the pub, she was fairly certain that she could do the same at home. But she didn't want to. She had grown accustomed to living by the rhythm of the winter days – rising with the dawn, working in natural light, sleeping when candlelight became tiring to read by. Since she'd mastered the Rayburn, there was plenty of hot water for showers. And she was genuinely excited at the thought of what her work would look like fired in the wood-burning kiln. It all just seemed to fit, seemed so right, somehow.

She leans into her run once more, allowing herself to go slowly, taking in the magical landscape around her. The sun is properly up now, the sky a sharp blue worthy of an alpine post-card, with the majestic mountains to the west offering very convincing snow-covered slopes. The water fowl glide serenely across the lake, apparently viewing the new surface of the shore with suspicion. After a short while, Tilda notices that Thistle is no longer with her.

'Thistle?' she sings out, her voice absorbed by the snow. She tries again, a little louder. 'Thistle? Come here, girl!' She slows to a walk, squinting back into the low sunshine to the east and then turning to scan the fields and the edge of the woodland. She spots her now, by the water's edge, digging at the ground, sending up a shower of mud-speckled snow behind her. 'What are you doing?' she asks, jogging over to get a closer look. By the time she reaches Thistle, the dog has unearthed something, which it holds tightly in its mouth. 'What have you got there? A stick? You want to play fetch?' But Thistle bounds away, showing an impressive burst of speed, tearing round in a large loop, back legs powering, her hind paws hitting the ground impossibly far forward of her nose with every stride, tail down, ears flat, round and round she goes. Tilda stands, hands on hips in amazement. 'Well, if you'd run like that after a hare you might have actually caught one. Daft creature. Come on, don't know about you, but I'm ready for some breakfast.'

As they approach Ty Gwyn, Tilda is cheered to see smoke rising from both chimneys. When she enters the kitchen it is to the sound of the kettle whistling and eggs being fried.

'Perfect timing,' says Dylan as she takes off her hat.

'Perfect house guest,' she tells him. 'Fires lit and breakfast cooked.'

He turns to grin at her and then freezes, staring. For an instant Tilda wonders if he has seen the ghost, such is the look of shock on his face. But no, she realizes, it is not horror, but surprise. And he is looking directly at her.

'I'm sorry,' he says, suddenly embarrassed, 'I didn't mean to . . . just wasn't expecting . . . I'm really sorry I did that,' he says, and busies himself with the cooking. 'Stupid of me. Sit yourself down, eggs are nearly ready.'

Puzzled, Tilda is about to do as he says when she remembers. *My contact lenses! I forgot to put them in this morning.*

She closes her eyes, trying to imagine how she must look to Dylan. He has only ever seen her with her coloured contact lenses, so her eyes have always appeared a light blue. Without them her irises are revealed in their true state, almost devoid of pigment, just the palest hint of blue tingeing their basic pinkness. With no colour to block out the blood vessels in the eye, the irises appear pink in some lights, almost transparent in others. Either way, they are startlingly unusual. She has worn lenses since her teens, in order to appear less different. More normal. But today she went out without them. The light was still winter-daybreak soft so, that even with the snow, there had been no glare to remind her to use them. Only when the sun had properly risen had she begun to squint, yet even then she had not thought about her lenses. This strikes her as odd now. Whilst part of the point of wearing them is cosmetic, and another part to cut out the harshest of the sun's rays, the lenses also have a prescription in them to help her weak eyesight.

But today I saw everything. I could see everything clearly without them!

She is still trying to take in this fact when Dylan puts the plates on the table. 'Here you go,' he says, 'best local eggs from freest of free range chickens. And crumpets, 'cos you're out of bread. And tea.' He looks up at her, grinning, determinedly looking at her but not staring. Tilda is touched by his consideration. She thinks of going to put her lenses in, so that he might be more comfortable sitting opposite her, but now she changes her mind.

No. It's okay. This is me. Let him see me.

'This looks fantastic,' she says, plucking off her gloves and sitting down. 'I haven't run in a while. I'm famished.'

'Was it slippy, running in the snow?' he asks.

'Not really. Anyway, it's so gorgeous out there, it was worth the risk. Thistle loved it too. Went all puppyish, didn't you, girl? Look, she's brought a stick home,' she says, waving her fork in the direction of the dog, who is already warming herself on her cushion by the Rayburn.

'That's not a stick.' Dylan peers over his mug of tea. 'Looks more like, I dunno . . .' He gets up and holds out his hand. 'Let's have a look, then, Thistle. Can I have it?'

The dog answers with a low growl, curling up her lip to show her fine, sharp teeth.

'Okay,' he says, backing away, 'I'll take that as a no.'

'Thistle! What's got into you?' Tilda goes over to the dog and gently but firmly takes the object from her mouth. She is relieved to find her dog does not growl at her and even beats her tail against the dusty cushion as she relinquishes her find.

Tilda takes the thing back to the table and studies it by the light of the window. 'You're right, it's not a stick.'

'What then, a bone, perhaps?'

'Yuck, no, thank heavens. It's metal of some sort. Wait a minute.' She goes to the sink and turns on the tap, holding the curved object under the running water, rubbing with her thumbs to get the soil and grit off the thing. 'I think it's a bracelet!' she tells Dylan, who has left his breakfast and come to stand behind her to watch. 'Yes, look, it's brass, or bronze, or something. It's not a complete circle; it's open, and there's a pattern worked into the metal . . . looks like . . .' Tilda stops, her breath catching in her throat. Suddenly she can hear her pulse pounding in her ears.

'What is it?' Dylan asks. 'Tilda?'

But she has gone, running, to the studio. He follows. Once inside, Tilda hurries over to her pots, the ones she has been working on all these weeks, the ones she has shaped and reshaped and carved and molded and coaxed into being. She rips off the plastic that has been wrapping them up, keeping them moist to avoid cracking while they wait for their first firing. She turns the nearest pot, the biggest and the most successful, so that it is facing the light of the patio doors. Her hand is trembling as she holds the bracelet alongside it.

Now it is Dylan's turn to gasp.

On Thistle's find, intricately and beautifully carved, is a singularly exquisite Celtic design, showing two leaping hares and a running hound. The limbs of the animals meld and intertwine in a highly stylized and complex pattern, so that where one ends, the next begins and where that one ends, so the next begins, round and round in a never-ending chase. On Tilda's pot, larger and clearer, is, twist for twist, curve for curve, exactly the same design, right down to the rolling eye of the racing hound.

11

TILDA

As the Land Rover slithers down the snowy road, Tilda is too distracted to be concerned about car crashes or flashbacks, though Dylan had sweetly checked that she was okay about getting in the vehicle again before they set off. The discovery that her own design matches exactly that of something dug from the earth beside the lake has shaken her. She and Dylan both tried to reason it out – common Celtic motifs, Tilda has a dog and recently saw a hare, both animals could have been found in the area anytime over the last several centuries. Perhaps it is just that Tilda has tapped into the language of the art of the place. Perhaps she simply saw an illustration of an ancient image somewhere and the similarities beyond that are born of coincidence. Or perhaps they are not. She cannot shake off the feeling that there is something more, some deeper connection between herself and whatever it is Thistle found.

One thing she and Dylan instantly agreed on was that the man to help was Professor Williams. Tilda had hurriedly put in her contact lenses while Dylan adjusted the stoves to work gently, before they jumped into the Land Rover, which, for all its great age and shabbiness, is perfect for negotiating the snow-covered slopes.

They find the professor clearing his garden path, shovelling snow and grit with surprising vigour for a man of his years. He greets them warmly and takes them indoors. Dylan and Tilda both talk over one another in their excitement, not letting up even as they take off their boots and he leads them into the sitting room, so that eventually he has to hold up his hands.

'I'm sorry, but all this clamouring is impossible to make sense of. Now, I suggest *one* of you take a deep breath and slowly tell me what this is all about. Whilst the other remains silent,' he adds quickly.

Tilda steps forward and holds out the bracelet.

'Thistle dug this up by the lake,' she tells him.

Professor Williams takes it from her, snatching up his reading glasses from the coffee table and setting them on his nose. He peers at the curious object, turning it over and over in his hands. Next, he abandons his glasses and from a desk drawer finds a photographer's loop, the lens of which will allow much greater magnification. He presses the device to his eye, holding the bracelet beneath a standard lamp. Which instantly goes out, as do all the other lights in the house.

'Damn!' says Tilda.

'That's curious.' The professor looks up. 'It's possible the snow has affected the power supply. Dylan, would you be so good as to check the fuse box for me, please?'

Dylan exchanges glances with Tilda, but goes to do his best with the fuses.

'Why not use the light from the window?' Tilda suggests, impatient for his verdict, and fearing the lights will stubbornly refuse to work while she is present.

'Yes, why not?' The professor leans as close to the mullioned glass as he can, positioning the bracelet so that the sunlight glints off it.

Once the professor's attention is focused away from her, Tilda is able to still her mind, close her eyes and bring her own thoughts to a single point. She imagines the power surging through wires toward the little house. She imagines a spark of electricity, a fizz of energy, as she wills the connection to be made once again. There is a pause, a flash, and then the lights go back on. Tilda waits, uncertain as to how steady the flow will be, but it seems as if it will hold.

The professor's mind is so absorbed by what he is looking at, he barely registers the working lights.

'My word, this is quite splendid. Where did you say your dog unearthed it?'

'Very close to the water, this side of the lake, just before you reach the bird hide. Do you think it's bronze?'

'Oh no, look at the purity of the metal. Look at the colour. Scarcely a blemish. There is only one element that can so resist the ravages of decay.' When Tilda looks blank, he explains. 'Gold, my dear. It is incorruptible.'

'Gold! But, it's really heavy; it must be worth a small fortune.'

The professor resumes scrutinizing the details of the treasure. 'Trust me when I tell you, if this is as old as I think it is, if its origins fit, well, the value of the material will be of secondary importance to its provenance. Ah! Lights again,' he exclaims, at last properly noticing the return of the power supply.

Dylan comes back into the room. He looks at Tilda, the question written plainly on his face. She shrugs and shakes her head. The bulbs in the room flicker but then steady again.

'The design,' Tilda has to ask, 'is it . . . is it common? I mean, hares and hounds were often depicted in Celtic art, weren't they?'

'They were, though it was more usual for the hounds to out-number the hares. That said, these particular beasts are more finely detailed than is common. See? Such delicate curls and lines, especially the faces, which were more ordinarily quite plainly rendered.'

'It's big for a bracelet,' Dylan puts in. 'Was it for a man, maybe? Or for wearing on the upper arm, d'you think?'

'It's possible.' His uncle nods. He places the find carefully on his desk and hurries to select a book from his collection. Jamming his spectacles back on his face, muttering all the while, he searches for an entry. 'Let me see, let me see, ah, here we are. As I thought: "Hunting dogs were often seen as a sign of status, and highborn men of the area would have regularly engaged in hare coursing or deer hunting not only to supply meat for the table, but as a sporting or social activity. However, when considering depictions of dogs, whether or not they are specifically hunting hounds, the more mythological significance of both creatures should be born in mind to avoid mis-interpretation of the work." Yes,' the professor says, nodding emphatically, 'particularly given the imbalance of numbers here. You see, hares are usually solitary animals, so the chase would be depicted with a single hare pursued by several hounds. This shows the reverse. Also, the attention to detail, giving such character to the faces, suggests something more personal, more individual, almost.' He snaps the book shut and removes his glasses. 'So, there you have it.'

'We do?' Dylan asks.

Tilda leans forward and picks up the bracelet again. The gold feels warm in her hand. 'So, if it's not showing a hunt, what, then?'

'Well, what is so special about your lovely object,' the professor tells them, 'is that it is a marvellous example of the importance of mythology among Celtic people. Each animal had its place in their beliefs, in their folktales, in their ancient stories. Owls, for example, traditionally foretold death. Horses represented the underworld, or departed spirits. These creatures' – he gestures at the bracelet with his glasses – 'are slightly unusual in that they both often represented the same thing.'

'Which was?' Tilda feels a nervous excitement charge through her body, as if someone has just startled her, or she has narrowly avoided a fall, or escaped a danger of some sort.

Professor Williams smiles as he explains, 'Hares and dogs are reliably accepted to represent witches.'

The next two hours are spent delving deep into the professor's library, searching for images or references that might give them clues as to who made the bracelet and who owned it. Every now and again the lights dim or flicker. Each time, Tilda takes a moment to calm herself, to still her mind, to allow the power to work. After a while she notices that she is concentrating her search on one detail of what the professor has told her: witches. She is surprised to find few mentions of them, but what is written seems to suggest an entirely different view than the one she might have expected.

'Professor, in the time we are looking at, let's say between 850 and 950 AD, were witches seen as good? I can't find too many references to them being persecuted or hunted the way they were in medieval times.'

'Not good, exactly, but an accepted fact of life. Christianity was well established in Wales by then, of course, and yet we read often that many still held the "old religion" dear. Paganism did not go away, and witches were very much a part of the older Celtic belief system. Many communities would have had a resident witch who might have provided spells and remedies for healing, or to assist warriors in battle. Some foretold future events. They would only have been prosecuted if they had been deemed to have used their magic against members of the community in which they lived – putting a hex on someone they took against, perhaps, making them ill, or causing their cattle to die, that sort of thing.'

'Do you think the bracelet could have been owned by a witch?'

'That seems a plausible hypothesis. Although, given the amount of gold needed to make such a thing, this particular witch must have been very wealthy. Or at least, had wealthy friends; someone who might have given the piece of jewellery

as a token of thanks, possibly. All in all, I can't say I am surprised to find evidence of such a person living by the lake,
whether at the time we are considering, or later, or indeed any
time at all. Greta always told me there were things history could
not explain. Things we would never find proof of but would
have to accept as inexplicable. Magical, even. No, I can't say I'm
surprised.'

Later, after copious amount of tea and some chunky cheese
and pickle sandwiches, Tilda thanks the professor for his help,
deciding it is time to leave. Suddenly there threatens to be an
awkward moment.

*Is Dylan expecting to come back to the cottage with me? Why would
he? Come to that, why shouldn't he?*

'I'll give you a lift home,' Dylan offers.

'Actually, I want to go down to the dig and have another
talk with Lucas.'

'Oh?'

'About who it is they are digging up. Though I can't imagine
they'll do much in the snow.'

'Ah, you might be wrong about that,' says the professor,
polishing off the last of his tea. 'The ground is actually less
frozen now than it was a few days ago, when it was actually
too cold to snow. My guess is, they might actually make some
progress today.'

'They could finally be removing the remains?' Tilda asks.

'It's possible.'

'I'll come with you.' Dylan walks with her as she heads for
the door. Tilda cannot quite decide if she feels pleased or put
off by how keen he is to spend more time with her. As if
sensing this, he adds, 'If things are moving again at the dig they
might want to put me to use. The snow doesn't settle on the
lake, after all.'

When they reach the site they find that the professor was
right. There is a buzz of excitement and activity around the

opened grave. A 4?4 vehicle is parked close to it, with a smart trailer attached, boxes of soil and samples already stacked in front of it. Around the dig site, three tall metal gantries hold powerful floodlights aloft – the kind used to illuminate foot-ball pitches. Molly and several of the other archaeologists are carefully packing things into crates, which are then lifted into the trailer. Lucas is directing operations with much arm waving and a fair bit of snapping at people. He does not look pleased to see Dylan, whom he all but ignores, but he does at least pause to greet Tilda.

'You've certainly got a knack for choosing the right moment to turn up,' he says. 'We are about to remove the top skeleton and then lift the coffin and its contents. You can't rush these things, you know. In the wrong conditions, one hasty move, and something that has survived for centuries can be destroyed.'

'But you can work in the snow,' Tilda says. 'Because the ground is not so frozen?'

'That's right. The snow acts as a sort of insulation. We had the lights set up a couple of days ago in case we have to work through the night. Once we get started, there's no turning back. We have to get everything, all the contents of the trench, lifted, packed, and moved into the trailer.'

'I'm surprised I haven't noticed the lights,' says Tilda. 'I can see the dig from my cottage.'

'We haven't used them yet. Tonight will be the first time. Or actually, this afternoon, the way the light is fading. We've got a bigger generator in specially.' He indicates a large metal box on wheels parked up by the main tent. 'You'll probably be able to hear that from your house when it's going, too.'

'Have you found out any more about the identity of the people in the grave?' she asks.

'Various theories have been put forward.' Lucas walks as he talks, picking up a discarded trowel and handing it to someone, tidying a loose coil of cable and generally fussing. 'We'll know more once we can open the coffin and see what grave goods are with the body. That the uppermost remains are those of someone convicted of a crime of some sort seems to be the most likely explanation, but there is another factor that we are looking into.'

'Something to do with the way they were executed, or who they were?'

'Both, in effect. Turns out pinning victims of burials in place – whether they were alive at the time or not – was not the only reason tenth-century lake dwellers might have dropped such a huge flat stone on top of them. It was common practice – so Molly assures me, and I've never yet had cause to doubt her research – in the burial of a witch.'

Tilda feels a shiver that has nothing to do with the snow chase down the length of her spine. Without really knowing she is doing it, she takes hold of the bracelet nestled in her coat pocket. She catches Dylan's eye. He looks serious for once.

'Uncle Illtyd might support that theory,' he says quietly, more to Tilda than to Lucas.

Although it is still early in the afternoon, the winter sky is filling with new snow clouds, and the dwindling daylight is already causing difficulties for the diggers. It is decided to fire up the generator and switch on the lights. There is a fair amount of running around and shouting. More than once Lucas instructs anyone not directly involved in lifting the remains to move away from the trench. After a couple of failed attempts, the generator powers up, its engine noise thudding through the still air, black smoke chugging from its exhaust. A switch is thrown and the overhead lights flare into action, casting their intense artificial brightness directly down onto the grave and its surrounding area. Tilda blinks, shading her eyes as she steps a little farther away. She is torn between wanting to see what is going on and not wanting to interrupt the functioning of the lights. She stamps her feet to ward off the cold that is beginning to penetrate her boots and thermal socks. She is aware of a dizziness, and knows that this time it has nothing to do with low blood-sugar levels or tiredness. It is the grave, or rather, whatever, *whoever*, is in the grave, that is causing her to feel light-headed, to feel somehow distant from the people around her. She is able to hear things above the thrumming of the generator. She can make out the heavy lapping of the water upon the shore, the chattering of a squirrel in a nearby tree, the beating wings of swans out on the lake. All her senses appear to be heightened. She is able to smell not only the acrid diesel fumes of the engine, but the mixture of sweat and body spray coming from the diggers as they work, the musty dampness of the branches of a large oak to her right, and the pungent odour of the ancient earth that is being, inch by inch, ever more disturbed. She can almost taste the moist, cold air on her tongue. The juddering of the generator, the stomping footsteps of those workers, the slight fizzing that runs down the metal supports of the arc lights – all these vibrations pass through her body.

And then come the visions. At first she sees just a jumping of the sharp-edged shadows cast by the lights, so that the abrupt change between the floodlit ground, tinged orange, and the cool blue of the natural snow, seems to jitter and shake. Then there are glimpses of movement away in the middle distance, as if shy creatures are breaking cover and darting across the wintry ground. And next come the swirling shapes, twisting and changing, in the sky above Tilda's head. Looking up, she can see figures forming and reforming, as if made from clouds that have fallen from the heavens to a height barely above the tallest of the trees at the edge of the meadow. Tilda gasps as a figure swoops low, diving at her and then flying away at the last moment. The form is vague, indistinct, its limbs dissolving into vapour as it passes. Then comes another and another.

Dylan has noticed something is wrong. 'Tilda?' he asks. 'What's the matter?'

She does not answer him. She cannot answer him. For now, she can see a dark shape beginning to rise from the open grave. Lucas, Molly and two more archaeologists kneel in the trench, and between them they lift the great slab of stone that had been holding down the bones of the deceased. They stagger under its weight as they lift it and tip it up on end, to one side of the body. Now, the skeleton is exposed. From where she stands, in the harsh lighting, Tilda can clearly see the broken bones of the corpse, its limbs lying at impossible angles, its skull tipped back, its jaw smashed, its brow cracked. And she sees the dark mass rising up from it, pulsating and undulating, and she knows that she alone can see it as it settles into the now-familiar form of the fearsome ghost that has been haunting her. It turns its gory face toward her, and Tilda watches as a hideous grin stretches across its shattered features.

They mustn't let it out! I have to make them stop.

'Don't!' she shouts out before she has time to think about it further. 'Put it back!'

'Tilda?' Dylan puts a hand on her arm. 'What is it? What's wrong?'

'They mustn't let it out!' She turns to him, shaking her head, trying to make him understand. 'They're setting her free. We have to stop them, Dylan. Before it's too late! Lucas, wait!' she calls out, running forward. As she does so, the apparition above the grave grows bigger, blacker, denser, so that she cannot believe no one else can see it. 'Lucas, you mustn't . . . !' She stumbles, slipping in the snow that has been compacted by so many booted feet over the hours. She slides forward, all but falling into the trench. Lucas bellows at her.

'What are you doing? I told you to stay back.'

'You don't understand, you have to stop what you're doing. You mustn't set her free!'

'What are you talking about? We've been waiting to raise the find for weeks.'

'But the grave . . . the body . . . Molly was right. It was held down for a reason. You're letting it go, don't you see?'

'Get out of the way. We need to get this stone into the trailer.'

Dylan calls down from the lip of the hole. 'Tilda, come away . . .'

'No! I can see her. This is what she wants. She's angry and she's wicked and once she's set free who knows what she'll try to do!'

Lucas is incredulous. 'Have you been drinking, or are you just barking mad?'

'Hey!' Dylan jumps down into the trench. 'Don't talk to her like that.'

Lucas narrows his eyes, looking from Dylan to Tilda and back again. 'Why don't you take your girlfriend home,' he hisses at him. 'I don't need hysterical women messing up months of work . . .'

Dylan scowls at him. 'Why don't you stop being such a pain in the arse?'

As the two argue, Tilda notices the witch's form circling above them, around the three lights, faster and faster, until it is a blur of speed and dark energy. One of the floodlights begins to wobble and threaten to tip forward.

'For God's sake, put the stone back where it was!' Tilda yells, but nobody takes any notice. She knows she must act, must do something. Swallowing panic, she scrambles back out of the trench and stands beneath the nearest light. She stares up into its beams the best she can, forcing herself to keep her eyes open. She breathes deeply, then faster, imagining she is running, imagining she is trying to send all her strength powering through her body, the heat and force of her own energy feeding her mind. Feeding whatever it is inside her that allows her to influence things in the way she believes she can. Her eyes start to water and sting, her mind fills with the beating of her own heart, pain builds in her head until she fears she may start screaming, or look away and give up.

I must not! I will not!

Still, she does not seem able to do what she needs to do. Still, nothing happens, except that the swirling mass of the witch's ghost grows ever bigger and darker and spins ever faster. Just when she feels sure she will fail, something compels Tilda to take hold of the gold bracelet in her pocket. She grasps it, amazed to find it is not just warm, but actually hot. She holds on to it tightly, willing herself to ignore the pain as it begins to burn her palm.

And then it happens. The light she is staring at explodes, the bulb and glass bursting, sending shards and splinters showering down onto the snow beneath it. Dozens of lethally sharp slivers slice into the ground around her, but not a single piece touches Tilda. Before anyone else has a chance to react, the second light blows in the same way, and then almost immediately the third. There is sudden silence as the generator splutters and fails. The area is plunged into darkness. Twilight fell while the excavation was in progress, and the sudden contrast with the earlier artificial light has left everyone temporarily blinded. Shouts go up, as people scramble for torches, amid cries of warning to watch for pieces of glass and hot metal in the snow. The diggers in the trench have no option but to set the stone back down on the ground. It is not in its original position exactly, but it is back in the grave, covering the main part of the skeleton once more.

As Tilda watches, the pulsating form ceases to grow. Instead it quickly shrinks and pales until it is just a faint, misshapen ghost again, slowly sinking down, down, down toward the grave. The hideous face turns to Tilda as it passes, spitting unintelligible words filled with venom. As the last of it is pulled back beneath the stone, a movement to her left catches Tilda's eye. The gantry holding the second floodlight is teetering.

It's going over!

'Look out! Dylan!' she shouts, as the hefty metal tower lurches and then begins to fall. Everyone on the ground scatters as they glimpse movement and hear Tilda's warning. Everyone except Dylan. He appears transfixed, staring up at the light as it hurtles through the half-darkness toward him. If he does not leap from its path it will hit him. Unless Tilda can stop it. From where she stands she is too far to reach him, so there is no possibility of her pushing him out of the way. With no real idea of what it is she is doing, she grips the bracelet in her hand, wrenching it from her pocket, even as the gold seems to sear into her skin, and holds it aloft. She focuses on the light as it topples over, keeping her glaze fixed upon it. In the seconds it takes to fall, she forces herself to will it to change direction. She conjures an image of it veering to one side, so that it will fall harmlessly beside Dylan instead of hitting him. She pictures it doing this, pictures it thudding into the snow with him standing, unharmed, next to it.

But none of this happens.

What happens is that the tower stops falling. It comes to a halt inches above Dylan's head and simply stays there, suspended by nothing. Nothing except Tilda's will. Gasping, she staggers forward, takes Dylan's arm, and drags him away. They have not gone more than two paces before the floodlight continues its journey and crashes noisily onto the ground, breaking into pieces and sending fragments of glass and metal bouncing across the snow. Dylan is jolted back to his senses. Tilda still has hold of his arm. He looks at the mangled remains of the metal tower, at the place where he had been standing, and then at her. Neither of them speaks. He pulls her to him, and the two stand there in silence, holding one another, as slowly everyone else returns to the trench to examine the chaos that has just rained down upon them.

12

SEREN

After the feast, after Hywel's mistimed toast that drew such unwanted attention to me, I walk through the snow to the western shore of the lake. Heavy clouds have gathered once more, and as I reach the furthermost point from my home the sky can hold its burden no longer. A steady fall begins, undisturbed by so much as a breeze, plump flakes of snow adding to the layer that already smothers the ground. The stiller edges of the water start to be coated in a topping of slush, as the snow decides whether to freeze or to melt. After hours cooped up in the company of so many, with endless noise and doltish behaviour, I feel the need to stand somewhere quiet and solitary. The need to look upon the ancient lake and feel its strength. Its magic. I require it to reassure and remind me that the foolish ways of men are but passing moments, shorter than the life of a single snowflake when compared to the existence of the lake. My boots are sheepskin, the wool on the inside keeps my feet warm, the tough leather on the outside offers sturdy protection. I am glad of my wolf skin to night, and draw it around me as I stand on the shore. With so much cloud there is little moonlight, what there is descending in brief glimpses of clear sky, so that I stare through one level of darkness out over another. From here I can discern the flames of the crannog torches, though most are going out now. What light there is finds a glittering surface in the white snow, and glimmers more flatly upon the lake.

I feel the peace of Llyn Syfaddan enter my soul. All that I am has come from this place, and one day I shall walk into the waters and let them take me, so that in the end I shall be as one with the Afanc. The thought forces me to recall my vision. Did it foretell Brynach's death? I have pondered this question over and over, and I think not. Water in my visions often signifies rebirth, or at the very least, a significant change. I have convinced myself that this is the case. Or, in truth, I continue to try to convince myself. Could it be that I am simply unwilling, unable, to accept the alternative? Can I not allow myself to read properly my own prophecy? Could it be that my heart is too tender where Brynach is concerned, and such feelings as I have for him are clouding my insight? Must I always be a Seer first and a woman second? Of course, I know the answer to this question. I take a step forward, so that I move from the softness of the snow to the grit of the shoreline, cold water lapping at my boots. If I am wrong, if the vision showed me my prince's possible death, then I must warn him. What is shown need not be the outcome of events, not if the prince is furnished with foreknowledge, so that he can act, can prepare, can protect himself. I stoop low and dip my hand into the lake, lifting the water in my cupped hand to take a sip. It is cold enough to make my belly knot, but there is a sweetness to it that can be found nowhere else. As I crouch, my eyes are close to level with the surface of the lake, and I detect the faintest movement farther out. A series of ripples, but not spanning outward as if a stone has been dropped from a height. Rather, these form an arrowhead, giving away the motion of something under the water.

Something slow.

Something heavy.

Something great.

And there is only one thing, one being, of such stature living in Llyn Syfaddan. My heart quickens and my blood warms at the thought that she is near. I dare not move, but remain as I am, waiting, hoping. The lake in front of me seems to flow this way and that now, as if it were a river undecided on its course. I can hear nothing, but I sense her presence. With care, I straighten, standing to better view the lake. A tense stillness descends. Even the restless owls in the woodland behind me cease their hooting and hunting. Small creatures in the undergrowth stop their scurrying and burrowing through the snow to listen, paws raised, noses twitching as they sniff the air. When she arrives, when she breaks the surface and raises her glorious, proud head high, it is the most graceful of actions. Water falls from her noble head, but it does so softly. She blinks slowly, her indigo eyes looking directly at me. She is the only Afanc upon which I have ever laid eyes, but I know in my heart she is the most beautiful that ever was. Her long neck is elegantly curved, down to her broad shoulders just visible above the surface. She gently moves her powerful limbs to keep herself afloat. Though this night I cannot see them, I have done so before, and know them to be immensely strong, ending in broad webbed feet. She is the length of half a dozen horses from the tip of her upturned nose to the end of her sinuous tail. Her hide is not quite skin, not quite scales, but made of an ancient matter that lies between the two. Even though light is scant, she has a sheen to her, so that her whole being glimmers like the wing of a kingfisher, one minute blue, the next green, then black. She is by far and away the most wonderful, the most magnificent thing that I have ever seen or will ever see in this earthbound life.

I stretch out my hands toward her and take three steps closer, into the lake, stopping when the water reaches my waist. The cold chills my very bones, but I do not care, for I am happily enchanted by the water-horse. I can smell her scent now; she smells of pebbles and reeds and bulrushes. She smells of an age before memory. Of centuries of lives lived and lost. Of her own deep, unchanging world. She stretches forward, lowering her head, and I am able to touch her gentle face. What ancient wisdom this fabled creature has! What timeless magic! As my frost-nipped fingers stroke her iridescent cheek, my soul sings. I am blessed indeed to have the trust of such as she.

'What should I do, my glorious Afanc? Should I speak to the prince of my fears, or is it better I hold such uncertain prophecies to myself? Tell me, mother-of-the-lake, what must I do?'

It may be that she is about to offer me a sign, something that will help me make the right choice, but I will never know, for at this very moment we are disturbed. The Afanc is the first to become aware that someone approaches. I cannot hear, nor see, anyone, but I can feel the horses as they draw near. Their hoof-beats spread through the ground beneath my feet like ripples through the water. The Afanc turns, lowering her head beneath the surface of the lake, and in one swift, silent movement, she is gone, vanished into the depths once more.

I hurry back to the shore. Who would be abroad at such an hour? Other than myself. Surely the inhabitants of the crannog will be settled in their ale-heavy sleep by now. And yet here come two riders, at some speed. As they approach I see they carry swords, and their faces are masked by the metal guards of their helms. Are we under attack? But no, these are not Vikings, nor do the horses show signs of having travelled any distance.

'Who comes there?' I call out, sensing that the danger is very real. I am trapped against the lake. I cannot run from them, and even if I attempted to do so, their mounts look fast and strong and would soon be upon me. 'Give your names, if you are not afraid to do so,' I demand, hoping to goad them into revealing their identities.

But they do not speak. They urge their horses on until they

circle me so close I am flecked by foam from the mouths of the destriers as they champ their iron bits. The silence of the men is menacing. It is clear by the way they watch me, drawing nearer and nearer, that they are not on some night hunt, nor making a journey, but they have come in search of me. And now I am found. I take my blade from my belt and turn as they circle me, trying to watch both riders, but they dig their spurred heels into the flanks of their increasingly agitated horses, spinning about me, faster and faster. Had I time to prepare, I might have cast a spell to protect myself. I could have transfixed their horses, or sent an apparition to confuse my assailants, or disguised myself. But I am caught unawares, alone, away from my home, my back to the water.

'What do you want from me? Who sent you?' I shout, for it is plain they are here on the instructions of another. These are not schemers or planners, not men of thought and guile. These are brute weapons, wielded by one who hides in safety while they go about his or her work. These are nothing more or less than instruments of death.

The first blow misses me only because I hear the sound of the sword cutting through the air as it descends, and spring to my right. The first rider wheels his horse about, while the second charges straight at me. I time my jump poorly, and though his sword does not find its target, his horse catches me a glancing blow and I am knocked to the ground. I leap to my feet, slicing at the leg of the nearest attacker. He screams curses. I press home my advantage, raising my arms and shrieking a hex as I run at his horse's head. The animal is spooked by the combination of my voice, the harsh words and my wolf headdress, sending it skittering sideways, so that the rider momentarily loses control of the horse, distracted as he is by the blood that begins to gush from his wounded limb.

I spin about, ready to face the second man, but I am too late to avoid him this time. He is already so close that I snatch his horse's bridle, forcing the animal to twist as it slithers to a halt. The attacker has no room to swing his sword about, so instead he brings the hilt down upon my head. His aim is expert, so that he avoids my headdress, which might have afforded me some protection, striking me through only the skin of the wolf. The crunch of my own skull as the force of the metal connects with it echoes through my head, and I crumple to the ground. The snow softens my fall, but the blow has left me helpless. That I should be rendered defenceless with a single strike! I feel anger at myself. I let down my guard, and now I am paying the price. My would-be assassin looms above me, his horse's ironclad hooves churning the snow to a filthy mush as it fidgets and stamps. He cares not if it treads upon me. My eyes start to fail, so that everything swims before them, shifting and blurring. I can discern the movements of my attackers, and I feel the thud through my body as the nearest one dismounts and strides toward me. Who is it, I wonder idly, who wants me dead? Who have I angered so? Who has most to gain? Had I time, I could seek out the answers. But my life can now be measured in seconds. Through the cloud that drifts before my eyes, that has come to claim my final vision, I see the henchman stand above me and raise his sword in both hands, high above his head.

There is a cry. From the second rider. The swordsman hesitates. He looks away from me, first toward his fellow, then forward. He does not bring down his mighty sword. He does not deliver the fatal blow. Instead he staggers backward, in such haste that he stumbles, dropping his weapon and falling onto the snow, only to scramble as quickly to his feet once more. Both men are shouting now. As my attacker hauls himself onto his whinnying horse and whips it into a gallop, I hear a low rumble behind me. With failing strength, I roll to my side and push myself up onto my elbow, raising my shattered head as best I can. Now I see what has driven terror into their black hearts – the Afanc! She has returned to save me! She rears up, high above the water, lifting her head and letting loose a blast of sound unlike any that exists apart from within her. Her noble face is the last thing I see before I slump into the snow and drift into the comfort of the beckoning darkness.

On my bed of snow, the winter air filling my lungs, the cold masks my pain. I do not suffer. I could slumber here, as I fade to eternal stillness, and not experience any agony of death. It is tempting to do so. To allow myself to be drawn to that place where I may at last take my ease, no longer troubled by the woes of the world, the quarrels of men, the ravages of age, the ache of my own foolish heart. Yes, it is tempting. But what of my prince, then? If he is truly in danger, and now I must believe him to be, who else but I can warn him of the treachery that will see him dead? I must tell him of my vision. I must show him what happens to those who point the finger of suspicion at his nonblood kin. I must speak to him. I must go to him.

But my senses are numbed, my limbs doubled in weight, my will draining away with my blood into the snow. Such a cumbersome thing, the body of a human. Too much reliance lies in the head. Too much. We have let our frames become frailer down generations, in favour of our seething minds and greedy hearts. Instinct has been dulled by thought. I cannot get to my feet, let alone drag myself back to the crannog. As I am, I am finished. My only hope, then, is to become other than I am.

I have none of my shaman's tools to aid me. I am away from my potions and infusions. I do not have the luxury of time to conjure or spellcast. I must act quickly, before the cold that holds me so softly hastens me to my end. I must make that leap, as I have done so many times before, but this time I make it unaided. And I must do so not in a vision, not leaving my womanly body to sit by the fire while my spirit travels where it will. Not this time. This time, my transformation must be complete. I must take my damaged body with me. I must shapeshift to my other self, my stronger, lighter, fleeter self, which will be able to withstand the wound, to carry me on lithe limbs, quickly and silently across the snow to the crannog. To my prince.

No rituals can help me now. No ancient words or incantations will work. What must effect my change is pure nature. What lies within me. What magic spark I was born with, when I was kissed with the blessing of my visions and given the name Arianaidd. I form no thoughts. I call upon no deities or forces. I merely allow myself to change. Change or die, for the two paths sit side by side, and I could with the greatest of ease slip along the wrong one, never to return. I feel my hands and feet twitching, my muscles tense and jerk. Are these the beginnings of my transformation, or of my death throes? There is a burning in my chest now, as it squeezes in upon itself, robbed of air. Am I shrinking to my other self, or have I drawn my last breath in any earthly form? I feel as if I am falling from a great height, and there is a rushing sound in my ears, as if the waters of the lake were flooding into me, into my body and my soul. The darkness presses down on me. Whatever alterations are taking place, I cannot resist nor influence them, but merely be carried by them.

And I am changed!

As I am, I can raise myself from my death-cold snow bed and stand, teetering, on four paws. My head hurts me, but my strong new body is better built to withstand such pain, better made to run than to think. The winter air has cooled my wound so that the blood does not flow from it. I am unsteady. I am still a broken thing. But I can carry myself. I can! My fur is so wonderfully warm, and that warmth revives me. My low stance means the top of the snow is level with my eye, so that I must stand up on my hind legs, using my short tufted tail to help me balance. Now I have a clear view of the land around me. I hop cautiously away from the lake, for I am not a creature of the water. How strange to move across the ground on silky paws, ears flicking to pick up sounds, to warn me of danger, of swooping owls, of hungry foxes. With every tentative step, my courage builds so that soon I am bounding toward the crannog, covering the distance in no time, the speed making my tiny heart beat like a war drum, and my spirits lift. It is a joyous thing to be so nimble. I am so revelling in my new-found strength that I am at the wooden walkway to the crannog before I notice my wound is bleeding again. I can feel the hot blood, sticky on my fur. I must go on. The watchman is pacing along the boards, blowing into his hands to keep them from freezing. He looks this way and that as he is bound to do, but his line of vision is well above even the black tips of my ears. I move swiftly across the construction that links the crannog to the shore and slip behind the smithy's workshop. I know where my prince lies sleeping, and I take the most direct path to the great hall. Everyone else is in their bed. A lazy cattle-dog in the doorway to a barn raises its head from its paws as I pass, but tonight he has no appetite for a playful chase, and a belly too full to care that a meal is walking past. The door of the hall is closed. I wonder how I will get in, but at this moment it opens. One of the villagers has come out at the urging of his bladder. While he stands facing the wall and lets loose onto the snow-white ground a stream of steaming yellow, I slip inside unnoticed. It is so very hot in the hall, though the fires have burned down to nothing. There remain several torches burning low in sconces fixed to the walls. So many men, women and babes lie packed within, snoring and filling the borrowed air with their stink. How base humans can be! I glide between their slumbering forms, taking particular care not to wake the sleeping hunting dogs by the hearth. At the far end of the hall sits the stately royal bed with its heavy drapery. I wriggle between the closed curtains. Now I see my prince, still dressed, as are most following their lengthy celebrations. He lies atop the coverlets, his princess sleeping beside him. Will he know me? How will he react to find me as I am? Will I succeed in making him understand or will he fear he is in the grip of a nightmare? I have no choice but to try. For his sake, if not my own. He sleeps with one arm flung out so that it dangles from the bed. I reach up my nose and sniff his palm, letting my whiskers tickle his skin. He flinches, the sensation stirring him. I raise my front paws up onto the bed beside him and nudge his arm. He shifts, pulling his hand in from the cold to tuck it beneath his head as he turns on his side. At least now he is facing me. I hop up beside him and for a few seconds watch him sleep. The notion of lying down next to him is an appealing one, but it would be my last act. Droplets of blood from my broken head spill onto the prince as I lean over him, dropping onto his cheek. He murmurs, and his eyes open. He peers at me through the smoky gloom, frowning. I see that he is about to swat me away and go back to sleep. How can I make him see who I am? If I cause a commotion and the hounds awake, that will be the end of me. When he tries to shoo me from the bed I do not shy away, as he might expect, but sit tight. His frown deepens as he raises his head, puzzled by my curious behavior. He puts his hand to the blood on his cheek and then sees the gaping wound between my ears.

'Be gone!' he whispers, batting me lightly with one hand while pushing himself up with the other. A way off, on the other side of the curtains, I hear one of the dogs stir upon hearing his master's voice. I must do something to make him understand, to make him see me, but what? A giddiness is swamping me now, my limbs losing their wild strength. Soon I shall succumb to my injury. I open my mouth, but as I am I cannot speak. There is only one path left to me. I pray my actions will not be too slow. I dare not leave the prince's side, for his dogs would surely find me now. Quickly, I stretch out beside him. He is too bemused and too sleepy to react roughly, and before he has time to push me from my place I close my gimlet eyes and let myself fall backward, away from this furry form, back to my true self. I am in darkness as my shape shifts once again, so that I am not able to witness the astonishment on my prince's face as he watches the small

*woodland animal at his side quiver, fade, and pulsate as it dissolves
and then, miraculously, reforms.*

'Seren!' I hear him gasp. And then I feel him take me in his
strong arms as the agony returns to my head and I slide back
into oblivion.

The first of my senses to return to me as I wake is that of smell.
Wood-smoke. Boughs of oak, hot and slightly bitter, with some
green hazel, hastily gathered and hissing as it burns. Beyond this
I detect male sweat, both sweet and sour at once. And broth of
some sort, several days old. And, oddly, lavender. Such a fra-
grance does not seem to fit. I try to open my eyes, but this
causes me such pain, any brightness as my lifted lids allow sting-
ing my eyes and sending a bolt of heat through my head. I
remember now my injury, and attempt to raise a hand to
examine the wound. My limbs are leaden, my movements
clumsy. The effort of such a small activity causes me to cough,
spluttering at the dryness in my throat, the fire smoke irritat-
ing me further as I gulp air.

Suddenly there is someone leaning over me, grasping my
wrists, preventing me from moving! I hear mumbled words and
am unable to discern their meaning. I struggle, but am weak as
a newborn lamb. My eyes, painful or not, spring open. A man
kneels beside where I lie, holding me fast, determined I should
neither raise myself up nor wriggle away from him. He speaks
more loudly.

'Be at ease, woman. You are safe. All is well,' he says.

The voice is familiar, but in my addled state I cannot place
it. And I doubt the truth of his words. I want to respond, to
shout at him, but can manage only a croak, whereupon my
captor fetches a beaker of water and bids me drink. I discover
I have a fierce thirst, and would drain the vessel if he did not
stop me.

'Not so fast! Ha,' he grunts, taking the cup from me. 'I never saw a person so happy to drink something that wasn't ale.'

My breathing is easier now, my throat soothed. My eyes begin to find their sight once more.

'Hywel? Is it you?'

'Aye.' He climbs stiffly to his feet. 'For my sins, Prince Brynach insisted he would put you in the care of no one else. Though heaven knows I make a poor nursemaid.'

I see now that I am in my own little house, and the realization brings me comfort. How I got here I do not know. The last I recall I was in the great hall, shifting from hare to woman, and on the point of death.

'You brought me here?'

'The prince did. I assisted him. He would not leave your side until he could be convinced you would live.' Hywel frowns down at me, his bushy brows and unkempt beard wriggling as if they have life of their own as his face expresses his displeasure. 'And well you might not have, the wound you had. I gave you up for dead more than once, but the prince would not have it. Bid me try anything and everything. Even sent for Nesta and her herbs, but Princess Wenna would not let her come. That displeased him greatly, I can tell you. Man was fit to tear his own teeth out when he thought you'd die. Don't know why you didn't, truth be told. Still, here you remain.'

'Yes,' I say, dragging myself a little more upright and pulling the woollen blanket around myself. 'Here I remain.' For a while I watch Hywel tending the fire, content to allow him to go about his business while I try to order my thoughts. 'How long?' I ask at last. 'How long have I . . . slept?'

'Five nights, if you count the one we found you. And I'm not likely to forget that this side of a harvest moon! Naked in the prince's bed! With half the village sleeping two strides away. Ha! How we took you from there without raising merry hell I shall never know. He wrapped you in a blanket and carried you himself, kicking me from my dreams on his way out. Says he knows not how you came to be there, nor who it was inflicted such harm upon you. Whoever it was, there is no doubt they supposed they left you dead. 'Tis a miracle you are not.'

'A miracle or your tender nursing,' I find I have the strength to tease him, at least.

'In me our prince found the person he could most trust with your safety. And I've dressed more wounds on the field of battle than any other living, I'd wager. And that' – he indicates my injury with a wooden spoon – 'well, you did not come by that falling from a tree or stumbling in a rabbit hole. Handle of some sort, most likely a sword hilt. Though how you came to be engaged so closely to one who wanted to kill you that he could not use the blade is another mystery.' He turns his attention to the stewpot suspended above the fire, stirring the contents with some effort, so thick and uneven are they.

I force myself to remember the events of that night. The snow. The riders. Their murderous intent. And the Afanc. Tears of gratitude come without warning. I know how she guards the secret of her existence, and yet she risked discovery for me. My sniffing brings an anxious glance from Hywel, so that I wipe my face with my blanket quickly, lest he think me a flimsy child. I become aware that beneath the blanket, save for a grubby tunic, I am naked. Has Hywel really tended me all these days and nights? He is a good man, but to have him be so intimate . . . But I am being foolish. His skills have saved my life as surely as the Afanc's appearance saved it earlier. 'I am in your debt,' I tell him.

'There is nothing I would not do for the prince. You, of all people, know what that means,' he replies without looking at me. He hands me a bowl of stew and a spoon.

'Yet it was to my benefit. And I am grateful,' I say. 'And thankful that Nesta did not put a hand on me!'

Hywel regards me closely now. 'You do not trust her?'

'Her loyalties lie with her mistress.'

'As they should.'

'So long as the princess's loyalties are also correctly placed.'

He ponders this statement for some time while I chew the grey meat that swims in the oatmeal broth in my bowl. An attempt has been made to disguise its flavour with the liberal use of garlic. I recall the lavender. 'Tell me,' I ask him, 'do you burn lavender on the fire?'

'Burn it? No. I used an oil infused with the flowers and leaves. To speed the healing of your head wound.'

'I am impressed.'

'A soldier who can keep other soldiers alive is more likely to live to see old age himself,' he explains. I might have questioned him further on his remedies but the door opens and Prince Brynach steps inside. Hywel scrambles to his feet, but the prince barely notices him the moment he sees that I am awake. Even in the firelight I can see he is tired and troubled, but his face is transformed with a broad smile now.

'You have decided to rejoin the living,' he says, coming to sit on the floor beside my bed.

'Only for Hywel to try to kill me off with this terrible stew.'

Brynach laughs, but Hywel bridles. 'I am expected to be cook as well as nurse and protector! Ha!' Muttering about, needing some air to breathe and snow to piss in, he goes outside.

'It gladdens my heart to see you well,' the prince tells me, taking my hand in his. There was a time I would have pulled back, but such closeness with death has, perhaps, made me keener to savour life's sweeter moments, so I let him hold me, let him softly caress my hand with his fingers.

'I wonder that you do not find yourself . . . repulsed . . . having seen me as I was,' I say, trying but failing to imagine his shock at seeing me shifting before his eyes.

'I have always said you are like no other, have I not? Why,

then, should I not accept all the strangeness that comprises you? I care only that you are returned to health. Despite Hywel's cooking.' He smiles.

'He is a skilled healer.'

'I have seen him bring back men from the brink of death. And I knew he would let no further harm come to you.' He hesitates, then goes on, 'Seren, did you see who it was? Did you see who attacked you?'

'They wore helmets with visors or crosspieces. And they did not speak. Nor did I recognize their horses. But . . . well, it was not the men who sought to stove my head who wished me dead. That is, not beyond doing the bidding of whoever sent them.'

'But who would wish harm to you? Why?'

'Answer the "why" and you will have the "who". There are those who see me as an obstacle in their path to greatness. If they remove me, they have an easier route to you.'

'Me?'

'I warned you, there is a traitor among those you name loyal.'

'You cannot believe Wenna had a hand in what was done to you!'

'The princess came to me, a short while ago. She asked me to help her.'

'Asked *you*?'

'It was indeed a measure of her desperation. She . . . she wanted to know if she would ever give you an heir.' He draws back a little from me now, his face glum. 'I sought answers to her question in a vision.'

'And what did your seeing tell you?'

I hesitate, but I must speak plainly. 'She will never bear you a child. That part was clear . . .'

He keeps his voice level, but I know this is a blow for him every bit as painful as the one I have endured. 'And the other part? You suggest there was more.'

'I saw men, an army; they were attacking the crannog. They were chasing you. They were relentless. They drove you into the lake . . .' He lets go my hand at last. He is quiet for a long time before he asks, 'This vision foretold my death?'

'I cannot be sure. There are other ways to read what I saw.'

He gives a mirthless laugh, standing up and pacing around the room. 'Soldiers hunt me to a watery grave? Such a vision speaks clearly to me.'

'Which is why you have me to interpret such seeings for you.' I try to get up, but the pain in my head is so sharp it is as if I have been struck anew. I clutch at the wound. Brynach hurries to my side.

'You are not yet healed. Do not trouble yourself with . . .'

'With your safety?' I gasp as he lays me back on my bed. 'It is my purpose, my prince.'

'And one which I pray you live to fulfill for many years, but that will not be the case if you struggle from your sickbed too soon.' He attempts a smile. 'Consider how grumpy that would make Hywel, after all his hard work.'

'Very well. I would not inflict his temper on you without me to protect you. I will rest a little longer before we talk. But talk we must.' My efforts to cease his flapping around me like a mother hen are poor. Another thought occurs to me. 'Have you been seen coming here? Hywel says you stayed with me. Were you not missed?'

'Seren, when I thought you were . . . when I feared I would lose you forever, I vowed to any gods who cared to hear me, if you lived I would have us deny each other no longer. I would not keep from you, would not continue my life without you. No matter the gossips and whispers. No matter the disapproval. And I will discover who it was who wished you dead.'

Such a declaration moves me so that I must bite my lip to staunch tears I do not wish him to see. 'Such behaviour might provoke another attack,' I whisper.

'You will not be unguarded.'

'Am I to be bait, then?'

He takes my hand again. This time he lifts it and presses it to his lips. I feel the softness of his kiss and the heat of his breath against my skin. 'My love. My love. *My love*,' is all he says.

The following days and weeks pass in a heady mix of pain, indolence, and delight. Every day my prince comes to my home and sends Hywel away. For a few hours he is mine. If it is daylight we sit by the fire in my house and talk. If it is night-time we go out and walk beneath the stars. Slowly my head heals and my strength returns. He courts me as if we were care-free youngsters, and always he is respectful, gentle and proper. He kisses my hand, but no more than this.

This evening has a special beauty about it. The snow has gone and there is a smell of spring in the air. We walk under a full moon so bright it casts sharp-edged shadows. I lead Brynach to the lake and show him the perfect double of the moon that floats upon the water on such nights as this. We sit atop a smooth rock that juts out over the lake and peer down to study our own faces, side by side, slick and darkly mirrored on the silky surface.

'No copy of you can be as wondrous as you truly are,' he tells me.

'I think it is a flattering likeness,' I disagree. 'The years have been kinder to me in the lake than out here. But it makes you look sorrowful, my prince.'

'I am only so when I am away from you, my prophet.'

'You have your princely duties,' I say, and neither of us will choose to name these.

'Would that you could be my princess,' he says suddenly, a bitterness to his voice that I have not heard before. I put my hand on his.

'Let us not waste our time together wishing for what can never be. I am content.'

'I am not!' He throws a stone into the water and our faces are broken to pieces by the disturbance. He stands, still holding my hand, and leads me back from the shore into the cover of the woodland. An owl swoops by as we slip between the trees. Somewhere near a hedgehog snuffles, newly emerged from its winter sleep. Prince Brynach stops when he comes to the shelter of a mossy oak, pulling me to him in a swift movement, finding my mouth with his. His kisses are deep and taste of passion, of want, of longing. For a moment I do not respond, my mind forbidding me, years of trampling my own desire beneath the heavy tread of duty keeping me from expressing my own desire. But my body acts as if cut loose from my control. I feel my need for my prince's love burning hotter than a fire of oak, and such heat melts my resistance and my reserve.

'My love!' he murmurs, shaking my hair free of its bonds and running his hand through it. 'My living ghost, my silver goddess, my shining heart . . .' He kisses my eyes, my face, my throat, hungrily, eagerly, the waiting and wanting of years at last overcoming him.

My hands trace the muscles of his back as he presses me against the trunk of the great tree. So much strength turned to gentleness. So much power brought to sweetness for want of me.

'Let me love you,' he whispers in my ear. 'Be mine now. Forever. I cannot live otherwise. I swear it.'

I gasp, unnerved by the force of my own desire for him.

He undoes the brooch that holds my cape, and slips the tunic from my shoulders, exposing my bare flesh to the moonlight. He touches the drawings on my pale skin, following the dark curves of the ink patterns.

'I would know all of you, in all your wonder,' he says, dropping to his knees to press his mouth to my quivering belly.

And I know I can deny him no longer. I know I can never again turn from him. Let the future judge us as it will, the present is ours, and it is glorious!

13

TILDA

They are both so shaken by the events at the dig that neither speaks on the journey back to the cottage. Lucas was in a state of understandable rage over the condition of the dig, the broken lights and the failed attempt to raise the remains. He didn't blame Tilda outright, after all, how could he? And yet a large part of his anger was directed at her. If he could not say exactly how she had been connected to the calamitous occurrences that had so completely wrecked the dig, he clearly knew she was, in some crucial way, involved. There had been so much confusion, so much panic when the lights had started exploding, with people scattering in all directions, that nobody save Dylan and Tilda had seen the last falling light halt halfway to the ground. Or if they had, they had not believed what they saw, and quickly allowed themselves to banish the image from their minds and address the more tangible, pressing issues to hand, such as clearing broken glass and checking mangled equipment in the half-light. When Lucas's language and demeanour became almost aggressive, Dylan was quick to defend Tilda, the two men nearly coming to blows until she simply turned and marched over to the Land Rover.

She is hugely relieved to be home again. As they approach the cottage she can hear Thistle howling, and the second she opens the door the dog bounds out, greeting her with such exuberance she is nearly knocked off her feet.

'Okay, girl,' she says, kneeling to hug her tightly. 'It's okay,' she repeats.

Dylan shuts the kitchen door behind him and leans on the Rayburn. He pushes his mop of hair back from his face. 'Right,' he says, the tension showing in his voice. 'I really need to know what just happened.' When Tilda says nothing, he tries again. 'Look, maybe I'm just shaky because I narrowly missed having my head broken open, but I'm having trouble making sense of things. What I do know is, I'm in one piece, nothing smashed or crushed, no bones snapped, standing here in your kitchen pretty hale and hearty, and the fact that I am is down to you, Tilda. It's because of something you did.'

She gets up, leaving the dog, and busies herself with finding small logs from the basket.

'Tilda?'

'I don't know! You think I can explain it? Any of it?'

'Any of what? This has something to do with what you saw in the Land Rover, doesn't it? Did you see the same thing again, down there at the dig? What made you jump into the trench like that?'

'This is going to sound completely crazy.' She shakes her head, pulling open the fire door and jamming wood inside. Smoke billows into the room.

'I'm prepared for crazy,' Dylan assures her. 'I just felt crazy whistle past my ear. I just saw crazy stop a heavy object in midair.'

'What makes you think I have the answers?'

'Okay, stop. Just stop.' Gently, he shuts the stove door, takes Tilda's hands in his and makes her stand and face him. 'Small steps. First, what did you see?'

'Lots of things. Moving about. Swirling. There was so much happening, so much that was so powerful and strange. Maddest thing is, it wasn't scary, not that, but then . . . I saw . . . someone. Someone . . . bad.'

'The same someone you saw before? In the back of Linny?'

Tilda nods.

'You think they came out of the grave?'

'I think she was trying to. I think she would have if they hadn't dropped the stone back in place.' She meets his gaze now. 'I think she will. When Lucas opens that grave again she'll come out. And I won't be able to stop her. And she's dangerous, Dylan. Those lights didn't fall on their own. We both know that. There was no wind, no one knocked them over. It was . . . whoever, *whatever* came out of that hole in the ground.'

'But you . . .' he squeezes her hands. 'You did something . . . amazing. How . . . ?'

'I don't know.'

'Have you ever done anything like that before?'

'Of course not!' she says, more sharply than she meant to.

'Oh? So are we not, even now, going to talk about a boat motor that wouldn't and then would start, or a clock that keeps stopping, or power supplies that blow?'

'That was . . . is . . . different.' She pauses, then explains. 'I can control that sort of thing now. Most of the time. If I put my mind to it. Or rather, if I let my mind . . . I dunno. It's not something I can put into words.'

'Have you always been able to do that stuff?'

'Only since I came here.'

'You think there's something about this place, something weird?'

'Not this place, but *me* in this place. I don't mean the cottage, but, well, around here. And that terrible ghost, whatever it is, the way it seems to seek me out . . . But mostly, it's something about being near the lake that has . . . changed me. No, wait, it's not that.' A moment of clarity makes her smile, despite her rattled state. 'I'm not different now I'm here, I'm more me. More my real self. More how I should be.' She searches his face for understanding but sees only bewilderment.

And who can blame him?

She rubs her temples. 'Look, I'm sorry, you don't have to stay . . .'

'Do you want me to go?'

'No. It's just, well, I want to load the kiln. I want to fire the pots tonight.'

'Now?'

'I know this'll sound ridiculous; I don't fully get it myself yet. I don't have it all worked out, I only know that the bracelet helped me today. Down by the lake, I couldn't have done whatever it was I did without the bracelet. And the drawings on it match the drawings on my pots. It's the connection that makes everything work . . . makes me able to do . . . things.' She sighs heavily. 'Trust me, I'm finding this as difficult to grasp as you are,' she tells him. 'If I try to figure it out any more I shall lose what sanity I have left. Right now I need to *do* something. Something I believe might help protect us from that . . . *thing*. And this is what I know how to do, okay?'

'Then let me stay. Let me help.'

'You sure you want to be near me? Seems stuff . . . happens around me.'

'Or perhaps the only place that's safe is with you, have you looked at it that way? I mean, you saved me tonight, no question.'

'But I'm the one who saw the . . . ghost, apparition, *thing* that came out of that grave. I'm the one it keeps leaping at, keeps trying to scare the life out of.'

'Safety in numbers then, better stick together. Yeah?'

She hesitates, then picks up the basket of kindling and thrusts it into his arms. 'Have it your way. You can set the fire in the kiln while I get the pots loaded.'

The moment she steps back into the studio Tilda finds her

mood shifts, as she knew it would. To engage in her creative endeavour is to lose herself in that act of creation, even when attending to the seemingly mundane process of preparing for a firing. As she carefully takes the wrapping off her pots and reveals them in their raw, unfinished state, she feels once again that powerful connection. A connection to the result of her own artistic effort, but also, this time, a connection to the ancient patterns and symbols she has worked into her pieces. She takes a minute to gaze at the bounding hares and the chasing hound. To let her eyes travel along the lithe, supple limbs, feeling their easy movement, imagining the strength of the muscles propelling the animals forward across frozen ground, immersing herself in the idea of their running free and wild, so that soon she is convinced she can hear the dual rhythms of their heartbeats, the hares' fluttering and fast, the hound's slower, but every bit as urgent and vital.

It is past midnight by the time Tilda and Dylan are able to step back and look at the smouldering kiln, watching as reassuring amounts of smoke pour steadily forth from its short chimney. The construction looks home built, but nonetheless robust, and the mortar appears to be set firm in the gaps between the bricks. The snow around it has melted, so that it sits, stout and russet, standing out against the stark whiteness its glow illuminates close up, fading into the darkness a few strides on. It took them two hours to carefully load the shelves with Tilda's pieces, and another to get the fire properly going so that they could then seal up the door.

'You know, I think it might actually work,' says Dylan.

Tilda nods emphatically. 'It will work,' she says. 'It has to.'

At last, with the fire beneath the kiln packed with as much wood as will fit into it, Dylan is able to convince Tilda it does not need to be watched. They decide to go inside, get something to eat and come out and check and re-stoke the fire at regular intervals through the night.

The cottage has warmed up in the hours they have been busy. The Rayburn fills the kitchen with a slightly smoky but welcome heat, so that the freezing temperature outside is kept at bay. In the sitting room, Tilda takes the bracelet from her pocket and puts it carefully on the small table by the window before laying a fire in the hearth and putting a match to it. Dylan fetches what food he can find from the kitchen.

'Here we are,' he says, setting down a tray on the coffee table. 'Bread, past its best, but still brown rather than blue; cheese, a tub of coleslaw, two packets of crisps, some chocolate biscuits and' – he waves a bottle triumphantly – 'the remains of the brandy.'

'I'm not sure I can cope with booze,' says Tilda, settling herself next to Thistle on the sheepskin rug in front of the fire.

'Yes you can.' Dylan gets glasses, then sits as close as Thistle will tolerate. 'It is a known fact that a little alcohol is good for shock and exhaustion.'

'That is rubbish.'

'Really? Can all those Saint Bernard dogs with their little barrels be wrong?'

Despite herself Tilda smiles. The events of the day have left her drained, and she is glad not to be alone.

No, more than that; I'm glad Dylan is here.

This realization is comforting and unnerving at the same time. She takes a proffered glass from him and sips it, leaning back against the base of the armchair and gazing into the dancing flames in the hearth.

'We will need to check the kiln in a few hours,' she tells him. 'We have to keep as even a temperature as possible.'

'For how long?'

'Well, ideally, twelve hours.'

'Okay, we can measure that by daylight, given that we can't reliably keep a clock or watch working around you.'

'Thanks for reminding me.'

Dylan takes a swig of brandy. 'No problem. We'll go by the position of the sun. We must have set the thing going near eleven. Daybreak is about seven-thirty this time of year. As long as there's not too much cloud we should be able to tell when the sun is directly overhead. What will we do then?'

'Rake out the fire and let the temperature drop slowly. We should be able to open the kiln about noon the following day.'

'Wow, that's a long time to wait. How can you resist having a peek?'

'Easily, seeing as to do so would wreck the firing. If the temperature inside the kiln drops too quickly the pots could crack or shatter, never mind what it would do to the glazes.'

They sit in peaceful silence for a while, sharing the simple food, gradually letting the alcohol and the warmth of the fire take the tension from them. At last, Tilda can feel her feet again properly and her shoulders start to ache less as she relaxes them. Her eyes are gritty from tiredness, the drying effects of the cold weather and the irritation of the wood smoke. She finds herself rubbing them.

'Why don't you take them out?' Dylan asks.

'Sorry, what?'

'Your lenses. If your eyes are sore, you should take out your lenses.' He shrugs. 'You really don't need them anymore, do you?'

She opens her mouth to protest, to explain, to make the case for the covering up of her strangeness, but thinks better of it. Instead, she does as he suggests. The relief is instant and she stares at the shiny little discs of plastic in her palm, hesitating only a moment before flinging them into the fire. They hiss and flare, making Thistle start.

'No more hiding,' she says.

'I'll drink to that,' says Dylan, clinking his glass against hers. 'No more hiding!'

'It . . . it's just the way I've been for a long time. The way I deal with . . . this.' She flaps a hand in a gesture that encompasses herself, head to toe.

'If other people have a problem . . . well, let them handle it. You're you. You're . . .'

'Please don't say special.'

'How about challenging?'

'Sorry.'

'Don't be.'

'It's just that, well, I wouldn't expect you to understand. What it's like . . . to be looked at like you're something . . . weird. Like you don't fit.'

He raises his eyebrows at her and gives a pointed shake of his shaggy curls, making his hair fall into his green eyes, turning slightly to profile so that the slender straightness of his nose is unmissable, grinning broadly, his teeth startling against his dusky skin in the low light. 'Yeah, right,' he agrees with a sarcastic edge to his voice, 'I have no idea what that might be like.'

Tilda blushes. 'God, how crass of me. Sorry. No, I'm really sorry.'

'Like I said, don't be. Let's just say we both know what it means to be outsiders.'

'Professor Williams told me you were born in Barbados. Is that where your mother comes from?'

'My father was a diver – I have him to thank for what I do – he met her when he was working on a wreck in the Caribbean. They got married over there then tried to live here, but she couldn't take to it. Dad wanted me to have a British education. God knows why! So, they moved back home, and when I was eleven I came to live term time with Uncle Illtyd.'

'You don't look much like your uncle.'

'That's because he's my uncle by marriage. My father was Greta's brother, not his.'

'Oh, I see. I just assumed . . . And do you call Barbados home?'

'I do, or at least I did. My dad was killed in a diving accident when I was twenty-two. Mom wanted me to give it up but, well . . . when you find the thing you were meant to do . . .' He drains his glass. 'I come back here as often as I can. It's been hard for Uncle Illtyd since Auntie Greta passed on. Fact is, I don't know that I feel at home anywhere except under the water.'

Tilda gives a gasp, shaking her head slowly. 'Well, that is somewhere we definitely differ. Nothing would induce me to go diving. Or swimming. Or even get in a boat if I can avoid it.'

'Landlubber.'

'Water baby.'

'Maybe I can help you with that.'

'Not a chance.'

'Have you ever seen the Caribbean? It's not like the sea here. It's turquoise, not grey. And *warm*!'

'Me in that sort of sun? Do you know how much sunblock I have to wear even in this damp, cloudy country?' She picks up the poker and chivvies the fire, encouraging more flames.

'Which is why you run at dawn,' he says, looking at her as if another piece of the mystery that is Tilda has just fallen into place.

'Easier on my skin and my eyes.'

They sit together in silence again, and Tilda notices she has been able to almost forget about what happened earlier in the day. The respite was helpful, but could only ever be brief. She looks at Dylan again now.

'You know, they will move that body. From the dig.'

'Oh yes. Lucas will make sure of that.'

'And when they do' – she searches for the words – 'they'll set her free again.'

'Who in God's name was she?' Dylan asks.

'I don't know.' Tilda runs her hand through her hair, tugging it out of its plait in her exasperation. 'I don't know who she was and I don't know why she seems intent on terrifying me. All I do know is that once that stone is taken off her again, somehow she is going to be let loose. And I have to be prepared for that. I have to be ready for her.'

'We.' Dylan puts his hand on hers. 'You aren't facing this alone, Tilda. I promise you.'

'Being with me nearly got you killed today.'

'But you saved me. You can beat this . . . creature. I know you can. And I'm going to help you. But tonight you don't have to worry. Tonight you're safe.' He lifts his hand and strokes her hair. 'It's like spun glass.' He touches her cheek. 'You are the most incredibly beautiful woman I have ever seen,' he says, and leans slowly forward to kiss her.

Thistle has other ideas. She growls and snaps simultaneously, missing Dylan's face by the narrowest of gaps.

'Thistle, no!' Tilda screams at her.

Dylan leaps to his feet, backing away. 'It's okay. I'm fine. No harm done. It's okay.'

'No, it is not okay! Bad dog! What is the matter with you?' Tilda opens the door and sends the dog out. Thistle slinks past and scurries up the stairs to the bedroom. 'Dylan, I'm so sorry.'

'Again? We've been through this.'

'It's not funny. She really went for you. She could have seriously hurt you. Here, let me see.' She ignores his protests and studies his face and hands.

'See?' He smiles at her. 'Told you, I'm fine. She's just jealous. She's used to having you to herself. I shouldn't have invaded her space.'

'*Her* space? This is *my* house.'

'She was only trying to protect you.'

Tilda reaches up and touches his face. 'There are plenty of

other people she can bite if she wants to. You, I can handle myself.'

'You want to bite me?' He laughs.

Tilda smiles. 'You think you're so clever,' she says, planting the lightest of kisses on his lips.

'I'm currently being kissed by the most desirable person in the room. I'd say that was pretty clever,' he tells her. And then he slides his arms around her waist and holds her close, and he kisses her, and she kisses him back. And Tilda finds she is hungry for him. That she can still feel passion, longing, want . . . and it is Dylan she wants.

Yes. Dylan.

Suddenly all the long, lonely months that have gone before this moment melt away. There is nothing but here and now. This man. This connection. She pulls him closer, holds him more tightly, kisses him with increasing fervour. And he returns her passion, so that soon they are tearing at one another's clothes, laughing as they tumble over the sofa, as they roll onto the rug in front of the fire, greedily snatching kisses, pulling at each other's seemingly endless layers of garments. Tilda wonders fleetingly if she is reacting to the trauma of the day; a need to affirm life after a brush with death. She is too lost in her need for Dylan to want to analyze how she feels. Soon they are both naked, the firelight dancing on his mocha dark skin and flashing on her ghost pale flesh. Their burning desire blocking out the cold of winter that has already coated the windowpanes with ice.

It is Tilda's concern for the kiln fire that eventually pulls her from their slumbering embrace. She sits up, gazing down at Dylan.

'It will need more wood. I daren't leave it any longer,' she says.

He touches her shoulder and lets his fingers travel the length of her arm until he takes up her hand and holds it to his lips. 'You taste as good as you look,' he tells her. When she shrugs self-consciously he adds, 'No more hiding, remember?'

'Not everyone sees me the way you do.'

'Their loss.'

'Not so long ago I'd have been called a witch.' She gives a light laugh, but the notion feels far from funny now. 'Maybe they would have had a point.' She gets up and pulls on her underwear and T-shirt. The clouds outside have cleared at last, so that moonlight falls through the little window and finds the bracelet on the table, causing it to shine and glint. Tilda picks it up and studies it.

Dylan props himself up on one elbow. 'You really think that helped you somehow? Down at the dig? You think it made you . . . stronger?'

Tilda nods. 'It did. I know it did. It was scary, the way it made me feel, but I know I wouldn't have been able to do what I did without it.'

Where did you come from? And why do I know I have seen these hares and this hound before?

The gold feels cool in her palm, the worn surface smooth save for the fine lines of the engraving. She turns it over and over and a faint but distinct ringing starts up in her head, as if a far-off glass wind chime were being moved by a sudden breeze. She takes a breath, and then slips the band over her hand and onto her wrist. It is too big, so she slides it up, wriggling it over her elbow until it sits comfortably around her upper arm. The metal presses gently against her skin, quickly losing its coolness as it takes up some of her own body heat.

And then all hell breaks loose.

The room is filled with a light so white that Tilda throws

her arm across her face in an attempt to block it out. The ring-ing sound grows in a crescendo so fast and to a volume so loud that when she screams, she cannot hear her own terrified voice. Blinking through the pulsating light, she sees Dylan thrown back against the far wall. He reaches out to her, but cannot move forward. The harmless flames in the fireplace swell and grow, burning with an unnatural brightness as they lick at the mantelpiece and begin to climb the wall of the chimney breast. The air around Tilda seems to swirl and move in great waves. She is buffeted by it, pulled this way and that, her hair whirling wildly about her, until she, too, begins to spin. She is power-less to stop. And as she spins, a vision forms in the blur of her sight. She sees herself, standing tall and straight, her hair twisted with leather braids, her eyes painted darkly with kohl, her skin bearing bold tattoos of heavy black ink, her body clothed only in leather armour, a dagger at her hip. This shimmering, fear-some version of herself raises her hand, slowly, reaching toward Tilda, who cannot move, either to take her hand, or to shrink from it. She knows she must do something, something to make it stop. Something to gain control. The fire is beginning to catch the wooden mantelpiece and sparks are setting the rug alight. Dylan's eyes are closed as if he has lost consciousness. The sensation of spinning is causing Tilda to fear she, too, will soon pass out. And then there will be no one to stop the spread of the fire.

Dammit, this is my house! My home! I won't let this happen!

With huge effort, she forces herself to lift her left hand and clutch at the bracelet. For a moment she fears she will not be strong enough. Smoke is beginning to make her cough. She can smell burning wool. At last she grasps the bracelet and wrenches it from her arm, flinging it across the room.

And everything stops.

She falls to the floor. The vision has vanished. The terrifying noise has ceased. She can move again. She snatches up a blanket from the sofa and smothers the flames around the hearth. Dylan splutters and clambers to his knees. Once the fire is out, she goes to him.

'Dylan? My God, Dylan . . .'

He looks at the devastation around the room, the upturned furniture, the broken ornaments, the burned mantel and carpet. He coughs and says shakily, 'Remind me never to piss you off.' Then he looks at Tilda and his eyes widen. 'Wow,' he murmurs.

She stands up, catching sight of herself in the mirror. Her skin is more than flushed, it glows with an eerie light. Her hair fans out, rippling and flowing, moving as if she were underwater. And her eyes shine like diamonds.

14

TILDA

Although the skies remain clear, what snow lies on the ground has frozen, gaining a crisp crust through which it is impossible to walk quietly. Tilda and Dylan have wrapped themselves against the cold and set about the task of extinguishing the fire in the kiln. Thistle frolics in the snowy garden as they rake out the ashes. Overhead, the noonday sky is Alpine blue and so bright it hurts Tilda's eyes now that she is without the protection of her tinted lenses. She had a moment upon waking when she feared facing the world undisguised might prove too difficult, but it soon passed. She already feels confident she can handle it. The way Dylan looks at her certainly helps, but more than that, she is aware of a subtle but crucial change within herself. As if she is more complete, somehow. As if she is stronger in an intangible way she would not be able to explain to herself, much less anyone else. It had taken her a while to realize that it was not fear she felt when she put on the bracelet and felt its power. True, she was afraid for Dylan, and the fire had been very real and very dangerous. But what she had experienced, what had coursed through her veins in the moment when the ancient band was on her arm, that was not terror, it was power. An awesome, magical power. Dylan had been quick to identify the bracelet as its source, but Tilda knew different. The precious metal against her skin, with its mysterious symbolic carvings, had most definitely triggered something astonishing, but she knew it was something that was already in her. The power came not from the bracelet, but from her. To be so out of control of such a force, to fear it might hurt someone she cared about, that it could be destructive, had scared her. The power itself, however, the overwhelming feeling of something magnificent inside her being ignited, that was the most profound, the most exhilarating, the most thrilling experience she had ever had. Dylan had been genuinely spooked by what had happened and had warned her against ever risking wearing the thing again.

But she knows she wants to.

She knows one day she will.

If I could learn to control it . . . if I could find a way.

'Are you okay?' Dylan put an arm around her shoulders. His expression is a mixture of concern and delight. 'I'd be feeling pretty shaken right now, if I were you.'

But you're not me. You didn't feel what I felt.

She smiles. 'I'm fine. Just a little tired. We didn't get much sleep, one way and another.'

'One way and another.' He grins.

'You know what was the weirdest thing about everything that happened? Seeing myself . . . like that.' She had spent some time explaining to Dylan in detail what she had seen while wearing the bracelet. However crazy it sounded, he had listened. He had believed her. And that meant a lot. 'I looked like me, but, well I was so *different* too. Those weird clothes, the knife . . .'

'Don't forget the tattoos. Perhaps it was your fantasy self, you know, the way you'd secretly like to present yourself to the world.'

'I have never in my life wanted a tattoo. But, wait a minute!

Why didn't I think of that sooner? I've seen her . . . me . . . like that before. The woman in the boat!'

Dylan does his best to keep up. 'Sorry, what boat?'

'I haven't told you? No, why would I have.' She takes a breath, trying not to trip over her words in her eagerness to clarify the point, to herself as much as to him. 'The day I met your uncle, just before I bumped into him on the footpath, I'd had a . . . a vision. I saw this woman, in a boat, with two men. She was someone ancient, from a different time.'

'And scary, like the ghost from the dig?'

'No.' She shakes her head. 'She wasn't . . . isn't frightening. She's not threatening. With her it's different, somehow. But I know she is who I saw here, this time. Thing is, she looked so like me, perhaps it wasn't a ghost. Maybe I was seeing, I don't know, another version of myself, in another time?'

'Are we talking reincarnation here?' Dylan looks uncertain.

'No. At least, I don't think so. To be honest, the more I think about it, the less sense any of it makes.'

From the open studio door comes the sound of the telephone ringing. Tilda knows before she lifts the handset, which is gritty with clay dust undisturbed by use, that it will be her father. Her postcard might have held her parents off for a few days, but they were worried about her.

'Is your mountain very snowy, Little Rabbit?' her father asks.

'It is. The whole valley is thick with it too. It's very beautiful.'

'Are the roads clear? Less than a week until Christmas. Your mother and I thought we might bring it to you this year. Turkey, mince pies, mulled wine, crackers, appalling jumper, carols on tape, DVD of *The Sound of Music*, the whole festive circus delivered to your door.'

'Oh, Dad . . .'

'It'd be no trouble. Truth is, your mother feels the need for a bit of clucking around her only daughter.' He pauses, then adds, 'We got rather used to having you here.'

Tilda can hear the loneliness in his voice and feels bad. While she might happily convince herself that her mother can manage perfectly well without regular contact, she knows her father misses her. But the thought of them coming to stay, with all that is happening to her, fills her with panic.

I can't do it. I can't cope with them, not here, not now, not like this.

'I'm not sure about the roads . . .'

'We can check the forecast.'

'My lane is definitely blocked.'

'Even your mother can walk a short distance if she's well motivated.'

'The power's unreliable right now too.'

'Again? I thought you were getting that fixed.'

'Must be the snow.'

'How are you managing?'

She pauses, unsure whether telling him about Dylan will make him worry less or more.

'I built a wood-fired kiln,' she tells him.

He laughs. 'That's my girl. Pots first, domesticity sometime never.'

'Pots first,' she agrees.

'Are you pleased with them?'

'Haven't opened the door yet.'

'Ah,' he says, sufficiently well-versed in the expectation that hangs on that moment to understand something of Tilda's nervousness about it.

They agree to watch the weather and leave things undecided beyond that. The idea of a visit is not as scotched as Tilda would like it to be but, as always, her father's gentle concern fills her with warmth and guilt simultaneously.

When she goes back outside she is struck by how clear the air is, how sharp the colours, how pure the sound of the birdsong. It is a bright day, and the landscape is looking its most beguiling. The lake appears sapphire blue set off by the whiteness around it. Even Thistle's mood seems to have lightened, and she is allowing Dylan to throw snowballs for her to chase.

'You're winning her over,' she tells him.

'She's not keen to share you, but every dog has its price.'

'A few snowballs? Some might call that cheap. My father would probably woo her with mince pies.'

'Are your family coming for Christmas?' It is a perfectly natural question, but it makes Tilda uncomfortable.

'The roads are blocked.'

'Only the lanes. The snow's not that bad.'

'We might have more.'

He looks at her curiously. 'We might not.'

'But, we might.'

'Okay.' He thinks for a moment and then says, 'Of course, if the roads *are* blocked, if your parents *don't* make it up here, well, you'd be welcome to spend Christmas at the Old School House with us.'

This is an entirely different prospect. The coziness of the professor's home, his unquestioning acceptance of her, Dylan's company and support, all sound so much more appealing than her parents' well-meant fussing. She doesn't have to hide what is happening from Dylan. Having him know, having him understand, means so much to Tilda. And the opportunity to spend time searching though Professor William's extensive library is an added attraction. The more she delves into the past of the lake, the more likely she is to find out the identity of the body in the grave, and to start making sense of what is happening to her.

'Won't your uncle mind?'

'He'll be thrilled skinny. Why don't we go down and tell him now?'

'Oh, actually, I'd like to spend a bit of time here. You go.'

'Want rid of me already, huh?'

'No, of course not, it's just that . . .' She can't find the words to explain that she is used to being on her own. That now, more than ever, she needs a little solitude. 'You know, girl stuff. Might crank up the Rayburn, get some hot water together for a bath, wash my hair, shave my legs . . .'

'Okay, I get it!' He raises his hands, smiling. 'Linny will manage the snow no problem with her chunky tires. I'll come back later with something edible from the village shop.'

'Tomorrow?'

'Morning?'

'Let's make it afternoon, shall we?' Seeing the poorly masked hurt on his face, she adds quickly, 'I'd really like you to be here when I open the kiln.' It isn't true, but she knows it will matter to him.

He pulls her to him and kisses her lightly. 'Brilliant idea,' he says, holding her close.

SEREN

We lie in a tangle of limbs, my prince's lean and muscular, my own lithe and pale. We are twisted as ivy through oak. Brynach has added a fine fur to my bed; a fur from a far-off land, the pelt of an animal I have never seen and will never know. I am grateful for the comfort it affords me now. It is noon, near enough, and the door to my little home is propped open to allow in the soft summer breeze with its scent of meadow hay, and the familiar voices of the waterbirds. Of late, I have submitted to a slowness that at first was frustrating and bewildering. I have come to see that nature has her own notion of what is best for me now, and I am in no position to argue.

'Are you thirsty?' Prince Brynach asks me, leaning over to smile down, studying my face, now my throat, now the curve of my shoulder.

'I am not. I wish only to stay here and watch the sun fall behind the mountains.'

'Are you hungry?' he asks, running his hand over the impossibly full curve of my belly, stooping to kiss the taught skin, following the now-distorted lines of the drawings on my flesh with his mouth.

'I am not, though I know you would feed me six times a day like a farrowing sow if you had your way.'

He smiles at this. 'The sow is sensible. She knows she cannot grow her young without sufficient fodder.'

I laugh. 'One look at the bulbous thing I am become will tell you I have allowed neither myself nor my unborn to go without.'

'Young princes grow large in the womb. It is often said.'

'And young witches too. Though this is not often spoken of.'

He tilts his head. 'Will our child be a boy prince or a girl witch?' he asks. 'Tell me, Prophet, what do you see?'

'I see that my baby likes to keep secrets. Though one thing is certain, I will give you no prince.'

His face clouds, but I speak only the truth. Whilst he has been as good as his word and made our love known to all, he remains married to Wenna. I am not his wife. Our child will be a bastard, and never a legitimate heir to his realm. And my vision remains true: the princess continues to be childless. How she must despise me now. Where I might have been tolerated as an amusement for her husband, now I am a threat to her position, her marriage, everything. There have been no further attempts on my life. It was many weeks before Hywel was freed from being my protector, and only then because the prince had issued a declaration condemning my attackers, swearing vengeance should anything more happen to me, and letting it be known that I would always be guarded. I have found it irksome, these past months, to forever have a shadow, however they tried to keep a respectful distance. I begged Brynach to take away whichever trusted soldier he sent, but he would not hear of it. If he feared for my safety before, he has become even more determined to have me protected every minute of every night and day since I told him that I am carrying his child.

I attempt to sit up, my movements clumsy and awkward. Brynach offers me his arm but I wave him away, turning onto my knees to right myself with much puffing and little dignity. 'I can manage,' I tell him sternly. 'Though I shall be glad of the day when I no longer lumber and lurch. I cannot so much as gather wild garlic or pick mushrooms in this condition.'

'How can you tolerate such restrictions?'

'Do not mock me, my prince. They may seem trifles to you,' I say, pulling my kirtle over my head, dusting myself down and slipping my swollen feet into my deerskin boots, 'but I am unaccustomed to being so . . .'

'Fat?' He pretends seriousness but only succeeds in doing so with difficulty.

I scowl. 'I am able to throw things still,' I warn him. 'My aim remains good.' I move to lean against the door frame, my eyes shaded against the sunshine, taking in the prettiness of the day outside. The lake shimmers. A lanky heron stalks fish in the shallows. A family of young grebes swims past, heads nodding in their distinctive, comical manner. Brynach appears at my side. He starts to speak, but the sound of approaching horses stops him. Two riders draw near. We recognize both at once: Rhodri and his green son, Siōn. They are dressed in their habitual finery, even though there is no one who cares here to see it.

'Good day to you, Prince Brynach,' the princess's brother hails his master cordially, bowing elaborately in his saddle, yet treats me as if I were not visible. He succeeds in deferring to his prince whilst wordlessly insulting me. Such subtle talents demonstrate skill born of a lifetime of diplomacy. 'And what a very fine day it is.'

'A fine day for a ride out,' Brynach agrees, pointedly slipping his arm around my waist. The action is not lost on his brother-on-law, but he masters his displeasure and conceals it well.

'Indeed,' he agrees, 'Siōn has a new horse and we wished to test his stamina. We took him atop Mynydd Moel and let him have his head.' Here he pauses to beam proudly at his pimply offspring.

'It is a well-formed animal,' says Brynach.

'It must have cost you dear,' I point out.

Rhodri would prefer to ignore my comment, but his son's vanity will not be easily controlled.

'Quite so,' he agrees brightly, 'Father gave more gold for him than for any other horse he owns.' Siōn crows, not seeing the flash of irritation on Rhodri's face.

His father is forced to laugh in an offhand manner. 'It is the way of parents, to indulge their sons,' he says.

Brynach smiles and nods. 'I look forward to spoiling my own child similarly very soon,' he declares.

There is a crackling quality to the air around us. This is as close to a challenge on the subject of my baby's place in the world as the prince has yet laid down. Rhodri, of all people, knows the importance Brynach will place on the child if it is a boy. Regardless of its illegitimacy, if this is the only son the prince is ever to sire, it may never become noble, but it will be his heir. Rhodri's tactic is to continue to ignore my very existence.

'Siōn,' he gestures toward his son's horse, 'your mount is cooling and must be tended to.' He turns a slippery smile in Brynach's direction. 'We will take our leave, my prince,' he says with another bow, expertly making his horse back away as he speaks.

We watch them go. I feel Brynach's arm tighten around me. I know he would protect me with his last breath. I pray it never comes to that.

15

TILDA

The night after the firing, Tilda finds it hard to sleep. The upstairs of the cottage is so cold she and Thistle opt for the sofa in the warm sitting room, keeping the fire well fed with logs. The woodshed is worryingly low, and Tilda knows she will have to restock it soon if she is to rely almost entirely on wood for her heating. She is aware that she could most likely restore the power supply, if only patchily, but finds herself reluctant to do so. She has become accustomed to working to the rhythm of the short winter days, functioning in the low light of candles and lamps, reading by the narrow beam of her battery head-lamp and doing without the computer.

Am I hiding, being like this? Am I putting off reconnecting with the world? Am I building up reasons not to have my parents here? Do I want to hide from the world?

She has to admit to herself this is a possibility. After all, it would be useful to search the Internet for information about the body in the grave, about the crannog, about the people who lived around the lake centuries ago. And yet, she is resistant.

What don't I want to see? What am I afraid of finding out?

She snuggles deeper under the duvet. Thistle gets up from her place in front of the somewhat blackened fireplace and climbs carefully onto the sofa.

'Really? You think there's room for both of us up here?' Tilda protests mildly, secretly glad of the comforting company of the dog. Her emotions are in turmoil after her night with Dylan. If anyone had asked her, she would have said she wasn't ready for another relationship; that her heart had not yet healed after losing Mat. And yet, being with Dylan had felt right. Had felt special. Had made her feel so much better. As if she had taken some crucial step. She knows that it is a step away from Mat, and that thought brings sadness with it, but in her heart she also knows such distance is inevitable. By clinging to the memory of Mat she is holding on to her grief. A twist of guilt knots her stomach.

Am I being disloyal? Is it too soon?

With a sigh she reaches out and strokes Thistle's ears. 'What d'you reckon, girl? Make any sense to you?' In the uneven light from the fire she fancies she can make out the dog's patient expression. 'No need to be jealous, daft pooch. You should like him; he was the one who got you out of that pink collar.'

She closes her eyes again and lets herself replay the events of the previous night in her mind. She remembers slipping the bracelet onto her arm. She can clearly feel the cool metal against her skin. And then so many conflicting thoughts and sensations come flooding back to her it is hard to make sense of them. The blinding white light. The feeling of being lifted off her feet. Dylan being thrown against the wall. The ringing noise. The swirling spinning that almost made her pass out. The fire, growing and leaping from the hearth, threatening to set the whole room, the whole house alight. And the vision. This . . . version of herself, standing so tall and serene and strong.

Could that really have been me? Do I even believe in reincarnation?

Beyond this, any of this, there was something else. Something that both thrilled and frightened her. It was the overwhelming, intoxicating, mind-blowing sense of power that had surged through her. She had never experienced anything like it. The fact that it was out of her control was what made it terrifying. But the energy, the force, whatever it was, that itself was glorious. And though Tilda hardly dares acknowledge the fact, even to herself, she knows that she wants to feel that power again. That she has to. That something about her, something in her, has connected with an amazing force, the like of which she cannot understand but which she cannot turn her back on.

The bracelet still sits on the table beside her. She has not dared put it on again, but she is frequently drawn to it, wanting to touch it, to hold it. Dylan had offered to take it to his uncle to see if he could shed any further light on its possible origins, but Tilda would not hear of it being taken anywhere. She wishes sleep would give her some respite from the turmoil in her head. Different concerns, each one perplexing enough to keep her awake, chase one another round and round in her mind. Dylan. Being with Dylan. Letting go of Mat. The ghost from the grave. The mysterious properties of the bracelet and the way it affects her. And the firing. She decides that, for now, she will concentrate only on the firing. Tomorrow she will open the kiln and see if weeks of work, if her hopes of transforming her ideas into something wonderful, have been successful or come to nothing.

One step at a time. Just like running. First step, the firing. And beyond that, right now, I am too tired to think.

But still, sleep will not come. As the dark hours crawl by Tilda becomes increasingly restless. Increasingly disturbed. She fidgets and moves about so much that Thistle eventually gets off the sofa and curls up on the hearth rug instead. With a sigh of exasperation, Tilda throws back the duvet, pulls on more clothes and lights a candle. She sits on the arm of the sofa, staring at the bracelet, watching the dancing light of the candle flame as it plays upon the warm gold. The flickering illumination appears to animate the drawings, so that the hares and the hound seem to first twitch, and then, gradually, the harder she stares, to start to run. She cannot resist reaching out to touch the bracelet. As her cold fingers connect with the hard metal she experiences something close to an electric shock charging up her arm, causing her to gasp aloud. Thistle wakes up, jumping silently from the rug to come and stand next to her mistress.

'What do you reckon, girl?' Tilda asks her, still keeping her hand on the bracelet, realizing that she *wants* to touch it. That she *wants* to feel connected to the strange magic it holds.

But is it in this beautiful, ancient thing, or is it in me? Does it affect me, or is it the other way around? How can I know?

It occurs to her that neither Dylan nor the professor felt anything unusual when they held the bracelet. She picks it up, and instantly becomes aware of the distant ringing sound she heard before. Her heart pounds running-hard as she recalls how utterly out of control she felt the last time she wore the heavy gold loop. At the same time she vividly remembers the pure energy that had surged through her body. It had been terrifying, but also intoxicating.

Looks like you've got me hooked.

Without allowing herself time for second thoughts, Tilda stands up, pulls off her fleece and slips the bracelet over her hand and onto her arm. This time she does not push it up beyond her elbow, but allows it to rest loosely around her wrist. Again she feels the warmth of the thing; an unnatural, fierce heat. She resists the urge to snatch it off, quells the panic that is rising from the pit of her stomach.

Steady now. No running away. Feet firmly planted. If it's me that makes the thing work, then I should be able to control it. Stands to reason.

She closes her eyes. Thistle moves even closer, so that she can feel the dog's tense body pressing against her. She drops her hand to Thistle's head.

'You and me together, then,' she whispers, her own voice

sounding oddly echoey and unfamiliar, as if coming from a long way off. She opens her eyes again. Although it is still nighttime, and the room is lit only by the single candle, she is surrounded by a pale glow. It does not come from the bracelet, she realizes, but from herself. It grows stronger, until the whole room is soon brightly lit. So brightly that it makes her squint. Alarmed, she wonders if it will become too harsh for her unprotected eyes to cope with, but she senses a steadying in the pulsating aura.

It's okay. It's okay.

As her vision adjusts to the glare she can make out shapes moving on the edge of her sightline. Things blur and jump fractionally beyond the reach of her imperfect eyesight. She turns her head this way and that, trying to focus, to catch one of the phantom shapes more clearly. Thistle's ears prick up and she, too, turns to look.

'You see them too?'

Remembering something about magic-eye pictures requiring the viewer to half close their eyes, Tilda tries this technique, but still the objects are blurred and malformed. She blinks and then, instinctively, shuts her eyes once more.

'Oh!' She cannot help exclaiming aloud, for with her lids tightly closed she is able to see the apparitions clearly. They are no longer fleeting glimpses of something, but clearly defined, and brilliantly coloured. There are two hares, their eyes bright and fur dense and luxuriant. Birds swoop and soar – she counts two owls and a hawk before becoming distracted by a white horse. It gallops across the hectic scene, riderless, mane flowing, silent hooves pounding the insubstantial ground. She tries to follow it, turning, but senses it is passing beyond her reach. She cannot stop herself opening her eyes, at which point the horse fades to a mere shadow. She shuts her eyes again quickly but the horse has vanished.

Damn! I should have known.

She is entirely lost in the beauty and wonder of what she is seeing, as the hares and the birds continue to dance and fly. Only gradually does she become aware of the ringing noise again, growing steadily stronger. And as it does so it alters, shifting in both pitch and tone. Soon it is no longer bell-like but an eerie wail, distant and distorted by a flat echo.

Like the singing of a mermaid! Or whale song!

The volume of the sound increases, and as it does so the vision changes. Gone is the light. The woodland creatures disappear, to be replaced by deepening darkness and a sense of plummeting that makes Tilda feel both dizzy and a little sick. She forces herself to stay with whatever is happening, to follow where she is being taken. The bracelet on her arm is getting hotter again. The strange sound is so loud now she instinctively puts her hands over her ears.

And then she sees it.

Huge and heavy and ancient beyond memory, powering up toward her through the darkness. Its skin has an iridescent sheen – blue, green, purple all at one time. It moves incredibly swiftly for something so enormous, its graceful neck stretched forward as it scythes through the gloom. It has a noble head, with a wide brow and huge eyes, shining and fathomless, deep set and ink-black. Tilda looks into those eyes and knows – just *knows* – that as clearly as she sees this magnificent creature, as surely, she herself is being seen. As the mysterious beast swoops upward and over her, Tilda fears she will be knocked down by it, crushed and broken, so that she opens her eyes, stepping backward, falling to the floor. The room is filled with swirling colours, but beyond this there are no more apparitions. The creature is not there. Tilda scrambles to her feet, putting her left hand over the bracelet so that she can hold it in place, but also so that she might pluck it off quickly if she needs to. But the vision is fading. The curious cry of the fabulous being she has just encountered weakens and dies away, as if the fantastic beast were travelling at great speed, singing all the while. Tilda stands for several minutes as everything around her returns to a more normal, everyday shape and state. Dawn is nudging its way above the hills outside, and shedding a weak daytime light through the small window. It is some time before Tilda feels ready to slip the bracelet off her arm. She finds she is both exhausted and exhilarated. Gently, she sets the precious band down on the table. Thistle has decided the excitement is over and climbs back onto the duvet. Tilda rubs her chilly arms, fighting an overwhelming fatigue, as she climbs back under the duvet, snuggling close to the dog, falling quickly into a deep and dreamless sleep.

The next morning when Tilda goes outside the coldness of the air and the beauty of the countryside take her breath away. There has been no further fall of snow, but the mountain has snagged a passing cloud, which has paused long enough to coat every gatepost, branch, twig and leaf in its vapour. And that mist has since frozen. Tilda has never seen anything so enchanting. Wherever she looks there are ice crystals, pure and sharp and delicate, frozen to every surface, even the wool of the Welsh mountain sheep as they chomp their hay from the equally frosted feeder in the field next to the cottage. Now a ceiling of high cloud diffuses the sunlight, softening it and removing the colour from the sky. The lake itself is covered in a layer of ice that appears from Tilda's viewpoint to be black. She knows this is an impossibility, and for a few moments is unable to do anything other than stand and stare at the wondrous scenery.

Thistle has no regard for such things, and busies herself following mouse tracks through the snow in the garden. The kiln has cooled completely now, and Tilda suffers a flash of worry that the winter weather will have caused the temperature to drop more suddenly than is good for the ceramics inside the little oven. She places her hand on the frost-topped brickwork. More than just a few pots depend upon the results of the firing. Her future livelihood is at stake, it's true, but there is something more. Her hopes for these special pieces are linked to all the strangeness of this magical place. To all the curious things, the changes that have been happening to her. Will the designs have the quality, the impact, the strength, that she is praying for? Will she be able to make something of the strange connection she feels to the lake, its past and its people? She has slipped the bracelet into her pocket, feeling a need to keep it close. Taking it out, she holds it up so that the soft morning light picks out the hares and the hound, locked in their eternal chase. She considers putting it on again, but knows that the moment is not right to explore the secrets it holds.

Not now. Not yet.

She is still giddy from the events of the previous night. Still stunned by her experiences. Still in awe of the wonderful things she was shown. She has not yet had a moment to try to make sense of it, and a part of her does not want to. Does not wish to taint the beauty and power of what she saw, of what she felt, with the application of reason and plain old-fashioned good sense. She holds on tight to the belief that by pressing on with her work, by bringing her art to life, she is strengthening the magical connection that the designs on the bracelet and her pots share. The thought of that connection thrills her. And scares her too, though at this moment she chooses not to dwell on that. She shades her eyes with her hand and squints up at the sky in search of the sun. It is still obscured, but the brightest of the gloom is not yet directly overhead.

Too early to open the kiln yet. And too slippery for a run.

She is about to go back indoors when she notices a figure trudging up the snow-covered path toward the cottage. At first she thinks it is Dylan, but as the walker draws closer she recognizes Lucas.

Lucas? Why would he struggle all the way up here to seek me out?

He looks up, sees her, and waves. She waves back. Thistle pads over to the garden gate to inspect their visitor.

'Good morning, Lucas.'

He stops, bending forward to catch his breath before speaking. 'Don't tell me you actually run up this hill,' he gasps.

'Not lately.'

He turns and takes in the view. 'Okay, I get it. That is spectacular.'

'The lake is completely frozen over today,' Tilda points out. 'Doesn't happen very often.'

'When I set out I thought it was cold enough, but now . . . *phew!*' He unbuttons his coat.

'No work on the dig today, then?'

He shakes his head. 'Everything is glued together with ice. And we've had to sort out the lights.'

'Ah.' Tilda cannot meet his eye. There is no reason he should think any of the chaos at the dig site was anything to do with her. No reason beyond her own behaviour, which must have looked nothing short of hysterical to Lucas.

'Actually,' he says, reaching down to casually pat a compliant Thistle, 'that's why I came up here. To tell you that we've rescheduled the lifting of the remains for two days after Christmas. I . . . thought you'd like to know.' He pauses, then adds, 'And I wanted to apologize. For getting so . . . cross. With you.'

Tilda smiles at the quaintly inappropriate word.

'Forget it,' she says. 'Everything was a mess . . . all your hard work. It was understandable.'

'All the same, I shouldn't have barked at you like I did. I'm sorry.'

She looks at him carefully. The fact that he has considered her, considered how she feels about the dig, that he has trekked all the way up the hill to talk to her about it, shows a side of him she had not given him credit for before. And now she sees he is looking directly at her, levelly and openly, and she is no longer wearing her tinted lenses.

'Coffee?' she offers.

He nods wordlessly and follows her up the path to the kitchen door.

'I've only just got the stove going,' she tells him. 'It'll warm up in a bit.' She pushes the kettle onto the hottest part of the Rayburn and fetches mugs and coffee. Lucas takes off his coat and scarf and sits at the table.

'Don't you feel a little isolated?' he asks. 'I mean, all the way up here on your own . . .'

'I like solitude.'

'A true artist, then.'

'Not a very productive one recently. Until today, actually.' Tilda is surprised to find herself telling him about the wood-fired kiln and the firing. He accepts her explanation that it was an artistic choice not to use a conventional kiln, and for a while the two talk about art and what it is she does and how she is both nervous and excited about opening the kiln. Eventually, though, the conversation falters and she knows they must return to the subject of the dig.

'I'm sorry,' she begins, 'about . . . the other day. When you were lifting the stone . . . I didn't mean to wreck things for you.'

'You didn't. It wasn't your fault the lights blew out.' He sips his coffee and then adds, 'You were very . . . upset.'

'I can't explain. Well, if I do, you'll think I'm crazy.'

'Do you care what I think?'

She smiles. 'In a small place like this gossip spreads really fast. I don't want to be written off as the mad potter on the mountain just yet.'

'Ah.'

'Look, I'm not an academic, I haven't studied the area for

years like you have, I don't really know anything about anything, it's just that ... well ... there is something bad in that grave. Something really bad.'

'And I'm setting it free?'

'It's not your fault.'

'But that's what you said, when we were raising the stone. Those were your exact words, if I recall.' He wraps his hands more tightly around his coffee and breathes in the steam.

He's scared. My God, he hasn't dismissed what I said as the ravings of a madwoman. Not completely.

She hesitates, and then asks, 'Have you ... noticed anything? Felt anything, while you were working on the site? Anything ... strange?'

'It would be easy to get spooked by the idea of disturbing a grave. It's not something any of us does lightly. We try to treat the remains with respect. They were a living, breathing person, once. We are digging them up from their place of rest.'

'Except that this one wasn't resting peacefully, was she?'

'It certainly looks as if she came to a highly unpleasant end,' he agrees.

'That's putting it mildly. You think she was buried alive. And that the stone held her in place while they shovelled earth on top of her. It seems so terribly cruel, whatever she had done.'

'It's a mistake to read the past with our twenty-first century sensibilities.'

Tilda shrugs. 'They are the only ones I've got.'

'We've had some of the test results back from the samples Molly sent off to the lab. We can pinpoint the date of the grave, almost to the year.'

'I know you're dying to tell me.'

'We think 910 to 920 AD. And the body is certainly that of a woman, aged between thirty and forty. She was healthy, in life. As we've already established, she didn't die of natural causes. Her diet included fish, from the lake, of course, but also high levels of protein from grains and regular meat. She was not some lowly peasant, whoever she was. She must have enjoyed quite an important position on the crannog. Until . . .'

'What did she do? What *could* she have done to deserve such a punishment?'

'We will know more when we get to the grave beneath her. Once we know the identity of the person she was most likely accused of murdering, we will know more.'

'He or she must have been important, you reckon?'

'More than likely.'

Tilda swallows more hot coffee. She sighs, unsure how to tell him more. Uncertain just how much of the craziness he will be able to accept. She considers telling him about the bracelet. He might well have some ideas about its origins, and she knows it would be of serious interest to him. Perhaps even important to the dig. But she cannot be sure how he will react.

What if he decides it constitutes some sort of national treasure? He might make me give it up. Might take it off to be analyzed. I can't let him take it. I can't risk him doing that.

Into the hesitation in their conversation comes the sound of an engine labouring, growing louder. The noise is familiar to Tilda by now.

'That'll be Dylan,' she says, getting up and slipping her coat back on.

The aged Land Rover makes short work of the wintry conditions and powers its way up the hill. He gets out with his habitual energy and upbeat manner, but even from where she now stands in the garden, Tilda can detect the change in his body language at the sight of her visitor. She feels uncomfortable at him arriving and finding her with Lucas, though she knows she has no reason to. After all, this is her house. And Dylan has no cause to be jealous. Besides, it is far too early in their new and faltering relationship for anyone to be laying down conditions or becoming in any way possessive.

'You're early,' she says, sounding cross when she hadn't meant to.

'I wanted to come and help,' he says, looking a little hurt. 'Sorry.'

'No, I'm sorry.' Feeling bad, Tilda tells him, 'Lucas came to tell me they are resuming the dig. A couple of days after Christmas.'

'We can't stay here much longer,' Lucas explains. 'Digs are costly. And it's not doing the contents of the trench any good having them exposed to all this weather. Really, the sooner we get everything out and back to the university the better.'

'Can't argue with that,' Dylan says, rather pointedly greeting Tilda with a lingering kiss on the cheek. 'Are you going to open that kiln up?'

'Oh, it's too soon, I think.'

'It's gone twelve.'

'Already? I hadn't realized.' She looks from one man to the other, wishing them both somewhere else. Neither has any idea how significant this moment is for her.

'I might leave it a little while,' she says.

'Really?' Dylan is genuinely surprised. 'It must be cool by now,' he points out, and then, seeing her reluctance, adds, 'but it's up to you, Tilda. This is your baby,' he says, smiling.

Tilda glances at Lucas, hoping against hope that he might decide he has something better to do and take himself off.

No such luck.

Dylan follows her gaze and says baldly, 'Haven't you got a hole to dig somewhere?'

'Not today,' he says.

Despite herself, Tilda feels the need to defend him. However much she might want him gone at this moment, she dislikes Dylan taking it upon himself to dismiss her visitor.

'It was good of Lucas to come up and tell me about the plans for the dig. He . . . he knows it matters to me.' An uncomfortable silence follows, which is not helped by Thistle slinking away from Dylan's outstretched hand. 'Oh, let's open the damn thing!' Tilda says quickly, unable to stand the strain any longer. 'Dylan, could you pass me the chisel and hammer, please? They're next to you, in the toolbox.'

He scrapes snow off the lid and takes out what Tilda needs, handing the chunky tools to her. She rests the sharp end of the chisel between the bricks of the door of the kiln, where the mortar is thinnest. Taking a firm swing with the mallet, she starts to tap, each strike growing a little stronger. Soon there is a gap forming. She works her way along until there is a space running along two sides of one of the smaller bricks. Soon she is able to wiggle the brick loose and then remove it altogether. She repeats the process with the next door brick. And the next. It is warm work, and her hand is beginning to blister, but she turns down Dylan's offer of help. She works on. As the opening becomes larger, the pots inside can be seen.

Are they okay? Has it worked? Has the firing worked, or have I ruined everything? Oh, please don't let them be a mess. I should have fixed the electric. I'm a coward. Why did I attempt this?

'Can you see in there yet?' Dylan asks, peering over her shoulder.

'A little. Just need to get the next two or three bricks out . . .'

At last, the door is completely dismantled. Tilda puts down the hammer and chisel, whips off her fingerless mittens and drops them into the snow. She kneels down in front of the kiln. Something of her own anxiety has passed to the men, so that the three of them stare in tense silence as Tilda reaches inside the makeshift oven. Slowly, with the utmost care, she takes hold of the first of the pots and lifts it out. She turns and sets it down on the small patch of ground close to the kiln, which is free from snow because of its proximity to the fire. She sits back on her heels and stares at the large, bulbous ceramic pot in front of her. For what seems like an age, nobody speaks. And then, without warning, Tilda's eyes fill with hot tears.

Oh my God.

'Tilda.' Dylan puts a hand on her shoulder. 'Tilda, that is bloody fantastic.'

'It is,' Lucas agrees. 'I've never seen anything quite like it. It's incredible.'

They are right. Through the blur of her tears of relief, Tilda can see that they are right. The kiln has done its work. The cold clay and gritty glazes have yielded to the heat and been transformed into something spectacular. Something magnificent. The base colour is that of the rich brown soil of the lowland meadows. The rock salt Tilda applied so cautiously has pitted and pocked the surface, giving a wonderfully rugged, natural texture to the pot. The glazes have oxidized perfectly, so that the subtle colours she selected for the running hound and hares seem to flash and flare even in the low light of the overcast day. And through it all, woven into the intricate pattern the chasing animals form, there is the glimmer of gold, snatches and splashes of the precious metal, causing a magical sparkle and brilliance set against the dark background.

Thank you!

She forms the thought without considering who it is she wants to thank, but as she kneels there, the cold beginning to work its way to her bones, Dylan's hand still on her shoulder, she knows that she has not created this wonderful, unique piece of art alone. Someone helped her. Someone sparked the ability within her to be able to do such a thing. Someone or something. She slips her hand into her pocket and takes out the bracelet, holding it close to the pot. The designs match even more closely now that the glazes and gold leaf have brought her own creation to life. And for a moment, for an instant, Tilda fancies she sees all six of the mysterious ancient creatures in front of her move, their ribs rising and falling, their eyes glinting as they run, run, run.

SEREN

It is nearly dawn when I rise from my bed. The summer moon was bright as a coin only a short time since, but now it pales in the lightening sky as an eager sun begins to make its presence felt. The young guard appointed to keep watch outside my house is sleeping peacefully as I step over him. He has not failed in his duty through indolence but because of the draft I gave him in his portion of the stew we shared last night. I knew my time had come. I knew also that I required no men to come running in attendance, with their inevitable panic and posturing and noise. This is a moment for myself and my babe, though I know the prince would have it otherwise, were it in his power to influence the event. He is not quite lord of everything, whatever he and his followers may believe. There are yet domains he does not rule, and the birthing of a child is one such place.

The birds are already awake, sweetening the air with their song. Nighttime animals scuttle to their burrows and lairs, making way for the heavier tread of those who go abroad in daylight hours. My progress is slow, as I must halt frequently to allow my body to cramp or surge. I am wearing a loose linen kirtle and carry a soft woollen blanket and my knife. I need nothing more. Placing my palm over my heaving belly I whisper, 'Be patient, little one.' I continue through the copse to the secluded spot on the shore of the lake I have chosen. Here the ground slopes gently into the water, and the earth is sandy with few stones and no reeds or rushes, so that after some effort I am able to lie down comfortably enough. The second I immerse my body in the silky waters of Llyn Syfaddan, I feel my pains ease. The child continues to move inside me as it should, but my suffering is greatly reduced by the magical properties of the sacred lake. I have foreseen this moment. I have nothing to fear. And whatever my prince might secretly wish for, I know that my babe is a girl. I have chosen not to share this knowledge with him. Let him hold his infant in his arms, let him gaze into her eyes, let him feel her tiny heart beat strong and brave in her breast – he will have no room in his soul for disappointment then.

As I work to bring my child into this world, I can feel vibrations through the water and I know the Afanc is near. She has come to witness the birth of a new witch. Knowing that she is with me gives me strength. I do not want to cry out, for to do so might give me away. There have been no further attempts on my life, but I have scarce been on my own, and here and now I am certainly at my most vulnerable. I close my eyes and quiet my clamouring thoughts. I bring my will and my strength to bear and with neither fuss nor ceremony my daughter slips from me into the life-giving lake water. I quickly lift her up. Oh! She is a most miraculous thing! So small and yet so fierce. She is the mirror of myself. I see the light in her soul shining from her. Like me, she has been kissed with magic. Like me, she will be a child of the moonlight. Like me, she will be under the protection of grandmother-Afanc.

'Welcome, my little one,' I kiss her brow. She does not cry, but looks about her, tiny fists clenched, calm but aware even now of where she is. Of what she is. And my joy manifests itself in a glowing light, tinged blue, that surrounds myself and my babe.

The surface of the lake bubbles. I hold my breath. Will she come closer? Will she show herself, even as the day brightens and she could so easily be seen? I take my knife and swiftly cut the snaking rope that has nourished my infant these long months. I wrap the child in the woollen blanket and hold her to me as I stand. Together we watch and wait. There is a stillness in the air, as if the very woods were also stopped from breathing. The birds hush. Ripples spin out across the lake. And now, silently, with such grace as to move the hardest of hearts to weeping, the Afanc rises up from the deep. She is even more beautiful revealed in the early sunshine! I lift up my newborn, holding her high. She neither wails nor whimpers. She is not afraid. The mother-of-the-lake lowers her noble head to inspect this tiny new prophet.

'She will keep your secret as I have done,' I promise.

The Afanc sighs, looking deep into my eyes a moment longer, and then moves back, causing gentle waves to lap at me. Without a single splash she slips beneath the surface and is gone.

I kiss my child, holding her close to me again. 'You are fortunate indeed, my young witch, for the blessing of the Afanc is the greatest protection of all.'

16

TILDA

Tilda glances in the direction of the setting sun. As it drops behind the snow-covered mountains beyond the lake, it bleeds its colour into the winter sky. Such a spectacle would, ordinarily, have halted her in her work, causing her to gaze in wonder. But today it serves only to remind her that the day is nearly over, and time is slipping through her fingers. It is now only two days until Christmas, and she has promised to celebrate with Dylan and his uncle, so she has only a few hours left before she will have to tidy herself up and tear herself away from the cottage. More important, she will have to put away the bracelet. Or at least, resist wearing it. The thought brings an anticipatory pang of longing. She marvels at how quickly she has moved from being afraid of what it brings her to being ecstatic about it. After the firing, Dylan had suggested a celebratory meal in the Red Lion. She had felt his disappointment when she had invited Lucas, and his relief when Lucas had declined the offer, saying he had more things to take care of at the dig site. In truth, she would rather have stayed at home. The success of the firing and the bewildering vision had ignited all her creative impulses to bursting point. She wanted to lock herself in the studio and draw what she had seen. Wanted to capture the image of the incredible creature that had appeared to her. Wanted to record all the minute details of what had danced and leapt before her eyes. Wanted to compare again the intricate design on the bracelet with her now-finished, glazed and fired artwork.

And she wanted to wear the bracelet again.

But not with Dylan there. Not with anyone there. So, she had gone to the pub with him, eaten a late lunch she scarcely tasted, drunk beer she hardly noticed, done her best to behave like a normal, reasonable, sensible person. Except that she didn't feel normal anymore. At the end of the evening she had gently but firmly sent Dylan away, flinching at the wounded expression he had worn as he left. She had tried to explain that she needed to work. Just these few days, she had assured him. They would see each other again on Christmas Day.

'I've lost you to a lump of clay,' he told her.

'I'm sorry,' she said, 'It's just that . . .' she left the sentence unfinished.

'Look, I'm pleased you're happy. Glad to see you thinking about your work instead of . . . well, other stuff.'

Tilda could only nod. She allowed him to believe that the success of the firing had turned her attention away from all the strange and frightening things that had been going on. Even though he had witnessed what happened the first time she'd worn the bracelet, she still felt a reluctance to talk about it with him. She hadn't even told him about the second time, when she had had the vision of the Afanc. She knew him well enough to be sure that he would not make light of it. That he would listen. That he would believe her. And yet, while she was able to be intimate with him, and even to have him share in her work, the way she felt when she wore the bracelet, when she connected with whatever it was she had found, it was just too personal to share. It was something she needed to explore on her own.

Now, at last, she is alone again, save for Thistle, who has

become even more her shadow than usual. Tilda turns her back on the sunset and goes into her studio. The shelves on the right are now filled with the gleaming new pieces, fresh from the kiln. She runs her fingers lovingly over the surface of the nearest one. She could never have hoped that the glazes would work so perfectly, the colours fusing and melding, making the Celtic animals on each pot stand out, and yet at the same time blend into their backgrounds. The technique of applying salt to the glaze and packing it with reeds from the lake has produced stunning results. The salt has expanded and melted, creating warm, coppery splotches and splatters in random patches around the pots, with a swirling smokiness produced when the reeds burned away. The animals themselves Tilda had picked out and highlighted by hand painting them with a copper wash before firing, so that now they gleam and glitter. Looking at them calms her. Touching them makes a tingle spread lightly through her body.

I know you. I know you all. And the Afanc? She came to me. She sought me out in that vision. Where does she fit into all this, I wonder? If hares and hounds used to represent witches, what did she stand for?

She hurries back to the sitting room and takes the bracelet from the high bookshelf where she had put it for safekeeping. She does not put it on – making a silent promise to herself that she will do so very soon – but tucks it into the pocket of the oversize tartan shirt she often wears to work in. Next she fetches the books loaned to her by the professor and returns to the studio to sit at her workbench, wrapping a woollen blanket around her shoulders. The stove in the studio is lit and burning quite well, but the single-glazed glass doors of the studio let out far more heat than they keep in. She puts a match to the wick of an oil lamp beside her and turns through the pages of the first volume, uncertain of what she is searching for, simply trusting that she will know it when she finds it. Thistle lies down on the rag rug at her feet, curling up tightly, her nose beneath her wiry-haired tail, the better to keep warm.

'Let's see, girl, what have we here?' A section in the book of Welsh legends and folklore comments on the collection of famous and ancient tales known as the *Mabinogion*. A detail regarding shapeshifting into different animals catches Tilda's eye. 'According to this,' she tells the dog, 'changing into other creatures went on quite a lot back in the day. Listen: "The Story of Taliesin" – it tells about this boy who accidentally tastes a magical potion in a cauldron. He gets chased by the woman who made it, called . . . here it is – Ceridwen. The boy is known as Gwion. She is seriously angry with him, so he runs away . . . "But Ceridwen was fleet of foot and so furious that she quickly caught up with the child, so Gwion changed himself to a hare; and she, seeing this, became a black greyhound. On they ran. Gwion fled to the river, and at the water's edge he did become a fish, but Ceridwen pursued him as an otter, so that still he was in danger. In fear for his life he leapt from the river, taking to the air as a bird. Ceridwen would not give up and turned herself to a hawk to hunt him down. Gwion was terrified, and saw a pile of wheat. Swiftly he dropped into the heap, becoming one of thousands of grains. But Ceridwen saw what he had done. She, too, changed again, this time into a recrested hen, which swallowed the grain. It went into her womb. Ceridwen became a woman again, and nine months later she gave birth to a child so beautiful she could not bring herself to kill him. Instead she placed him in a leather bag in a coracle and set him adrift on the lake." Good grief.' Tilda lets her eyes scan the following pages, but the shape-shifting has stopped in this story, and there is no mention of the Afanc. She finds again the legend of the water-horse, and reads how it was tempted from the lake by the song of a brave girl from the village. 'Always a girl that has to do these things. Leave it to the women to sort out, eh Thistle?' But the dog has fallen asleep and snores softly. There is an illustration of the *Afanc*, showing it as a fearsome creature, all scales and teeth and jagged edges. 'But she wasn't like that at all,' Tilda murmurs. 'She was beautiful.'

Excitement tightens her belly as she pushes the books to one side and grabs a block of drawing paper and a stick of charcoal. She works quickly, narrowing her eyes, making bold, fast strokes of smudgy black on the page as she strives to capture what it was she saw in the vision. The graceful arc of its neck. The proud bearing of its head. The deep-set, luminous eyes. The muscular limbs that powered it silently through the water. After half an hour of sketching she stares at her work, biting her bottom lip thoughtfully.

Yes. Or at least, almost. Won't know until I go further. Too soon to tell.

Jumping from her stool, she hurries over to the bin of clay and takes out a large lump of the gritty brown earth. This binful has already been wedged and pummelled so that no air remains inside, so that it should not pop during firing and explode the piece. After a few moments of kneading and turning, the material is sufficiently malleable to be used. Tilda pauses, brushing her hair from her face with her arm, her hands already sticky with clay. The uneven light from the oil lamp glints off the inch of bracelet that peeps out of her shirt pocket. She nods.

'Okay,' she says to herself, to the slumbering dog and to any other souls who might be listening, 'let's begin.'

SEREN

They are not expecting me. As I walk toward the crannog amid the softening light of dusk I allow myself a small smile at the thought of their surprise. It would not do to become such a creature of habit that all my actions might be anticipated by others. Though, in truth, they *should* expect me, had they sufficient wits. The prince has, of course, met his infant daughter. He was so attentive throughout the months the babe grew within me, so happy at the prospect of at last having a child of his own, it was only natural that he should want to take her in his arms at the first opportunity. He bestowed such a look of love upon her that day that I am certain, in my heart, he will never turn from her. She cannot ever claim a place as princess, but short of this he will give her every honour, every protection, every care. It is not the prince I come to exchange words with this evening. I know there are whisperings, there is gossip, there are tongues wagging at every hearth hereabouts, concerning my child. Our child. I care nothing for the idle musings of people of no influence or importance. Tanwen, as time passes, will win over the people she will one day serve, I have no doubt of that. What concerns me now is the plotting and scheming of those who place themselves close to the prince. They continue to do their utmost to come between us. In this, they will not succeed. Nor will they ever convince him to denounce his daughter. The matter for me to address is this:

When they come to see that he will not turn from us, and they recognize that more power lies with this babe – and therefore with me – than with all of them put together, when that moment arrives, Tanwen is in grave danger.

Although the late summer day has been warm I wear my red cloak, so that I am able to conceal my child snug and safe beneath it. She is not some entertainment for the villagers to gawk at. Let them wait. The guard on the causeway permits me to pass without questioning my right to do so, averting his own eyes from my steady gaze, then quickly looking again when he thinks I will not notice. I was once asked if being feared leads me to loneliness. My reply was that I have known no other way of being. Now, with the warm, smiling, bright-eyed result of my prince's love held close to my heart, I would say that the fear of many serves only to heighten the experience of *not* being feared. So that the love I share with Prince Brynach, and the love I feel for my babe, is the deepest, the strongest, the most blissful love possible.

On the little island, people are going about their everyday business. With night approaching, mothers call in their children. Men who have livestock return from the fields: the shepherds leaving their sheep to sleep in the grassy meadows next the lake, the cattleman bringing the best of his beasts into the safety of the byre. Women walk briskly, their arms filled with firewood, or trudge beneath the weight of yoked pails of milk. The blacksmith tamps down his forge, taking care no stray ember or spark escapes to kindle a blaze among the dry wood of the palisades or the thick thatch of the roofs. A herding dog slinks around my heels, nervous of my confident stride but drawn to the snuffling sounds from beneath my cloak. I drop my hand to my side, low and still, and he sniffs it, wagging his tale in acceptance of the gesture of friendship. Smoke is already rising from the hole in the roof of the great hall. I can picture well the assembled company, gathered for their evening of talking, and eating, and drinking. It is in these close moments that syrupy words are poured warm and winning into my prince's ear. It is the oldest, simplest magic: Give a man a bright fire to stare at, a tankard of fresh ale to drink, a place of comfort to take his ease and a bellyful of good meat, and he will listen to the rankest rubbish and think it sweet.

I am, nonetheless, shocked to find no guard at the entrance to my prince's dwelling. I am able to pass over the threshold without the slightest hindrance. Inside, all is so exactly as I had known it would be it is as if I had experienced a vision of it. A table runs along the far wall, on the other side of the fire, and at it sit Prince Brynach, Princess Wenna, Nesta, Rhodri, Hywel and Siôn. A page pours ale, and fetches meat from the fire. Two soldiers feed logs onto the base of crimson embers. Other warriors and members of the royal household sit and eat in quiet corners, each lost in his or her own world of worries and wishes, with scarcely a glance at their prince, and not one of them noticing an unannounced visitor come standing among them. Until I speak.

'Must I stand here so long my feet take root before I am acknowledged?'

At the sound of my voice several of Brynach's men jump startled to their feet, or hurriedly drop their beakers of ale, attempting to make themselves appear worthy of the name guard. One draws his sword in a futile show of strength.

'Save your blade for another day,' I tell him. I sweep the room with an angry glare. 'Had I been minded to harm the prince your actions would have come too late to stop me.'

Brynach stands, holding up his hand in a gesture that aims to both steady his men and calm me. 'Peace, Seren Arianaidd. All is well. My men were rightly at their ease, for there is no danger near.'

'There is *ever* danger near.'

At this, Rhodri rolls his eyes. 'Alas, I fear our venerable Seer, for all her gifts, has not the art of relaxation, my prince.'

Wenna smiles. 'But brother, it is her role, to warn us of the darkening skies that herald the thunder, of the departing geese that foretell famine, of the sickening mouse that speaks surely of broad disaster.' She keeps her words gentle, but the mockery is plain for all to hear. That I failed to help her conceive a child of her own is not a matter she will forgive. That I have since provided her husband with a daughter is more than sufficient cause for her to loathe me forever.

Nesta laughs loudly, even though her mouth is stuffed with bread. Siōn joins in, his boyish sniggering and red cheeks making him appear younger and sillier than ever.

Hywel bangs his tankard on the table. 'Page! My vessel is empty, and the prophet has been offered neither scat nor refreshment. See to it!'

There is a deal of scurrying as a chair is brought and a boy hastens to fetch victuals for me. I shake my head.

'I have no need of rest or food.'

The Prince is watching me closely. 'We are, as ever, honoured by your presence, Seer, but I wonder what it is that has brought you here?' he asks, the formal way he is bound to receive me clearly causing him discomfort.

Rhodri gives a bark of laughter. ''Tis not for the pleasure of our company then?'

The women find this remark amusing. Siōn, evidently still too green to hold his ale well, is emboldened by his parent's lack of respect for me.

'Oh, father, I know! She has come to dance for us! A merry jig and a cheery song to brighten our day!' He laughs at his own cleverness, hiccupping as he does so.

I refuse to be baited like a bear. With one flowing movement, I throw my cape back over my shoulder to reveal Tanwen. I lift her high, holding her up and turning slowly so that all in the room may see her. There is a collective gasp. Though her birth was not a secret, this is the first time my child has been seen by any besides myself and her father. She has known no more than two moons, and has still the purity of the newborn about her. I have dressed her in a simple muslin shift, so that her plump, pink arms and legs wriggle free, her paleness – *my* paleness – clear. Young as she is, she has a head of hair soft as thistledown and white as cotton-grass. Already her stout heart and singing soul are evident, for she is not afraid, but gazes about her with interest, happy and curious. There is a tension in the room now. All eyes are upon this tiny likeness of myself.

'Bear witness to the coming of a new Prophet of Llyn Syfaddan! Behold Tanwen! Destined to one day hold the position of Shaman, Seer, Prophet. Born in the magical waters of the lake, carrying the ancient magic in her blood. Descendant of the revered witches of Llyn Syfaddan. Blessed by the Afanc herself. Daughter of our noble ruler, Prince Brynach!'

There is a louder gasp now. For all the rumours and tittle-tattle regarding my child's parentage, to hear Brynach so boldly named as her father shocks them. Wenna's expression tightens. Rhodri scowls, not so much as attempting to mask his displeasure. There are murmurings all around, and people shift and shuffle, the better to see this strange and wonderful child. I lower her and step forward until I am standing directly opposite the prince. We are separated by the worn wooden table, and by centuries of tradition that dictates a noble man must take a noble wife. I offer Tanwen to him.

'Will you hold your child, my Prince?'

The murmuring and fidgeting behind me stops instantly. The room is filled with such a silence as might be found in an empty tomb. I would swear an oath that Wenna is holding her breath. I can clearly see Rhodri mouthing soundless curses at me. For this is a moment heavy with meaning, and all present know it. Tanwen can never be a titled child in the royal household, but in the absence of a legitimate heir she does have a position, an unassailable place, as the only offspring of the prince. To acknowledge her now would be to underline this, would bestow a measure of status upon this little one that could never be taken from her. Were Brynach to spurn her, however, were he to lose his nerve, to falter in his deep love for her, to be swayed by the vitriol and ambition of his wife and her family, then Tanwen would never know true respect. Would never be able to claim her rightful place. Would be banished to the shadows and margins not only by her physical heritage, but by the bastardy of her birth.

He hesitates. The pause stretches too long and too wide. And I become aware of something else. Of another level of influence at play. At the far edge of my thoughts, where my mind melts into my ancient soul, I hear whispering. Whispered words that are urgent. No, *vehement*. I pay heed to them, straining to catch their meaning and to discern their origin. And now I have it! A hex! Clear as a full moon in a summer night's sky. Dark magic, sent to turn my prince from the path of truth, to bend his will and plant black-hearted notions in his mind. Nesta! This is her wicked work!

I put my eyes on her. My eyes and my own sharp-edged will. She does her best to look away, to evade me, but she cannot. Her wavering gaze is locked into mine, and I send to her − *into* her − such a shock of magic, lake born and nourished, fierce with the ancient enchantments I have been blessed with, that she cannot continue with her loathsome efforts. The whispers cease.

Prince Brynach blinks away his confusion. He smiles. He reaches across the table and takes Tanwen in his arms and the two exchange the sweetest of glances. He bends over her and kisses her tenderly.

'Hurrah for Tanwen!' The cheer goes up and others join in the cry. More ale is called for, as Hywel demands a toast to the new babe, and the room is filled with good wishes and merriment. Amid it all Wenna remains still as a standing stone. I pity her. I admire her quiet dignity. Nesta's face blackens with fury. Rhodri gets to his feet, muttering his refusal to be a part of such outrage. But Brynach notices none of this, for he has eyes only for his beautiful baby daughter.

17

TILDA

For Tilda, the garden feels like the best place to try out the bracelet again. Being outdoors makes sense, feels curiously safer. As if the energy the thing unleashes is too much to manage when confined. Better not to have heavy stone walls boxing her, and it, in. She has kept it with her, in her pocket, or sitting on the worktop in the studio while she works, but has resisted putting it on again. Until now. She feels as if she has been holding back from indulging in a delicious treat, but at the same time she is more than a little apprehensive. Her memory of the strange visions and sensations wearing the bracelet caused is a powerful one; her belief in her own ability to control such a force and stay safe has dwindled somewhat. The recollection of the first time she wore it, of the fire, of Dylan being flung against the wall, of the giddying chaos, lingers in her mind still.

I'm alone up here. If something went wrong . . . But then, at least I won't be putting anyone else in danger. Not risking someone I care about. Better this way.

Tilda has also been surprised that there have been no further scary visitations from the ghost from the grave at the dig. At first she thought it might be because the stone had been firmly put back in place, but then she remembered the earlier apparitions happened before it had been moved. Thinking about it, she feels certain now that the bracelet has something to do with it. Or rather, what happens when she puts the bracelet on. And if that is the case, then she needs to learn how to withstand the disturbing force it unleashes. Needs to see if there is some way she can harness it to protect herself and Dylan.

The snow still lies thick and frozen. Everything in the little garden, from the low stone wall, the wooden gate, the flagstoned path, the small lawn and the slumbering flower beds, to the frozen birdbath, is coated in a crisp layer of icing white. The valley below, and even the lake itself, sit snugly beneath their sparkling new coat of frosting. The distant mountains appear almost Alpine. Tilda tugs her beanie lower on her head, does up the toggles of her duffle coat, and moves to stand in the centre of the lawn with her back to the house. Thistle watches her quizzically. Under the holly bush, a robin searches for something to eat. In the meadow farther down the hill, sheep bleat as they follow the farmer on his quad bike, eager for the sugar beets he is doling out of sacks into long dark lines on the snow. All is as lovely and as normal and as typical a scene of the countryside in winter as could be. All except for the shiver that travels down Tilda's spine as she takes the bracelet from her pocket. A shiver not brought about by the cold, but by a thrilling blend of anticipation, excitement, wonder and fear.

She wriggles the bracelet over her hand, her fingertips showing blue-tinged cold out of her fingerless gloves. With awkwardness, she pushes the gold band up under the sleeve of her duffle coat, beneath her fleece and thermal T-shirt, until she feels the metal's now-familiar warmth against her flesh. The transformation is immediate. Straightaway, the bracelet's charge, its energy, courses through her body, banishing the chill of the December day, filling her with a warm strength. Where the gold sits against her bare skin she feels as if she is being burned, feels certain that this time there will be a mark, a scarring from such heat. And yet she has no wish to stop it, to remove the bracelet. The pain is a price she is more than willing to pay.

She starts to hear whispering voices and to see the flitting figures and shapes once more, always moving, always on the very periphery of her vision. Beside her, Thistle begins to whimper. Tilda is aware of her dog's anxiety. She wants to say something to comfort her, to reassure her, but no words will come. Her whole being is overwhelmed by the tumultuous experience wearing the bracelet triggers. Once more, she becomes aware of a change in the quality of the light around her. Even here, outside, in the brightness of the day. There is a phosphorescence to the air that surrounds her. More movement disturbs her vision, and again the lurching giddiness threatens to take control of her stomach.

Tilda closes her eyes tightly and the shapes become instantly clearer, sharper, bolder. She sees the hares again, running, ears flat, twisting this way and that. And the hound, silent and swift. And birds again, cawing crows this time, and a buzzard casting a broad dream of a shadow with its majestic wings. Tilda searches for faces. And for the *Afanc*. She longs to find the magnificent creature. Wants to experience again its ancient, magical presence. But today it is absent, and the dancing animals move ever faster, increasing her dizziness. The ringing in her ears is building, too, quickly reaching a painful level.

It's too much. I can't control it!

Instinctively, she opens her eyes. The supernatural brightness is shocking, making her blink and gasp, her sensitive eyes smarting, her vision blurring. For a moment she fears she will fail; that all she can do is snatch off the bracelet to make it all stop. She has her hand on the gold loop, ready to wrench it from her arm, and yet she pauses.

It's not the bracelet . . . it's me. This is in me, somehow. And if that's true, then I must be able to handle it. I must!

Slowly she takes her hand away, holding her arms out to balance herself. No shapes appear in the blinding whiteness that reflects, dazzling, off the snow. No diamond-eyed woman. No mythical water-horse. Just glare and noise, both painful and overwhelming. Tilda can feel her heart thudding, the beat of it pounding against her ear drums, blood surging, the sensation of plummeting threatening to make her pass out.

No! Dammit, no!

She flings her arms wide and her head back.

'Stop!' she shouts, the word echoing around the valley, rebounding off the hills again and again, repeating and insisting. *Stop! Stop! Stop!*

And it does. Or at least, the unmanageable parts of it do. The deafening ringing noise ceases at once. The strobing whiteness fades to a softer glow. The swirling sensations and the bewildering giddiness abate, so that she stands steady now, stable, strong. She is aware of a powerful tingling in her hands and feet, and when she looks closer she sees that her fingertips are fizzing. Tiny blue flashes crackle from them, like the arcing of circuits shorting out. Tilda steps over to the snow-covered stone bird-bath on the wall and reaches out to touch it. As her fingers get close the snow recedes, melting as quickly as if she had touched it with fire. Cautiously she brings her fingertips to her cheek. There is a zinging vibration, but no pain, no burning. She looks around the garden. Thistle stands close by, her eyes never leaving her mistress. If she is frightened she does not show it.

'What is it?' she asks herself as much as the dog. 'What am I supposed to do with . . . *this*?' She flicks her right hand outward as she speaks and a burst of something invisible yet tangible flies from it, a pulsating wobble through the bright air. It connects with the holly bush, causing every flake of snow on it to explode into a million white crystals before they melt into nothing. The little plant stands out oddly, its prickly leaves glossy and green amid the whiteness. Tilda tries again. This time she carefully waves her hand at the garden bench. Although she stands three long strides from it, it is as if she is sweeping it clear of snow with a heated broom. In seconds the worn wood is exposed, and the snow at its base recedes to reveal the yellow-green grass of the lawn.

Tilda laughs, self-consciously at first, and then joyfully; a wild, visceral sound. Thistle reacts to the break in the tension and bounds about the garden, chasing the clumps of snow Tilda now flicks off the cottage roof, leaping at the showers of ice she causes to rain down from the branches of the apple tree, biting at the dozens of snowballs she hurls through the air without moving a single step from where she stands. Using nothing but the magic that fills her to the brim. Revelling in the warmth and the joy of it. Laughing through it all, happier and more complete than she has been in a very, very long time.

Christmas morning sees a cheerful sun lifting over the hill behind the cottage, its rays bouncing off the crisp layer of snow that still coats the landscape. Tilda can no longer put off leaving. She picks up the bracelet and slips it into her fleece pocket, zipping it in securely, enjoying the thrill of having it close again. Since the success of wearing it in the garden she has put it on twice more, both times outside, each time gaining a little more control, becoming a little braver, discovering more ways to use the wonderful, inexplicable changes it brings in her. She cannot bear the thought of going anywhere without it, but she knows she is not ready to tell anyone of how it changes her. Not even Dylan. More than ever she wants to know, needs to know who it belonged to. Where it came from. Why she has it. Why it releases what it does from somewhere deep inside her that she never knew existed.

In her bedroom, she stands for a moment in front of the mirror. She realizes she has not exactly dressed up for the occasion, and the thought comes to her that Dylan has only ever seen her in running gear or working clothes. Or naked. She smiles at the thought. On impulse, she undoes her hair from its plait and shakes it loose about her shoulders. It looks fine, but she knows it will be a mess by the time she reaches the Old School House. She turns to her bedside locker and slides open the drawer in it, taking out a small velvet pouch. She hesitates only a moment before shaking the contents onto her hand. The silver hairpin feels cool in her palm. It consists of delicate strands of silver worked into a beautiful Celtic knot. A present from Mat. The last thing he ever gave her. A talisman for their new life in their new home. She has not had the courage to so much as look at it since he died, but now she can. Now feels like the right time to wear it. Deftly, she twists her hair up, threading it loosely through itself, and then securing the updo with the pin at the nape of her neck.

You look okay, Tilda Fordwells. You look okay.

She has already shut down the stoves in the house and studio, so that they will still be going when she returns. She collects Thistle and a tightly wrapped package from the kitchen, locks the back door, and sets off down the hill. Thistle bounds happily at her side. The energetic pace the dog enjoys reminds Tilda how long it is since she has been for a run.

I miss it. But I'd be risking a broken leg in these conditions.

'A brisk walk will have to do us today, girl,' she tells Thistle, smiling at the animal's antics as she frisks about in the snow.

The Old School House is picture-postcard pretty, its low roof and deep-set windows thick with fluffy snow, and every plant in the garden similarly frosted and sparkling. Tilda feels a pang of guilt at having put her parents off coming. They had been disappointed, but had accepted that the roads were still bad and the weather unsettled. At least she had been able to reassure them that she was spending the day with lovely neighbours, successfully painting a picture of rural friendliness and

community spirit to comfort her father so that he wouldn't
worry about her. She takes a breath before knocking on the
arched front door.

It is Dylan who opens it. He grins at her and steps back to
let her into the hallway.

'Wow,' he says, staring at her. 'You look . . . incredible.'

Tilda shrugs. 'It's my very best duffle coat,' she tells him as
she pulls down her hood, though she knows he is not com-
menting on what she is wearing. Knows that she appears altered
in some indefinable but unmissable way.

'Merry Christmas,' he says, pointing at the mistletoe suspended from the ceiling above them. He takes her in his arms,
gently pulling her close for a warm, unhurried kiss. It feels
good to be enfolded in such easy intimacy. To be held again.
To be wanted.

'Your hair is different today,' he says, touching the pin that
holds it. 'This is pretty. It suits you.'

She feels no awkwardness at the blurring of the lines: a gift
from Mat, a kiss from Dylan. She mattered to both men, and
they both matter to her. She is relieved at how natural that pro-
gression feels now. She returns his kiss, the two of them only
jumping apart at the sound of Professor Williams's voice.

'Ah! Our guest has arrived. Splendid. A very happy Christmas to you, my dear,' he says, extending a hand and then smiling
broadly when Tilda steps up and gives him a peck on his
whiskery cheek. When he draws back and looks at her again she
sees surprise on his face and remembers her uncovered irises.

'Happy Christmas, Professor,' she says, taking off her coat.
She hands him the parcel.

'A present! My dear, we agreed not to. Dylan told me . . .'

'I know.' She smiles. 'But I wanted to. It's just a small thing,
really.'

The professor looks at Dylan, who gives him an I-knew-
nothing-about-it shrug. He takes off the brown wrapping and

finds one of Tilda's earlier works, a little pinch-pot, smooth yet irregular, the finished article still bearing the potter's thumbprints, glazed in a deep burnt umber, rich and textured.

'Well! What a truly delightful thing,' he says, beaming. 'Thank you so much. It will take pride of place on my desk. Now do come through to the sitting room, it is warmer in there,' he tells her. 'It is so very good for we men to have company today, else we might have let the occasion slip by unmarked. As it is, my brave nephew has risen to the challenge of preparing the feast.'

'Have you been trawling the shelves of the village shop again?' she asks Dylan.

'I'll have you know I went to the farmer's market for the turkey and veg, and the best baker's in town for the pudding.' He takes her coat and notices her glance at the grandfather clock.

'It's not working,' she says, a note of panic in her voice.

The professor shakes his head. 'Would you believe Dylan suddenly found himself unable to sleep through the chimes? They were practically the lullaby of his childhood, and yet now he can no longer tolerate the sound. The poor boy begged me to do something about it, so I've given the clock a week off over Christmas.'

Tilda silently mouths a thank-you to Dylan, who simply shrugs.

She reminds herself that Dylan cannot possibly know how much has changed – how much *she* has changed – in a few short days. Not so long ago she would have been nervous about causing the power to fail at the Old School House, but not now. Now she knows she is in control. Knows that it is her choice whether or not to influence such things.

'We've put up a tree,' the professor explains as he leads the way into the sitting room. Thistle makes straight for the hearth rug where she stands and shakes, sending snow and ice from her fur hissing into the fire. There is, indeed, a Christmas tree squashed into a corner, finding a space where previously there was none. It sports an eclectic selection of decorations, some evidently family treasures, others, Tilda suspects, hastily bought additions. Some rather brash tinsel is draped over the lower branches, and the look is finished off with a glitter-encrusted gold star. The effect is wonderfully homely and unpretentious.

'Not my forte, I fear,' Professor Williams apologizes. 'Greta was a whizz with such things, and I'm afraid I haven't bothered much in recent years.'

'It's lovely,' Tilda tells him. 'I haven't even put a sprig of holly up in the cottage. In fact, I think Christmas might have passed me by completely this year if I hadn't been invited here.'

'If you want something to eat,' Dylan tells her, 'I'm going to have to see to things in the kitchen. And, by the way,' he adds as he reaches the door, 'our cooker is an Aga – oil-fueled and gravity fed. Doesn't need electricity to run. Thought you'd like to know.'

Tilda is touched by his thoughtfulness.

'We shall manage without you,' the professor insists, picking up a bottle of sherry from the sideboard. 'Now then, what can I offer you to drink, and are you keen on games of any sort? I'm afraid I'm a little rusty, but I have been known to play a passable hand of Canasta. And I believe there is a box of Monopoly hiding somewhere in the house . . . ?' He stops, looking at her more closely, and noticing something more this time, something beyond the naked colourlessness of her eyes, making her wonder just how altered she appears.

Eager to smooth over the moment Tilda says, 'That book you leant me . . . the one about the myths and legends of the lake . . .'

'Ah yes, I thought you might like that one. We are not all about dates and battles, we historians, you know? My interest is in all aspects of the past. Greta being an anthropologist opened my eyes to so many things. History is primarily about people. And people are complicated beings, who lead wonderfully complex lives. A belief system, rituals, magic, things beyond rational explanation . . . these are as much a part of what has gone before us in this mysterious place as any victorious army or change of political allegiance. Dear me, I seem to be giving a lecture. I do apologize, it's just so stimulating to be in the company of someone with a genuine interest. I am enjoying researching the lake anew.'

Tilda smiles. 'Have you discovered something more about the woman in the grave? Or about the bracelet?'

'Not yet, but now that you are here to help, I believe we will make progress.'

'It would be really, *really* helpful if we could try to find some more answers about who is in that grave, and who the bracelet belonged to.'

'Excellent!' He snatches up his reading spectacles, fetches two schooners from the sideboard, and quickly pours two generous measures of treacly brown sherry. 'Here we are, let this be our concession to the festive merriment. Your very good health!' he declares, raising his glass.

Tilda gulps the sticky drink and follows Professor Williams to his desk. 'I've brought this with me again.' She takes the gold bracelet out of her pocket and puts it on the ever-present map. She is disconcerted to discover how much she hates being separated from it. 'In case we want to check the design again,' she tells the professor.

'Splendid. Now, I did come across something the other day . . . where did I put it? Oh, and you might want to have a look at this.' He hands her a book declaring itself to be *The Anglo-Saxon Chronicles*. He talks on as he searches through a pile of papers and volumes stacked on the floor and reaching half-way up the overstuffed bookcase. 'In there you'll find one of the only mentions of the crannog as inhabited. I've marked the page . . . Ah, yes, and this might be useful . . .'

While he digs on, Tilda turns to the relevant entry. 'This bit here? Yes, I see . . ."AD 917. This year was the innocent Abbot Egbert slain, before midsummer, on the sixteenth day before the calends of July. The same day was the feast of St Ciricius the Martyr, with his companions. And within three nights sent Aethelflead an army into Wales, and stormed Breconmere; and there took the king's wife with some four and thirty others." Okay, Breconmere is one of the old names for Llangors Lake, Llyn Syfaddan being another . . .'

'You've been doing your own research, I see. I am impressed.'

'But can that next part be right? Did the Queen of Mercia really attack the crannog because of a murdered abbot?'

'That is what is recorded. However, Queen Aethelflaed had been at odds with the *Cymru*, that's the Welsh, of course, for many years. It may be she used the hapless priest's killing as an excuse to cross the border.'

'And thirty-four people, no, thirty-five, including the king's wife . . .'

'In reality more likely a princess,' the professor puts in. 'We know that the crannog was built for a Welsh prince, a gift from his father, who had a region of his own to the south to worry about. Eager to have his son settled somewhere, I should imagine. And married to someone politically helpful. In such unstable times any manner of alliance that could be formed was worth a try.'

'So the princess and these few people from the actual crannog, they were taken prisoner. What happened to the others? To the rest of the villagers?'

'We must assume they were killed in the attack. The settlement on the crannog was set alight, burnt down to the wooden piles and stone base that remain. I should imagine all the dwellings along the lakeside would have been put to the torch

also. These raiding parties were not in the habit of leaving anything much aside from devastation in their wake.'

For a moment Tilda is assailed by images flashing through
her mind of what such an attack must have been like. Women
and children running. People taking to the fortified island for
safety, only to find themselves trapped. So many people killed.
In a few short minutes, everything gone. And what of the
woman in the boat? What of this other version of herself? Had
she been one of the survivors?

'Professor, is there a list anywhere that tells us about those
who were taken prisoner?'

'Not that I have been able to find, though there are some
new documents being archived at the National Library of Wales
in Aberystwyth even as we speak. The collection is being
digitalized, so that at the click of a button one can be reading words written over a millennium ago. Astonishing. Truly
astonishing.'

The professor pauses as the standard lamp beside him fizzes
alarmingly.

*No, not now. Steady. Let them work. All I have to do is let them
work.*

Tilda eyes the bracelet anxiously, wishing she could snatch it
up and hold it close, but aware that to do so would look more
than a little weird. The bulb in the lamp gives a fat popping
sound and goes dark. The rest of the lights in the room, however, brighten once more and remain steady.

'Now, this might be of interest to you.' Professor Williams
lifts up a dusty, leather-bound book and angles it so that the
light from the window falls upon the page. 'I'd quite forgotten
I had this until the other day. Written by a fellow called
Humphries. Goes on a bit, he was an expert on Ogam text.
Not much survives, but he busied himself translating whatever
he found. All sorts of snippets. He places this as dating around
914 AD, although I have to say that's probably an educated

guess. Ah, here, an entry in the monastic records of that time, curiously not in Latin, for reasons we may never discover. The writer is unknown, but he mentions a feast held by Prince Brynach ". . . on the crannog of Breconmere, and in attendance was the entirety of the village, for all were made welcome to celebrate their good fortune, and the guest who was honoured for her part in protecting the crannog was the Seer, Seren Arianaidd." There, you see?'

'Do I?'

'Your woman in the boat, I think. The one you mentioned you'd seen a picture of.'

Tilda remembers telling him this half-lie, and is at once ashamed of not trusting him with the truth, however bonkers it might have sounded at the time.

'The way you described her to me,' the professor continues, 'suggests the garb of a shaman. One given to having and interpreting visions. A very important member of society at that time. Do you recall what colour her hair was?'

Tilda hesitates. The woman in the boat had been wearing an animal skin headdress, so her hair was not visible. The vision Tilda had seen when she had put on her bracelet, that other version of herself, had, of course, had silver blonde hair the same as her own. She cannot imagine trying to explain all this to the professor as he watches her over his reading glasses, waiting for her answer.

Were there two different women, or one? Who am I looking for, myself, or a ghost, or an ancestor?

'I'm not sure,' she says at last. 'The first time I . . . I saw her, her hair was covered. After that . . . I'm not certain.'

'I only ask because, well, there are clues here as to what she must have looked like, not least in her name.'

'Really?'

'"Seren" is still a common Welsh name. It means star. Rather lovely, don't you think? "Arianaidd" on the other hand, is very unusual. I've never heard of anyone else being called that. It means "Silver". So, she was known as Star of Silver. Which suggests she would have been very fair. Not unlike yourself.'

A chill wriggles down Tilda's spine.

'But we don't know if she survived the attack on the crannog.' She sighs, then a terrible thought occurs to her. 'Lucas said something about the body in the grave at the dig. He said that sometimes people were buried with heavy stones on top of them if they were thought to have been witches. When the crannog was inhabited, would someone who had visions have been thought of as a witch?'

'A difficult question to answer. The custom of foretelling the future is such an ancient one, and one that is found in so many diverse cultures. The early Celts certainly had their shamans, and they were important people, but seeing the future was not seen as magic. More a talent, or a gift.' He gives a chuckle. 'They might perhaps have been viewed more as our weather forecasters are today.'

'So not witches, then?'

'Ah, well, witches abound in Celtic literature and many other ancient Welsh stories. And there is nothing to say a Seer cannot also be a witch.'

Tilda feels suddenly weary. She drains her glass, letting the syrupy sherry pleasantly ease her tangled thoughts. 'I'm beginning to think the more I find out, the less I understand.'

At this, the professor laughs more heartily. 'My dear girl, welcome to the world of the historian!'

Dylan has returned to stand at Tilda's elbow.

'Is my uncle making your brain ache?'

'He's trying to help, but I can't expect sensible answers if I can't even form reasonable questions,' she tells him, running a hand through her hair.

'Perhaps another sherry would help?' Professor Williams suggests.

'Wow.' Dylan is horrified. 'No wonder you're struggling. Sit yourself down. Lunch will be ages yet. I'll open a decent bottle of wine, and between us surely we can work out what it is you need to know. Okay?'

Half an hour later, at Dylan's insistence, Tilda has made a list. She is reluctant to read it out.

'It looks even crazier written down.'

The professor smiles. 'If I have learned anything from my years of study, it is that what at first appears incredible, often, when looked at from the correct angle, comes to seem entirely plausible.'

Tilda can't help wondering if his credulity would stretch far enough to believe what happens to her when she wears the bracelet.

Dylan gently takes the list from her. 'Let me,' he says. 'First up, who was the woman in the boat, and is she the same as the woman you saw the other day when you put on the bracelet?'

Tilda grimaces. 'See, I told you.' She glances at the professor. *Here goes nothing. If I want him to help me I'm going to have to tell him.*

'Professor, something strange happened when I was wearing it,' she explains. 'I saw . . . things. Saw a woman. And yes, I do think I've seen her before. That morning when I was down by the lake.'

'The morning we met, I believe,' he replies. 'I didn't know you then, of course, but it was clear to me something had shaken you.'

'I wanted to tell you, but . . .' She leaves the sentence unfinished as the professor nods his understanding.

Dylan reads on.

'Next, who is the woman in the top half of the grave being dug up? Third, were they the same person? Why is the frightening ghost trying to attack you? What was she saying when she

259

leapt at you in the studio? And last, but not least, who did the bracelet belong to?' He waves the piece of paper. 'Simple.'

'Says you.' Tilda swigs some more wine, ignoring the growling of her empty stomach. 'Actually, I don't believe the scary creature that keeps threatening me can be the same as the woman in the boat. She is terribly disfigured, her face all broken up, but no, now that I really compare the two, her body shape is all wrong. She is shorter. Fatter. And darker, I think.'

'There you go,' Dylan says. 'One question answered already.'

'So now I'm definitely dealing with two ghosts. Great. Oh, and there is something else. The scary ghost; I've been thinking about the words she spat at me in the studio. They were Welsh, I think, and very hard to make out. All I could get was something that sounded like "bewit"? Or "buwid" could it have been? I've looked, but I couldn't find anything.'

'Hmm,' the Professor, without so much as questioning the fact that Tilda is talking about more visions, more ghostly women, closes his eyes, mumbling words over and over until he comes to one he thinks could fit. 'How about *bywyd*? It means "life".'

Tilda nods. 'Yes. That could be it. She . . . the ghost . . . she said it twice.'

Dylan looks at her. 'A life for a life?'

There is an uncomfortable silence. At last, Professor Williams picks up the bracelet from the desk. He fetches a magnifying glass from the mantelpiece and sits in the armchair beside the fire to examine it again. 'I do feel some of the answers you seek lie here,' he says. 'This is a very fine piece of jewellery and would have been of considerable value. It must have been owned by someone important.'

Dylan tops up Tilda's glass. 'Do you remember seeing it on any of the women in your visions?'

'No. I'm sure I would have remembered if there had been anything like it.'

The professor holds it up to the light. 'It occurs to me that it is rather large.'

'It is.' Tilda nods. 'When I put it on, it was much too big for my wrist. I assumed it was meant as a band to wear on the upper arm.'

'Possibly.' He sits up, an idea striking him. 'Of course! It isn't a bracelet at all.'

'Not?' Tilda is confused.

'It's a torc. Look. How dim of me not to see it before. Dylan, pass me that book on the end of my desk, would you? The one with the red binding. Thank you.' He flicks through the tome until he finds what he is looking for. 'Here, see? These are plain, I know, not beautifully decorated as yours is, but the shape is identical. A loop not completely closed, rounded edges, with slight thickening at the ends. It is a torc, meant to be worn around the neck. I'm certain of it.'

'But, I'd never get that around my neck,' Tilda points out.

The professor whips off his glasses with a smile. 'That my dear, is because you are an adult. This marvellous object was made for a child.'

SEREN

Another winter has come and gone and life around the lake feels as settled and timeless as ever it was. It is hard to imagine we lived on the edge of fear for so long, anticipating disaster, awaiting danger. Is this a trick played on us all by fate? She can be a cruel mistress. Are we lulled to softness, our sword arms weakened, our vigilance dulled, only so that we may be easier prey at some future date? I am still assailed by visions of my prince's descent into the water, but it has become impossible for him to believe the threat is real. And how can I argue otherwise? As the weeks turned into months, and the seasons swing full circle once more, and life continues undisturbed, my prophecies lose their weight. Other smaller seeings have come to pass, and I continue to work my minor magic as is required of me, but on this one matter my opinion no longer holds sway. I see Rhodri plumping himself up with each passing moon, never missing an opportunity to remind Prince Brynach that it was he who brokered the deal with the Mercian Queen, he who helped him bring about this time of peace. He is ever at the prince's side, and with him Wenna, quick to parade the family bond. It is as well for her that her brother is seen as so successful, so useful, in the prince's eyes, for that other vision of mine has proven true. She has given him no heir, nor will she.

And yet, of course, her husband has a child.

Our child.

Today I have taken my daughter out fishing on the lake. She is nearly a year now, well-grown, with a head of spun-silver hair, eyes bright as diamonds, and already teetering on her feet. In the canoe she enjoys the feeling of swift movement as we paddle through the water, and later she will be rocked to sleep curled up in the bottom of the boat. She is at home near, on, or in the lake, and that is as it should be. This is our favoured hour, with the sun dropped behind the mountains, the cool of the early evening, the softened light, the day grown lazy and yawning into twilight. Only the fish are busy now, nipping at buzzing flies that hover above the surface of the water.

'Not too far, Tanwen,' I tell her as she leans over the side of our little boat to dip her fingertips in the water. She smiles up at me, and I see her father in that smile. I named her White Fire, for it suits both her appearance and her nature. A tug on the line I hold in my hand alerts me to a catch. I wait until I am sure the fish has taken the bait, and then quickly pull in the line, hand over hand, holding it high at the end so that the fine young perch dangles and flips in the air. Tanwen laughs and claps as the dappled fish showers her with droplets of water. I lower it to my feet and strike its head one clean blow with the handle of my knife. It lies still. Tanwen is not distressed by this. She has witnessed the transformation from life to death, creature to food, so many times. She understands the order of things, and she is fast learning her own place within it.

A movement on the shore takes my attention. Brynach has come to find us. He stands tall, a strong, dark figure in a wood-land lake of bluebells.

'Look, little one, there is your father,' I tell my daughter as I pick up the paddle and steer the boat across the lake. Tanwen gurgles happily as we draw closer to where he stands. He has tied his horse to a tree and waits for us, watching us closely. Or rather, watching Tanwen. Was ever a father more adoring of his child? When the boat reaches the shallows he can wait to longer, and wades into the water to greet us.

'Here come my fisher-women! What have you caught for your supper, daughter?' he asks her, grasping the prow of the canoe and scooping Tanwen from her seat with one strong arm.

I lift up the shining fish. 'Enough for three,' I tell him. The invitation to supper is as much a challenge as an offer of hos-pitality. I do not fight for his company only for myself now. I know that Wenna and Rhodri do their best to find ways to keep him from us.

He steadies the boat while I climb out. 'If it can be served without a helping of rancour I will join you,' he says. When I do not answer, he regrets his words and leans close as I tie the boat to its stake. He nuzzles my neck. 'Time spent with you is ever more memorable than time spent elsewhere.'

I push him away, more playful than sulking. 'Is my cooking so exceptional?'

'It is not,' he concedes. 'So it is a mystery why I cannot stay from you without feeling hungry.' He grabs me again and nips at my ear, jiggling Tanwen as she sits in the crook of his arm, making us both smile.

He picks a bluebell for her, handing her the pretty flower before he sits our child in his saddle, and we walk side by side as he leads the horse slowly back to my house. When I have rekindled the fire and set the fish to cook, he takes something from his saddlebag and offers it to me. It is a small object, wrapped in a piece of cloth. The wrapping itself is so carefully stitched, worked in patterns of animals with thread of gold and red and blue, that I am content to admire it without giving in to my curiosity over what it conceals.

'This is beautiful indeed, my prince. There is silk here, is there not?'

He smiles. 'The cloth is for you, my seer. A token of my love. A keepsake. Its contents are for Tanwen.'

I unfold the silky needlework and take out a smooth, heavy piece of gold, the glint of which causes me to gasp. It is a torc, fashioned with such care and artistry, I have not seen its like in my life. It bears carvings showing two running hares and a hound. Their legs, tails and heads are entwined and twisted, so that they continue on and on, with no beginning or end.

'Oh.' I find my voice at last, turning the torc over in my hand, marvelling at it. 'My prince, such a gift . . .'

'It pleases you?'

I look up at him and his face is that of a young boy, desperate for praise, so eager to please, his expression moves me more than I dare tell him. I smile and nod, and he leans over me, pointing.

'Here, this hare, that is you, see the lithe limbs and the look of courage greater than on the face of any warrior? This smaller one, that is our little witch, springing forward into life.'

'And the hound who would have us for his dinner?'

'No, he does not seek to catch you, he runs *with* you. See? He shows no teeth, and his eye looks back, not forward. He is your protector.'

'So much gold. You could feed an army for the price of this.'

'My daughter is a princess. She should be adorned as such.' He takes it from me and kneels in front of Tanwen. He lets her touch the torc, shows her the pictures, talks softly to her, making gentle, cooing noises. He lifts the golden ring and fits it into place with such care and delicacy that our babe does not protest. She puts her fingers to it, exploring the smoothness of the precious metal, picking out the carved lines upon it. But she has a young mind, and her attention is caught by a caterpillar crawling near her foot, so that she forgets what she is wearing, and hastens to catch the little creature instead. Brynach sits back on his heels, gazing at her. 'I know she is a child of the moonlight,' he says, the sadness catching in his voice. 'I understand she must live as you do, making friends of shadows and shade, happiest and safest in the soft hours of cool darkness. I know this.' He turns to me. 'But I live my life by day, Seren. And though she is in your image, she has my blood.' He nods at the golden necklace. 'Now I know she will forever have a drop of sunshine with her, however deep the night. Forever.'

18

TILDA

By the time Dylan drives Tilda home a sudden thaw has begun, so that the Land Rover swishes and slithers through slush. The cottage is dark, but the fire in the kitchen stove has kept in well, so that the house feels welcoming and warm. Even so, Dylan suggests they would be warmer in bed.

Upstairs Tilda is embarrassed to find she is nervous. Their first lovemaking had been spontaneous, without time for awkwardness. Somehow the whole business of undressing and getting into bed together is painfully intimate. She has become so used to wearing her thermals at night and having Thistle curl up on her feet. She is unsure how to behave.

Long Johns and a hairy lurcher could be passion killers. Or should he just see the real me? Whatever that is.

Picking up on her nerves, Dylan takes her hand in his. They stand beside the bed. She is in her T-shirt and underwear. He has stripped to his jeans, his body gleaming in the faltering light of the candle that burns on the bedside table. He gently unclips her silver hairpin and puts it on the bedside locker before running his fingers through her loose hair, following the irregular waves it has gained from being pinned up. 'It's been a special day,' he tells her. 'Spending Christmas with you . . .'

'The food was great,' she says, aware she is talking to fill any possible silences. 'And your uncle is so sweet. He's been such a help.'

'You saved us from a sad bachelor Christmas.'

'Thank you for the clock, what you did. Thank you for . . . everything. Putting up with all the weird stuff. Listening to me going on and on about ghosts and witches and heaven knows what . . .'

'Hey, I want to spend time with you, Tilda. I want to be with you.' He pushes her hair back off her face. 'But I know things have been tough for you. I don't want you to feel . . . pressured.'

'I don't. Oh, look, let's just get into bed, shall we? It's bloody freezing up here.'

Laughing, they dive beneath the duvet, holding each other close. Thistle comes to the side of the bed, sniffs, and turns away grumpily.

'Oh dear,' says Dylan, 'she's really going to hate me now.'

'She's gone back to the kitchen. It's warmer in there. She'll be fine.'

'And what about you?' he asks. 'Are you fine?'

She hesitates. At this moment, his arms enfolding her, safe and snug, still comforted by the kindness of the professor, Dylan's continuing help with all the frightening things that have been happening, her body well fed, the fading effects of the wine still taking the edge off her worry, she does indeed feel fine. Her answer is a slow, sensuous kiss.

'I'll take that as a "yes",' he murmurs. He pulls back to look at her in the low light. 'I know it's rude to stare,' he teases, 'but I can't stop looking at you. You are . . . fascinating. So beautiful. You look delicate, fragile, but you're one of the strongest people I've ever met.'

'It's a common misconception,' she tells him, trying not to sound like some sort of information broadcast. 'People with albinism are often seen as frail. It's one of the things other people find scary about us. About me. They are afraid I'll break.'

'But you won't. You can run farther and faster than just about anyone I know. And I've seen you wield a pick axe and a lump hammer.'

'I do have to stay out of the sun. A summer's day can make me blister, though there are some pretty good sunblocks out there now. It must have been difficult in years gone by. Imagine what it would have been like all those centuries ago.'

'You think the woman in the boat had the same condition as you?'

'Whoever I saw when I put on the bracelet – the torc – she showed every indication of having albinism.'

'It must have been hard. I mean, nobody would have understood. She would have been singled out for being so different, surely.'

'It's odd, but that would have been less problematic than it is now. It's a modern reaction, stigmatizing people who don't fit the general idea of what we should all look like. There's evidence that through the ages people who stood out were often thought of as being of special importance. Something *more* rather than something *less*.' She pauses to consider this for a moment and then goes on. 'If Seren Arianaidd was like me, and if your uncle's right and she was the local shaman, she would have been revered and respected. No, for her the hardest part of having this condition would have been protecting herself from the sun. She may have had problems with her eyesight too, but not all of us do.'

'You don't need your lenses anymore. Your eyes have got better, since you moved here.'

'Yes. They have.' She snuggles closer to him. 'You have no idea how wonderful it feels not to be hiding behind them anymore.'

A thought occurs to Dylan. 'Uncle Illtyd says the torc was

made for a child. If it has all those witchy symbols on it, and it has such an amazing effect on you when you wear it, it makes sense to think it belonged to the woman you saw, if she was a shaman and possibly a witch. So . . .'

'So she must have had a child. So, did either of them survive the attack on the crannog?'

He kisses Tilda's brow, her face, her throat. 'Because if they did,' he whispers, 'then maybe, just maybe, Seren also had grandchildren, and great-grandchildren.' He kisses her collarbone, slipping off her shoulder straps, moving lower, 'and so on, down, down, down through the ages, generation after generation, until we get to . . .' He looks up at her, smiling.

Tilda smiles back. 'Me. Until we get to me.'

SEREN

Tanwen plays happily with the flowers outside our little home. There is such joy to be found in watching an inquisitive young mind snatching at everything life offers. Her fascination with the petals of a buttercup, her wonder at the wings of a butterfly, her fury at the sting of a nettle – with each new experience she grows. Already I can see the light of magic in her eyes. She was blessed by the Afanc and she is my daughter, but more than this, she has the gift in her own soul. I will nurture it as I cherish her, and one day she will be my worthy successor.

She hears, no, *senses* someone approach. I follow the turn of her head and soon spy Nesta tramping into view. I am quick to attribute my child's sharpness to her singular blood, but in truth, a cloth-eared drunkard at the bottom of a barrel could hear the princess's maid stumbling along the path. She is carrying a wicker basket holding something heavy within. The day is falling into dusk, but still I can make out an uncharacteristic smile upon her plump face.

'Good day to you, Seren Arianaidd,' she calls. 'And to you, little one. How pretty she is grown.'

I raise my brows. This attempt at cordial behaviour toward me – toward us – is as easy to see through as a glassful of lake water. When I do not return her greeting, however, she does not let slip her mask of friendliness. 'Forgive me for not calling upon you these long months past, Prophet. My mistress likes me ever at her side.'

'And she did not wish to visit?' The mockery in my question is a challenge, but one she is clearly prepared for.'

'On this occasion,' she says, lowering her voice a little, 'I act of my own accord. My mistress knows not of my wish to speak with you. I have slipped away unnoticed.'

This I find hard to believe, but I will play the game and see what it is she wants of me. For Nesta does nothing that does not forward the cause of Nesta, however indirectly.

'Won't you sit?' I gesture at the blanket upon the ground. It is too warm for a fire yet, but there are cushions and it is a pleasant spot to rest. With some huffing and puffing, she lowers herself onto the red and green wool. She smiles at Tanwen, who stares back for a moment, decides the woman is of no interest and goes back to her flowers.

I sit opposite Nesta. 'You are not given to visits without purpose,' I point out. 'What is it you want of me?'

'Oh, nothing,' she protests. 'That is, nothing for myself. As I have said, I come here without my lady's knowing, but it is for

270

her benefit I come. And for yours too, I believe.' She pauses to order her thoughts, or possibly recall a speech committed to memory, and then continues. 'My mistress does not, for reasons you will understand, feel she can come to you herself. That does not mean, however, that you are not in her thoughts.'

'I am certain she has an opinion of me. I'm not certain I need telling of it.'

'Yours is, after all, a . . . prickly situation.'

This makes me laugh aloud, causing Tanwen to look up and smile, and making our visitor scowl. 'You have many skills, Nesta, I will allow that. But diplomacy is not one of them. It may be the princess should have sent her brother to pour syrupy words in my ear.'

'I tell you, the princess does not know I have sought you out.' This time her voice has her more customary sourness in it. Her patience is already wearing thin. 'I have come because I want only what is best for my princess. And I come to speak to you as one witch to another.'

Now it is my turn to frown. 'Witch I may be, and you have a skill with potions and poultices, but do not confuse your talents with my gift, maid-of-the-princess. I would not lower myself to whisper the dark words you call magic. It is a base and dangerous art. You and I are not equals, nor will we ever be.'

Nesta squirms upon her ample backside, her fierce dislike of me doing its best to claw its way to the surface, while some pressing need for her to remain pleasant pushes it back down.

'Forgive me,' she simpers, 'My eagerness to win you to my cause is making me clumsy.' She hesitates and watches Tanwen for a moment. 'She is so very like you,' she says, 'and yet, there is something of her father about her also. It is there for all to see,' she adds, turning her piggy eyes back on me to make the point.

'Her parentage is no secret,' I say.

'Indeed it is not. And my mistress has accepted this fact.'

'Has she a choice?'

'She has . . . allowed things to be as they are.'

'How could she do otherwise?'

'She could put more obstacles between you and her husband. See that he visits you less frequently. Find further ways to hinder him coming to your door.'

'*More* obstacles? *Further* ways? You give the truth an airing with every word you utter, despite your attempts to the contrary. The princess tolerates Prince Brynach's love for me and his desire to be with his daughter because there is no alternative available to her.'

'She endures the situation with dignity, as befits a princess!'

'Should I be grateful for it?'

'Do you steal another woman's husband with such an easy conscience?'

'Prince Brynach is not anyone's possession that he might be stolen. He bestows his affection where he chooses. He spends time with his child, as any loving father would.'

'And any loving mother would want the best for their daughter, certainly.'

'Of course. I am no different from any parent in this.'

'And yet, perhaps you do not see how you stand in the way of your child's possible betterment. Of her birthright.'

Now we are come to it. There is weight behind these words, and Nesta sees that I have felt it.

'I have at the heart of my every waking moment a fervent wish for all that is good for my daughter. I am ever striving to see her well fed, well clothed, well loved. She wants for nothing, and she learns what she needs to learn.'

'It is true you equip her to be a shaman. A witch. To live apart as you do. To follow the path of your life, and yet . . .'

'And yet? Spit out what it is you came to say, Nesta Meredith, before it sticks in your throat and chokes you.'

'There is a way you can do what is most generous for all concerned in this matter. A way you can make an easier life for the prince. A happier life for the princess. A royal life for your precious child.'

She waits while I sift through the grit of what she is telling me. Of what she is suggesting. My mouth dries at the thought of it. My heart pounds. I pray my face does not betray my anger. My fear.

'You have come here, to my home, to tell me I should give up my child? Give her up to Wenna?!'

'Think of it. Do not let your heart rule you, but only think of it. Your daughter has royal blood in her veins. She is of Brynach's line. You and I both know Princess Wenna will never give him an heir. He adores the child. She is his *princess*. And my mistress is not as cold as you would have her be. Her longing for a child is only in part to secure her position. She is a woman, and she craves a babe to hold in her arms, to mother. She would take her husband's child into her home, she would raise her as her own, even as she is . . .'

'Even as she is!' I can contain myself no longer and leap to my feet. 'In one breath you bid me part with my very heart, and in the next you pierce it with your barbed observations! How could Wenna love a child that is the reflection of the woman who has her husband's desire, his passion, his love? How could I give up my own blood into that nest of vipers, none of whom would truly accept her as their own, but always see her as something fearsome? Something from another realm altogether. I would not condemn her to such an existence for all the gold and furs and fine silks such privilege could bring. You talk of her birthright, well it is here. With me! She is a born witch, she has the gift of magic in her, even you can see that. And I will raise her as a shaman, which is what she is destined to be!'

Nesta's face sets hard. Her mouth closes in a firm, thin line. Her eyes are like currents in dough. She looks away. Her shoulders slump. She is defeated.

'I see your mind is fixed,' she says quietly. 'You are not to be persuaded, not even for the sake of the child.'

'It is for the sake of the child that I refuse such a proposition.'

She nods, slowly. 'I had hoped to return to my mistress with my task a success.' She smiles almost wistfully. 'Imagine how such news as I would take her would gladden her poor heart! She has been a good mistress to me all these years, never belittled me, always treated me with kindness. Affection, even. I had so hoped to bring her joy, to see her happy again.'

'We are each mistresses of our own happiness. We ought not to look to others to supply it.'

Nesta gets stiffly to her feet. 'I see that you will not consider the merits of my plan, and it is clear you refuse me not from malice or spite, but for love of your child. I believe you are wrong, and that she would fare better in life were she to take her place with the prince, but I cannot deny your intentions are true. You act as your own conscience bids you.'

'I do,' I say, instinctively stepping between Nesta and Tanwen.

The woman picks up her basket and holds it to me. It is made of plaited wicker, with a curved handle, the top narrower than the base, and has a cloth tucked over the contents.

'At least take this token from me, to know that there is no ill will left after my . . . disappointment. You may refuse me the status of your equal, my seer, but you will surely not deny we are women both, at the mercy of those we love, working only to protect and care for them. Here, some beer and honeyed bread for yourself and the babe.'

I want nothing from her, but nor do I wish to inflame her dislike of me further. I reach out my hand toward the basket. As I do so, Tanwen stops playing and looks up at me. Her bright eyes are wide and fierce, and as she stares at me I experience a sudden wild seeing. There flashes before my eyes a vision of startling clarity, fleeting, but powerful. I see a scarlet sky, the red of pain, with black tendrils of a monstrous ivy twisting and tightening, robbing the air from the night, bringing death with them. I gasp, and stay my hand.

'What manner of gift is this? There is agony and death in that basket, wise-woman!'

Her face darkens and she opens her mouth to speak, but her words are silenced by the thundering of hooves as Hywel and a fellow soldier come riding to my door. He springs down from the saddle, surprisingly nimble for one so large. I no longer have a guard watching over me day and night, but still Hywel takes it upon himself to see for himself that I am safe whenever he can.

'What strange alliance is this?' he asks. He knows well that I do not trust Nesta, and she has never made any secret of her hatred for me. I wonder if word had reached him of her making her way to my house.

Nesta backs away. 'I came to visit Seren Arianaidd, bringing my mistress's good wishes.'

'Ha!' Hywel barks, 'that is not a thing I find easy to believe!'

'Liar!' I spit at her. 'You claimed the princess knew nothing of your intention to put your cruel plan to me. And when I would not listen you sought to do me harm.'

'That is not true!' she protests. 'I came in good faith. I brought a little bread I baked myself . . .'

'And what poison did you add to the mix?' I demand.

'None! See here . . .' She pulls off the cloth cover and breaks off a piece of the honeyed bread, stuffing it into her mouth before she can be stopped. She chews noisily, and swallows. We watch, waiting for some dire effect to take place, but nothing happens. 'See?' she sneers at us. 'You accuse me falsely! The princess will hear of this. Your treatment of me will not go unnoticed.' She makes to push past us, but Hywel blocks her way.

'Why the sudden haste to leave, if your calling on our prophet was such a friendly event? Here, let me try that.' He reaches into the basket and helps himself to a mouthful of bread. Nesta does not attempt to stop him, but I see her eyes widen.

'Hywel,' I say, 'do not . . .'

But he is already chewing thoughtfully. He shrugs. 'In truth it is good. Try ...' He takes the basket from Nesta and plunges his hand into it once more to fetch a piece of bread for me. But this time he cries out, frowning, snatching back his hand. 'What is this?!' he roars.

And then I see what it is. I see the two tiny wounds upon his flesh, neat and deep, where the fangs of a viper have pierced his skin. Chaos enfolds us. Hywel curses, clutching at his hand and letting go the basket. The soldier leaps from his horse, but knows not what he should do. The snake wriggles from beneath the discarded basket, sliding toward Tanwen.

Nesta cries out, 'The babe!'

But I have no fear. My daughter watches the adder slither over her bare feet but she neither screams nor cries. She knows instinctively that this creature should be shown respect, but that it will not hurt her if she does nothing to scare it. The soldier has no such understanding and raises his sword. I would save the poor thing, but he is too swift and in a second has cut it in two. Hywel writhes on the floor, trying to take his knife from his belt to cut out the poison, but his agony is too great.

'That is no ordinary snake!' he bellows. 'No viper ever gave such a bite! That witch has hexed the thing.'

I drop to my knees beside him, taking my own blade from my hip and slicing into the already purple flesh around the wound. But Hywel is right in what he says. This is no common poison. Nesta has done something to make the snake more powerful, has worked some wicked magic, dark and strong. The matter makes sense to me now, for the snake was intended for my hand, was meant to sink its fangs into my flesh, and she knew she would need something more deadly than a lowly adder to take my life. Behind me I hear her lumbering through the tall grasses as she tries to flee. Let her try. The soldier will soon have hold of her, and she will be dragged back to the crannog for justice. My concern is for Hywel.

'Lie still,' I tell him, as he tries to rise.

'I never in my life fought a battle lying down!' he argues.

'This once you must!' I push him firmly back onto the grass. 'Cease struggling, Hywel. The poison must not be made to flow more quickly through your body.' I steady my mind. I need to summon my witch's strength, to cast my own spell to counter that of Nesta, but there is no time. No time to prepare a potion to help him. No time to call upon the old gods to assist me. No time to undo what has been done. Even now an evil stench begins to pour forth from Hywel's hand, and his skin is turning blackish-brown down the length of his arm.

'The crone has done for me!' he yells through teeth clenched tight.

'No! Only give me time . . .'

'There is none.' He clutches at my arm. 'Seren Arianaidd, this death was meant for you! The woman brought that cursed creature to send you from this world. Argh!' He breaks off, his face twisted in pain. I start to recite an ancient prayer of protection, tripping over the words I know so well in my haste to help him, to do something to ease his suffering. 'Beware!' he growls. 'She will not have come without her mistress sent her. The princess wants you dead, girl. Be ever on your guard.'

'I will have you to protect me awhile yet, Hywel,' I tell him, placing my hands over his heart, calling on the magic of the lake and the gentle presence of the Afanc herself to come to my aid and rid this poor, dear man of the vile substance that seeks to silence him.

He shakes his head, wildly thrashing from side to side, foam flecking his beard, his eyes, burning, raging against death's approach. He has been a warrior all his life, and knows nothing but to fight until his last breath. 'God's truth! Let that witch be put to death so she may do no more harm. Yet even then you must not turn your back on Wenna for an instant, for she will be ever waiting, dagger raised. The prince needs you. He needs the child. You cannot let down your guard. You must not. Give me your word!'

'But Hywel . . .'

'Your word!'

'You have it!'

He beats his fist upon the ground, roaring, defying death to the very end. And at the last he does not seek comfort, does not search for pity, but raises his one good hand in a salute and bellows into the fading summer day, 'Prince Brynach! My Prince! Prince Brynach!' And even as light of life leaves his eyes his battle cry continues to echo, on and on, around the shores of the lake.

19

TILDA

The day after Boxing Day Tilda stands shivering at the bus stop in Llangors, her stomach turning over as she waits for the bus that will take her to Brecon. She thought of asking Dylan to take her. Thought of asking the professor. Even contemplated seeking out Lucas in case he could help. In the end though, this is something she needs to do on her own. For many reasons, not the least of them being her need to prove to herself that she can.

Don't need my hand held anymore. A short bus ride, slow and safe, most likely lots of other people on board. Got to be independent. I can do this. I managed in the Land Rover.

In fact, when the bus arrives, the only other passengers are two holiday-bored, stir-crazy teenagers no doubt desperate to escape the slow pace of life in the village for a few hours. Tilda buys her ticket and sits at the front, near the driver, silently chiding herself for feeling as nervous as she does, but noticing that she is less anxious than she expected to be. It could be the sedate speed the bus moves. Or the fact that, ghostly apparitions aside, the journey to Brecon with Dylan was manageable. And yet, she knows that in fact it is something else. There is another change. A fading. A lessening. The sharply painful memory of Mat's death is receding into the past. Her grief for him has become more distant. For a moment this makes her feel sad, as if she is losing the last of him, but the panic passes. It is as it should be. It is time.

The countryside that moves slowly past her window is still snowy, but has lost much of its festive charm. There is a sense of the thick layers over fields and hills shrinking and shrivelling, rather than melting softly away. The result is a muddy mess in gateways and on tracks, and grey slush alongside the gritted tarmac of the roads. On the broad oaks, branches poke their elbows through worn, snowy sleeves.

Her second reason for wanting to make this trip alone has to do with her purpose in going to town. The curator of the museum had been surprised to get her phone call on the dot of nine o'clock, pointing out that they had very few visitors or enquiries at this time of year. It had taken some persuading to agree to allow Tilda access to the archives. Most members of staff were on holiday, he had explained, and as this was the quiet season many of the exhibits were being restored or cleaned. Tilda had pleaded her case, telling him of her ceramic art, of an upcoming exhibition, of her urgent need for details and references as far back as possible connected to the crannog. In the end her sincere interest in the subject and her fervent desire to discover hidden facts had appealed to the archivist in him, and he had agreed to her request.

I told him it would be just me. I know if I'd told the professor what I'm doing he would have wanted to come, and I can't risk the curator changing his mind.

She feels bad about being secretive. Both Professor Williams and Dylan have been so supportive, so understanding. But that is the other point; the other reason she needs to go alone. If the bracelet (or the torc, as she must now think of it) can cause such mind-blowing reactions in her, what if there is something in the museum collection, some seemingly simple object, that connects with her in a similar way? She needs to allow that

link to be made, to pick up on whatever is there. More important, she needs to be able to stay in control of whatever happens.
She knows she will be better able to do that if she is on her
own.

The journey takes only twenty minutes, but still Tilda is
relieved when the bus swings into the line of bays near the
main car park that constitutes the bus station. As she steps out
through the automatic door she finds her palms are damp with
sweat and her knuckles white from being clenched. The short,
chilly walk to the museum helps to calm her a little. There is
scarcely anyone about, the streets all but empty save for the
occasional dog-walker or bleary-eyed holiday maker clutching
top-up supplies of bread and milk from the ever-open supermarket. Tilda is only vaguely aware of the curious glances
thrown in her direction. Her hair is mostly covered by her
warm hat, and her duffle coat and scarf hide her further. Only
a person passing close by on the pavement would be able to
see the strange paleness of her skin and the startling trans-
parency of her eyes. She is, as she had anticipated, the only
visitor to the museum. Mr. Reynolds looks up from behind the
reception desk, sees her, reacts minutely, recovers himself and
musters a practiced smile.

'Good morning,' he says in a tuneful, youthful voice, despite
clearly being near retirement age. He is tall, angular, with a
lifetime of careful reading etched into his lean face. 'Miss
Fordwells, is it?'

'Please, call me Tilda.' She offers her hand and he shakes it
briefly, falling into distracted chatter, as many people do to
cover their unease on first seeing her.

'As I mentioned on the telephone, we seldom have visitors
so close to Christmas Day. I only open up because, you know,
I have things to do, and if I'm here we may as well be available to the public. Now, if I can just ask for £3.50 for your
admission ticket . . . ?'

'Of course.' She fumbles for the money with cold fingers. 'It's good of you to give me access to the archive. I really do appreciate it.'

'We are here to assist in any way we can, and my goodness, if we can't help a local artist draw inspiration from our heritage then we wouldn't be doing our job at all well, would we? You say your particular area of interest is Llangors Lake?'

'That's right, and the crannog. I'm really keen to find out about the people who lived there right at the end. Just before it was attacked by the army from Mercia.'

'Ah, Aethelflaed struck a cruel blow. It was never inhabited again after that, you know?'

'I understand the buildings were destroyed. Everything was burned, wasn't it?'

'They could have been rebuilt. And the crannog itself remained intact. As I'm sure you will have seen. No, I think it was the thought of that terrible day. So many slaughtered. There simply wasn't the desire to live there anymore. Now, I'll just drop the latch on the door for five minutes while I take you downstairs.' He picks up a large ring of keys and a clipboard with papers and pen attached. 'Follow me, please.'

He leads the way briskly through the main exhibition area of the museum. Tilda has to almost trot to keep up. They pass back through history with each exhibit, the Victorian schoolroom, the agricultural implements, the historical mountaineering, the shepherds and the drovers, all a blur of telescoped time as they descend to the basement.

'Ordinarily,' Mr Reynolds explains, 'the artifacts and objects from our early medieval lake exhibit are kept in the blue room, on the second floor, but that is currently being refurbished. We have brought everything down here for safekeeping for the time being. And we're taking the opportunity to give some items a bit of a once-over.' He comes to a halt and gestures at a dowdy-looking mannequin dressed in a rough woollen kirtle and cape. 'Poor old Mair could do with a bit of TLC. I don't think the real inhabitants of the crannog would have been as troubled by the moth as we are!'

'No?'

He shakes his head. 'Much too cold, and their homes far too draughty and damp. Well, here we are.' He throws numerous switches and now Tilda can see large boards showing artists' impressions of how the dwellings might have looked on the crannog in the tenth century. There are three other models, all similarly dressed to Mair, sitting or standing in disconcertingly lifelike poses, as if they are patiently waiting to be spruced up and put back on display. There are boxed up, labelled parts of the collection stacked at the end of the room, and several small display cabinets containing fragments of pottery or jewellery or weapons.

'These might be of special interest to you, I believe,' the curator tells her, removing a pile of leaflets from the glass lid of one of the displays. 'Some rather fine examples of Celtic knot-work here. And the fabulous remnant of gold-threaded cloth that was found on the crannog itself. Quite remarkable.'

Tilda is doing her best to listen, and to appear attentive, but in truth she cannot take her eyes off the main exhibit, which currently stands along the right-hand wall of the basement room.

'Ah, I see you like our canoe.' There is unmistakable pride in Mr Reynolds' voice. 'So marvellously preserved. Hardened and brought to such a shine by its centuries in the water.'

'It's incredible. Is it really over a thousand years old?'

'Carbon dating says so, and science is rarely wrong in these matters. I think we can safely say that Mair here might have gone fishing on the lake in something very similar.' He glances at his watch before holding the clipboard out in front of Tilda. 'If you wouldn't mind just signing this. We try to keep paper-work to a minimum, but still we need forms and signatures, no getting around it. Here, and here, thank you. Just to say you are who you are, and at the address you gave me over the phone. Then if the canoe goes missing we'll know where to come, won't we?' He laughs merrily at his own joke and then hastens away, eager to unlock the door again in case another visitor should appear. 'Come up when you're ready,' he calls over his shoulder, closing the heavy basement fire-door behind him.

Once he has gone, Tilda slips off her duffle coat, draping it over a nearby chair, and steps closer to the slender dugout boat. Its centuries in the water have darkened the wood to a rich, treacly brown, with what she sees more as a gleam than a shine. The grain of the wood is still detectable, the narrow-spaced lines forming flowing patterns along the length of the canoe. She knows at once that this is identical to the boat she saw on the lake. The boat in which she first saw Seren. It is about ten feet long and just wide enough to sit in.

The information note beside it says it could carry three people, and that it would have sat very low in the water. Already she can hear the now-familiar distant ringing noise. She has the torc in her pocket, but does not dare take it out for fear of damaging any of the exhibits. Tentatively, she reaches out and lays her fingertips on the smooth edge of the boat. It feels warm, and hard as stone. There is a vibration running through it, as if someone has struck a tuning fork. Even this feels some-how distant, not in space, but in time, as if the thrumming of the wood is an echo of ancient days when the canoe was paddled across the lake. She can almost hear the sound of the silky water lapping and rippling as the boat cut through it. She begins to feel light-headed and quickly steps back, turning away from the dugout.

Stay focused, girl. You're here for a reason.

Tempting as it is to spend her allotted time connecting with the wonderful relics and finds in the archive, she has only a few short hours, and a glance at the rows of books and files on the shelves tells her she has her work cut out for her. She begins scanning the titles, searching for data specific to the sacking of the crannog, and the prisoners being taken by Queen Aethelflaed's men.

Who survived? Did Seren? Was there a child? And if there was, did he or she make it off the crannog, or did they perish too?

Tilda already knows from her conversations with the professor that the prince for whom the royal dwelling on the crannog was built is thought to have fallen in the battle. There is no record of him living beyond that date. What seems certain is that his wife, the princess, was among the prisoners.

But who else? Who else?

She pulls a box file of dusty documents from the shelf declaring themselves to be pertinent to the lake and bearing the dates *900–920 AD*. It seems as good a place to start as any. She finds a chair and pulls it up to one of the sturdier display cabinets which she uses as a desk, spreading out the papers and files, poring over them, her eyes straining for mentions of crannog dwellers, prisoners, and, ever hopeful, shamans and witches. A plain-faced clock on the far wall marks the passing of the first hour. And the next. Tilda works on, taking care to replace the documents in the order she finds them, making notes in her notebook of any details that seem relevant or helpful, though it is hard to find anything beyond what she and Professor Williams have already unearthed. The chair soon becomes cripplingly uncomfortable, and she wishes she had brought more than a bottle of water to sustain her. She repeatedly stumbles upon the reference made in the *Anglo-Saxon Chronicles*. She knows how many people were taken, and where they were taken to. But then the trail goes cold. She sighs, stretching her aching back.

Nothing. Not a single, solitary damn clue.

She turns to look again at the boat. There is something so beautiful about its simplicity of design coupled with the certain solemnity given it by its great age. Tilda cannot resist going back to touch it again.

'Are you Seren's boat?' she wonders aloud, her voice startlingly loud in the hush of the basement. She is suddenly seized by the urge to climb into the canoe. Experiencing a flash of terror at being caught taking such a liberty with a priceless museum exhibit, she knows as soon as the idea comes to her that this is what she must do. She pulls off her shoes and carefully steps into the shallow hollow of the narrow boat, steadying herself on the side, and desperately hoping that the stands on which the thing is displayed are strong enough to support the extra weight. There is an alarming creaking sound, but once she is sitting still the canoe feels stable. Once again the boat starts to sing, and soon Tilda's vision starts to blur and she begins to feel dizzy.

Just like with the torc. Should I put it on? Dare I?

It occurs to her that the combined effects of the torc and the boat together might prove overwhelming. The thought should terrify her, but it does not. In a moment of shining clarity she sees what it is she has to do. Sees how it is she will find the answers to her questions. Taking a long, slow breath, she removes the torc from her pocket and slips it onto her arm. She keeps her eyes open as long as she can, bracing herself against the swirling, lurching sensations and blurred sounds that assail her. Her mouth is horribly dry. Her brow is damp with perspiration. The lights of the basement room flicker and their artificial illumination is replaced by a brightness so white and so strong it makes her flinch. Her fingers begin to tingle, the sensation quickly increasing to an uncomfortable level.

Okay. I'm ready. Show me. Show me Seren's child! Show me what happened!

Tilda closes her eyes.

There is a shocking sensory assault as images of indistinct faces, of malformed animals, of eerie sounds and distorted words engulf her. A fleeting sight of the terrifying face of the witch from the dig almost startles her into opening her eyes, and she fights the urge to cry out, but it passes quickly. One moment the spectre is there and the next it is gone again. Tilda forces herself to keep her eyes shut tight. For she knows this is how she will see, will *truly* see. She struggles to make out definite shapes among the phantasmagoria that dances in her pulsating vision.

'Where are you?' she whispers. 'Where are you?'

And as suddenly as the mayhem began, it subsides. Images recede, colours fade, until there is only a gently undulating blue light. And into this light comes a figure. Tall. Slender. Her hair braided with leather. Her eyes dark with kohl. Her skin patterned with bold tattoos.

'Seren!'

Seren walks toward Tilda, her piercing eyes aglow, holding Tilda's own bewitched gaze, demanding that she continue to look. Tilda gasps as she sees that Seren is holding a small child by the hand. The little girl walks calmly beside her mother, her own silvery hair loose and wild, a happy smile upon her lips. The pair stands for a moment until the picture begins to shake and to judder and there comes the sound of thundering hooves. Seren lets go of the child's hand and clutches at her stomach. Appalled, Tilda watches as blood pours between her fingers, soaking her hands, flowing unstoppably, so that Seren staggers backward, growing fainter, melting into the darkening blue behind her. The child remains, continuing to stare at Tilda. All sounds cease. The vision becomes clear and still. For a blissful moment, Tilda looks into the eyes of Seren's daughter and finds a connection of such sweetness it makes her cry.

And then it stops. Everything stops. Tilda opens her eyes, wiping her tears on her sleeve, blinking as her sight adjusts to the more ordinary light of the museum basement. The vision was so strong, so vivid, so loud, that she is amazed to find that it has not brought Mr Reynolds running.

But he couldn't hear it. Of course he couldn't. Only me. I saw them. I saw them both.

On returning to the cottage, Tilda feels completely exhausted. She phones Dylan to put off his visit, claiming a light cold, and takes a long shower in an attempt to shake off the curious sense of dread that the vision has left her with. Her mind is a whirl of confusing thoughts. She should be so happy that she has seen the child, Seren's child, but that happiness is tainted by the sight of Seren dying such a brutal and violent death. Tilda goes back into the studio and tries to work, but nothing will go right. She replays in her mind the scene she witnessed, over and over. She knows now, beyond any doubt, that Seren had a little girl. And the vision seemed to suggest that the child did not die with her mother.

But does that mean she survived the attack on the crannog or not? I still can't be certain.

Later, she takes Thistle for a walk. She deliberately avoids the lake, mostly because it would be more than a little awkward if Dylan were to see her out and about, but also because, just for a while, she needs a bit of distance between herself and all that the lake signifies. Needs a break from the intensity of it all. She and the dog tramp up through the watery snow, following the sheep track behind the house. They climb for nearly an hour before resting on a crumbled bit of stone wall. The view of the valley is quite magnificent, even as the snow recedes and decays by the minute. The lake looks so much smaller from such a height, giving Tilda just the perspective she needs at this moment. From here the grave at the dig is hardly visible at all. As if it had never been found and disturbed. Or as if it had never been there in the first place. She wishes that were the case. She knows, deep down, that she will have to face whatever lies there. It will not leave her alone unless she does. It will have to be confronted.

But not today. Not now.

She sits and takes in the magical landscape for as long as her woolly layers keep out the cold, and then descends to the cottage to stoke the fires and make something to eat.

Come the night, despite being exhausted, Tilda's mind is working too fast, trying to make too many connections, for her to be able to rest. An hour before dawn she gives up and gets out of bed. Thistle raises her head and wags her tail.

'Don't get up, girl,' Tilda tells her. 'It's silly o'clock. I'm going to make tea.' But the dog won't be left behind and pads down the stairs after her. In the kitchen, Tilda puts the kettle on the heat and takes a poker to the Rayburn to ginger it up. The smouldering logs give out more smoke and then splutter into hungry tongues of flame. Staring at the play of orange against grey, Tilda contemplates her next step. She had left the museum disturbed, saddened, and yet encouraged. There *was* a child. That much is clear. What is equally obvious is that she will get no further tracing the little girl by digging around in the museum archives. She reached the end of that particular trail.

But where else do I search? I've tried the records and writing about the Mercian court, but the captives are never mentioned again. There's a heap of stuff about the queen and what she does, but not a word about the people from the crannog.

A spitting log causes a spark to jump out of the open door. Tilda searches for it on the floor and is surprised not to be able to find it. It was a large, glowing lump of wood, and she is certain it landed by her feet, but it is nowhere to be seen. Following the smell of burning dog hair, she goes to Thistle's cushion, and is surprised to discover the spark quietly setting fire to the fabric. She picks up the cushion and flicks the little ember back into the fire, musing at how far from the Rayburn it travelled. She rubs at the cloth with her thumb. There is a small hole and a scorch mark but no real damage. Suddenly, something in Tilda's mind shifts.

Of course! I'm looking in the wrong place! The prisoners aren't written about by people who documented the life of Queen Aethelflaed because they weren't with Queen Aethelflaed.

She peers across the gloom of the kitchen. Her laptop is still sitting on the worktop where it has been for weeks.

Could I get that thing to work? I haven't tried for a while. Could I keep it working? Of course I could. Just an hour or so. Piece of cake.

Before she has a chance to change her mind, Tilda snatches up the laptop, sets it down on the table, opens it and presses the on button. There is a pause, then a hopeful whirring, and the computer begins to fire up. She backs away, making the tea quietly, as if the slightest sudden sound or movement on her part might shut the laptop down again. By the time she has stirred milk into her drink, the screen is cheerfully displaying her chosen wallpaper; a photograph of the sun setting over the frozen lake.

And now I need Wi-Fi. Which means I have to get the electricity running again.

She goes into the hallway and stands under the fuse box. She has grown accustomed to living in the house without power, and the main switch is still in the off position where she left it weeks ago. She bites her lip, willing herself to stay calm. Stay focused. Holding her breath, she takes hold of the lever and pulls it down. The lights come on. The long-forgotten fridge hums. Next to the telephone socket on the hall table, the Internet router blinks into life. And then there is a sharp snap, and everything goes dark once more.

Dammit!

She stands there in the darkness, quelling the urge to scream. *How can I be so useless? Why can't I control this thing? The power stayed on at the professor's house. And I stopped that floodlight falling. This should be easy.*

The realization comes to her. She is not wearing the torc. She hurries into the kitchen and fetches it from her bedside table.

'Right, Thistle,' she says as she passes the dog on her way back to the hall, 'hold on to yourself.' With a determined step, she goes straight to the fuse box, clutching the torc tightly in one hand, and throws the switch a second time. The power is restored. She nods.

Good. That's good. Okay.

Back at her computer she is uncertain as to how best to hold the piece of jewellery and type at the same time. She is reluctant to put it down, feeling the need for direct contact with it, but at the same time she doesn't want to put it on again. She can't imagine trying to search the Internet in the midst of the magic released by the torc. She settles for resting the thing in her lap as she works. Within minutes, she has found a plethora of historical Websites dealing with early ninth-century Britain.

So much information! Getting through this lot could take forever.

With a sigh, she ploughs on, scrolling through document after document, frustrated by wrong turns and details that seem to duplicate themselves. She reads on, her eyes watering a little at the unfamiliar brightness of the screen. Half an hour passes. An hour. She makes a second cup of tea and works on, encouraged by the fact that the power has remained stable, but daunted by the size of the task she has undertaken. She returns to her seat and continues. She learns more and more about the people who lived around the lake in the early years of the tenth century. About how hard their lives were. About how they lived, and what dangers they faced from warring armies, harsh winters, and disease. She reads about how they dressed, what manner of music they made, and their beliefs. She has just reached a file containing information regarding the final attack on the prince's dwelling on the little island when the lights flicker ominously.

No, not now! Not yet.

She reads on. She finds the extract from *The Anglo-Saxon Chronicles* that the professor had marked for her, telling of the prisoners taken from the crannog.

'Thirty-four, plus the princess,' she reads out to a slumbering Thistle. 'Yes, I know, I know, but who were those prisoners? Were any of them children?' She reads on, but can find nothing. The same dead end she came up against at the museum. Nothing more. She leans back in her chair, the hard wood beginning to make her back ache. Setting her mind to the problem, she pictures the small group of villagers as they were taken away from their homes. She knows they would have been a pathetic collection of people. People who had just lost everything. Many would have seen their loved ones slaughtered. Some might have been injured. Their lives were in chaos. They were being dragged away. But how long did they spend at the court of the Mercian queen?

Basically, they were slaves, and slaves get sold. So where did they go next? Who was trading with Aethelflaed? Where would she have got a good price for them? I just need to look in the right place.

She tries a different search, using the words *slave, Cymru, Aethelflaed* and *trading*. Reams more of irrelevant data unscrolls in front of her. A page detailing the queen's origins catches her eye. Aethelflaed was the daughter of Alfred the Great, and originated in the south of England. She lived there until she entered her arranged marriage into the Mercian dynasty.

Which means she would have had strong connections with the area. Probably relations still living down there too.

She shifts the region of her search to Wessex, the ancient collection of counties that included the city of Winchester, where Alfred came from. An essay on the family of the famous English king shed some light – there were certainly several cousins from the same generation as Aethelflaed, and they lived on in Wessex. A small, slightly clunky Website run by a group of Alfred enthusiasts and re-enactors snags her attention. There is an account of a household near the city, known to have royal connections, giving an insight into the everyday lives of the highborn of the time. Tucked away in all the data regarding births, marriages, wars and burials, there is a seemingly insignificant account of a party of visitors arriving from Mercia.

Bingo!

A small file, summarizing a change of ownership attached to four slaves, sent as a gift from the queen to her cousin in Wessex. In 918 AD, less than two years after the attack on the lake settlement, she sent a present of a handful of young slaves to Egberta of Wessex, who had a home midway between Winchester and London. Tilda squints at the screen, her eyes smarting now, blurring her vision slightly.

'Here it is! "One young man, with red beard; one boy not yet fifteen, but strong . . ."'

There is a fizzing sound and the screen goes blank.

'No!!' She looks up. The power is still on, but the lights flicker and stutter. 'Not now!' She takes a deep breath, knowing she must not get upset, must stay steady and calm, but it is so hard to do so.

I need to know who else was on that list! For God's sake, just a few more moments!

Thistle gets up from her bed, coming to nudge Tilda's leg.

'I can't keep it working! I can't keep the fucking thing working!' She stands up, gritting her teeth. 'Okay. If that's what I have to do . . .' She picks up the torc and quickly pushes the heavy loop of gold onto her wrist. She waits. Nothing happens. Everything is quiet.

Too quiet.

It is the in-breath before the scream.

The room is filled with the roaring of a fierce wind, a sound from nowhere, a cacophonous noise that makes Tilda throw her hands over her ears. Thistle dives beneath the table. Tilda can feel the force of a gale against her face, but sees that this time nothing in the kitchen is being disturbed. Everything remains still. No cups crash to the ground, no books fly from the shelves, even the undrawn curtains do not so much as flutter. And yet she is painfully aware of a brutal force pushing against her, a pressing down, a buffeting and pounding. But it is only she who feels it. Only she who finds herself pulled this way and that, the breath all but knocked from her, the shrill sound growing inside her head. And then come the faces. Two, three, ten, dozens of faces, flashing before her, some old, some laughing, others crying, all with eyes staring intently at her, into her, questioning, probing. And their voices, mangled words and utterances in many languages, all gabbling and spitting at her, demanding of her, though she cannot understand what it is they are saying, what it is they want. She fears she will go mad, will finally lose her mind. She lurches forward, the whole room spinning, or is it she who spins? Nausea threatens to swamp her. A dizziness begins to take hold. In desperation she grasps the torc, ready to pull it from her arm. But then she sees another face among the many. A face she knows. Pale, and beautiful, and steady, returning her own gaze, unfaltering, knowing, strong.

Tilda chokes down panic and forces herself to let go of the torc. She pushes against the table, making herself stand upright, straight, using the power of her strong body to hold herself steady.

'Enough!' she shouts into the maelstrom. 'I've had enough!'

It is as if all the air has been sucked from the room. There is a dazzling flash of whiteness. And then nothing. Silence. Everything as it was. Except that the laptop beeps gently back to life.

Tilda slumps onto the kitchen chair and frantically clicks points on the screen, searching for the document she was reading, dreading that it will somehow be lost.

'No! Here it is, here! "... a boy not yet fifteen but strong and with green eyes; a woman past thirty but with good teeth; and a girl child, no more than three years, very pale, with hair clear as glass and eyes to match ..."' Tilda leans back in her seat, a tearful smile tugging at her mouth. 'Found you,' she says quietly. 'I've found you.'

20

TILDA

Pulling on her running thermals and outer layers, Tilda deftly secures her hair in a single plait. Dylan has stayed the night again and is still sleeping deeply. It gives her such comfort, such joy to see him lying there, familiar, strong, peaceful.

And mine? Is he mine? Have we really come so far so soon? I should be panicking, surely. I should be, but I'm not. And that's bloody amazing.

The previous night he had arrived with the dusk, the old Land Rover skidding up the lane over the dwindling snow. He had brought beer and a takeaway curry, which they had shared in front of the fire in the sitting room. Tilda had wanted to tell him so much about what had happened to her since she last saw him – about the way the torc brought about such changes in her and the incredible things she was able to do when she wore it. But sitting there, devouring the delicious, spicy food, relaxed by the warmth of the fire and the strong bitter ale, she could not bring herself to ruin the peace of the moment. Could not embark on the difficult task of explaining the inexplicable.

Instead, she had told him about her discovery regarding Seren's child.

'So you really could be her descendant?'

'It is possible.'

He grinned. 'So you really could be a witch?'

Tilda tried to find something flippant to say, something that would mask how much this question disturbed her. Nothing helpful offered itself, and Dylan was quick to pick up on her silence.

'Tilda?' He shifted his position next to her on the sofa, drawing back a little so that he could study her expression. 'You have seriously been thinking about that, haven't you?'

She shakes her head and takes another swig of beer. 'It's ridiculous. Impossible.'

'Yeah, right. Just as impossible as whatever it was that flung me against that wall. Or set fire to this room. Or made those lights fall on me.'

She turned to face him quickly. 'The lights fell because of whatever . . . whoever it is in the grave.'

'A witch, we think, don't we?'

'So you're saying I could be like that? Do stuff to hurt people? Terrify people the way that ghost does?'

'Whoa! No, of course not.'

'Because sometimes it does feel as if when people are around me . . . bad things happen.' She had said it without thinking. Without realizing that she was talking about Mat as well as Dylan. And that he didn't see that. How could he?

'That's rubbish,' he said.

'You don't understand. It's not just you. My husband, Mat . . . the way he died, in an accident . . .'

'Tilda, an accident is nobody's fault.'

'But, perhaps . . . if there's something bad in me . . .'

He put his hands firmly on her shoulders. 'Listen to me. Lots of people feel guilty when someone they love dies. It's a natural reaction, but of course it wasn't your fault. And it . . . your husband's death, it has nothing to do with what happened at the dig, Okay? Bad things happen to good people, that's all.'

'You can't know how much I need to believe that. I don't feel anything . . . bad.' She hesitated, still unsure how much she wanted to share with him. Still aware, even with what he has witnessed, of how crazy it would all sound. 'What I felt when I put the torc on my arm . . . that time in here with you . . . What I'm saying is, it wasn't *bad*. Scary, yes, a bit, and weird, God knows, but not bad. Do you understand?'

He nodded slowly. 'There is nothing bad in you, Tilda. If you've found some, I dunno, let's call it *magic* in that bracelet, that torc, then it stands to reason it would be something . . . wonderful. Like you.' He paused, then went on, 'You must miss him very much. Mat. It can't have been easy for you, starting a new life here without him.'

'It wasn't. It took me a long time to feel . . . right. But, you know, I do think I belong. I always thought that. And now it makes more sense. And . . .'

He waited, watching, and she could sense how much what she was saying mattered to him.

'. . . and it is getting easier,' she told him, with a faltering smile. 'I do feel differently now.'

Later, in the quiet watches of the night, she had thought about how deeply she had come to care about Dylan, and how much the fact that he tried to understand meant to her. She had at last begun to let go of Mat, and it was Dylan who had helped her do that. She decided that it was up to her to act. To protect them both. She knew he would want to help, but she knew also that she was not going to put him in danger. Being close to her put him at risk, the falling lights had shown her that.

Once downstairs she hesitates, but there is no decision to be made. She knows what she has to do. Tomorrow Lucas will resume the dig and remove the body. She has to act now. She slips the gold torc into her fleece pocket and jams on her beanie. Thistle stretches elaborately and stands wagging at the back door.

'Okay, you can come, but it's been thawing, there's not much snow left to play in,' Tilda warns her. She crouches down and hugs the dog. 'You know what? I could do with a bit of help today.'

Outside, the snow has shrivelled off the tarmac of the lane, but remains in slushy lumps on the fields and paths. By the time they reach the track around the lake, a steady drizzle has begun. Tilda regrets not putting on a waterproof jacket, but knows her fleece will keep out the wet for the hour or so she plans to be out, and she can move faster like this. If Thistle minds the rain she doesn't show it, but bounds happily along beside her mistress.

It is so good to be running again! Come on, fleet, old feet. Pace, push, breathe. Pace, push, breathe. One step at a time. That's how to tackle stuff. One thing at a time.

She runs on. The countryside looks drab as the snow is melted by the rain, turning the scenery from white to grey. On the lake, geese take to the deeper water, grateful for the thaw, untroubled by the lack of sparkle or sunshine. A long-legged heron prods around in the shallows. Tilda allows herself to revisit what she's learned over the last couple of days. Seren did not survive the attack; she has to accept that was what she was shown in the vision in the museum. She had a baby daughter, and that child was taken prisoner, and later sent to live in Wessex.

So, the line continued. It really can be true. They are my ancestors. My family. All this crazy stuff, all the different ways I have felt connected since I came here — the designs on my ceramics and the torc; what the torc does for me; what I've seen; Seren, even the terrible being from the dig — it's all because this is where everything started. This is where I started. This is where I belong, and where that mad spark of magic in me came from. Seren. The Afanc. The lake. Me. Here.

The notion that she is descended from the woman she saw in the boat, from the woman who she sees when she puts a loop of gold around her arm, somehow this makes sense of everything. She was meant to live here, in this magical place. She was meant to reconnect with her heritage. She cannot believe that coincidence alone has brought her here. She and Mat had visited the area several times before buying the cottage, and she had always felt an inexplicable affinity with the place. An affinity that surprised her, given her fear of water. When they had found Ty Gwyn, the cottage had felt so right, almost as if it had been waiting for them. But she had dismissed this feeling as one hundreds of house hunters experience after months of looking for their perfect home.

Only for me, it was more than that. This is my home.

And Thistle had found the torc.

And I found Thistle. Or did she find me, I wonder?

The timing of the dig seemed to be another factor that had heightened the chances of such a strong connection being made with the past. The ghost of the person in the grave was being disturbed, and that disturbance had led it to seek out Tilda.

Why me? What did my ancestor have to do with the person in the grave? There must have been something that happened, something huge.

She stops running. Thistle stops too, looking at her, ears pricked, waiting.

'We have to go to the grave.' She forms the statement aloud to the dog, but it is herself she needs confirmation from. 'Tomorrow they'll lift the body out. After that, well, there'll be no getting the genie back in the bottle. Think I'd rather face her now, when that heavy stone weighs things a little in my favour.' She turns down the path that will take her to the dig site. The going is horribly slippery, and the rain has increased so that it is starting to work through the fabric of her clothing.

She spits away the water that courses down her face and increases her speed. As she approaches, she is relieved to see that the site is deserted. She imagines everyone will be away celebrating Christmas with their families for as long as possible before returning to raise the remains. There is something eerie about the empty tent, the abandoned trench and the general feeling of loneliness that permeates the place. She sets her mind against the wriggle of fear that is working its way in.

This is no time to get jittery. I can do this. I have to do this. That thing has got to see that I'm not going to be terrified by it anymore. That it has to leave me alone. I'm ready for it now. I'm not the defenceless person it thinks I am.

She reaches the grave. Lucas has covered it over with polythene sheeting, pinned down with tent pegs and weighted at the corners with hefty stones. The earth around the whole area is horribly churned up from all the activity of the preceding few weeks, followed by the harsh weather, and now the sudden thaw and heavy rain. Thistle stands close to Tilda, her body tense.

'It's going to be okay, girl. You'll see,' she assures her, hoping the dog cannot sense the extent of her own anxiety. She pulls out the pegs, moves the rocks and peels back the plastic. It makes an unpleasant rattle as she folds it into an untidy heap, a sound that seems startlingly loud amid the quiet of the early morning. Now the large, flat stone that pins the body in place is revealed. Tilda quells a shudder at the thought of what that stone signifies, of what must have happened.

Now, what? Do I stand here and talk to . . . to what?

She waits, astonished to find that she actually wants the fearsome ghost to appear. That unless it does, she cannot confront it. She feels her stomach turning over. It would be so easy for her nerve to fail her. So easy to turn and run back along the shortest route to home.

But I can't.

She closes her eyes for a moment, trying to picture Seren.

Are you here? I need you now. I need your help to do this. Isn't this what you want? Isn't this what you brought me here for? Where are you?

She opens her eyes again. Nothing stirs, save a noisy mallard in the reed beds behind her. With a sinking heart, she realizes what it is she has to do. If she is to confront whatever lies in the grave, she is going to have to set it free herself. She jumps down into the trench and kneels on the slimy mud. Thistle begins to whimper. Tilda ignores her and takes hold of the edge of the stone, pushing at it with as much force as she can muster. It does not move. Not one inch. She redoubles her efforts, tries again, gasping and cursing as she strains against the hateful stone.

It's not budging. Dammit. I need a lever.

She looks around and spies some tools leaning against some stacked boards by the fence. There is a broom, the handle of which is only wood and would surely snap under such pressure. There is a spade with a good sharp blade, but still, she fears, it would not be up to the task.

'Look, Thistle, this will do! A pickaxe. Just the tool for the job.' She knows she sounds ridiculously cheerful.

And it's fooling no one.

Back in the trench she works the point of the pickaxe beneath a corner of the stone, then she stands on the other end of the metal head, using her weight to try to pry up the slab. This time it gives a little. Not enough to open the hole properly, but enough to fidget and nudge the stone a fraction to one side. Even so, with this method it will take more time and more energy than Tilda has to remove the thing completely. She steps back, using her soggy sleeve to wipe rain and sweat from her face. There is nothing else for it, she will have to use the torc to help her.

She takes it out of her zipped fleece pocket. She is not wearing gloves, and the moment it touches her skin, she feels a zing of energy pulse through her. It makes her hesitate. She begins to doubt her ability to control its force, to steer its power in the direction she needs it to go. In the kitchen she had marshalled it, had mastered it, but only just. And that was at home. This time she is standing in the grave of someone who wishes her ill. Her running clothes are properly saturated now, and she starts to shiver.

'This is rubbish,' she declares. 'I'm cold, I'm tired and I'm scared. Let's get this thing done.'

So saying, she shoves the torc over her wrist. It catches on the fluffy thickness of her fleece, so that she can jam it no farther than her wrist. She hopes it will stay in place. All at once there comes the swirling sensation, as if she is on a fairground ride, and everything around her blurs and spins. She plants her feet firmly on the uneven ground, taking hold of the pickaxe once more. This time, coloured light pulsates in front of her.

Wow. This is what I imagine a bad trip feels like. Okay, just ignore it; stay focused.

As she slides the iron spike under the stone she can hear her own heartbeat echoing in her ears, pounding erratically and at a worrying speed. She tries to ignore it, pulling all her attention to shifting the heavy weight at her feet, willing herself to use whatever it is that is inside her.

'Come on!' she shouts through the lashing rain. Setting her teeth, she hauls on the axe handle. 'Move, you bloody piece of . . . Move!'

There is a grating noise, rough stone sliding over grit and mud and bone, and then it is done. The momentum of the slab's own weight once it is in motion carries it over the edge of the grave so that it slews sideways into the dirt. And the tangled skeleton, twisted and broken, is exposed.

Tilda is just on the point of crouching down, reaching her hand toward the dark, stained bones, when she is knocked off her feet. She is flung backward, and lands heavily on the hardest, stoniest part of the trench. Winded, unable to draw a breath, the air driven from her lungs by the force with which she struck the ground, she clutches at her chest, struggling to make her body work again and take in oxygen. As she thrashes about in the freezing earth she turns onto her stomach, pushing herself up onto her knees, and all the time she can feel it coming, can feel the rotten soul of the long-dead witch in the grave rising up to loom over her.

Thistle barks madly, the only time in her life she has ever made such a sound. Tilda at last gulps air and leaps from the trench at the very moment the pickaxe swings through the air, embedding itself in the ground where only seconds ago she had been. She tries to see where her assailant is, to pinpoint its shape among the dark, choking mass that has risen from the grave. She cannot make out a proper form, but only glimpses part of a smashed jaw here, a blood-filled eye there, a gaping, broken mouth in front of her one minute and vanished the next. It takes a superhuman effort for her to hold her ground, to stand straight and tall and force herself to remain where she is. The dog is snapping and growling at nothing, driven almost insane with fear and an instinct to protect its mistress. Suddenly the ghost's face takes shape and spews forth ancient words, some Tilda recognizes as Welsh, others that seem even more ancient, all spat with the same hot hatred and rage.

It's too strong! I shouldn't have let it out. I was stupid to think I could deal with it on my own!

The apparition comes closer and closer, thrusting its face at Tilda. She is too petrified to move. She tries to do whatever it was she managed to do in the garden when she used the torc's energy to clear the snow, or in the kitchen when she used it more subtly to control the electricity, but her head is filled with the screaming and screeching of the ghost, her body weakened by terror and by the numbing cold that has taken hold of her.

'What do you want from me?!' she yells into the chaotic,

shifting being in front of her. 'Whatever happened to you has nothing to do with me, you hear? Leave me alone! Leave me alone!' As she screams at it, she clutches at the torc, raising her arm, hoping against hope that it will protect her.

The ghoulish being screams back at her, repeating the words she had spat in her face the time she appeared in the studio.

'I don't understand! Stop it! Seren, where are you? Why don't you help me?'

At the sound of the shaman's name, the ghost from the grave roars with fury, sending one of the trench planks flying through the air to strike Tilda fiercely across the knees. She falls to the ground, groaning in pain.

And the torc falls from her wrist.

The ghost storms forward, raising up the pickaxe once more, this time gripping it in its phantom hands. Tilda can't get up. She gropes in the mud, searching desperately for the gold band, but can't find it, expecting at any second to feel the steel of the axe chopping into her back.

With a fierce growl, Thistle attacks the fiendish thing that is trying to kill her beloved mistress. The dog hurls itself at the ghoul, snarling and biting and tearing at the insubstantial substance of which the terrible creature is made. The brave hound cannot hope to inflict any real injury on such a spectral form, but her actions cause it to pause, to turn. Tilda scrambles to her feet, abandoning her hunt for the torc, and sets off running as fast as the slippery ground will let her. As she looks back she sees with horror that the ghost has changed the swing of the pickaxe so that it descends in a swift, deadly arc, that finds its end point in the soft, yielding fur of the dog. Thistle lets out a heartbreaking yelp and falls to the ground.

'No!!! You cruel bitch!' she screams, maddened by sorrow for her dog and frustration at her own powerlessness. Without thinking, not stopping to consider what she is doing, she turns again and runs at the witch.

The ghost turns its mangled, pulpy face to Tilda and grins a terrible, joyless grin. It slowly spreads its arms wide and then brings them forward and up in one sudden movement. Tilda skids to a stop and watches in horror as the metal tent pegs that had been securing the polythene rise up from the ground. They hover in the air and then turn, their points facing her as if directed by some unseen magnet. The quiver, all two, maybe three dozen of them, and in that half second she understands what is about to happen and throws herself onto the ground. She feels the whooshing of the steel spikes as they fly over her head. Peering up, she can see Thistle lying lifeless in the sullied snow. The evil witch lowers her head and begins her charge. Tilda hauls herself to her feet and she runs. She runs faster than she has ever run before, arms and legs powering her over the stony, icy path, lungs working hard and furious, head down, not once pausing to look back, for she knows to do so would cost her precious seconds.

She takes the lower path, the easiest route back around the lake. The creature is gaining on her with every step. More and more objects are flung at her, stones, lumps of wood, whistling past her head, some striking her back, her elbow, her leg. She can see the disused boat house to her left.

Can I get to it? Would I be able to keep her out if I got in there? Would it make any difference?

There is no time to even think of an alternative. She breathes deeper, faster, pushing herself into a sprint. All the time she is aware of the creature behind her getting closer and closer. Soon it is so close she can smell its foul breath and feel the heat of its unnatural form. Tilda reaches the door of the boat house and yanks the rotten handle, scrabbling to pull the door open on its rusted hinges. It drags against the mud, so that she is only able to open it a few inches. She has no choice but to force herself through the gap, scraping her face, her hands, her leg as she flings herself inside.

She turns to try to pull the door shut, but to her amazement the ghost does not attempt to follow her in. Instead, it slams the door behind her. Slams it with such force that the entire building shakes. There follows the sound of stones and mud and wood being thrown against the door. Piled up against it. The door buckles and creaks, some of its planks splintering, but it holds.

And suddenly there is silence. Only the sound of the rain pounding on the old tin roof, and Tilda's own ragged, near hysterical breathing. She waits, listening. But she knows, just *knows* that the thing from the grave has gone. Cautiously, she tries the door. It is stuck solid, completely jammed by the weight of all that has been stacked up in front of it.

It doesn't want me dead. Not yet, at any rate. It wants me trapped. But why? Why?

SEREN

We meet at dawn. And what a violent daybreak greets us, the sky streaked crimson and scarlet, as if the day itself is full of pain and rage. It is close to midsummer, so that the night is confined to the smaller number of hours, and we are up from our beds early this morning to lay Hywel Gruffydd in his final resting place. Every man, woman and child has turned out to pay their respects. The procession makes its sorrowful progress from the crannog and along the shore of the lake, coming to a halt but a few strides from my own house. There was much said and many voices raised in the choosing of the site for Hywel's grave. He lived his life a Christian, and the priest argued he should be given a place next to the church, so that he might be in God's keeping, he said, and comforted by the sound of the monks' prayers.

Brynach wanted a warrior's burial for him in a grand tomb. I told them Hywel did not require comfort but vengeance. On this point we finally agreed. When the punishment for his killer was decided, there was no question of him being buried with the Christians. Their god has not the stomach for the punishment meted out by the Old Religion. The priest backed down quickly enough when he understood what is to be done. What has to be done.

Hywel had neither wife nor children of his own. He saw his prince as his reason for being on this earth. He and Brynach loved each other as warriors, as brothers, and now the prince is bereft. His heart will ache, and there will forever be a space at his table now. When all are assembled at the appointed place, Hywel's coffin is lowered into the deep wound in the earth that awaits it. The priest stands close and says his words. Many of the women and children weep. Brynach and his soldiers stand steady and quiet but they cannot hide the pain of loss they are suffering. When the Christian rites have been observed I step forward. I am not wearing my ceremonial headdress this day, for the occasion is too sombre, too personal. Instead I have dressed in my red woollen cloak, my hood up to cover my hair. I lead Tanwen by the hand, moving slowly so that she can walk the short distance to the grave. She, too, wears a cape of red wool, given her by her father, to match mine, but her hood is down, so that her bright hair gleams in the sunlight, as does the golden torc at her throat. It is fitting that we should act for Hywel together. He loved her, and he died protecting me. She will one day take my place as shaman. There is much she must learn.

The hole has been dug deep. The lid of the coffin remains drawn back so that we might say our farewells. Hywel lies, arms crossed, his sword in his hand, grave goods placed all around him — silver plates, goblets, weapons, a fine robe — he will not want for anything in the afterlife. He did not fear death. No man who still has the Old Religion in his heart has reason to. He knew he would be welcomed, be revered. The sadness for him was that he did not die a warrior's death in battle. And that he has left his prince's side. The bitterness we must live with is that he was so cruelly sent from this world by wickedness. And I, I must endure the knowledge that his life was forfeit for mine. Nothing Brynach says can remove that painful truth from me.

There is silence as I pray for his soul, as I ask for him to be honoured in the Otherworld. Tanwen is sensitive to the mood of the gathering and to my own disposition. She, too, stands quietly, peering down at the figure she knows so well, her expression questioning his lack of movement. At last she squeezes my hand a little tighter and whispers, 'Sleeping!' Together we kneel on the gritty rim of the grave. Tanwen drops in a single white bloom, lily of the valley, for its purity and its sweet scent. I lean down and carefully put into Hywel's hand a small stone jar with a wooden stopper. This is no ordinary pot. It contains a potion heavy with magic. I have worked a spell into it, fixed with poison from the deadly nightshade, and drops of juice from the roots of the oak, and water from the very bottom of the sacred lake, and magic words older than any of these things. Magic to keep him safe in his slumbers. For to gain his justice, his vengeance, he must withstand such evil company that he cannot be left unprotected. Tanwen and I return to stand at our place close to the royal party. Wenna does not meet my eye. How could she? She and I both know who sent Nesta with her cursed serpent. Still Brynach does not wish to hear ill of his wife, and chooses to believe that the maid acted on her own, out of ambition, and out of jealousy of me. I have no proof, of course. He is deaf to this particular truth, and I fear this is in part due to the guilt that gnaws at him every time he looks at the barren wife he does not love. Every time he turns from her to me. But I have seen the truth of it now. Rhodri's success in negotiating a pact with the Queen Aethelfaed was to further his own ends, for he knows his wife's marriage is no longer sufficient to secure his family's position of power. Nesta came to me at Wenna's behest; and Wenna was acting on her brother's urging. The peace Prince Brynach is so content with is built on ground less firm, less stable than the sucking marshes on the north side of the lake. If Rhodri cannot be rid of me, and rid of Tanwen, the Queen of Mercia will act. I know it. I have seen it. I understand my vision clearly now. This truce has served only to allow time to pass. Time that has no doubt served the Mercian ruler's own needs as she builds her army. Rhodri has betrayed his brother-in-law, I am certain of it. The man stinks of betrayal.

Two carpenters drop nimbly into the grave and hammer on the lid of the casket. Once they are out, a layer of good Welsh soil is spread atop it, packed gently, and covered with small stones from the lake, and yet more earth.

Now the mood of the assembled company changes. They are no longer here to say good-bye to the prince's most trusted swordsman. They are no longer here to mourn their friend and send him to the Otherworld with their prayers and their blessings. Now they are here to see justice done. A high price will be paid to avenge Hywel, the suffering will be great, but it is no more than the wretch who murdered him – who would have murdered me – deserves.

Brynach raises his hand as a signal. 'Bring forth the witch!' he commands.

From the very back of the crowd three burly soldiers emerge, dragging Nesta between them. Her hands are tied behind her back, and her mouth is tightly gagged. She has spent these past days chained in a pig sty, coming out only for the swift trial where no one spoke in her defence. She raged and howled and insisted she was doing only as her mistress bid her, and that as a maid she had no choice but to obey. She might have saved her breath. Prince Brynach called such words treason and vile betrayal. Told her she was wicked to her bones and sought only to further her own cause by killing me. Nesta wept and begged to see the princess, refusing to accept that her mistress had abandoned her to her fate. All the while I had to remain vigilant, offering my own words of prayer and protection, surrounding the traitorous witch with lake water and blessed bones to prevent her using her dark magic. Nesta's guilt was never in question. Sentence was passed. And now her hour is come.

It is Rhodri who stands and delivers the reasons for the woman's execution. His voice is stern, clear and forceful. He serves his office well. How does it sit with his conscience, I wonder, knowing that he is as much responsible for Nesta's end as his sister? If justice were truly to be served, Wenna and Rhodri would also be facing their deaths now, hands tied, fear loosening their bowels. Instead, as the strong hide behind their privilege, yet again it is the weak who must pay the price.

Nesta shakes her head and cries out through her gag. The prince indicates that it should be removed.

'Say what you must,' he instructs her.

She turns, weeping, to the mistress she professed to love. I do believe she was sincere in this, at least until the point when the princess chose not to defend her, not in any way to help her, if only to lessen the severity of her punishment.

'My Princess,' she trembles as she speaks, 'have I not been a true and loyal servant to you all these years? Does it count for naught that I have tended to you, comforted you, been your helpmate and your friend through so many travails? Have I not kept your secrets safe and done everything I could for your happiness? Can you not find it in your heart to help me now? Will you not speak for me?'

The princess does not answer, only turns her head away.

Nesta cries out. 'What manner of woman are you? Have you no pity?'

'Enough!' Rhodri seeks to silence her, bidding the guards replace her gag, but Nesta wriggles from their grasp long enough to say more.

'You!' She directs her rage at me now. 'If you had only thought of someone other than yourself Hywel would still be alive. This need never have come to pass! None of it! It is your selfishness, Seren Arianaidd, that has been the cause of this!'

'Be silent, woman!' Brynach tells her. 'Let the execution proceed.'

Nesta snarls, her face contorting. The sky darkens as a flock of rooks rise up from the woods and fly so thick and so many that they block out the sun's rays. She raises her voice, fuelled by hatred and her own fear. 'A curse upon you! A curse upon all your children, and their children! May they never know peace. May they none of them live to see their own young grown! May they die in terror and screaming, each and every one of them!'

It is a terrible curse. Such a legacy of dread and sorrow! All around people gasp and cry out, some of the children weeping. And all of them look at me, for had she not seconds before named me as the reason for all that we stand witness to?

'Silence her!' Brynach shouts.

But I know the truth of it. I saw where she directed her nightmare curse, I saw whose eye she hooked with her wild stare, whose future she blighted. And the words were not meant for me, but for Wenna and her brother, and his son.

The guards, aided by a shaken Rhodri, grapple with Nesta, tying her gag so tight as she struggles that I hear the cracking of her jawbone. They spin her on her heel and push her head-long into the grave. Quickly, they turn and lift the great flat stone that lies upon the grass beside the grave. We can all hear Nesta's muffled cries as she tries to get to her feet, but before she has time to do so, the stone is dropped into place on top of her. Mothers cover their children's ears. Some among us cheer, letting go their grief at losing Hywel, finding a way to vent their impotent rage. Others fall silent, lowering their heads, sickened by the suffering man is able to inflict upon his own kind. The priest prays. The soldiers in the ranks behind where the prince stands bang their shields with their swords, drowning out Nesta's pitiful cries and moans. Noises that are soon enough smothered by the soil and stones shovelled into the grave. In less than two minutes it is done. The opening is closed. The earth has swallowed two more bodies. Hywel will have made his journey a hero. Nesta will stay where she lies. And the rest of us must continue with our lives, bearing our loss and carrying our guilt. And Rhodri must live in hope that our prayers and that brutal stone are sufficient to trap the witch's magic, else her curse will be visited upon his family, and I would not place a wager on Siōn living to see another summer.

21

TILDA

Now she begins to examine her prison. Her eyes adjust to the gloom so that she can make out a corrugated iron roof – which resounds to the beating of the relentless icy rain upon it – and wooden walls on three sides, one containing the barred door. The small window above where she sits is too narrow to pass through and too high to reach. The slimy floor on which she sits is actually a platform, an indoor jetty providing covered access to the space where a boat could be moored. But there is no boat, has not been for years. Decades. Just an empty rectangle of dark, evil-smelling water that laps at the rotting planks only a few short yards below Tilda's feet. This entrance to the boat house may once have let in light, but was long ago boarded up, from the ceiling to the water, so that only an uneven sliver of grey, a subtle lightening of the gloom, can be seen. The water at this point is overgrown with a tangle of reeds and rushes, so that it resembles more a swamp than a lake. With mounting horror Tilda realizes that the only possible way out is through that deep, weed-filled, treacherous water. She sits, benumbed by what has happened, stunned into motionless terror, her ears filled with the near-deafening sound of the incessant rain beating upon the old tin roof.

No one would hear me above the noise of this rain, no matter if I screamed my head off. And who would there be, anyway? In all the time I've been running this way, I've never met anyone so far from the footpath.

It is as if she has always known that one day it would come to this. One day she would have to face it. Her darkest fear has been there to test her from a distance all her life. Years of imagining, thinking, wondering what it would be like to be swallowed up by the waves, or swept away by a fast-flowing river, or held beneath the sunny surface of a sparkling swimming pool, all have led to this place, this moment.

Gingerly, she moves toward the edge of the jetty. Her fingers are already losing their colour in the damp chill. She crouches then sits, lowering her feet into the water. The intense cold is a shock. Her breathing accelerates as she twists around and lowers herself over the edge and in. The jetty is slimy with algae and her fingers start to slip. She gasps, clawing at the wet wood, but cannot get a firm grip. With a feeble splash she slides into the water, bursting into tears of relief and terror as her feet find the silty lake bed. The water level is just above her waist. Raising her arms, elbows bent, she edges toward the entrance, inching her way along the uneven surface. The sloping uneven surface. By the time she reaches the gable end of the boat house the water is up to her armpits. She knows she is in danger of hyperventilating. Of being sick. Of fainting.

No, no, no, no! Mustn't trip, mustn't stumble. Small steps. Come on feet, pretend we're running. Running in slow motion. Fleet feet. Strong steps. One foot in front of the other.

She pushes through the reeds, causing small waves to bounce back at her from the timber walls. She raises her chin as the water sloshes against her face. With every step she fights rising panic. Panic that threatens to send her falling into the water. Panic that might be the finish of her.

She reaches the low boards that block the exit. The moment has come. Now she must dive beneath the water, push through into the unknown, fight the tangle of weeds and swim to the outside. She knows if she thinks about it longer she will not move, so in one desperate, sudden action she forces herself under the surface. The sensation of going beneath the water is more that she can stand. She loses her balance, falling through the twisted undergrowth, her feet sliding so that she disappears into the brackish blackness. She reacts as she has always feared she will, as she has always imagined so vividly in her night-mares. She inhales. The mouthful of water becomes a lungful in a soundless scream of terror. Tilda feels time stop. Her intel-lect tells her she must get up, must break the surface, must push up, grab something, find air. Her instinct tells her to fight and flail and clutch and claw. But the blackness is enticing, the silence seductive. And the cold, the bone-deep cold, has her in its tight embrace, numbing her will as well as her body.

As she sinks down deeper into the cold blackness of the lake, Tilda thinks about how people say you see your whole life flash before you when you die. But no images of her childhood appear, no snatches of teenage romances, or family moments, or first foreign holidays. Nothing. It is more, she decides, as if she is watching her own death from a distance. As if she is a detached witness to the event, rather than the main player. She is not aware of any fear, nor pain. Just the seductive power of the cold, and the light-headedness a lack of oxygen is currently bringing about. She knows time must be passing at the usual rate, and that all she is experiencing is happening in seconds, and yet it feels as if these particular seconds have been stretched. As if down here, in the quiet darkness, everything moves to a different rhythm. Even her own heartbeat, which echoes softly against her ear-drums, seems to have slowed effortlessly.

Her mind is able to drift back to the moment in the boat-house when she knew she could not wait for rescue. She had sat and shivered on the wet, slippery boards of the small building, trying to see why the ghost had not killed her. Without the torc, without poor Thistle, Tilda was defenceless. She was easy prey. And yet the apparition from the grave had chosen to leave her trapped, rather than deliver a fatal blow. It made no sense, after all the other attacks, after what had happened when Lucas had lifted the gravestone, the way the creature had menaced and hounded her, why had it pulled back this time? She had made herself find possible explanations.

It only wanted to scare me. But why? And it certainly felt like it was going to kill me when it swung the pickaxe at me. But perhaps I could have still reached the torc. Is that what it wants? The words it shouted at me, Life for a life, *the professor said. But is it likely Seren killed the woman in that grave? If Lucas's theory is right, and she was being punished, I don't see how Seren can have been responsible for putting her there, so why would she come after her descendants?*

The more she had turned the matter over and over in her mind, the more she had heard those words. *A life for a life.*

She wants someone dead, but not me. Wants someone's life, but not mine. Who, then? Who else can have a connection? Professor Williams says his family came from north Wales, not around here. And his wife, Greta, she and her brother, Dylan's dad, they came from Winchester. Not Wales at all, but Hampshire.

It was then she had seen it. A possible link. A small, fragile thread, but something that just might tie the past to the present in a way none of them had thought about before.

Winchester. The capital of Wessex. The place of the Queen of Mercia's birth. And the place where she sent some of her slaves. Not just Seren's daughter, but others from the crannog. Who were they? I must be able to remember. A middle-aged woman, and a teenage boy. With bright green eyes. Like Dylan's. Oh my God! All the time, the link was there and I didn't see it. Professor Williams said Greta had wanted to move to the lake. That she had felt an affinity with it. She was researching the crannog and she must have got so close to finding the truth about what happened. And then she died, before she could find the final piece of the puzzle. Did she know? Had she realized the connection her own family had with this place? I wonder.

Tilda had found it. Dylan was the descendant of the other slave sent to Wessex from the crannog. It must have been his ancestor who had in some way been responsible for the terrible end that the woman in the grave had suffered. It was Dylan's life she had come back for. Now that she had that piece, more fell into place. The witch's ghost in the Land Rover had been trying to get to him. The falling lights at the dig were meant for him.

Dylan!

Now, in the water, it is the thought of him asleep and defenceless in the cottage, unaware of what terrible danger he is in, it is this thought that sparks panic inside Tilda. Only a few seconds ago she had been content to let go, to drift ever downward and become part of the lake. To accept her fate. But now, realizing that she alone can save Dylan, she is forced to fight for her own life.

I couldn't help Mat. I'm not going to let Dylan die too. I am not!

She starts kicking. Her legs are strong, but the cold has numbed them so much she can barely feel them. She uses her arms in a desperate attempt to halt her descent, to propel herself up. She can still just make out the light above the surface, but there is so much dark water between herself and that soft glimmer. There is pain in her chest now, and a buzzing in her head, all telling her to take another breath. But she knows that to do so now, at such a depth, would be the end.

Come on, girl! Just like running. You can do it.

She has succeeded in stopping her fall. She is at last moving up rather than down, but her progress is so slow. Too slow. She can feel her lungs burning and her strength beginning to fail.

Seren, where are you? Why don't you help me? Please!

But no vision appears to lead her to safety. No tall stranger, the image of herself, comes to her rescue.

Is this it? Is this how I fail? Will Dylan and I both die today because of something that happened over a thousand years ago?

And yet, even as this desperate thought forms in her head Tilda feels something shift, something change, as if the very water has taken on a different composition. As if her own body has altered so that it is no longer something in the lake, but it is *part of* the lake. Suddenly she feels that she is not flesh and bone, but liquid, her whole being melded and merged with the chill, pure water. She has lost all sense of being separate from it. She has lost her fear. The realization that she is no longer afraid, after a lifetime of fear, now, as she faces her own death in the way that has always terrified her, shocks her but curiously feels right. As if all along, down the years, she has been reading her reaction to water wrong.

Not afraid, but awed. Not fear, but wonder. Not revulsion, but . . . what? A need? A longing, somehow, that twisted my stomach to knots and made my pulse race. A yearning. All that time, all those nerve-tingling moments, not terror of the unknown then, but the rekindling of a far-distant memory. A memory that should have been passed down to me, but got lost, got confused along the way.

She does not see anything in the water beneath her. She is not aware of another presence. The first thing she feels is pressure against her back. Feels herself being moved through the gloom, being moved upward! Her mind is spinning, free falling, on the verge of losing conscious thought, so that she is unable to make sense of what is happening. All she knows is that she is being pushed up, through the choking water, toward the day that waits beyond the surface. When she is almost at the top, she can feel the immense strength of whatever it is that has lifted her at such speed, so that an instant later she surges up, breaking the surface in a great wave, gasping and gulping air the moment she is free of the water. Her throat burns and she coughs, spluttering, ridding her body of the water she had taken in when she plunged into the lake. She thrashes wildly, fearing that she will sink again, but she is sitting on something that keeps her safely afloat. She wipes water from her eyes and tries to see what it is that is now taking her to the shore. Instinctively, she grabs at the solid mass beneath her, and is astonished to feel flesh, warm and firm, and to see what can only be a neck lifting up in front of her. The creature raises its head now too, and uses its powerful limbs with their webbed feet to swim gracefully and easily toward the shallows.

The Afanc! My God, the Afanc!

If she wasn't already so shaken, so shocked and battered by her experiences, by the bruising blows from the ghost, by the deadly cold, by the bellyful of water, by her own terror and by that final alteration in her very being, Tilda might have laughed, might have considered herself finally crazy. But she has no strength for such rational reactions. She is able only to slide from the back of the magnificent beast and crawl on hands and knees through the shallow water and onto the lakeside. When she turns, gasping, head aching and fit to burst, it is in time only to catch a glimpse of the Afanc's tail as it disappears beneath the surface of the lake.

SEREN

The dream precedes the vision.

In my sleep I imagine I am lying in my prince's arms, in his fine bed, a fire burning in the great hall, with no one to disturb us, no one to tell us this is not meant. Not right. But then there are noises, commotion, shouts outside. The raised voices grow more frightened and more urgent.

I sit up, awake, shaken from my sleep by the sense of menace that had descended upon us. And now, my eyes open, aware that I am in my own small house, my own small fire burnt low, my own small babe slumbering softly beside me, the vision takes the place of the dream. Unbidden and unsought it comes to me, with bright colours and loud clamourings. A seeing as bold and clear as any I have had. Armed soldiers, pouring down the valley pass, encircling the lake, loosing hundreds of arrows toward the crannog. They spur their horses recklessly into the water between the island palace and the shore. Many are cut down by the spears and arrows of Brynach's defending men, but the numbers of the attackers are so great, they are a swarm, endlessly running between the mountains, galloping on, stopping for nothing, so that soon they ride over the bodies of their fallen brothers, over the still-warm horses that lie bleeding in the water of the lake.

I leap to my feet, causing Tanwen to stir, rubbing her eyes to see what it is that disturbs me. The vision has ended, but my heart remains heavy with dread. This was not some shadowy view of the distant future. The threat is real. The threat is now.

I sling my cloak about my shoulders, fastening it with a pin, and take Tanwen onto my hip. Outside, the night is still and warm. The moon sits atop the hills behind us, its silvery beams lighting our way, my own shape described in shadow in front of me as I run to the crannog. To the prince. Already I fear I will be too late. I can sense danger closing in, and soon I know the thundering of an army of war-horses will shake the ground beneath my feet.

The guard on the walkway to the island regards me with surprise as I dash past him, but makes no move to stop me. I run, breathing heavily now, straight to the great hall. Two soldiers stand at the door.

'Out of my way!' I all but scream at them. 'Wake the prince!'

These two are not so ready to let a wild-eyed woman run into their master's home, however much they secretly fear me. However much they know about the child that clings to me as I run.

'Hold fast, Seren Arianaidd.' The bravest steps in my path, his spear angled across the doorway. 'What is your business with Prince Brynach? Give me a message, and I will take it to him,' he offers, his voice gentle, his aim to placate.

I step closer so that only a hand's span separates our faces when I speak. The guard's eyes waver but they are locked in my gaze. There is nowhere for him to hide.

'Tell him the Mercian Queen broke her word. Tell him to call his men to arms. Tell him death is coming to Lake Syfaddan, riding on swift horses. Tell him it *is* come!'

He hesitates, for he cannot sense what I sense, cannot feel what I feel. He glances at his fellow soldier and sees fear there. This decides him.

'Wait here,' he tells me, hurrying inside.

I hear voices, footsteps, weapons being taken up, and the prince appears, his expression grave. He knows better than to doubt me.

'How long?' he asks me. 'How long before they are upon us?'

Now that my prince stands before me, my heart aches to think of what lies ahead. Although I cannot accept the thought, cannot allow myself to truly believe it, I know that I have foreseen his annihilation. What words can I offer now? What purpose do I serve if I have failed to shield him from this moment?

He sees what is written in my eyes and need not question me further. He shouts orders to his men, sending them to man the palisades, to rouse each and every one able to wield a sword or loose an arrow. He sends two scouts to ride to the top of the pass and keep watch. He orders the walkway to be chopped, cut asunder.

The door opens again and Wenna steps out, alarmed by the shouts and the seriousness with which her husband issues his orders.

Turning to me, Brynach clutches my arm. 'Seren, take the babe, leave the crannog. Go deep into the woods and hide yourselves there.'

'But, my prince . . . !'

'I will hear no argument! This is not the moment to defy me.' He closes his eyes briefly, snatching up my hand. When he looks at me again I see the sparkle of tears. 'Take our child. Keep her safe. For me. And Seren –' he pauses, glancing at his wife before letting go of my hand –, 'take Princess Wenna with you.' When I gasp he says softly, 'She is in your care, and you in hers now. Do this for me.'

I nod. I do not trust myself to speak, for my heart is breaking. Brynach kisses Tanwen's pink cheek and then turns and strides away, doing what a prince must do, even when he knows all is lost.

The three of us leave the crannog, as behind us men take axes to the wooden boards. In seconds the link to the shore is gone. Brynach and his men remain on the island, the villagers huddled in the hall, ready to face what is to come. For so long such a tactic has proved effective. Warring parties, opportunist bandits, even roving Vikings have been deflected and defeated in this way. But I know that this time will be different. The force that even now thunders into the neck of the valley is too great. This time the defences will not hold. I know this, as does my prince.

'Come!' I bark at Wenna, holding Tanwen close. We set off at a run, but before we have reached the flimsy safety of the woods the earth shakes and we hear the battle cry of our foes as they descend upon the settlement. We keep running. We are nearly to the trees when Wenna stumbles and falls. Looking back I can see she has landed awkwardly, her ankle damaged. She cries out as she struggles to get up. My instinct is to run on, to leave her, to get my child away. But I cannot. I hurry back, and as I help her to her feet we both witness the terrible onslaught of the Mercian warriors. My vision did not lie. The forces sent are more than Brynach will ever have faced before; the odds are impossible for him to overcome. The crannog is soon under a ferocious attack, with the Mercians using flaming arrows to strike at the settlement. I can see our people running to fetch water to dowse the flames, and being cut down by yet more arrows as they do so. I see Brynach leading his brave men. My soul screams out for him, for he can do no more than lead them each to a warrior's death.

As we watch, Wenna cries out, pointing to a small group of riders who have detached themselves from the main body of soldiers and are moving in our direction. I haul her to her feet and we make our unsteady progress toward the shelter of the woodland. Tanwen, unnerved by such torment and destruction all about her, begins to cry pitifully, but there is no time to stop and comfort my poor infant. Even as we blunder on, it is clear we have no chance of hiding before the riders are upon us. I push Wenna behind a blackthorn tree, making her climb in beneath its low branches, its barbed boughs a strong defence. I pass her Tanwen.

'Take her!' is all I have time to say before I start to run for the lake. My aim is to lead the soldiers away from my child, to divert them, so that perhaps, if we are blessed with the smallest scrap of good fortune, she will not be discovered. To do this I must make myself a prize they will be determined to claim. As soon as I am close to the water I turn and stand. They have already seen me, but I must be certain they are entirely engaged in their dispute with me.

'What are you waiting for, sons of whores?' I scream at them, throwing off my cape to reveal my hair, striking in the strengthening dawn light, and the patterns on my flesh, so that they might see me for what I am. Shaman. Witch. I take my knife and brandish it, raising my arms. 'Does the Queen of Mercia suckle cowards at her poisonous breast? Does she feed her men on lies and beer only? What sickly creatures does she dare send to face Seren Arianaidd?!'

There are six of them. Two, those of the hottest blood and lowest belief in themselves, urge their horses on and approach me at the gallop. The first is easy to dispatch, for his horse is a knot of fear and fatigue. I catch its eye and send it a sudden vision of slavering wolves that causes it to swerve at such speed that it falls, landing heavily upon its rider, who does not move again. The second soldier presses on. I wait until he is close, his broad iron sword raised, murder glinting from behind the face piece of his helm. I fight my instinct to move and instead hold my place, only ducking at the last second, using my blade to slice through the cinch of his saddle as I slide beneath his horse's hooves. The animal's first thought is to save itself from a fall, so although its ironclad feet flash about me, none strikes me. As the rider leans on the reins to turn his mount and shifts his weight, the girth gives way under the cut I made and his saddle swings around, throwing the soldier into the reed bed, where he lies yelling, clutching his shoulder. He is no threat to me now. I turn back to the others. Three more come at me, though with more caution and guile than their fallen brethren. There are shouts of 'Take the witch alive! Rope her!' and 'She will make a fine gift for Our Lady!' They have made a dangerous decision to try to capture me. If they truly knew me, they would be content to try to kill me only. They circle, then charge, seeking to knock me down. But I am more nimble than any they have encountered before, stepping this way and that, evading their charges. Enraged, one of my attackers swings his sword, aiming at my knife hand. He is rewarded with my blade in his thigh and retreats screaming, his life blood gushing from him, his hopes of home going with it.

On seeing their fellows so stricken the others change their minds.

'Kill the evil creature!' one yells, and the rest roar in agreement.

I am ready for their charge, but I can do nothing to evade the arrow that is loosed by the archer who sits still and quiet upon his horse whilst the others bluster and thrash about. The arrow that cuts through the moist morning air silent save for its whining song of death. The arrow that, as I leap from the path of the black warhorse, finds the end to its journey deep in my belly. I fall to my knees, dropping my knife to grasp the shaft of the arrow with both hands. I know it has struck a mortal blow, but I will not cross to the Otherworld with the instrument of my enemy's victory in me still. I wrench it from my body and pain sweeps through me like a wave of fire. I am aware of the men coming to claim my corpse, but I will not let them! Summoning my spellcraft, I compel my own fading limbs to raise me up, so that I might stagger into the sacred waters of the lake.

I know she is near. She could not save me this time, for with so many foes near to show herself would have meant disaster for her, but I know she has come to take me with her. The hour has arrived when I shall go to her secret home in the depths, and she and I will dwell there together. As I fall forward into the water the shouts of those earthbound become more distant and blurred. I can feel her beneath me know, gently lifting me, bearing me away from the cruelty of men and the suffering of this life. I move so that I can see the little blackthorn tree. Wenna is still hidden there, my babe in her arms, and I send her a vision and with it my words, speaking directly to her mind, letting her know my dying wish.

'*Tanwen is Brynach's child.*' I remind her. '*She carries his royal blood. She is his heir. Love her as such. For his sake, love her!*'

And now the cold of the water numbs my pain, and the soft swimming of the Afanc carries me across the lake. No more shall I walk these shores. My prince has gone, and I pray that I will find him in the Otherworld. My babe will live on, and I pray that one day she will return to the sacred lake to find me.

22

TILDA

Wet through, Tilda clambers to her feet. She begins to shiver uncontrollably.

Must get back to the cottage. To Dylan. So cold!

She knows her body is in danger of going into shock, but this is something she can deal with. What she must do now is force warmth into her trembling limbs, and the perfect way to do that is to run.

Come on feet, one in front of the other. Footsure. Step, breathe, step, breathe. I can do this. Run, girl, run!

She is soon racing along the rough path, the rain still falling heavily, streaming down her face, making the colours of the day weaken and merge. Suddenly, through this murkiness, she sees something on the track ahead of her. Sitting small and still in the centre of the path is a large brown hare, its fur surprisingly dry, its eyes bright and watchful. It does not run away. Instead it appears to block her route, carefully moving from side to side so that she has to go off the track to try to get round it.

'Let me by, bunny,' she says breathlessly.

But the hare won't get out of her way. Tilda stops and stares at it. Before she has time to question what she is watching the animal starts to grow, and to pulsate, and to writhe and wriggle.

Tilda steps back, wondering if near-drowning has starved her brain of oxygen and has sent her mad.

First the Afanc, now this! Am I dreaming?

In seconds the hare has gone, transformed into a strong, striking woman who stands as solid and real as anything else in the landscape.

'Seren!' Tilda's heart races. She is transfixed, but she is not afraid. Rather, she feels emotion threaten to overwhelm her. Now that she knows she is looking at her ancestor, and after all she has just been through, the connection she feels with the person who stands before her is so powerful it is beyond anything she has experienced before. 'You came' she sobs at last.

When Seren speaks, her voice is not some ethereal whisper, it is clear and firm, a tone not to be argued with.

'You must return to the grave,' she says.

'What?' Despite the doom-laden nature of the statement, Tilda understands this is not a threat. She knows Seren is speaking of the grave at the dig site. 'No.' She shakes her head. 'I have to get to the cottage. Dylan is in terrible danger. You must know that.'

'You cannot defeat Nesta without what is in the grave. Take what protection Hywel holds. Go now!'

And she vanishes. As if she never was. And Tilda is alone again. She gasps, trying to make sense of Seren's words.

Does she mean the torc? It's true, I was useless against the witch . . . she called her Nesta . . . without the torc maybe I won't be able to help Dylan. Oh, I'm going to be too late!

She sets off running again, faster this time, pushing harder, gulping air as she forges on, turning toward the dig site, all the time fearing that it will all take too long. That Dylan will die.

As she approaches the trench, she looks for Thistle and spies her bedraggled body in the muddy area beside the dig. Hurrying over to the limp dog, she falls to her knees beside her.

'Oh, Thistle! You poor little thing. You were so brave.' She puts her hand on the soggy fur on the hound's head. The blow from the axe did not penetrate the rib cage, but dug deep into her stomach. The earth beneath her is sticky with cooling blood.

But not that much blood. Why isn't there more?

She realizes that the cold must have slowed the flow. Quickly, she puts her ear to the dog's chest, searching for a heartbeat, praying that there might be something, even the faintest fluttering.

'Nothing. Dammit! I let you die too!'

And then it comes to her. An idea so crazy that even in a day of craziness it seems beyond sense.

But why not? Why the hell not?

'Okay, Thistle, listen to me. Your heart is a pump, right? Just a pump. A working part, like in an engine, or a bit of clockwork. And I can make things stop, and I can make them start again, okay? The torc! Where is it?'

She scrabbles in the mud, precious seconds ticking by, clawing at the gritty soil with her hands, trying to recall exactly where it was the gold band slipped from her arm.

'I have to find it. For Thistle and for Dylan!' She is nearing despair when she catches the glint of precious metal amid the grime. 'There! Yes!'

She drags off her sodden fleece and flings it aside. Now she is only in her vest, but bare flesh is warmer than having a wet jacket clinging to her. And besides, she wants to feel the torc against her skin. Needs that connection. She jams it onto her arm, fixing it firmly above her elbow, determined it will not fall off this time. Immediately she experiences a surge of power and warmth flowing through her body.

'Okay,' she says, as much to herself as to the horridly lifeless dog in front of her, 'I can do this. I can! Just letting something work again.'

She forces herself to calm down, to focus, to be quiet and still, to open her mind to the possibility of what it is she needs to do. Already her body is glowing from the magic of the torc. All she must do now is let her own ability work with it. She places both hands over Thistle's heart and closes her eyes. Images flash before her mind's eye. Hounds running. Fire. Water. The darkness of the lake. Seren.

Nesta in all her fury. The warmth in her body intensifies, so that for a moment she is afraid it will prove too much for her, that it might burn her up.

Mustn't stop. Must not stop.

She holds her nerve, clutching at the soft fur of the dog under her palms, willing her tender heart to beat again.

'Come on, Thistle,' she pleads. 'You have to come back. You have to want to.'

There is a loud crack, as if lightning has struck only paces away from where she kneels. A searing pain shoots through Tilda's hands. She hears a yelp, and the dog leaps to its feet, growling and sneezing at the same time, before recognizing its mistress and bouncing all over her.

'It worked!' Tilda is laughing, knocked onto her back by the exuberant hound. 'Good girl!' She gets up. 'Come on, Dylan needs us.' She makes herself go over to the grave and peer in. Half of her does not want to disturb it further; is fearful of doing so. She has the torc now. She has just done something miraculous.

Do I need anything else?

As much as she would rather hurry back to Dylan, she can hear Seren's voice telling her that she cannot defeat Nesta without whatever it is the man in the grave has with him. Tilda grabs a nearby spade and drops into the pit. The moment she starts to dig, Thistle joins in, so that it takes them less than a minute to scrape though the thin layers of stone and earth to the lid of the coffin itself. Rubbing away the dirt from the wooden planks she finds there are only holes where the nails were driven in to hold the top down, the metal having rusted away to nothing after so many years in the particularly wet ground. Whilst water weakens iron over time, it has hardened the wood of the coffin lid, so that she cannot break through it with the spade, but has to pry it up. Tilda is surprised at how light it feels, and at how easily she is able to remove it from the grave and cast it aside. It is only now that she notices the torc is doing more than gleaming, it is actually glowing, pulsing with its own light.

Is it making me work better, or is it the other way around?

Having removed the lid she nervously turns back to look into the grave itself. The sight that meets her eyes is so poignant she finds herself sobbing. There is a complete skeleton, bones all appearing to be strong and unbroken and laid out as the deceased must have been over a thousand years before, with arms crossed over his chest. The skull is encased in a finely worked helmet, and even in the rain and the dimly lit day, Tilda can make out an intricate brooch pinning the remnants of a cloak around his shoulders. Beside him is the handle of a dagger, and a sword, rusted, but complete. There are plates and dishes, too, and a goblet, all lovingly placed next to the dead man, furnishing him with wealth and plenty in the next life.

Thistle jumps into the grave and for an instant Tilda fears she might pull at the bones, but she does not. Instead she sniffs at the skeleton's left hand, her tail wagging furiously. Tilda thinks back to what Seren told her.

Take what protection Hywel holds.

'And you must be Hywel. What have you got there?' With great care she unfurls the finger bones and discovers a small, stoppered clay jar. It is intact, amazingly well preserved, but then Tilda is familiar with the enduring properties of ceramics. She gently removes the jar, the earthenware rough in her palm.

She looks at Hywel. 'I'm sorry,' she tells him, 'but someone I love needs this more than you do now.'

The run back up the hill to Ty Gwyn is the hardest she has ever run. Thistle, too, struggles, though seems remarkably sound and strong, considering her injury. For Tilda, each step feels leaden and slow, as if she is running in a dream.

Will I be too late? Oh, please don't let me be too late.

At last she reaches her own garden gate, a sharp stitch in her side causing her to double over as she releases the latch. She can already sense the witch's presence. It is as if dark dread emanates from the little cottage. She hurries toward the kitchen door at the back of the house but stops when she hears noises coming from the studio. Sounds of crashing, of things breaking, mixed with Dylan shouting.

He's alive!

'Stay back, Thistle!' she tells the dog sternly. 'She could hurt you again. You stay out here!' Tilda reaches the patio doors of the studio in time to see Nesta causing one of her best pots to rise up into the air. She sees Dylan, blood gushing from a cut in his cheek, dive behind the workbench. Tilda screams through the glass of the door. 'Leave him alone, you bitch!'

Slowly, with a low gurgle from deep in her broken chest, Nesta turns. When she sees Tilda, she hisses and lets forth a stream of Welsh too fast, too ancient and too distorted for any words to be made out. But her meaning is clear. In a heartbeat, the large ceramic piece — one Tilda had spent so much time and care creating — stops its journey toward Dylan and instead comes hurtling at Tilda. She has no time to do anything other than fling herself to the ground as the pot smashes through the glass, shattering the panes into a thousand slivers. She scrambles to her feet, unable to avoid cutting her hands on some of the shards as she does so.

'Tilda! Run!' Dylan calls to her. 'You have to get away.'

'No, it's *you* she's after.'

'What? I heard noises in here. I came looking for you . . .' Dylan breaks off as he is forced to crawl under the workbench and emerge on the other side of it to evade a collection of metal tools Nesta has flung in his direction. There is a series of thuds as the blades and sharp edges scythe into the wood of the bench. In another second, she has caused the heavy workbench to slide across the floor, so that it traps Dylan against the wall. He groans as the weight of it presses against him.

Tilda tries to get past Nesta to help him, but the witch hurls a chair at her. She fends it off with her arm and feels a sickening crunch as the bones in her fingers meet with the unyielding wood. The pain is such that for a moment she can scarcely breathe, much less move, and crouches on the floor trying to catch her breath. Nesta turns her attention back to Dylan. While Tilda watches in horror, the witch raises herself up, arms held wide, and slowly makes all the broken glass from the patio doors lift into the air. The pieces move upward as if on hundreds of invisible strings operated by an unseen, sadistic puppeteer. Within seconds, they are all poised and pointing directly at Dylan. He struggles against the workbench, but there is no chance of him freeing himself. Nesta begins to rave, shouting unintelligible words as she clearly believes her moment of vengeance has come. Tilda struggles to her feet with a scream, stumbling across the studio floor, putting herself between the deadly slivers and Dylan, spinning around to face them at the exact moment that Nesta, with a terrifying shriek, sends them slicing through the air.

When Tilda acts she does so out of instinct, as she has not time to consider what she is doing or whether it will work. She lifts her arm so that the glowing torc is held high. She closes her eyes and pictures as clearly and as vividly as she can what it is she wants to happen. What it is she *prays* will happen. There is silence. She opens her eyes. The glass has stopped. Every single, deadly sharp slice has halted in its lethal trajectory, so that hundreds of cruel spikes quiver in the air, only inches from her, pointing at her face, her eyes, her throat, her heart. She trembles at the thought that it is her own will alone that is keeping them there.

Enraged, Nesta swoops to the floor where she spins, spitting more spells and curses as she turns. The glass begins to move again, to twitch and vibrate, as if gathering power to surge forward once more.

'Tilda, get out of here. For God's sake, run!' Dylan shouts.

She cannot answer him. Dares not so much as shake her head. It is taking such an effort of will and concentration to hold off Nesta's magic that she fears any second she will lose the battle. Already she can feel her strength ebbing. Can see the shards starting to move.

She's too strong for me!

Just as she thinks she will fail and that both she and Dylan will die at the ghostly, mangled hand of this demented witch, Tilda thinks of the Afanc. On the floor, still wrapped in damp muslin, is the piece she has been working on ever since the time she wore the torc and the water-horse appeared to her. She risks closing her eyes again. Images loom and fade in her dark vision, but she ignores them, in the same way she ignores the cacophony of ringing and screaming that comes from inside her own head as well as from the fiend who would see her dead. She calls the Afanc. She wills it to come, to help her again.

I am a child of Seren Arianaidd, please help me once more!

She opens her eyes. The glass spikes quiver and twitch. Nesta is still ranting, still raving, still exerting her formidable power, full of hatred and rage. To her left, Tilda's creation starts to move beneath its dusty wrapping. Astonished, she risks shifting part of her focus, part of her will, onto it. The cloth undulates and shifts, as what was until seconds ago merely a quantity of clay shaped into a form, a piece of art, nothing more, writhes and stretches as it is filled with magic and brought to life. A second later it bursts from its covering, taking to the air.

'My God!' Dylan gasps.

'Yes!' cries Tilda. 'Yes!'

Nesta ceases her screaming and turns to look at the wondrous thing that now swoops and turns about her head. When she recognizes it she shrieks anew, only this time her voice is filled not with anger but with fear.

Dylan struggles against the workbench. 'What is that?'

'The Afanc!' Tilda is smiling now, though she still holds the torc high, still dares not move from the spot where she stands keeping the lethal glass at bay.

The clay model of the water-horse that Tilda had spent so many hours sculpting is a perfect representation of the Afanc of her visions. Of the Afanc that saved her in the lake. Not yet glazed or fired, it remains the colour of the earthenware clay, dark and mottled red, as if seen through storm-churned lake water, deep and muddy, but even in this unfinished state it is glorious. The magic that stirred it has given it a lustrous glow that makes it appear both miraculous and somehow dangerous; its eyes burning bright, its bared teeth gleaming, its body rippling with strength. It flies around Nesta, diving at her, snapping at her, as if it were swimming, its sinuous neck twisting as it turns, its long tail flicking and thrashing at the terrified witch. The effect it has on Nesta is immediate and striking. She is terrified beyond any thought except of escaping from this symbol of the lake witches, this guardian of the ancient magic, this creature she was told to fear all her life, as the only thing whose power was stronger than the power her own ancestors had given her. She spins and shouts oaths and curses, half dissolving once again into a bruise-coloured cloud of vitriol and wickedness, but the *Afanc's* avatar will not let her go. The glass spikes, no longer under the witch's control, fall, smashing to the floor.

Tilda has no way of knowing how long this animated replica of the Afanc will serve to distract the witch. Cautiously, keeping her movements small and stealthy in the hope that they won't be noticed, she slips her left hand into her pocket. The broken finger bones make her flinch and nausea threatens to overwhelm her, but she forces her hand into her pocket to retrieve the little stone jar. Slowly, haltingly, sweat breaking out down her spine from a mix of pain and sustained effort, she lifts the jar. She holds it close, prying off the stopper with her thumb, gasping as more needle-sharp agony shoots through her damaged hand.

Must not miss. One chance. I have to get this right.

She takes a deep, slow, powerful breath, smiles her best and brightest smile and calls out, 'Hey! Pick on someone your own size!'

Nesta ceases spinning to scowl at her, searching for the reason for her opponent's apparent glee.

Tilda continues to smile as she speaks.

'Seren says hello,' she states calmly, before flinging the contents of the jar at the ghostly witch.

The tiny amount of blue liquid seems too harmless and too small a thing to set against such fury and strength. Tilda and Dylan watch, openmouthed, as the potion exits the stoneware bottle and sails across the room in an unnaturally long and steady arc, before it connects with the startled witch on the far side. And the instant it does, Nesta begins to writhe. She tries to turn, to spin, to rid herself of the magic substance, but it has entered her ghostly form. The spell is strong, and there is no escape. The more she fights against it, the more she rages and curses and flings herself about the room, the more the liquid appears to swell and bubble until it entirely encases the hysterical witch. It is a terrible thing to witness, but any sympathy Tilda might have felt for the creature disappears when the ghoul reaches out a misshapen hand to snatch at the Afanc.

'No!' Tilda cries out, but there is nothing she can do. Nesta's poisonous grasp sucks the water-horse into the vortex of the spell, so that it merges into the mass of dark blue chaos. Within seconds the witch is reduced to nothing more than a part of a smouldering, arcane chemical reaction that ultimately, only moments later, dissolves her to nothing.

The instant she is gone, exhaustion overwhelms Tilda and she slumps onto the broken glass, too stunned to even cry out as she sustains more cuts. The workbench returns to its normal weight, so that Dylan is able to push it away and free himself.

'Tilda! Tilda.' He puts his arms around her and helps her to her feet, carefully removing pieces of broken glass from her hair and her clothes.

'I'm okay, really. Put me down, I'm fine.'

'You are far from fine. Your hand . . . and those cuts, there's glass everywhere . . .' Dylan is appalled at the state of her.

Tilda reaches up and touches his own damaged cheek. 'It's nothing. It will heal,' she says. He looks up at her and she smiles back at him. This time her smile is real. 'It's gone. She's gone. There's nothing to be afraid of now.'

'You did it,' he tells her. 'You beat her. You were . . . incredible!'

'I wasn't on my own. I had a little help,' she tells him as she stoops to retrieve pieces of shattered clay from the ground. She turns a portion of the Afanc's tail over in her hands. It still feels warm, still carries within it the vibration of something vital and at the same time ancient.

'You could make it again,' Dylan suggests. 'I mean, make another one.'

She shakes her head. 'No. I don't think so. She did what she came to do. What she needed to do. I think I should leave her where she belongs now.' She looks up and sees through the clearing rain the lake in the valley far below, the water starting to steam as the sun breaks through the clouds.

EPILOGUE

Tilda stands back and allows herself a moment to admire the completed pieces that now fill the shelves in the workshop. It has been a productive few months. After the dramatic events at the end of last year it had been bliss to sink herself into her art once more. In truth, she cannot remember a more creative time in her life. The connection she has found with the lake and all that it signifies now fires her artistic impulses. Her gleaming pots and wilder one-off ceramic pieces are fine creations. She feels it in her heart.

A tapping on the glass doors makes her turn. Dylan holds up two mugs of tea.

'Leave those for one minute and come out here. It's too glorious to miss,' he says.

She dusts the gritty glaze residue off her hands, brushing down her checked work shirt, causing specks of unborn colour to dance in the late-afternoon sunlight that streams into the studio. As she steps outside, she breathes in air heavy with the scent of blossom from the apple tree. It has survived yet another harsh winter and is now a mass of pink-and-white blooms. Dylan hands her the hot drink.

'You're right,' she tells him. 'Glorious. Completely glorious.'

Spring has transformed the landscape. The lake shimmers beneath the warming sun. Flocks of small birds have returned from their winter homes to build nests on the marshy shores. The larger water birds are busy gathering reeds and weeds for their own haphazard nurseries. The verdant meadows are dotted with clean white sheep and even whiter lambs, which rush about in unruly groups, leaping and jumping for the sheer fun of doing so. The week has been mild, but there is still a chill in the air, which gives it such a freshness, such a purity that it might be intoxicating.

Dylan slips his arm around Tilda's shoulders.

'Temperature's dropping. Might need a fire tonight.'

Tilda smiles at this. Her relationship with Dylan seemed to have begun in front of the very fire he is talking about, on the very rug on which he will no doubt persuade her to lie again. She knows it is still the place he feels closest to her.

'Oh, I think it's going to stay fine. The year is warming up. No need to waste firewood,' she teases.

A movement catches her eye. In the field below the garden a large brown hare lollops silently into view. Tilda gasps and her hand flies to her mouth. It has been so long since she has seen it, and now that it is here again she is taken aback by how happy she feels. The hare nibbles at the new shoots of grass beside the path. Before she can be stopped, Thistle has bounded over the wall and races toward it.

Dylan sees her. 'Thistle, no!' he shouts instinctively.

But Tilda puts a reassuring hand on his arm. 'It's okay.'

As they watch, the hound circles the hare before crouching down in front of it, ears flat, tail wagging, an open invitation to play. The hare regards the lurcher thoughtfully for a few seconds and then leans forward. The two sniff, nose to nose, one set of twitching whiskers, one bristly moustache. And then they start to run. They tear around the meadow, this way and that, along the hedgerow and back across the grass, down the steepest part of the hill, and back up alongside the path. The hare easily keeps ahead, but sometimes she twists and jinks back so quickly that Thistle ends up in front and it appears she is the one being chased. It is a sight both comical and marvellous.

Then, as quickly as it started, the game stops. The hare turns to look up the hill, up toward the garden wall, up at Tilda. She looks down into the bottomless depth of the animal's ancient, knowing eyes, and feels a pang of longing and of love.

Hello Seren. I've missed you.

The hare sits a moment longer, then flips around, bounding for the hedge, and is lost from view. Thistle returns to lie panting at her mistress's feet.

'Daft dog,' she says, stooping to stroke the hound's ears. The wound on her side has healed well, and the fur grown over it once again. Slowly, but in a similar way, the frightening aspects of all that took place over the previous Christmas have faded. Tilda's broken fingers mended. Dylan's cut face healed, leaving only a short scar, which he declared manly. The cottage is peaceful now, and full of new beginnings, for all of them. Tilda keeps the torc in a safe place, and often takes it out to hold. To gaze upon. To remember. She allows herself to wear it, to feel the magic it releases in her, but only when she is alone at the cottage. And every time she uses it, she feels more at ease with the gift she has been given. It feels meant. This is where she is meant to be. And every time she runs by the lake she says good morning and thank you to the Afanc, even though the mother-of-the-lake does not show herself, but remains hidden in the deep, mystical waters. Tilda knows she is there, knows that the Afanc is aware of her presence. And that is enough.

She smiles at Dylan and touches the raised mark on his cheek.

'Come on,' she says, 'I'm starving. Time to go in.'

Dylan grins, taking her arm as they head up the path. 'I'll set the fire in the sitting room.'

'I'll sit in front of it.'

'I'll make something to eat.'

'Thistle and I will eat it.'

'Seems fair,' he says as they enter the cottage.

Tilda turns, peering back down the garden path, scanning the sloping pasture, but there is no sign of the hare. She feels a stab of sorrow at the thought she might not see it again, but this is swiftly followed by a vision, clear and bright, of Thistle and the hare playing on the shores of the lake, at the edge of the woodland, the ground a vivid pool of bluebells.

ACKNOWLEDGEMENTS

My thanks, as ever, to the team at Thomas Dunne Books, and all at SMP who have helped to bring *The Silver Witch* into being. Particular thanks due to Peter Wolverton and Mary Willems for their enthusiasm for the story, their willingness to be taken on this strange flight of fancy, and their attention to detail that won't ever let me get away with seemed-like-a-good-idea-at-the-time.

My gratitude, also, to the designers for such a lovely cover.

The staff at Brecknock Museum was wonderfully helpful, giving me access to the valuable collection of artifacts discovered on or near the crannog dating back to Seren's day, despite the museum being closed for major refurbishment. I promise I never sat in that canoe!

DON'T LET THE
STORY STOP HERE